THE SOJOURNS OF ANTON REISEN

For Sabra,
In gratitude for
your gift to me.
Art Bridge
Nov 13, 2003

© 2003 by A.V. Bridge.
Cover art by Megan Murphy, 2003.
All rights reserved.
Printed by Lithtex Printing Solutions, Hillsboro, Oregon, USA.

Cesareo Gabarain, *Pescador de Hombres,* ©1979, 1987, 1989, published by OCP Publications, 5536 NE Hassalo, Portland, OR 97213. All rights reserved. Used with permission.

Manuscript edition.
For further information, please inquire at
avbridge_2000@yahoo.com.

ISBN 0-9743813-0-6 (pbk.)
1. Imaginative narrative and poetry. 2. Bibliography and endnotes. Bridge, Arthur V., 1949 –.

I will call the world a school—and I will call the child able to read, the soul made from that school—and I will call the world a school instituted for the purpose of teaching little children to read—I will call the human heart the hornbook[1] used in that school—and I will call the child able to read, the soul made from that school and its hornbook. Do you not see how necessary a world of pain and troubles is to a school and to intelligence and how it makes it a soul? The school of the world is a place where the heart must feel and suffer in a thousand diverse ways. Not merely is the heart a hornbook, it is the mind's Bible.

John Keats (1795–1821),
The Vale Of Soul–Making[2]

CONTENTS

Premonitions 3
Our hearts are given away.. 13
Complacencies before nightfall 21
Continual fear, and danger of violent death............................... 35
I saw Eternity the other night.. 39
You are searching for Aguilares 43
Gravity's graceful ways 51
Fire and water 65
Your hand presses hard upon me 71
A special Gospel, for the poor alone... 77
The bread of hospitality 83
Fire burns brightest at night 91
And the yoke shall be broken.. 99
Tools and life 115
Companions in memory.. 121
Out of the strong, something sweet.. 139
Spoken from everywhere and a dream..................................... 151
Their eyes were upon me 159
The quickening heart 171
Calypso's mantle... 185

Give me my soul again	197
Wind, sea and song	209
My thoughts are forged in your heart	223
Every breath, a thought of you	233
Our trials, thy pathway	245
Peace in a life of pain	259
His ear to hearken to my need	269
The Red Rose of Carmel	279
The timbre of her voice, nature's music	289
A feast as mends all length	301
Through the city to civilization	311
A meadow for the Muses	323
Lethe's elixir	331
Dreams, plays and sudden sight	343
"More light!"	359
Author's Note	371
Bibliography	375
Endnotes	381

THE SOJOURNS OF ANTON REISEN

In the end, modern man drags around with him a huge quantity of indigestible stones of knowledge, which then, on occasion, rumble around in his body, as they say in fairy tales. This rumbling reveals the fundamental characteristic of modern man: the curious disparity of an interior with no corresponding exterior, and an interior with no corresponding interior—a disparity that was alien to ancient peoples.

Friedrich Nietzsche (1844–1900)[3]

Salt is good: but if the salt has lost its savour, wherewith shall it be seasoned? It is neither fit for the land, nor yet for the dunghill; but it is cast out. He that hath ears to hear, let him hear.

Luke 14:34-35

Premonitions

THE DAY HAD COME when the faces in the class swam before him. His hand, squeezed into a knot, opened. His lecture notes dropped to the table. With a trembling voice, he said, "I have nothing for you today. I am empty. I am sorry." Then he left.

Anton Reisen shifted his backpack to allow the breeze to run across his back and neck.[4] In his pack he carried an extra pair of jeans, a sweater and heavy winter jacket, cap and gloves, and a few other essentials. He walked eastward along Santa Monica Boulevard, wending his way through groups of people, around food stands and construction sites. At every cross–street, cars jostled and inched forward like objects on an assembly line. His senses were assaulted on every side. The barking of car horns mingled with the clatter of doors on beer trucks. Heavy trucks sent blasts of compressed air from their brakes and set the concrete to shaking as they rolled by. Engines roared anxiously as the traffic prepared to race off the mark to a hasty stop at the next light. Car exhaust mingled with the indefinable heaviness in the air that precedes an early winter rain.

To rest his eyes from the glint and glare of chrome, Anton looked down the line of trees that pointed the way to the interstate. Like dreadlocks of tall maidens observing the mêlée below, the fronds of the palm trees were lofted by the gathering breeze of the early afternoon. Anton walked on, past bus kiosks, through more intersections, along the storefronts proclaiming car parts, carpets and low cost bail bonds, past the car dealers in white, short sleeved shirts lounging in the shade of their showrooms, past movie theaters with their posters of angry heroes and vapid and grinning models, and past faceless and withdrawn specters carrying their life possessions in grocery carts.

Along the way he could hear short, crisp phrases in the English, Russian, and Vietnamese tongues. Women of Mayan descent spoke Spanish and Catchua to their children as they waited for the bus, plastic grocery bags in hand. Anton thought of Cortez and Pizarro, the brigands who had sailed from Spain to the western continent so long ago, and whose technologies of war and imported diseases had all but wiped out the thriving civilizations of the time. How long, he wondered, can we maintain our faith in our technologies to hold the night's darkness and nature's wilds at bay? What will be the sound of our language after the tinny trumpets of our proud, carefree civilization are silenced and the festive lights of our prosperity flicker out? The breeze, the breeze—. Would that I had my own sails to set! To rise upon the surge of the sea, to hear the low moans of the deep as it embraces my own boat and sets it to creaking!

The breeze pushed gently at his back. He walked east, away from the ocean. Here, near the coastline the air was fairly clear. Fifty miles further east the soot and grime from the city packed up against the San Gorgonio and San Jacinto mountains, where on bad days it rested like a reeking, fetid blanket over the cities of Colton and Riverside. The aerial effluent then made its way north, up the San Fernando Valley, to be disgorged onto Palmdale, Bakersfield and the Mojave. Anton walked before the breeze.

Fifteen years at a small, prestigious college had persuaded Anton that he was a teacher. There he had gathered students into little conversation circles to puzzle over life's questions. With learned diligence he would disturb them with such questions as, What would our political culture look like if governmental leaders pursued the truth with the relentlessness of an Oedipus? Or: what drove Antigone to scatter the forgiving earth over her dead brother Polyneices, rather than leave him "unwept, untombed, a rich sweet sight for the hungry birds' beholding," and so risk her own sorrowing life?[5] And: where do you find yourself in Plato's Allegory of the Cave—locked in shackles, or scrabbling through the rubble of life toward some dimly perceived light? Further: could Hamlet be persuaded today to receive talk–therapy and medication for his melancholia? Was Machiavelli, who saw the Church as nothing more than one political entity among many, a partisan for the people or a teacher of tyrants? And what is the condition of the human soul in Eliot's *Wasteland* and what new vision is the poet suggesting?[6]

As a professor, Anton had immersed himself in classical literature, the texts that raise up such questions yet never allow them to be put to rest. He had offered the questions to young students as inspirations of intellect and insight that have instructed and guided innumerable generations. He had thrown himself into the service of these questions, believing them to be wandering and homeless spirits that can only find peace and refuge in the souls of vibrant and receptive minds. The furrowed brows of his students had reassured him of the seriousness of his project, as had an occasional affirmation from a student who thanked him for sparking a personal awakening. He would use these precious moments to further convince himself of the necessity of delayed gratification in the learned life; this idea, like many others, he brought as a noble and necessary sacrifice to the altar of the liberal arts, and so consoled himself in his pleasant routines. The walk to the office along shady arbors, the warmth of his wooded study, the predictable rhythms of committee meetings and course scheduling, and the higher and more complicated rites of accreditation and peer review felt so gratifying, after all. He had never thought of his ordered life as a placebo, a substitute for the more bracing elixir of real experience. The real work, he told himself, was in the classroom, with his students and the Ideas. There he strode, day after day, week after week, year after year with his notes in hand. Until the end.

The end came disguised in the malaise of doubt on an ordinary day in Ordinary Time. For much of Anton's professional career he had been haunted by a distrust of his own pedagogic enterprise. The trappings of professional prestige and a collegial conspiracy of silence had helped him stave off personal doubts in this area. Radical doubt itself even held an honored place in his tradition, as long as it was reserved to earlier adventurers of the intellect like Descartes. It would then be up to later savants like Anton to correct and overcome their errors and myopia, to tame the fury of this organized assault from the intellect, and to domesticate it in survey courses in Western thought. Thus dulled, the dangerous tool of doubt lost its ability to cauterize the flabby mind, and became no more than a quaint and innocuous footnote in the history of consciousness.

Still, the question had always lurked in the back of Anton's mind: what is the price paid by the human soul whose leisure is invested in the contemplation of abstract, disembodied questions? Can the passions of the heart and the deepest movements of the psyche even be approached through the medium of text and narrative? Is not the reaching of judgments about life through books, even the most sacred books, among the most bizarre of human delusions? Can joy and suffering ever be comprehended in the ordered syntax of rational thought? Is it not wiser and more truthful to shelter and protect these profound movements of the human soul in poem, parable and song? What other medium can trace them to their source and track their course in tears and even honor the salt left once the tears have dried? And when, pray Heaven, have I last uttered a song?

Unconsciously these misgivings insinuated themselves into Anton's mind and became manifest in his teaching style. By nature he was not one of those mesmerizing professors whose bombast and sheer command of a discipline convinces everyone that he knew something about everything. His delivery never sought to envelop the listening student in a tidal wave of erudition. He appreciated the fragility of speech and the protean nature of argument. He was daunted by the notion that learning demands more than words alone—that touch, sound, sight, and even smell are powerful agents of natural intelligence. He was also conscious (and this was his uncomfortable secret) that his own belief would not support half of his assertions. Against this he consoled himself in the creed that "students need to know these things," and that the Canon of the Liberal Arts, in all its majesty, contained everything an educated person might need—except experience. And was not reading and talking about human suffering far more pleasant than experiencing it? His convenient life helped him avoid the same questions about human companionship, for how much easier it is to smile at the wiles and foibles of literary characters than to experience—in one's own self—the rush of anger and the ache of love and longing. As for the ecstatic joys of intimacy and mystical experience, such extremes seemed remote to a life well practiced in moderation. His intellectual culture added its share of lassitude to his cherished conveniences. Much as it despised noisy talk and undisciplined verbiage, it feared silence and solitude more. That culture suggested that everything worth knowing deserved to be shared through publication. However, had not everything important already been done and published? What creative work could he imagine for himself? All of these possibilities seemed safely closed away to him, the don living comfortably in the rarified atmosphere of higher education.

The seed–bed of Anton's discontent began to bear its unwonted fruit during a lecture that he gave in the middle of the fall term. Apropos to his course title, "Thresholds and Turning–points in Ancient and Modern Thought," he was attempting to draw students into the light–and–shadowed world of early fifteenth century Italy. In particular, he was describing how Giovanni Francesco Poggio Bracciolini had excused himself from the political moils of Rome during the interregnum of Pope Alexander V and the "anti–Pope" Baldassare Cossa (self–proclaimed as John XXIII) in order to explore the library at Cluny, itself nearly five hundred years old at the time. With nostalgic pleasure Anton described Bracciolini's delight as he beheld the deteriorated manuscripts of several of Cicero's speeches, heretofore unknown to Italy; how Bracciolini carried them back to Florence; and how he implored the *condottieri* Cosimo de Medici to pay for their transcription and preservation.[7]

All of these and similar noble and delicious deeds had for years secured Anton's service and devotion to the Republic of Letters. All greater the shock, when at the moment he could have been swelling with vicarious pleasure to the urgent proclamations of Cicero, that patriot and master of political oratory, Anton lost his footing. He suffered a loss of mental discipline. Simply put, his imagination wandered. His subconscious mind reached forward in the political and cultural history of the West to his own time. He thought of the freeways lacing the Los Angeles basin, much as Roman roads had traversed the empire, the one carrying commerce and an enterprising populace, the other perfectly designed to carry a phalanx of legionnaires. He thought of the canals bringing Sacramento River water to the desert city of Los Angeles, much as the graceful, arched Roman aqueducts supplied the thirsty imperial city with water from the outlying territories. He saw the ruin of the ancient engineering achievements, and felt crowded by growing awareness of the inevitable decline of his own city's fortunes.

While these intrusions from his imagination were being forced upon him, Anton felt thoughts piling on thoughts as he spoke to his class: "Pericles' Athens is gone. Hamilcar Barca's and Hannibal's Carthage is gone. So too Caesar Augustus' Rome. Yet their memory endures. They even live in us, whether we know it or not. There is a story told of Bracciolini's portraying Manlius Boethius sitting amid the fallen walls and columns of conquered Carthage. In the dust and wind arriving from the desert, Boethius hears the whisper, *'Cartago delenda est,'* Carthage is destroyed!, uttered by Scipio Aemilianus in 146 bce in fulfillment of the command of Cato the Elder. Finally the Romans are relieved of the terror of the marauding Hannibal who had routed them at Trasimene Lake and Cannae! They go on to raze the buildings and even salt the ground of their fearsome Carthaginian adversary. Yet, so the story goes, as Manlius sits amid the shattered Carthage five hundred years later, he contemplates his own losses, and sees himself equally dashed to the ground. From being a friend and honored advisor of the emperor Theodoric, Manlius sees himself plunging into obscurity and death; he feels it coming! In this turn of the wheel of fortune and misfortune, Bracciolini's portrait of Manlius amid the ruins of Carthage offers a portent of his own fate. Did not Bracciolini himself feel it wise to flee Rome to avoid being consumed in the political troubles of the Vatican?"[8]

Even as he shared these wonderings with his students, Anton felt himself for the first time to be one of Bracciolini's kin. The thought, Would that I too could flee!, welled up in him. But where? And to what avail? Bracciolini had seen his fate in Manlius, and now Anton and even his young students at a prestigious and comfortable private college were seeing it as well! Is this the fate of those who simply delight in the discovery of other persons' works and never their own creations? Where in this well–trodden world could he go?

Anton finished his lecture, but the eruption from the hidden depths of his unconsciousness had only begun. He knew his history. In fact, he was imbued with it. He knew that an answer to Bracciolini lay two generations ahead when another Florentine, Niccolò Machiavelli, would suggest that Fortune could be controlled by the ideal man, rich in *virtú*, strong and daring like the *condottieri* Cesare Borgia. Treat *Fortuna* like a woman, with firmness, with a heavy and even violent hand, counseled Machiavelli.[9] So was launched the modern project of guiding the wheel of Fortune with its worship of success and its central maxim that "the end justifies the means." Before long the project would be dedicated to "relieving the inconveniences of the human estate," as Francis Bacon would say. How shocked would even that ambitious Englishman have been at the sight of the immense engineering projects known as the Industrial Revolution. In this new dispensation, it is no trivial matter that Nature, everywhere honored in the feminine metaphor, would be governed by the marketplace. From Machiavelli's personalizing of *Fortuna* with feminine semantics, to the assault on the earth and the desacralizing of "matter" itself—*matter*, the word whose origin lies in the ancient Latin for "mother" or *mutter*—these were easy steps. Anton felt himself grieving the decline of the city, while holding out some hope that Nature would restore her claims with dirt, vines and weeds. Yet even these natural realities were vivid only in his imagination, for years had passed since he had felt their gritty edge and fragrance.

Beyond that unwelcomed moment that triggered Anton's malaise, it was an encounter with the "Sad Reflection" in Kierkegaard's *Journals of 1850–1854* that indicted him completely. One day in the middle of the fall term, he chanced upon the morose reflection –

In one of the Psalms it is said of the rich man that he heaps up treasures with great toil "and knoweth not who shall inherit them." So I shall leave behind me, intellectually speaking, a capital by no means insignificant, and alas, I know full well who will be my heir.

It is that figure so exceedingly distasteful to me, he that till now has inherited all that is best and will continue to do so: the Docent, the Professor.

Yet this also is a necessary part of my suffering—to know this and then go calmly on with my endeavor, which brings me toil and trouble and the profit of which, in one sense, the Professor will inherit. "In one sense"—for in another sense I take it with me.

Note. And even if the "Professor" should chance to read this, it will not give him pause, will not cause his conscience to smite him; no, this too will be made the subject of a lecture. And again this observation, if the Professor should chance to read it, will not give him pause; no, this too will be made the subject of another lecture. For longer even than the tapeworm which recently was extracted from a patient...even longer is the Professor, and the man in whom the Professor is lodged cannot be rid of this by any human power, only God can do it, if the man himself is willing.[10]

This encounter with the loquacious Dane prompted the insidious question: "Are you, Anton Reisen, an authentic human being? Are you a genuine seeker? Are you even a Bracciolini, who served all of history with his remarkable finds and who connected a forgotten past with an unimaginable future? Perhaps you, Anton Reisen, are merely a mouthpiece, an *epigone* of the beautiful thoughts of others...thoughts that make no claim on you, because you have no Self for whom these thoughts are very Truth and Life. Are you not going ever deeper in self–important foolishness, taking yourself with such seriousness as paves the way to perdition?"

The question pried open his eyes to his ivied setting, staid, secure and ordered under the aegis of academic freedom. If he were truly free, why be so hesitant to seize the offered hands of great adventurers of the spirit? Kierkegaard had asserted that when one wills one thing, all roads lead to God, even the dangerous and painful road taken by "the repentant one who wills the one thing."[11] But Anton began to wonder how he could be "willing one thing" when his comfort and sense of competence within the institution were as important (and probably more important, were he to be honest with himself) than his engagement with Life. Could he exchange comfort and competence for a hard, uncertain path in the maelstrom of the modern world, even if it did lead to the God of Life? And what is Life but the fertile ground of love and terror, the space and time of ecstasy and ever–returning cycles, the setting for ultimate beauty suggested in a silhouette, the raw and humble earth and daily surrender to the mystery and grandeur of cosmic intentions lying forever beyond our understanding and grasp? Life!

These baleful questions precipitated the acid of doubt onto his comfortable self–concept. In the days that followed, his enthusiasm began to darken like a slow eclipse of the sun. Nothing had prepared him for this strange cooling of his day's energies. No one had let slip the secret that questions contained only in the mind might bring the ruin of his health. He became distracted and moody in his relations with other faculty members. When one student struggled with his authority, he grew exasperated and judged the student to be rude and disrespectful. When another student challenged his teaching methods, asking fretfully why she had to perform certain tasks (originally conceived by Anton as high and noble exercises in scholarship), he felt scalded and diminished by the criticism. When the college provost talked about the employability of various college majors, patience abandoned him. When other faculty members became passionate about their plans and projects, his mind wandered and he wished the interminable conversation would end. He wanted no part in such a bland, saltless affair. Not that he felt alive with ambition and plans for action, No: he simply felt that he had lost all energy for listening and could hear no more.

Anton turned his growing annoyance on himself. What is the name for someone who believes that by looking at words he understands the things themselves? Effete intellectual, Sophist!, he lashed at himself. His credentials, earned in this early enthusiasm for the antiquities, were beginning to feel like an obituary. Even the books, silent on their shelves, accused him. Among them he saw his doctoral dissertation, entitled *Psyche and Thumos in Homer's* Iliad *and* Odyssey: *An Evolving Conception of the Human Soul*.[12] What is the value of this? he wondered. How can my own soul feel untouched by Homer's two timeless themes of anger and war, homecoming and love? Truly, I beheld Homer's great teaching in the frieze of the Parthenon; its light helped me see my way through the writing of my early work. But it now serves no one, not even the rarified culture of classical scholarship that received it. Is the mold gathering between its pages simply nature's claim and valuation of my all–too–human work?

In these condemning thoughts Anton felt himself sliding down to the brink of despair. The man who had been coasting under the momentum of his youthful passions and institutional security was slowly, slowly coming to a stop.

Getting and spending, we lay waste our powers:
Little we see in nature that is ours;
We have given our hearts away, sordid boon!
This Sea that bares our bosom to the moon;
The Winds that will be howling at all hours
And are up–gathered now like sleeping flowers;
For this, for everything we are out of tune;
It moves us not,—Great God, I'd rather be
A pagan suckled in a creed outworn;
So might I, standing on this pleasant lea,
Have glimpses that would make me less forlorn
Have sight of Proteus coming from the Sea
Or hear old Triton blow his wreathed horn.

> William Wordsworth (1770–1850),
> *The World Is Too Much With Us*

O Fortuna velut luna statu variabilis, semper crescis aut decrescis; vita detestabilis nunc obdurat et tunc curat ludo mentis aciem, egestatem, potestatem dissolvit ut glaciem.

O Fortune, like the moon you are changeable, ever waxing and waning; hateful life first oppresses and then soothes as fancy takes it; poverty and power it melts them like ice.

> From "Fortuna Imperatrix Mundi,"
> *The Carmina Burana*

OUR HEARTS ARE GIVEN AWAY

THUS, IN THIS STATE during his last lecture of the fall quarter, his class became a placid sea of faces. He stood looking at the students and felt his remaining passion being quenched like a sputtering candle. He raised his notes closer to his eyes. His heart quaked. He dropped his hand and mumbled, "I have nothing for you today, nothing..." He found his way to the door and staggered back to his office.

The word quickly spread through the academic halls. "Have you heard? Something's happened to Dr. Reisen..." Young people who had long lived within the walls of formal learning felt their ground shifting. Anxious freshman consulted one another. Complaisant sophomores who had resented his arcane assignments felt vindicated: "Sexist antiquarian... he faces his own extinction," they said sardonically.

For their turn, his peers in the faculty believed that one of their own secrets had been revealed: that what begins as a romance of ideas might wane into a flat and insipid affair with a faithless mistress. A younger colleague, not yet understanding this, muttered something darkly about Anton's "overheated brain." Others, goaded by guilt and fear, urged the academic dean to give Anton a vacation, medical leave, a sabbatical,— anything and quickly! lest the contagion spread. With one eye out for a lawsuit and the other at the cost of a replacement faculty member, the dean reluctantly agreed. With a supercilious half–utterance about Anton needing "The Grand Tour of Europe," the dean relieved him of his professional responsibilities. "Just get your grades in," were his parting words.

Back in his small apartment, Anton rankled under the words. "A Grand Tour!" What's that supposed to mean? Another "sentimental journey" of a precious epicure? Me, a despicable Tristram Shandy?[13] I've been to Europe twice!, he thought, once bringing back shining memories, the second time, a heart scarred with punishing regrets. What does this mean? Buy a ticket to a land of memories and incantations, museums and tales that tire and grow stale when read from old men's lips? Won't my condemnation become final as I behold battles, woes and rites that trivialize my own agonies?

Fretting over these questions, Anton wandered around his apartment study, a cluttered reliquary of student papers, journals, books and artifacts. A picture of Beethoven with Hellenistic curls glared across the room at an unshaven Rousseau leaning against a tree. A photo of a bust of Homer presided impassively over the chaos. Anton reached for Goethe's *Faust* and read,

> They call me magister, Doctor, no less
> And for some ten years, I would guess,
> Through ups and downs and to's and fro's
> I have led my pupils by the nose
> And see there is nothing we can know...
> All delight is in me shattered;
> I do not pretend to worthwhile knowledge,
> Don't flatter myself I can teach in college
> How men might be converted or bettered.[14]

Faint consolation in Faust's adventures and discoveries...The old and familiar awe at the *magnum opus* of Goethe rose in Anton as he traced Faust's fatal and destructive swing from pure contemplation to raw experience: Gretchen, a tender and simple naïf, never appreciated, never honored, the victim of Faust's cravings, her plea for heaven the last expression of her darkened mind; her mother dying in obscurity; the ignoble death of her brother; the plight of Baucis and Philemon, the frail and ancient couple who resisted Faust's engineering projects; the final apotheosis and invocation of the saving Feminine at the end of the protagonist's life. He heard Goethe's lament for the disenchantments of modernity in the person of Faust's father, the alchemist who was honored for having saved a village from the plague, while Faust himself looked like a dissolute Don Juan and wastrel. Where is the magic and even the whimsical and diabolical genius of Mephistopheles to invoke in today's enlightened age? What has become of us, Faust's unknowing children?

And Faust was a professor, a *literati* who had also caved in under the burden of his disciplined learning! One could see where a wandering mind led him! In Anton, the noble virtue of prudence had swung to the vicious extreme of hesitancy and caution that was paralyzing his limbs.[15]

Looking within he saw rhetorical finesse and skill with the *bon mot* that hid his true meaning. Looking around he saw selfishness masquerading as pragmatism, while "adventure" and "romance" could be purchased in convenient, air–conditioned, two–week excursions. His own academic setting seemed more and more like a huddled refuge of lettered grant–seekers and unjustly paid office workers. Where was the service to the freedoms earned from the blood and sweat of radicals and freethinkers renown and forgotten? Where was the passion that led men and women to the barricades and the bullhorns in more seminal times? In the faculty offices all he heard were insipid complaints about classroom sizes and plodding computer networks. In the locker room it was rumors about the improved "benefits package." Even once–lofty conversations in the hallways slipped into silence with the first appearance of college "governance." Thus was his privileged professoriate wallowing along in the drifting vessel of its own inertia.

And the paper! He and his colleagues had been devouring paper like a herd of dyspeptic goats munching discarded books. And the student essays! Rather than original if clumsy and uneven displays from within the portals of the students' thought, they were all too often plagiarisms of anonymous on–line essays. Even the articles submitted by his peers to professional journals tended to say more and more about subjects of less and less general interest. What was that horribly humorous expression from Nietzsche in his rebellious period, in the *Untimely Meditations?*—that modern scholars, for lack of more profitable employment, were becoming "experts in the intestines of leeches"? Was all this writing, including his own, worth the paper it consumed? Was his own writing nothing but tracings in the rulebook of the cynical game of "publish or perish"?

Thus, the three mainstays of his profession had slackened: reading had become nothing but the illusion of experience. Writing for publication seemed either a flight from silence or a mockery of genuine competence in important things. And lecturing was becoming an exhausting, mind–numbing sophistry offered in a pretentious style that discouraged anyone from revealing its patent nonsense.[16]

So, what to do? Succumbing to a Rousseauan sentimentality felt unmanly, a collapse into biliousness and egotism. A Buddhist renunciation of desire and emotion, an equanimity smiling in this direction and that, felt like the approaching chill of death. And going on was impossible.

For hours these thoughts raced around in Anton's mind, colliding with each other and bouncing off the numb walls of his fatigue, growing all the more intense with every realization. Perhaps, he thought, I have been seduced by sirenic music, only to have run aground, there to be devoured by an intricate and inflexible system of commitments...And my school: its landscaping is beautiful and the floors are always polished and all the rooms have computers, but where is the raucous vitality of youth in this shrine of luxury and pride? Where is the spirited indignation that raises its face to the banality and injustices of the world? Hah! In our time the rabelaisian abandon that inspired the *Carmina Burana* would be a scandal. Everyone a bookworm or a Babbitt! Everywhere neo–classical devotionals to Apollo, and burgeoning prisons for Dionysus![17] This Anton knew well enough from close, if indirect experience: one of his own brothers was completing a minimum mandatory sentence at Folsom State Penitentiary for the crime of protest, vagrancy (which he laughingly called "idleness on public grounds"—leaving the ambiguity intact), and general disrespect for institutions.

As he wandered around his small abode Anton allowed his feelings to gnaw their way to consciousness. Through the window he could see the hub of land ending at the line of blue drawn by the Pacific as it spread away to the west. It was mid–day in a deserted neighborhood. Everything was still. His home was still. Professionally pruned trees and shrubs stood like lifeless paintings on a canvas of artifice. He strained his ears to hear a human voice. Only the traffic noise from the highway below and the rising thunder of a jet leaving the international airport reached his ear. There is no one here, he thought; I am not even here. Perhaps I have missed the most important thing. What are we supposed to be doing?

What do I want? What is it? Or, Who is it?

Questions leading into deep obscurity..."The unexamined life..." Socrates had said that it is worthless! Think of it: a life not worth living! But could the "over–examined life" be an even greater curse? The thought of the old, shabby and famously ugly avatar of the intellectual quest smiling benignly over the whole enterprise became suspect. Was that a hint of malice in his sparkling eyes?

Maybe I have it wrong, Anton whispered to himself. Socrates seems sleepless most of the time...I am like him in that, sleepless...But behold the man: voluntarily poor, with no title or position, no institutional security, indeed, threatened by institutions; everything about him for truth, for clarity, for intimate, passionate relationships. And oh, look at me: compartmentalized and sanitized, scheduled, organized and delivered! Socrates: a gadfly and irritant and reproach. Me: a socialized and polished pseudo–sage in tweed. Him: so frustrating and irritating, courageous in his confrontations, firm at his post in war and politics, sneering at danger, so inured to the cold and ardors of the battle that even hardened infantry were embarrassed by him. Me: a dilettante, probably the butt of secret jokes, a coward afraid of my own forgotten shadow, at the front line, first among those to flee.[18] What inner *daimonia* did Socrates discover in his relentless pursuit of the truth of his life? Spirits of negation and affirmation that he failed to tell us about? What was the price of his vaunted self–knowledge? No wonder the sage was famed for his ugliness as much as his limpid clarity.[19]

As Anton mined his thoughts for something safe and secure, everything familiar slipped away from him. His certainties disappeared one after another behind impenetrable veils. For the first time in his life, he knew the meaning of existential anguish.[20]

Then, during this trial of the spirit, he dreamed that he was sitting on the roof of a very wide and tall barn–like building. It was night. Dim, flickering and smoky torches provided an uncertain light. He was surrounded by other people, also sitting. No one was moving. Gingerly he took a step toward the top of the roof, then realized to his dismay that the roof was simply a thick, loose layer of dirt. When he moved, he began to slide. The harder he pawed his way up, the more the whole slope moved—down, down! After a moment of futile grasping and groping, he surrendered and plunged off the roof. He landed in foliage, still wet from a recent rain. He rested there. When he awoke from the dream, he was aware of only one possible movement: down, down.

The crisis loomed upon him during his waking hours and weighed on him in his sleep. Neither his piles of books, nor the library rising majestically near the college quadrangle; neither a solicitous counselor who, with calm, professional empathy, could point out and catalogue his "issues" and "projections"; nor a caring friend and colleague—none of them could supply the needed balm to his soul. I am disappearing into the vacuum which nature abhors, he thought with horror. I must breathe! I must renew! Somewhere beyond this gauntlet of despair must be the fruit of victory, a renewed soul.

For the first time in many years, Anton knew that only Life—living itself—could speak to him. He had to see life from ground level. Practical judgment having deserted him, he cast about for a destination. A visit to his father's home? Not likely: there he could expect neither sympathy nor understanding for the ambiguity that was claiming his soul. The home of his eldest brother in Fresno? Images of the man's somber countenance and dim eyes, nearly blinded from an accident during the Vietnam War, dissuaded him. The brother who resided at the Folsom penitentiary would gladly regale Anton in his spartan cell, but his wife, a *non-pareil* of sudden rages and virulent attitudes towards children, would not welcome his spontaneous visit. San Francisco? That seemed reasonable enough: one of his brothers was a barista in a small but flourishing coffee bar in the Haight district. He was usually at work or at home and his life was diversionary enough. Plus, his female consort was an astonishing woman whose mind and spirit could certainly distract Anton from his own furies. No need to call them to explain. It would be only a day's drive. But wait: the car is in sore need of a tune–up. A friend's car? No: the dependency would only add to his embarrassment. The bus, then. No again: too many stops along the way, and strangers and dingy terminals. Hitchhike? Why not? He could be there in a day, two at the most, with a comfortable stay in a roadside hotel. With no more of a plan than this, Anton stuffed some extra clothing in his backpack, ordered his mail held at the campus post office, withdrew some money from the bank, and descended off the hill to begin his journey.

Human beings expect from the various religions answers to the unsolved riddles of the human condition, which today, even as in former times, deeply stir the heart: What is the human person? What is the meaning, the aim of our life? What is moral good? What is sin? Whence suffering and what purpose does it serve? Which is the road to true happiness? What is death, and judgment and retribution after death? What, finally, is the ultimate inexpressible mystery which encompasses our existence: whence do we come, and where are we going?

From *Nostra Aetate:*
On the Relation of the Church to Non–Christian Religions
Rome, October 25, 1965

COMPLACENCIES BEFORE NIGHTFALL

LIKE ANY ANGELINO, ANTON HAD ENTERED the stream of traffic up Santa Monica Boulevard and onto Interstate 405 innumerable times. Never before, however, had he dared to hitchhike along the broad avenues of concrete and steel that lace the metropolis. Positioned in hopeful waiting on the onramp, he was struck by the stagnation of the river of traffic that flowed past him. From his viewpoint as a pedestrian now, the unending cascade of cars and trucks of infinite sizes, shapes and colors seemed to pour and puddle its way down to the clogged freeway below. After an hour of waiting with his thumb poked out for a ride, Anton's legs and feet began to ache. He began to despair of any help and began to reconsider his hitchhiking idea in all of its derring–do. While he could see every face closely through the windshield of the car or truck, he felt plebian, as strangely distant and as personable as a wooden post. He disciplined himself in the art of hitchhiking, keeping his face uplifted to suggest safety and innocence, and maintaining a posture that conveyed casual insouciance and openness. This was not too difficult for Anton: clean shaven and attractively dressed in jeans and sweater, he did not present the cloudy and faceless appearance of many hitchhikers. A car's headlights flashed, and a wave of a hand invited him in.

"Where you headed?" the driver asked.

"San Francisco. Thanks for stopping." Anton looked at his benefactor, a man near his own age, perhaps closing on his late fourth decade. He wore a clerical collar and a camelhair coat. Cufflinks closed long, black shirtsleeves with subtle tastefulness. The priest's thinning hair was still dark, though touched with grey. He was stylishly handsome and seemed at home with himself.

"I have a brother living in the Bay Area," Anton continued. "I'm on my way up to visit him."

"You're hitching all the way? Kind of a late start." The driver appraised him calmly while glancing ahead at the slowly moving traffic.

"I know. I thought I would go as far as Valencia or Saugus near Six Flags, stay the night, and do the rest tomorrow. With a little luck I should get there by tomorrow night."

"Alright," the driver said. "I am going over to North Hollywood, but I'll drop you off at a good spot near the 170. Then you can catch up with the I-5 further north. My name's John. What's yours?"

"Anton. I haven't been to San Francisco for a long time. This time, I don't know why, I want to go more slowly. Hitchhike like I did when I was younger."

"There were a few more people hitting the road then," John said. "The times allowed it. Today…I don't know…People are getting pretty wary."

"I figure I'm pretty harmless looking."

John looked him over again with appraising eyes. "Hmm…'A man with no guile.' Harmless, but inviting, I'd say. Think about it: do you pick up hitchhikers?"

"Well, no. I usually avoid the freeways."

The conversation trailed off for a moment. The slowly moving traffic and the twinkling of car lights began to create a mosaic of memories in Anton's mind. "I once thumbed my way up to Berkeley, 1969, I think. I can't see why it should be so different today than in the sixties. Were you in California then?"

John nodded. "Seminary training at Menlo Park…The sixties: what a mess! Trying to study the systematics of the Church in the throes of the Vatican Council reforms—hah! A sorry situation…They thought they could run an organization with everybody 'having a voice,' as they now put it in polite circles. Thanks to Vatican II, being 'Catholic' means 'being diluted,' not 'universal,' if you ask me! We hardly recognize ourselves any more. How can you expect people to keep coming to Mass if you encourage individual 'spiritual search'? I know, I know, I'm supposed to give credit to other religions, no matter how bizarre. But that's a joke! Political correctness has given us all lobotomies! Didn't Jesus say, 'I am the way, the truth, and the life'? That's the end of the conversation, as far as I am concerned."

Marveling at John's heated and tortured mixture of sarcasm and grief, Anton was tempted to ask if Jesus really did say that. He wanted to venture the question of whether repeating the dictum was the true believer's subterfuge, a kind of ersatz spirituality that mocked the more difficult work of living the life of unbounded compassion and love. But he did not want to annoy the man, or worse, be dropped off at the next exit. He changed the subject.

"I was in college, too," he said. "Remember the People's Park thing at Berkeley? Kids today don't know anything about that."

"I remember it, vaguely," John replied. "I was still in high school, I think."

"I was just a college freshman then, and had some time on my hands during the spring break. I dropped in to see what was going on and got swept into a crowd on Telegraph Avenue. I can still see the smoke, the police, the National Guard. Everybody staking some claim for law and order, 'flower power,' free speech. The wretched parking lot, now just a weed patch. Hardly worth spilling your blood for. 'Where have all the young men gone?' And the young women?"

Anton paused, surprised by the tone of lament in his own voice. The memory of the low and fearful groans of the crowd rose in his consciousness. He remembered the howitzer–like thump of smoke grenade launchers and the grey clouds that billowed down Telegraph Avenue, pushing people ahead with an acrid hand. In his remembering his heart missed a beat: the young woman...Who was she, that young college student who had tripped against him in the crush? He had reached out and pulled her away from the gathering torrent of people who moments before had been heckling the police and now were stampeding away from them in anguish and panic. For tense moments they had stood in a side alley while the shrieking, trampling crowd, the sobbing women, the yelling and raging men pushed and fought their way from the smoke. He remembered the shimmering sounds of storefront glass shattered by rocks and bottles and the uneven popping of smoke grenades launched by the steely, determined and equally frightened police. Anton saw himself with the young student finding their way to the lawn above Sather Gate, collapsing with panting breath and pounding hearts, stunned and exhilarated. He saw himself holding her one last time before freeing her to an unknown future. What did we say to each other? Who was she? Would she remember, too? What of the gift of trust and gentleness shared by a young man and woman in the calm eye of a hurricane?

Anton shivered. In the darkening twilight he felt evening claiming the vivid memories of his past. Enough, he thought.

"What do you do?" he asked his companion.

"I work for a bishop," John replied. "I'm out of parish ministry, thank God! Did that for sixteen years. Assigned two years here, three years there. Total of five parishes, I believe. Two pastorates. All here in Los Angeles."

"What's it like to work for a bishop?" Anton glanced around the car for the first time. It was a late–model car, spotless, a compact disc player, telephone, a briefcase on the back seat. Other than these items, the car seemed empty.

"Couldn't ask for more," John sighed complacently. "The bishop and I share a house in West LA. Big place with a pool. Got a housekeeper, a woman from Guatemala, I think; I don't know. She'd been a coffee bean picker and needed a job, so we got her papers set up. The diocese gives me this car. No middle–of–the–night calls. It can be stressful on the weekends, keeping up with confirmation schedules. Sometimes we do two confirmations on a weekend. It's always the same. You know the drill: arranging things, making sure everyone knows what to do, parading in and out, a tight and eloquent sermon drawn out of the file as I fly out to the particular service. Eating too much afterward, or rushing off to the next appointment. We try to stay to talk with the rectory staff, over a glass of sherry if we are lucky, but even that's perfectly predictable: everything is dusted off and well–heeled businessmen run the finance council. Controversies in the parish council are being resolved in a collaborative manner according to the latest formula for lay participation, and to 'Father's' satisfaction, of course. Sunday attendance is increasing, the budget is in the black, and so on.

"But I still feel uneasy," John continued dubiously. "The rectories feel like polished mansions with one or two people in them who have to force themselves to have dinner together, and I know that not a few deal with loneliness by drinking alone. Sometimes I even prefer their company, because the 'hail–fellow, well–met' community organizing types who scratch your back today might just as well be stabbing you in the back tomorrow. Then we deal with this traffic. I sure wish the bishop and I had an airplane so we could zoom over the city without having to hassle with traffic."

Anton heard all of this with increasing astonishment. He forgot his own weariness in the presence of this modern–day Potemkin.[21] "Where do you think it's taking you?" he asked.

"Hmm?" John sent a guarded look at him.

"I mean, do people in your work have a sense of a path? Where they end up after all the work?"

"A path...I don't have the luxury to think about that any more." John's words sounded resigned, matching the grim expression on his face. He ran his hand through his hair. "When we were in seminary we talked about that with the vocations director, who was also the diocesan recruiter. With all the people leaving the priesthood it was hard to take seriously stuff about 'calling' and so forth, especially coming from a recruiter. 'Knowing yourself' came up a little later in my philosophy class, I think. Isn't that a quaint idea? We left it behind when we got to the real meat of ministry: theology. The whole goal is to make you effective for parish work, in three years' time, no less. We had to learn the tradition, you know, the encyclicals, exegesis, pastoral counseling, scripture. It comes in handy during those thirty second inquisitions when parishioners pin you to the cookie table after the liturgy."

As John paused in his reminiscence, Anton searched for some trace of the dignified and courteous medieval debate between philosophy and theology. Even that conversation seemed lost in the modern world, where pragmatism had replaced both disciplines in the courts of professional ministry.

John then laughed, and continued in the same vein. "Practically the only thing I remember from that whole time was the day when I was ordained. Before the ceremonies, you should've heard the hair dryers going! It sounded like a whirlwind! And the sun shining off our patent leather shoes!" He whistled and chuckled again. "As for where I'm going, it's just a matter of putting in the time. Either I'll be made a bishop in the next few years or I'll retire. Or I could be made a secretariat director."

"What's that?"

"Oh, a kind of department head. It's a great job for someone who has the system figured out. Just work with the system…that's my motto. Show up in uniform and be a good soldier. Deal with constant paper. Just keep it flowing. Don't let it settle on your desk to gather dust. I think that they have me in mind for the Finance Department. I've really got my stewardship pitch nailed down for the annual appeal. A seven minute homily…powerful and painless and just enough tingle to hold peoples' interest while we pass out pledge cards."

John continued to ruminate as the traffic picked up speed to a steady lope over the hill into the San Fernando Valley. "You see, you have to know your 'agenda.' That's the key word for working with the system. Even the people who hate the system know this. There's always too much to do, so you figure out what will get results. That becomes your agenda. For me, it means paying attention in meetings with His Excellency and the deans, listening to the news, the gossip—'theology in the hallways,' you know. That's how it is today: we trade the silence of morning prayers for the screaming headlines of the morning newspaper. Then we can tell ourselves everyday that we are being relevant, I suppose, and keep up on the 'theology of the gutter.' I've been around the block. I know what will get my head cut off and look out for that. Sometimes it's kind of laughable, or pitiful, to see the young guys learn those lessons.

"So, you asked if I have a sense of path, and I end up sounding like a careerist. How do you know if a path is going anywhere? Better to have a cause, a winning cause. Before the current mayor it was gun control. We got together with a lot of churches and had big rallies, even had some union people involved. We got some legislation passed that got assault rifles out of stores. Of course, they're still all over East Los Angeles and South Central. That can't be your cause for too long. It's too big.

"And I learned to steer clear of migrant labor issues. That's even more overwhelming! Too many people. All sheep and no shepherd. Now I know what is meant by 'the poor you will always have with you.'[22] In Texas they swim the Rio Grande, or slog across where it runs dry. The term 'wetbacks' hardly works anymore. Here in California, they creep over the border. It's like a sieve down there. You should hear some of the clergy in San Diego who work in the affluent neighborhoods on the hills. Their rectory windows have to look down on the tents and ponchos spread over the brush in the ravines. Talk about an annoyance! The Mexicans or Hondurans or whatever hide in the ravines below the red tile neighborhoods on the hills, camp out in the brush and create an enormous fire hazard until the county gets called in and they bring in bulldozers to clean up the mess. The clergy down there are getting all exercised because people are running across the freeway, sometimes getting hit. So they've had signs put up, like the ones for deer crossing areas, only these are signs with two people running, an adult and a kid, usually. It's crazy down there, total anarchy! Then the people go underground with relatives for a while. We know this happens because they're everywhere, stretched from San Diego to Seattle, and mostly along I-5 and up the valley. They're certainly not hanging around the camps in San Diego."

As Anton listened, he felt growing pressure on his chest, a clawing at his throat. He listened with increasing incredulity as his image of priest and pastor was being demolished by John's gnashings.

"So, what then?" John continued with heat. "They show up in church! Church facilities can't handle them, most of the clergy do not speak their language, so they wander off and join the Pentecostals and Jehovah's Witnesses. Really, they'll go anywhere where they can worship like they're at a fiesta. The rest of the week you'll see them on the street corners, waiting for someone to offer them a day job.

"County health and the social service agencies deal with the problem, but they have a good conscience. 'County' doesn't go looking for these people. They sit tight in their offices. If the immigrant comes in for services—which they will only do if they have immigration papers—'County' wears them out by hassling them with paperwork, fingerprints, and all that. Of course, somebody who has no papers will not dare to show up for help; they'd be back on a bus to Tijuana within the hour. That simplifies the county job by a long shot.

"Same situation in the hospitals: when one of these people shows up in the emergency room, they stitch them back together and put them back out and don't worry about what brought them there. Once an ER doctor told me that a Crips gang member who was getting stitched up for knife wounds had asked him if he would be on duty in a couple of hours. The doctor said, 'Yes, why?' The gang member shrugged and said it didn't matter much: no doctor would be able to stitch up the Blood who attacked him up after the Crips got through with him."

John's voice quieted for a moment as he pondered another image. "We people in church do things differently. We promise things, really great things, a hell of a lot more rewarding than a job or medical care. But the catch is that it's all coming in the next life. Our job is to assure people that it's so good it's worth waiting for, even when things here are absolutely miserable. I guess I have a bad conscience about this, but at least we don't hassle people with paperwork!"

John paused in his reflections to merge onto 101 eastbound. "Nasty traffic," he muttered as he inched and squeezed his car between trucks, taxis and commuter cars. While they were settling into the flow again, Anton's mind flickered back to a small, hidden sanctuary church, practically under the freeway somewhere in East Los Angeles. What was its name?...Dolores Mission...He remembered meeting a young Jesuit priest dressed in fraying jeans, a cotton shirt and a *sombrero*, as he painted the small play structure on the church grounds and fixed the piping for a shower for his guests. In his mind's eye he saw Mexicans and Central Americans from the public housing projects bringing beans and tortillas to the exhausted and frightened arrivals. He saw the busy kitchen and washing machine that never stopped, and the piles of blankets for sleeping on the church pews.

Now, here beside him in the car was 'Father John,' certainly no Prester John, the legendary Arthur of Abyssinia in the 1400s, a leader and statesman who had no agenda and no business meetings, yet whose kingdom was said to have no poor, no violence, and no thieves. Nor was this world–weary man a match for one of those prelates of medieval Europe who piled his pelf while conducting his affairs with a debonair cynicism that left him rich, rapacious and insolent. No, he is more like a Polonius, the pathetic and complaisant elder who mouthed platitudes like "To thine own self be true," little knowing that a sword was rising behind the arras where he stood.[23] Yet, Anton thought, I feel a certain kinship with this unhappy soul. Like me, he has had fleeting thoughts of an accomplished life, but has lost sight of it in his busy affairs. What a paradox, what a detriment to faith this despair is! Pascal had said it well: "Men despise religion; they hate it, and they fear it is true."[24] So, if we can't look in the obvious places like the churches and centers of worship, where is true faith to be spied out? In small clusters of people underneath the freeways, with paint brushes and plates of beans in hand? And what does this say of me? Am I not becoming a carping cultural philistine, a two–dimensional man? Could this individual beside me not be a strange gift, an insight into my own possible prognosis? Am I too a soul dying to the Great Romance? But for now some questions are best left unspoken.

Anton asked, "So, what keeps you charged up now?"

"Well, I'm not exactly 'charged up,' as you put it. Don't really want to be 'charged up.' The evil in me is that I know too much. The more I know, the less I feel like doing anything, and the less difference it seems to make anyway. Got to husband my strength at this point. You should know that. No wandering around the country hitchhiking for me." Anton felt John's glance appraising him and his graying hair.

"I had all of this figured a long time ago. I got permission for a three year leave and went back to school. Got a Doctor of Theology degree from Catholic University, then got appointed as the Bishop's theologian."

"That sounds like an enormous responsibility," Anton said, trying to fathom this ordered life. "How can you have a job as a theologian?"

"Don't laugh. It's not as hard as it sounds. We're mostly ghostwriters. We never say anything in our own names. The less you say, the better. You get to read a lot, and only have to work (I mean study and write), when the bishop tells you to. Mostly it's all been laid out for you in earlier pastoral letters or papal encyclicals. If you have to draft a pastoral letter, you have the pattern and a style ready–made: there's the lofty language of the universal Church, fraternal greetings to everybody, a web of Scriptural references that makes sense to other theologians, even if it annoys ordinary readers. Of course, when I say that it makes sense to other theologians, I mean the appointed academics who are doing the same thing as you. We all share in this conviction, that we are doing important work.

"Do you remember Oscar Romero?" John asked abruptly. "He was a 'do nothing,' academic bishop, a safe choice for El Salvador. When he put away his books and starting speaking out and showing up with the peasants at the voting places, no one backed him up and he got gunned down. I think he was gunned down before they shot him. Think I want that to happen to me? Better to write about peace and justice than to stick your neck out...Well, never mind all that. So, when you write, you defend your position; but of course you do not make it sound like 'your position.' Rather it comes as the inescapable conclusion of reason, the tradition of official pronouncements from the *magisterium,* and Scripture. We can write all this without bringing up the question of Jesus. Or if we have to mention Jesus, we make him say what we need him to say, because his job is to help our argument along. Of course, I know this is ridiculous: everyone who dealt with Jesus was completely brought to a halt and was unable to go on doing their usual thing. No one could trot him in 'to do their thing.' They couldn't even get close to tricking him. So, my job is to write letters that are really nothing more than footnotes to the old tablets. You do that right, and things won't change. How could things change, I mean really change, short of the Parousia, the 'Second Coming,' when it has been bumbling along for 2000 years?"

"Sounds pretty straight–forward." Anton said politely. This was a ride, after all. But my heavens, what I thought might be Dostoevsky's Grand Inquisitor is nothing but a jaded and cynical civil servant. The successor to the coldly principled despot is a fatuous bureaucrat or a pathetic Walter Mitty![25] But, Anton's thoughts wandered, if we dare ask for change in a time plagued with constant change, why not a change for justice and kindness, for a better world? If not for that, the whole life of Jesus is nothing but a sentimental spectacle. What would the world be like if people set aside just one week out of the year to emulate Jesus? But from the point of view of my companion, why change things when your bills are paid and you get a new car every other year? It seems so clean and clear to this fellow. My own life feels like a fiasco.

John suddenly changed the subject. "What really throws the whole thing off is women, the attractive ones, that is."

Anton's instincts fired into life. He said nothing, but gazed at his host.

"Women...they shake the whole thing up." John paused, testing the sympathies of his guest.

"I have no great wisdom about that," Anton said elusively. The movements of old sorrows stirred in his chest.

"Then I'm not alone...I've seen lots of my friends just cave in. For a long time I thought I would just tough it out, remain celibate, you know, hoping that someday it wouldn't matter anymore."

"They say that celibacy is meant to be a spiritual gift," Anton said, searching for safe ground. By no means was he going to offer a word from his own story to this troubled man. In a passing thought he remembered Sophocles' exasperation as an old man when he pleaded to be rid of amorous desires; but Anton said nothing.[26]

"Funny thing is, the hardest thing is not being attracted to women, or being attractive to them because you are unavailable. That made me crazy until I learned to run from the pain. What's really hard is preaching about the 'renunciation of pleasure,' although I never use so many words. Better to stand up as someone who has dedicated myself to 'another world,' which, in a funny way, includes so much of what is squelched here in this world. So, what is the 'other world'? (Here John threw up both hands, leaving his vehicle to steer along straight without guidance for a moment.) How can you even talk of the 'Kingdom of God' without irritating the radical feminists and the politically correct? I guess we could call it the 'commonwealth of Jesus and the poor' where everyone shares everything in common. The irony is, he wanted it for here and now, not for some other world. I know that I'm not dedicated to that. I didn't make a vow of poverty. Chastity is bad enough! If my celibacy is not a sign for that way of life, what is it?"

Anton felt cautiously for words. "I've never felt that the Church had it right when it equated celibacy with Jesus' way of life, at least the kind of celibacy that implies a lack of intimacy. What seems to have happened is that the loss of passion has taken refuge behind arguments for celibacy. It seems a shame that this aspect of his life, which seems insignificant, should become so overblown. Smothering natural passions only inflames them, it seems to me, or diverts them in unfortunate directions."

"Ho! I notice how delicately you put that!" John half groaned.

"Forgive me for sounding pompous. These are sensitive matters."

"Well then," John continued with heat. "Why hide the obvious? Look, there's Jesus, always with women, everywhere he goes. The Mary's, Martha, Anna, his mother, the woman caught in adultery—whatever that means—, the Samaritan woman at the well, the unnamed woman tugging at his cloak when he is rushing off to see Jairus. They are too many to be named. It seems like it's always a woman who stops Jesus in his tracks. They're the ones who sit at the foot of the cross until the very end. They're the first to see him and recognize him after his death. Seems to me that they could have written the whole story themselves. And I don't believe that women had to badger him for their attention: I think he really loved women, and was happy and peaceful around them. He didn't seem to care that the men around him were scandalized and irritated by the way he enjoyed their company."

Anton marveled at the pained self–disclosure being offered by his companion. He was on the verge of complimenting him for his pastoral conscience when John's tone changed. His voice became nearly inaudible.

"In fact, I am perfectly comfortable with the idea of Jesus as a lover…a man of passion! That is something I have a hunch about."

"Do others feel that way?"

"I would never try to find out, not in this job! And if I did, I sure wouldn't offer it as an arguing point in a pastoral letter! Frankly, it's a career–limiting move just to be seen in a car with a woman, unless she is really along in years, and never, heaven forbid, a young woman or a teenager. Why, even with my brother priests and a carafe of wine, the subject hardly comes up. So I try to forget about it and remember that I'm an official and not a man and human being." John gave a slight shudder, almost a paroxysm at the thought of the condemnation and suspicion that would descend upon him.

At this, a vague memory of something called "learned ignorance" passed through Anton's mind: untruths spoken and recited over and over again until they sound and feel like truth.[27] What can I possibly say to this? he wondered. Some trite comment about "ordering our desires," when my companion here is wracked by doubts that consume his remaining years? Such a parade of vices tripping after an excess of virtue! How can the argument against the complete dignity and equality of women in heaven and on earth simply labor on? The very well–being of the planet depends on the end of the war of the sexes and the healing of its injustices. Here, escorting him along the freeways of the fallen City of Man, this unindividuated human being lives in this peculiar nightmare while knowing he is awake.[28] But who am I to criticize? Anton asked himself. It is said that the man who plays the fool is a God in disguise; how am I a fool to others? Anton did not know whether to feel pity or exasperation.

"I'll be exiting in a minute," John said. "What would you like to do? Shall I find you an onramp for the 170? Maybe you'll get lucky with someone going on up the I-5."

Anton looked around at the swirl of traffic and streetlights. Signs pointed away to Van Nuys, Burbank, North Hollywood, and Studio City. Faces on billboards stared down at him: one advertised a TV program about Hercules. Why do the old heroes look so stupid and malicious when used by sophisticates for entertainment? he asked himself. Not even the heroes can muster strength against the sordid forces of greed and anger, jealousy and laziness. They have become nothing but financial line items in the next profit report. This is no place for me to spend the night. Rather than get swallowed up in ugliness here, get out and move on, he thought.

"That would be fine. There's a lot of traffic going north. I would like to get up to Valencia for the night."

John wheeled his car smoothly through the traffic and stopped along the sidewalk. "Nice talking with you. Be safe."

"Thank you for the ride." With a wave, John disappeared again into the city, and Anton walked up to his next intersection.

Where every man is enemy to every man...there is no place for industry, because the fruit thereof is uncertain: and consequently no culture of the earth; no navigation, nor use of the commodities that may be imported by sea; no commodious building; no instruments of moving and removing such things as require much force; no knowledge of the face of the earth; no account of time; no arts; no letters; no society; and which is worst of all, continual fear, and danger of violent death; and the life of man, solitary, poor, nasty, brutish, and short.

Thomas Hobbes (1588–1679),
Leviathan XIII

CONTINUAL FEAR, AND DANGER OF VIOLENT DEATH

By now, the energy of Anton's exodus from the safe and secure college grounds was being replaced with a sense of heaviness and uncertainty. It was 6:00 on a late November evening with an unpromising sky overhead. From the buzz and busyness of its daylight hours, North Hollywood was decaying into a crashing, careening retreat, as though its citizens wished to reach the security of home and neighborhood before night had fallen. Caught on the sidelines of the frenetic rush from the city, Anton felt nameless fears and worries rising in him. While he had credit cards and cash he resisted the idea of stopping for the night. Better to continue further north to the lights and exuberant racket of the amusement park of Six Flags Magic Mountain. There would be families around and people having fun. A good dinner and night's rest awaited him, he hoped. He could wait for something to eat. Anton faced the traffic and put out his thumb.

He stood beside the road for an interminable hour and a half. The cold deepened and an occasional raindrop was a harbinger of an impending storm. Finally, when Anton was ready to surrender and seek a North Hollywood inn, a car slowed instead of accelerating by him. He felt himself being scrutinized by the occupants. The car stopped, and Anton opened the back door.

"Where you headed?" a woman's voice inquired. With the help of the freeway lights Anton made out the profiles of a man and woman in their mid–20s. They had the unkempt look of people on the move. The man behind the wheel wore a shabby–looking leather jacket. From his face sprouted whiskers that failed to convey that dismissive and charming contempt of the Bolshevik of old; he simply looked dirty and mottled with adolescent growth. The woman beside him had eyes like tiny black coals shrunken inside a huge clump of metallic red hair that had been teased into an electrified look. Her stone-cold mask for a face reminded Anton of the Medusa's head with its spitting snakes.

"The I-5 up to Valencia," Anton said. "I'm heading to San Francisco, and planning to spend the night near Six Flags."

"We're headed that way ourselves. Hop in."

Anton complied. As he seated himself he felt hunger and fatigue and a growing anxiety. The smell of cigarette ashes and unwashed skin assaulted his senses. A six-pack of beer bottles was lodged on the floor against the back seat. Several bottles appeared empty.

"A rough time of night to be traveling."

Anton agreed, expressed his gratitude for the ride, and shifted to make himself comfortable. The car moved on in silence above the dense neighborhoods and strip malls of Hollywood. His discomfort made him remember his little flat near the ocean, the clean, well-lit kitchen, the evening meal alone or with friends, the young men and women at the college rejoicing in their safe and creative community of learning, the peaceful routine of his collegiate life. Here in this car with these sullen souls, no amount of shifting could dispel his sense of being trapped. He settled into a tense vigilance, watching for familiar city and street names. The only sounds were the swish of the tires and the clicking of the windshield wipers as they swept away the rain.

Anton could not make out any of the conversation between the man and woman over the engine noise, although he could see their eyes connect for brief moments. They were not affectionate glances, but were pregnant with meaning. The woman leaned over to turn on the car heater, and hot, dusty air from the engine added to the oppressiveness.

As signs of the glittering profile of Six Flags Magic Mountain came into view, Anton spoke up, "I'm getting off at Valencia. I think the exit is the next one." The woman stiffened. The driver ignored him. The exit passed by. Fear surged up his backbone; he could feel it clamp his belly, wash up his shoulder blades and around his neck. He felt it tightening a freezing grip around his vocal chords. Six Flags with its huge roller coasters and blazing lights came and went.

"Sorry to bother you, but I need to get off now," he said, the tremble in his voice betraying his foreboding.

"Oh, right," the woman said, turning back to look at him. "How about handing over your wallet?"

The words hit him like a dagger. "You can't be serious! Give me a break!"

A clicking sound from the cocking of a pistol came from the front seat. "Hand it over!"

"In the name of God," Anton gasped.

"Oh, shut up. No angels here, you idiot. Maybe we're your angels!" came the man's sneering voice. *"Your wallet, slick."*

Anton's trembling hand reached into his pocket for his wallet. He gave it to the woman. What is happening to me? he anguished. "At least let me keep my credit cards," he begged. He felt dirty, ashamed, helpless. The woman's glare answered his entreaties.

The man pried open Anton's wallet. "Well, I'll be go to hell! Five hundred dollars! We can sure use this!" He shoved the bills in his shirt pocket, opened the window, and threw the wallet out into the rushing wind. Anton saw his identity cascade into the departing abyss of night.

"What are we going to do with him?" the woman asked.

"Keep an eye on him. You know what to do if he budges. Just don't mess up the upholstery," came the answer.

Anton felt animal fear. With a gun pointed at his chest, with the unblinking eyes of the horrible woman upon him, he felt frozen in a vice of terror. This is the emotion underlying the vile statement about life being "nasty, brutish and short."[29] Konrad Lorenz was right: The missing link between apes and the human race? Ourselves! At least I can protect myself with my pack, he thought. Beneath the woman's gaze, he shifted his pack around in front of his chest. He embraced the pack like a man clutching jetsam from a sinking ship.

The car moved rapidly through the darkened world, climbing steadily into the Tehachapis. In this frozen time Anton heard scattered phrases, "…back to Magic Mountain…really good stuff…woo-ey, stop tantalizing me!…he might recognize us…get it over with…don't chance it." The car battered on, a hot, fetid prison.

Suddenly: "Stop here." With an abrupt braking and swerve that threw Anton against the door, the car wrenched to a stop on the freeway shoulder. "Get out!" Anton flung open the door, gripped his backpack and winter jacket, and threw himself out. He tripped painfully on the asphalt, lurched to his feet and ran blindly away. The car with its monstrous occupants roared out of sight. Anton fell to his knees on the damp soil and his guts heaved.

If the nearness of our last necessity brought a nearer conformity into it, there were a happiness in hoary hairs, and no calamity in half senses. But the long habit of living indisposeth us for dying...

Thomas Brown, d. 1682

I SAW ETERNITY THE OTHER NIGHT

How long Anton remained at the roadside he did not know. It may have been no more than a minute. The freeway had become an avenue of trauma. Like the wild and abysmal river of Acheron flowing straight to Hell,[30] the road roared past him with an inhuman cacophony of sound. He could hear and feel nothing but the screaming whoosh of spinning tires, clamoring diesel engines, banking wind and flying dust and gravel. He could see nothing but the stream of car and truck lights blazing down on him in the night. No street or city lights could be seen, no signs, no telephones, nothing but a torrent of racing lights accompanied by the unearthly din of metal monsters.

At least the rain had stopped. Anton tried walking along the shoulder for a few minutes. Blinded by the headlights, he tripped on stones and felt pocked by sand and litter thrown by spinning wheels. A dull terror reeled around his chest and numbed his senses. The hunger in his stomach reached up to his mind like a vast emptiness. His emotions ran amuck, from shivering hilarity to exhausted relief. He felt disoriented and aimless, and ached with a weariness pumped into every nook and cranny of his being.

I have to get off this road, he thought. Feeling his way by waving his hands in front of his face, he squeezed through a barbed wire fence. Now the soft beam from the moon coming from behind broken clouds was able to light his way. Beyond the fence the hill sloped up to an indistinct ridgeline. Placing one foot gingerly in front of the other, Anton moved up the hill. Along the way he picked up a stick to help him find his way. In the distance he could see the faint glow of a settlement, too remote for a night trek. After walking, stumbling and groping his way over hundreds of yards, he found himself before a rocky outcropping. Here, on a huge, smooth granite boulder, he sought safety.

Quiet descended. The cold cut into him and edged around into sheltered places in his body. He donned his jacket over his sweater, and pulled out his clean shirt from his pack and wrapped it around his neck. He pulled his wool cap far down over his forehead. He listened. Nothing. No freeway sounds, no lights from cars. Nothing but the rocks, the hill fading into darkness, and the faint light of the moon.

Over the pounding of his heart Anton could hear small creatures moving with stealth in the brush. His heart quaked as the still air spread aside for an owl who came and went through the darkness, sending down a low, warning hoot to the rocks below. His ears began to make out odd clicks and whistles that shook the sheet of silence. The curtain of his senses rose and he became enveloped in the nocturnes of desert night. Time deepened in the waiting. Far away on some invisible hillcrest, a coyote lifted his voice under the dark canopy in the long trill of a lonely piccolo. His comrades joined in an invisible chorus, deepening the primeval drama of night. The yipping pierced and punctuated the darkness, then fell silent.

On his rocky bier above the desert brush, Anton's senses regained their primacy over his mind. Outwardly stripped of the armor of technology and familiar comforts, inwardly seared with the rush of adrenalin, hungry, stripped of all resource or a sense of direction, awareness overwhelmed him, weighed upon him, invaded him with shocking intensity. Huddling before the scrutiny of uncountable and unknowable beings in the brush and rocky crevasses, he experienced the world unfolding in his seeing and hearing. How much have I not seen nor heard, he said in his heart. Unlike the invisible creatures around me, I can keep my larder full. My habits are little more than instincts that have become lazy comforts. Not until tonight have I faced a predator. It was evil…He shivered in the cold.

Then he saw something move. The rustling in the bushes became silent. A line was being drawn in the sand. A long, dark snake glided noiselessly from underneath a mesquite bush and into the open. The moving line curved toward him to within ten feet. There he paused. Anton could see the V-shaped head rise urgently, staring with the total, timeless passion of the desert. The snake's tongue flicked in and out, probing some strange new smell. Anton tapped the rock sharply with his stick.[31] Instantly the snake coiled, his head drawing back to give forth a mighty bolt of animal energy. The castanets on his tail cracked the silence like the rattle of a snare drum. The snake stared at the intruder with wild, distant, yet benign objectivity. Anton sat very still. The man and the animal beheld each other for a long moment under the never-blinking eye of the moon. Then, the snake unwound and withdrew, leaving Anton breathing quietly on the rock.

Anton realized that the night action left no one as a spectator. The snake had ordained him as a participant. From this wild drama with no beginning nor end, the human imagination draws meaning: the silent, watchful owl taking flight in the dusk becomes the symbol of life's late wisdom.[32] So too, the snake lifted up in the wilderness both terrifies and heals; and the coyote draws the haunt of his voice from the spirit world. The words of Vaughan's old poem came to his lips in a voiceless whisper:

> I saw Eternity the other night
> Like a great ring of pure and endless light,
> All calm as it was bright;
> And round beneath it, Time, in hours, days, years,
> Driven by the spheres,
> Like a vast shadow moved, in which the world
> And all her train were hurled...[33]

In his solitude, immersed in the sound and movement of the desert and safe from brigands and night terrors, Anton awaited the dawn.

With great difficulty advancing by millimeters each year, I carve a road out of the rock. For millennia my teeth have wasted and my nails have been broken to get there, to the other side, to the light and the open air.

And now that my hands bleed and my teeth tremble, unsure in a cavity cracked by thirst and dust, I pause and contemplate my work. I have spent the second part of my life breaking the stones, drilling the walls, smashing the doors, removing the obstacles I placed between the light and myself in the first part of my life.

Octavio Paz[34]

You are searching for Aguilares

MORNING ROSE, cold, crisp and clear from the distant dark, lifting the veil of shadow from the surrounding hills. Anton maneuvered his aching body off the rock, and, watching for the snake, worked his way back down to the freeway. He set out, walking along the freeway shoulder in the direction of the glow of lights that he had seen the night before. He was again buffeted by the blasts of wind from trucks, and became gritty with sand in his eyes and hair and ears. He felt painfully hungry, begrizzled, and broke.

    Who in the world am I? he thought. Would the man who walked out of class the other day recognize himself? Am I going backward, or forward? When I get to that settlement up there, whom should I call? Who would come all the way out to the Tehachapis to pick me up? Anton knew that any of his college friends could be there in two hours, and that by noon he could be at home, clean, warm, and fed. But is this how I wanted to be seen, the urbane college professor, the man warmed and respected by the esteem of his family and friends, his colleagues and students? Hardly! I have embarked, the wordless thought came to his mind. What am I to learn?...Certainly that I am not master of my own fate, captain of my own soul!...But what else? I set off for a city named after a man of utmost peace, and have run head–on into bestial human beings. I have felt fear. I have felt the earth grinding into my knees. Is this why we light up the night skies with street lamps? Is fear the hidden heart of our longing for comfort? How can I now despise the Israelites who longed for the stability and comforts of old and familiar Egypt? I have something to learn, and I don't even know what my own questions are. The old ways hold nothing but the old answers. I will find my questions at the bottom of my cup, and I will drink it to the lees. Not yet: I am not ready to go back yet.

After walking several miles Anton arrived at a roadside truck stop. Two mechanics were conversing in Spanish. As he approached, they stopped talking and gaped at the tottering apparition.

"*Buenos días,*" he said, dropping naturally into the second language of California. "*Buenos,*" came the reply.

"*Amigos, necesito ayuda. Viajaba de Los Angeles a San Francisco. Tengo hermano allí. Algunos ladrones trajeron mi bolleta...por sus drogas, yo creo. Me empujaron en la calle en arriba dos milas, mas o menos. Estoy muy cansado y tengo mucho hambre.*" Friends, I need help. I was traveling from Los Angeles to San Francisco. I have a brother there. Some robbers took my wallet, for their drugs, I think, and shoved me out on the highway about two miles back. I am very tired and very hungry. The words flowed with much feeling, as though Spanish had been shaped to convey the passions and distress of the heart and soul.

"*¡Madre de Dios! ¡Qué suerte que no lo mataron! Esto pasa de vez en quando en la carretera.*" Mother of God! You were lucky they did not kill you; this happens from time to time along the highway.

Anton felt their sympathy. The conversation became too rapid for him to follow, but in the end, one of the men said, "*Venga conmigo,*" and began to walk down a side street from the main highway. The open air of the day, the graciousness of his companion, and his own hunger restored Anton's trust. He learned that his guide, Juan Carlos, was a Salvadoran immigrant who had found a job as a mechanic, and lived on the outskirts of the settlement. His wife worked as a housekeeper at the truck stop motel. Within a few minutes they arrived at a small house. At the sound of their voices, a woman opened the door. She held an infant held in one arm and a dishtowel in her other hand. A small child scurried behind her skirt. Juan Carlos introduced his wife Anita, whose eyes of an exile were both fearless and welcoming. She held the door open wide and invited Anton up the steps into their home.

The smells of the kitchen bathed Anton in an indescribable warmth. Anita gestured him to a chair by a small table. She laid the baby in a carrier on the table, where he began to chew on a toy and watch his mother with soft eyes. Anton removed his backpack and jacket and felt himself collapsing into safety for the first time in many hours.

"*¿Tiene hambre, No?*" she asked. You are hungry?

"*Oh, señora, mi estómago está vacio.*" My stomach is empty. But as he spoke these words he realized that he was also hungry for something that could not be satisfied by any food. He watched as Anita placed a pan on the stove, filled it with water and oatmeal, broke two eggs into it, and added salt, milk and honey. Within two minutes the steaming bowl was placed in front of Anton, with a cup of coffee and the words, *"Buen provecho."*

Anton took one bite and felt the warm nourishment reach through his mouth, throughout his head and weary eyes, and down, down into his chest and the empty empire of his stomach. He ate the meal with tears streaming down his face. In compassion Anita turned and busied herself at the sink. The little girl gazed at him with wide, curious eyes and an open mouth absent a few baby teeth. Juan Carlos smiled and said, *"A buen hambre no hay gordas duras."* Hunger is the best sauce. More rapid words were exchanged between the couple.

Juan Carlos laid his hand on Anton's shoulder and said, *"Puede lavarse en el baño. Después, descanse aquí. Está casa es su casa."* You can wash here in the bathroom. Afterwards, you can sleep in our room. This house is your house. Then he left.

Bathed, shaved, and settled onto the couch bed in the small trailer, Anton slipped into a dreamless sleep for the rest of the morning. When he awoke, the house was quiet and empty. Juan Carlos and his wife and children returned at noon.

"How are you feeling?" he asked.

"I am so much better. I cannot thank you enough," Anton said.

"It is nothing," Juan Carlos replied. "We have been helped many times to get here. Here, *cara mia,* let me hold the baby." He took the baby boy from his wife, kissed him, and stood aside while she began to take food from the small refrigerator.

"We have been separated from each other and our loved ones. I was once robbed by the *coyotes* at the border, and know what it feels like to be very, very hungry. Here we are safe, and our little girl can play outside and has friends. And look at our baby! He is so healthy and fat. We are very happy. In the spring and summer we can even grow some of our own food. Come, let me show you our garden while Anita makes lunch."

Juan Carlos bundled the baby in an extra blanket and the two men walked outside into the cool air of late autumn. "There is nothing here now, but in the spring I grow beans, corn, peppers and chilies, tomatoes, everything we like to eat. We have our friends over for dinner every few days, or we visit them. Sometimes the pastor from Valencia comes. We eat and tell stories. Sometimes we sing old songs or the new hits. The kids play and shout and the dogs run round around and bark, especially when we swing the *piñata*. We have a great time.

"Sometimes we talk about what we have left behind..." A shadow darkened his weathered, brown eyes. "We talk about our parents and our old homes and our childhood, and we remember those who did not make it...Sometimes some of the young men tell us about the women who cannot be with them...I think of my aunt who was killed down there. I too was a teacher, elementary school, and I miss my students very much." For a silent moment the two men felt the weight of life and the loss of what they had known and loved.

"Still, we laugh, too. Someday, *amigo*, we will laugh at what you looked like when you came into our station this morning. Like nothing on earth. Like a crazy man. Both sad and very funny. You're better, now, no? What are your plans?"

Anton looked out from the garden to the skyline above and listened to the quiet of the open horizon. "We say sometimes, 'I shall lift my eyes unto the hills, from whence my help comes.' Now I know what that means. You and your wife and little ones have given me a great blessing. Now, I must keep going."

"But how? You have no money. After yesterday, you think you can get to your brother in San Francisco by tonight? Does he even know you are coming?"

With a start Anton realized that he had not thought about the purpose of his journey since the previous night's ordeal. "No, he doesn't know." A long pause allowed Anton a growing realization. "Maybe I'm not supposed to go there."

"I think I understand." Juan Carlos leaned his elbows on the fence of his garden plot. "You need to travel, but you do not know where you are going, or how you are going to get there. All you know is that it is beyond, somewhere waiting. We have a saying for this in El Salvador: *buscando Aguilares:* 'searching for Aguilares.' Originally we knew Aguilares to be a little neighborhood in God's great neighborhood. We had *Padre* Rutilio Grande and the Jesuits who taught the people that the Bible is a call to human dignity: you know, being able to walk on the street with everybody else, and not having to walk in the gutter when the big shots come around. Christ the healer, the prophet and revolutionary had so much work to do in us, because we had become so accepting of terrible things. After Rutilio was killed, a hydroelectric plant on the Orellano hacienda displaced people who had lived there for fifty years. People had no where to go but to *El Norte*.[35]

"When thinking of the North, people would say, *'Los Estados Unidos es un lugar de mil maravillas':* the States is a 'place of a thousand marvels.' Also, there is a town of Aguilares in Texas, so people would put the two together in their mind. Then, people who made it to North America would realize that what they were looking for was even beyond the land of miracles. They knew that it was a place in the heart. So, they felt like eagles looking down, seeing the really big picture. 'Searching for Aguilares' means that people are looking for their rightful home, knowing that their true home is out there somewhere. For us, to go north on faith is a risk…Finding your true home demands still greater risks."[36]

"Leave home to find it. At what cost!…," Anton said.

"Not until you know you have a home are you able to take the greatest risks," Juan Carlos agreed thoughtfully. "But if you had not taken even this small risk, I would not know you, and I am grateful to know you."

"Wherever I go, whatever I do, I will need to find some work," Anton said.

"Hmm. Wait here. I have an idea." Within a few minutes, Juan Carlos returned. "I have an uncle living in Bakersfield. He has a restaurant and he hires people to work in the kitchen. I called him, and he says you can work for him for a while, if you want. You can make some of your money back. The restaurant is very busy. Minimum wage, but he has a bunkhouse, and you can eat in his kitchen. It is available."

Anton looked into the warm, brown eyes of the Salvadoran. For a instant he saw other faces, his students' concerned faces, the dean, the disillusioned priest, the merciless woman with the gun, Anita with the warm and savory food, the children. These are all my teachers, he thought. May I receive and understand their teaching...

"Yes. I'll do it. Thank you, *amigo*."

After eating lunch Juan Carlos returned to the garage. Anton rested. In the evening Anita and the children came home from the job at the motel. The little group ate dinner together, and Anton tried his simple Spanish with the child, who grinned like a pumpkin and hid her face behind her hands. He remembered magic coin tricks, and using some of his remaining change from his pocket, produced coins from her father's ears. The little girl giggled with laughter. Juan Carlos wrote directions to his uncle's restaurant, and everyone turned to sleep.

The next morning, Anita bade farewell to Anton at the door with, *"Buena suerte. Revuela algun día."* Good luck. Come back someday.

Juan Carlos said, "Come to my garage, Anton. My partner has been checking the brakes for a truck driver. He goes to Bakersfield. He says he will take you." Then, before entering the garage, he asked, "Do you have the directions?"

"Yes, here in my pocket."

The two men looked at each other for a moment. The Salvadoran then said, "I remember reading Cervantes when I was a younger man, Anton. At the end of all his crazy battles Quixote is a battered wreck, but everybody who knows him is somehow better. He says to Sancho, *'Morir es descansar, y vivir estar loco':* 'To die is to rest, and to live is to be crazy.' He's right, you know. But we know that God looks after children and homeless and crazy people. Thank you for coming into our home." He then embraced Anton and took him to meet the truck driver.

Twofold always, may God us keep
From single vision, and Newton's sleep.

              William Blake (1757–1827),
                  Songs of Experience

Gravity's graceful ways

AN ANCIENT PETERBILT in faded green rested outside the garage. It had long ago given up its polish and smooth skin to the mute dents and odd bucklings of steel plate and bodywork that accumulate with a million miles of road wear. The driver said, "So, you want to go to Bakersfield? Fine with me. Let's go!"

"If it's not a problem for you," Anton replied.

"Not at all. Hop in." Stepping on the runner over the fuel tank, Anton pulled himself up by a handle and opened the sturdy door. The gears engaged with a low protest, and the truck pulled ahead with a long tank trailer in tow. "My name's Rusty," the driver said. "It's a slow ride. Nice to have some company."

Anton could see that Rusty was little more than twenty years of age. He wore modish sunglasses with small oval lenses, a silver earring and a baseball cap with a well-curved bill. After introducing himself and finding comfortable contours in the springs of the seat as they responded to the waltz and sway of the truck, Anton said, "This is my first ride in a big truck. Come up here often?"

"Once a week for the last six months," Rusty responded, his voice raised over the insistent roar of the engine. "I usually go straight through, no stopping. Today I felt like taking a close look at my brakes, so I stopped back there at the garage. Everybody checks brakes at the summit up ahead, but I also wanted to look over the hydraulic lines. Everything checks out. It's no fun for 40 tons of truck to break loose on the Grapevine!" After passing through more gears, he continued, "The mechanic told me about you. Sounds like you've been through a lot."

Anton nodded. He learned that Rusty had dropped out of the state college after his freshman year and had been driving two-axle flatbeds before graduating to semi-trucks and tankers belonging to an agricultural chemical company. On this trip Rusty had two thousand gallons of insecticide in one tank compartment, and an equal amount of liquid growth hormone in the other. He had a credit card for fuel and lodging, and his dispatcher had assigned him a route through the farmlands in Tulare County. After delivering his cargo to ranches and farms in the valley, Rusty would "deadhead," or drive the truck empty of cargo back to his home base in the San Gabriel Valley.

"My boss always says 'Go slow' when it comes to the Grapevine," Rusty said. "Not to worry. It's an all–day drive, one–way. The worst is behind us. One hour in Los Angeles is like a whole day in the open country. It's good to have company. I get pretty sleepy out in the valley."

As he spoke Rusty drove with an effortless competence, his foot plying the throttle like an organist playing his pedals, his left hand riding lightly on the wheel, the fingers of his right hand moving the two gear shifts in a frictionless and coordinated dance. As the truck gained speed, Anton noticed that Rusty had not used the clutch once since he had left the first gear, and had synchronized the higher gears with an orchestration and grace that belied the huge size and noise of the vehicle.

"How was college?" Anton asked.

"I was clueless," the youth responded. He paused to look through his mirrors and signal in a passing truck. "...18 years old, thrown into that school, with all of those courses...no direction, no guide. I had done okay in the sciences, thanks to my high school teacher. There was some magic in that. But during my first quarter I took economics and couldn't get it, didn't want to get it. Heartless. Horrible. I flunked it and dropped out of school."

"That must have been rough."

"You said it! But there's no escaping the economy. It's all around, like the air we breath."

"They call economics the 'dismal science'," Anton sympathized.

"Science? It's not like the sciences I know! No life in it, no heart. Just charts and chants about money. When I listen to the financial news in my truck, it alternates between heavy omens from the Fed and chatter from silly commentators with their MBA's and jobs in the big brokerage houses. How could I have known this is where it led? Even my teacher had more hot air in him than my truck tires. Prick him with a little feeling and he would go flat like a slow leak! Ugh!"

Anton listened to the complaint and found it both naïve and refreshing. "Maybe it's not a science then. Maybe it's a religion, but with no deity. It does have an 'invisible hand,'" he joked, "all–powerful in our workaday world like the hand of God."[37]

"Puppets have an invisible hand above them, too," Rusty grimaced. "Is economics a science for puppeteers? It's the only science that makes me feel cynical. Something has to be wrong with it...."

Anton carried the conversation further. "Individuals don't count for much in economics. In that, it's like a science. But that rule breaks down when it comes to individual decision–makers with a lot of power and money. Free will comes rushing back in, and science isn't comfortable with free agents. Then, if it's a religion, it doesn't seem to have a god. Nor does it seem to recognize anything sacred."

"That's for sure! In the economic mind you can put a price on anything. 'Everybody has his price,' and that sort of thing."

"That's what I mean, Rusty. Once you start thinking like an economist, great absurdities—all very logical—come to your lips. Everything gets reduced to a utilitarian dimension. Even the earth and sun are demoted from divine realities. They're not higher powers, but are little more than energy sources. Even one of the most momentous experiences in our life—our dying—is trivialized. You know the expression: 'The only certain things are death and taxes.' Pretty boring way of thinking, I would say."

"And, about this religion of yours, Anton," Rusty said, gaining enthusiasm. "The Fed chairman learns to make pronouncements like any oracle: very guarded, ambiguous, full of meaning that only the initiated ones can fathom."

"Then the economists must be the temple priests. This is hilarious, Rusty! I have never thought of it this way. That would make employees the sacrificial offering, especially when they are laid off to help the company report better cash flow and thus become a more attractive stock option. That happens, too, although I have never fully understood why. So where's the salvation story, Rusty?"

"Consuming and spending, I suppose. Aren't we supposed to do that? Spend ourselves blue in the face to save the nation? Shopping is happiness itself! I've seen the bumper stickers on cars racing on to the mountain resorts: things like 'I'm spending my children's inheritance,' and 'The one who dies with the most toys wins.' Things like that."

"Poking fun is healthy, but the point is that none of it touched you. If you were attacking the system that employed you or secured your social status, then it wouldn't be any fun at all. That's when the radical critique begins. That's real detachment! But you seem to be enjoying your work now. You don't seem to feel exploited."

"I'm not exploited! I choose to do this. I get to cover the ground and see new places. Driving a big truck is fun. But you should see some of the people I run into in the valley. That's exploitation…It can be miserable in summer and winter out there. People living in barns with no plumbing, outdoor latrines, beds made out of hay, miserable wages.

"It's not just out in the country, either. I read in some protest literature back in Los Angeles about how everybody plays soccer on Saturday. They use a high–quality ball that costs forty bucks. Take a look at where the balls are made: Haiti. Some Haitian woman gets paid a dime for stitching together one ball. She needs to spend that dime for her bus ride from the slums to the factory. Five more soccer balls give her enough to pay childcare. Ten more bring in enough money for the one meal she provides for her family in the evening. Did you know that in Haiti, 'rich' people get three meals a day, 'middle class' people get one meal, and the so–called 'poor' people get a meal every two or three days? So the worker has to work like crazy to make enough balls to feed her family. Then the company that employs her can pull up the stakes at any time to move to another country to reduce wage costs! We kick people around like we kick that ball around. It's absurd…but it's called 'economical.' That's what economics has come to…" He stopped talking for a moment to downshift with the steepening grade.

"Where did you go when you were struggling with your courses, Rusty?" Anton asked.

"I didn't know that I was supposed to go anywhere. I saw my advisor once for fifteen minutes in the fall of my first term. A big man with big letters after his name, lots of books in his office. I felt ridiculous. He wouldn't know me if he saw me again." Rusty's voice grew fierce. "I'm not sure I want to go back to that college. I want to do something with my life, make a difference, but don't know how to do it or where to go and I don't see what college has to do with it!"

Anton felt his own frustration rising. "Look, I know this may be hard for you to believe, but I'm a college teacher."

"You're a professor? You gotta be kidding," Rusty said, his eyes widening. He drove in silence.

Anton felt some of his old sadness returning. "What you just said hit close to the mark for me. There are probably students who think about me the same way you think about your advisor and your teachers. But in spite of it, I believe in education. In college a student can find himself, build his identity, find that one thing that says, 'This is who I am; this is true for me.'"

"Well, if that's the case, I hardly scratched the surface," Rusty said. "What are you doing out here?"

"Same sort of reason as you. Taking a break. Something is really missing in my life. It's pretty grim to be a teacher who has lost his grounding. I got a real taste of despair, and that is pretty noxious. I felt that whatever was making me sick could start to do some real damage to other people. It was time to leave. Even in that, in leaving something, I found I had no savvy, no experience."

As the conversation faded, Anton thought, we give young people on the cusp of adulthood the power and skill to traverse the globe; we give them the keys and send them up and down the Grapevine! We give them comfort, sports, fast computers, everything their fancies desire. But do we give them a relationship for life or a commitment to a safe and nurturing world? They feel like strangers in the land which our generation and our century has created. And how will my century be remembered, except for the Great Depression and the dismal legacy of two world wars? May their world emerge unshaped by such catastrophe…

Soon the summit was in sight. Unlike the automobile drivers who began to gather speed and relax from the pressure of the climb, Rusty moved into a heightened state of alert. He changed to the far right lane reserved for low–speed trucks. At the crest he tapped his brakes once lightly, then again strongly, feeling for any swerve that would indicate loss of brakes on one wheel. Down, down he plied the gears with the great engine roaring its resistance to the remorseless hand of gravity.

Settled at ten miles per hour on the speedometer, Rusty relaxed and smiled at his companion. "Now we're set. Just go with the flow, and watch your rear view mirrors for anyone who cuts loose above you." Anton leaned closer to Rusty to continue the conversation above the compression braking of the engine.

During the descent Rusty asked Anton a battery of questions about his life. He wanted to know why anyone would choose a life of learning, and why anyone would want to study ancient literature written in forgotten languages. How could Anton know that he was performing meaningful work? How could one know what service is, anyway? He was hungry to know if the world had room for hope, especially for him and other young people. And why would one choose to dwell in the realm of ideas when tools and technique are what gets things done?

Anton tried to explain that the classics are the nursery for the enduring ideas that shed light on the human condition and the dilemmas of life. "I admit to you, Rusty, that I have done a disservice to them—the classics, that is. We present them like a one-sided conversation, like we're the ones asking the questions. Really, when we open them up, we find that *they* are reading us, and their questions make us squirm. The more uncomfortable we feel, the more valuable they are, the more we want to avoid them. So it becomes ever harder for the academics and the publishing industry to sell these texts. The classics come out in fancy editions, and are put in mandatory courses. Can you imagine? Not one of these authors would tolerate such treatment if they were alive today. We force-feed students like geese to be slaughtered for *pâté de foies gras.*"

Rusty also wanted to know how Anton's family felt about his venture on the open road. At the question, Anton shifted uncomfortably. His father was still very much alive and he did have three brothers whom he rarely saw and understood less. Nor could he point to a wife and contented children at his knees. For the young Rusty's benefit he simply said that he had never been married, and lived alone. Yet he wondered whether this young man was asking him to explore the mystery of love and the alchemy and spontaneous combustion of intimacy. In his heart he wondered why of the three cardinal virtues, love was so much more difficult to talk about than faith and hope.

But Rusty only briefly hesitated at this information, responding with "Oh." With his truck feeling its way down the steep hill, he tactfully raised other questions that occupied his young mind. "Driving a truck gives you a sense that you can do just about anything. I felt that way about some things in college. If you can understand calculus you can figure out anything. Taking physics seemed to prove the point. That's how it works, doesn't it? Everyone takes calculus so they can understand physics. I remember how excited I felt when we derived Newton's formulas for differential equations. I really got into that. It was beautiful. Maybe I was born at the wrong time. I probably belong in the 18th or 19th centuries. But then I would think that everything had been figured out and that there was nothing for science to do. I wouldn't know anything about what's happening in quantum theory. I listen to books on tape while I'm out here on the road. All that relativity and chaos theory and quantum cosmology: lovely stuff."

"I like the way you put that, Rusty: in physics, if it's not lovely and beautiful, it's not true."

"That doesn't make it easy to understand," Rusty replied. "You can't get cozy with it like you can with other beautiful things. One lecture I heard said that gravity may be due to gravitons, a fundamental particle that is its own anti–particle, with undetectable rest mass. Maybe gravity weighs as much as the vertical or horizontal dimension: it's right there in front of us (or underneath, or really all around), and we can snag it with a net or hit it with a baseball bat. That really clears things up, huh?"

"So it appears that we really are held to earth by an idea," Anton said. "I'm not surprised. The old notion was that things fell because they wanted to go home; things were drawn to the earth because the earth is our final home. In Einstein's universe, we've lost that old sense in spite of his fond hopes, so we are looking for a new idea, maybe even a new sense of home."[38]

"That's all very well," Rusty said. "But out here on the mountain, Newton is king. This is one big hill of potential energy, and all I have to do is put this old Peterbilt in neutral and we prove Newton right. We would become a big roller coaster to a messy end. For heavy trucks and me and you, Newtonian physics is true. It's the big things that count out here, and they're a matter of life and death. What do you think?"

As Rusty spoke, there echoed in Anton's mind the wordless, uncanny voice of nature in the hoot, howl and hiss that he had heard while alone on the rock two nights before. It was not the language of Newtonian physics.

"Newton gave us the equations for our structures that collapse into very big messes," Anton agreed. "But Nature alone never makes a mess. That's *our* handiwork."

"I still think that Newton is king. He has the last word out here. Newton...I know very little about him. He did explain the universe like no one had before, and he could concentrate a long time and had a terrific temper and pride. There's an old saying, 'God save me from Newton's sleep.' Was that William Blake? I wonder what he meant by that."

"Probably that Newton didn't get much sleep. Or maybe we would be shocked if we saw what was happening in Newton's sleeping mind. Newton's theory is right at home here, in the hills, and in hot brakes and escape ramps. Drivers out here (except for a few like you, Rusty) never think about Newton, but they really understand forces of acceleration."

"You're right about that! During the long stretch toward the bottom I talk to this old thunder carriage! I keep telling her to hold her horses, keep pulling them backwards against the hill, keep me slow when I can almost feel the pain in my red hot brakes. What a sweat!"

"That's what I mean, Rusty. Horsepower is something you can feel, almost smell. It was a common sense notion when horses were on the street. But Newton can't help you understand yourself or me or even why you are carrying this load up to Tulare. But that is not a criticism. I remember reading about the inscription on his tomb: 'Mortals! rejoice at so great an ornament to the human race!' It will always be true. Only a poet like Blake could add luster to Newton's work in science, and show that every soul is a center of attraction or repulsion. In the end, Newton knew that he was just tracing the fingerprints of the God who lay behind all the intelligibility and beauty. And the mathematics, calculus and the laws of motion, are nothing more than the tracings of the mind contemplating that beauty. Like you were saying, the elegance and obviousness of his formulas are a testament to their truth. But standing before nature herself, Newton thought of himself simply as a child at the beach who picks up shells and stones and marvels at them before tossing them back in the waves."

"So the great man becomes a little child. Human beings…we think so much of ourselves, but we mess things up so easily. Pretty pathetic."

"There's a lot more to it than that, in my mind," Anton rejoined. "I wasn't much older than you when I discovered that I was a human being. Isn't that the strangest thing you can imagine? I suppose you could say that I discovered the humanities, but that's not what I mean. I met a very old way of thinking that is very beautiful and alluring, even…," and here Anton paused in memory of his recent encounter with the thieves, "…tragic and terribly sad. Our humanity reveals itself everywhere we are. Even now, I feel I'm just beginning to see it, even though I have been looking for years."

"I feel surrounded by clues to what you're talking about," Rusty said, "but can't even begin to put my arms around it. I especially see it early in the morning, when I'm out in the valley and the sun begins to rise over the Sierras. It's beautiful. I feel it all through me."

Still the scholar, Anton continued his old habit of discourse. "Beauty is a portal to our true nature, Rusty. When I traveled to Greece I learned why the ancients turned their faces from ugliness. They had found the golden link between beauty, humanity, and education. One could be serene in the presence of tragedy. Even someone weighted down with utter misery can maintain his serenity. He can be beautiful to our mind's eye, like old Lear or the blind Oedipus. He will never be ugly, because he is living his truth. Funny, isn't it, that evil is filled with twisted truths that eventually add up to be boring and ugly—'banal,' as someone once put it[39]—but tragedy arises when the hard and unwelcome truths complement and enliven and ennoble even the beautiful truths."

"So beauty is not something on the surface," Rusty pondered. "I mean, it's more than a beautiful sunrise."

"What's beautiful appears so to the soul that is nobly made," Anton said. "That's why the ancient artists depicted humanity in such perfect proportions: not because of the beauty of the human figure itself, but because of the nobility of the moral idea. The tragic hero veers away from ugliness in his desire for perfect self–fulfillment. In that, he may fall into *hubris*, a fatal over–reaching of conventional limits. People warn him against being more than he is, but he can't settle for being less than he is. How can you know in advance where the fine line is, beyond which you trespass to your great folly? Most of the time, moral heroism is found in simply trying to solve the equation of your life, which has new variables appearing faster than the old ones are solved."

"This is amazing!" Rusty said with enthusiasm. "That's how I have been feeling about my own life! I have never heard things put this way. So, try as you might, if you let your soul grow ugly, you can never be the hero of a tragedy?"

"That's how the ancient mind had it," Anton agreed. "They thought it unconscionable for art to show a miserable, wretched person achieving happiness. If he did, it would not be great art, and even then, not much more than comedy."[40]

"You must have had some great teachers yourself."

"I did, without a doubt. We sort of stumble into each other." Anton shrugged in surrender to fortune's mercurial nudgings. "It feels pretty accidental. I can't offer this to anyone. I never really believed that. The classics say that this intuition is conceived within, and only in some souls and in certain moments in life. That's what caught me up, not so long ago. I knew that I had lost sight of it, that magical something, and began looking for it again. Then I had to ask myself, do I really know something I could lose so easily? After the last few days, I really don't think I know anything any more. I am really in the fog."

"Then why on earth are you out here, hitchhiking on the freeway? I thought that only big truck drivers were 'dromomaniacs.' You know: mad wanderers."

"I had to get away. I felt indicted and convicted by those I was trying to serve: not only the great thinkers, but even students and their parents."

"How's that?"

"Well, I don't think that we're completely honest with our students and their parents, who are paying twenty–five thousand a year or more for their kids' tuitions. Virtue and goodness and beauty can't be taught.

But what's more important for us to know? The scary thought hit me that we might be telling a not—so—subtle lie with our academic departments set up to 'teach the humanities'—whatever that means—to people who have not discovered their own humanity. What makes us think that students can discover this in a book or hear it in a lecture? It has to happen some other way. Maybe we merely prepare students for the discovery that comes later, in unimaginable ways: between a parent and a sick and sleepless child late at night; between a teacher and the student who claims the teacher as his own; between friend and friend; between lovers; between enemies on the field of battle: all in the doings of life. If I am not living this, how can I be teaching this?[41] Reading assignments are a pretty thin substitute for life experience."

"It's astounding how important books are in school," Rusty said. "There are so many of them! School seems to be only books and more books. How can you know which are really important and worth your time?"

"I know what you mean. How have books gained a life of their own? What would an ancient citizen say if he saw someone sitting with a stack of printed paper in his hand, turning them one at a time, lost in thought? He would think him entranced, mesmerized by something like sheep entrails, maybe even under the influence of malignant vapors that he could not see! Books are either like gadflies, irritating; or footnotes to life, or portraits of characters. I hate it when they become substitutes for the wisdom gained through living. Some people love the Bible, great book that it is, more than they love life; or the Quran, which they revere too much to ask about its origins—outside the *mythos* surrounding Mohammed, that is. For some religions, even asking questions about their sacred texts becomes blasphemy."

"I guess I don't have that problem," Rusty confessed. "I haven't read much of the Bible. My parents couldn't stand unquestioning fundamentalism or reading the Bible for some literal meaning."

"I can understand that. I don't think any literature, however true, is intended to be a template for life. Goethe taught me this. His Faust character knew everything, had read everything, could cite anything chapter and verse, but he could relate deeply to no one until he had suffered life in his heart and soul. Knowledge for him had become little more than a treat for a magpie, who samples this and that and flies off, sated but unchanged. That is why Plato said all genuine knowing is recollection, remembering some truth that had already been given to you.[42] Formal learning might help, but it just as often buries truth deeper and deeper. Real learning is bringing our truth to life, which is often a painful thing." Yet even as he uttered these sentiments, Anton wondered whether they would survive the test of experience, and whether they would always occupy such a central place in his thinking.

By now the steep incline had begun to flatten out in the long slide into the San Joaquin Valley. Rusty moved carefully up a couple of gears, and Anton could feel the sloshing of the load in the huge tank in tow. The Tehachapis rose and fell behind them in indistinct waves. The autumn sky itself was tinted light brown as it carried the city air north from Los Angeles.

"We made it," Anton whistled as the truck reached its highest gear.

"Good brakes. Like I said, on the Grapevine we pay our homage to Newton," Rusty said.

The two traveled on in silence. In the distance Anton could see the huge pipes of the Sacramento River water project that had lurched into his conscious mind not so long ago; they continued straight and gleaming over the rise and fall of the hills. Below them he saw the blue canal carrying the water from the river four hundred miles to the north. Soon they were on the valley floor and the flat landscape spread out beyond them, as strangely barren as the bottom of a tarnished frying pan.

"We're getting close," Rusty announced as they passed the small settlement of Weed Patch, a commercial oasis left ramshackle and parched by the siroccos that wither the slopes of the Tehachapis. "Where you headed in Bakersfield?"

Anton gave directions to the restaurant in the city. He could see billboards and isolated trailer homes on the barren land and an occasional water tower in the parched uplands on the south side of the city. Each freeway exit led to identical convenience stores, gas stations and restaurants for truckers and other travelers.

"See those oil derricks?" Rusty commented. "Some guys I know bring out a tank full of emulsifiers for separating out oil and water. Then they take the crude oil back to the refineries in Long Beach."

"And the water?" Anton asked.

"Dumped back in the ground, I guess. Right back into the water table, and up again into people's homes and faucets."

Soon they were in the stop–and–go traffic of the city suburbs. The cityscape seemed like bad prose to Anton—ideas thrown down in disorder with signs promoting claptrap and pointing to tasteless stopping points. Everything was artifice without plan or purpose, splotches of construction set up in haste to steal the attention of the traveler.

When they reached the main part of town described in Juan Carlos' directions, Anton prepared to disembark. "Thanks for the ride. I enjoyed our time together. Maybe I'll see you again."

"You know, I come through here every week. After Bakersfield, I head up to Delano and Visalia. Here's my phone number if you want to stay in touch."

"Thank you," Anton said, touched by the generosity of the young man. "Good luck, Rusty." With that, the old Peterbilt lurched forward, towing the tank trailer with its springs creaking and huge wheels crushing the gravel on the road.

"You are young," the old priest said, "young in soul, every one of you. Your souls are devoid of beliefs about antiquity handed down by ancient tradition. Your souls lack any learning made hoary by time. The reason for that is this: There have been, and there will continue to be, numerous disasters that have destroyed human life in many kinds of ways. The most serious of these involve fire and water, while the lesser ones have numerous others causes…"

Plato (427–347 bce),
Timaeus 22b[43]

Fire and Water

ANTON WALKED DOWN the main street, past small cafés, furniture outlets and collectible stores, "everything under a dollar" warehouses, florists, and small shops that posted bond and cashed checks. Durable plastic Christmas decorations, used year after year, dangled from streetlights, and holly and candy canes were placed randomly in storefront windows. Christmas is in the stores, but hardly in the air, Anton thought.

Soon he arrived at the restaurant owned by Juan Carlos' uncle. It looked like a going concern, its parking lot nearly filled with cars even at lunch time. In the window a blinking neon cactus plant with the words *Dos Equis* advertising a favorite beer. Entering through the front door, Anton breathed the thick air scented with salsa, sweat, dirt from the city streets, cigarette ashes ground into the carpet, and deep frying fat. The restaurant looked full, and a half dozen people were waiting to be seated. The warmth of the restaurant felt good, and Anton's mouth watered.

"*Buenas tardes.* Welcome." A young hostess greeted him with a friendly smile. She looked fatigued in the rush of customers.

"Hello. Would Luís be available? I believe his nephew told him that I might be coming to visit."

"Just a minute, please." The hostess left, and reappeared in a moment with an older man with a portly waistline and graying hair.

"I am Luís Quesada. How may I help you?" he asked.

"My name is Anton Reisen. Your nephew Juan Carlos said that you might be needing a worker."

"Yes. I was hoping that you would come. It is a perfect time. We are very, very busy with the holidays. We need a dishwasher. You can also help María, our hostess, set the tables. Can you do that?"

"I can do that."

"OK, then. Pay is five–fifty per hour, plus your meals. We have workman's compensation. Other than that, we have no benefits."

"That sounds fine to me."

"Juan Carlos said that you might need a place to stay as well."

"Yes, all my money was stolen outside of Los Angeles."

"I heard about that. A terrible shame. Come, let me get you some lunch, and we will start right away."

Leaving the dining room with its clean tables and candles of flowing, colorful wax, and the customers bending over their tamales, fajitas and enchiladas, Anton and Luís went through the swinging doors into another world. In a cacophony of rushing water, clanging dishes, sizzles from the stove and shouts from the cook, food was assembled on plates and ushered out with haste by four waiters and waitresses. Off to one side a slender, dark–haired man in a tee–shirt sweated in a frenzy of motion in front of a large, industrial dishwasher. Luís gestured to a table in the back of the kitchen, where Anton sat and removed his sweater. As Luís brought him a plate of tacos he realized that he did not feel as ready for this new work as he had imagined. He had never been in a restaurant kitchen before, and felt awkward and strange in this steamy hothouse. The flat spot where his wallet used to be reminded him why he was here. From his table Anton watched his new mentor scrape, rinse, stack and shove his way through the small mountain of dishes on the metal sink. Fifteen minutes later, Luís returned and took Anton over to the dishwasher.

"Hey, Nestor! This is your new helper, Anton," Luís announced.

"Hey!" the dishwasher shouted a greeting above the din. "Grab an apron. Here's what you do: take the dishes out of the machine, and carry them over there, where the cook can get them. Be careful of the plates: they are very hot." Nestor returned to his scraping and rinsing.

Over the next two hours Nestor completed his training. Anton also learned how working people sweat. In the round and emphatic style of his Sicilian ancestry, Nestor told Anton to be careful not to slip near the stove where grease and water flowed together, and to sort silverware before it was washed. He advised against touching the caustic soap with bare hands. Hang the ladles here, the spatulas there; store the knives in the woodblock; stack clean glasses. There's the switch for the disposal. The floor mops are hanging on the back porch to air out. Thus Anton began to learn the myriad and invisible details and motions that produced a clean and tasty plate for the customers in the quiet world beyond the swinging doors. Within these short hours, Anton was a trained and engaged scullion.

When the noontime rush abated, Nestor and Anton stopped to drink a cool glass of water, then reported to the cook, who set before them a crate of lettuce and a crate of onions for cleaning and peeling. Nestor placed the onions before a fan to blow away the fumes. He was a talkative, first–generation Sicilian who still called home to his aged parents in the southeastern city of Syracuse. With the finesse of a swordsman from the old world, he parried and sliced through the pile of vegetables. Nestor spoke of the busy restaurant season upon them, the cooling of early winter weather, and the relief from the heat of the summer, which, he said, reminded him of an erupting Mt. Etna. By two o'clock the kitchen was clean, the tables were set, and the restaurant sank into silence.

Luís came out from his office and took Anton outside to a separate building. "This is our bunkroom for the cook and dishwashers," he said. "You may stay here. I provide towels and soap. You can have that bunk," he gestured to the corner. "Breakfast is toast and coffee at 8. You and Nestor start work at 9. Break time is between 2 and 4. We start again at 4, and work until 11. One day off a week, which we coordinate with Nestor. You see why I needed another worker? It is a long day, so you should get some rest. See you at four o'clock." Then he left.

Anton collapsed on the bed and closed his eyes. It only seemed like a moment had passed when he felt a strong hand on his shoulder. He heard Nestor say, "Come on. It's time to go." They returned to their post.

So began Anton's initiation into the inner world of those who prepare and serve food, wash dishes and scrub floors. Over the next two weeks Anton washed more dishes than he could ever imagine. He came to see the noisy, brutally hot dishwasher as a perpetual–motion machine that transformed soiled plates into hot discs that gleamed and clanged and mounted into teetering columns beside the black stove, only to fall into a greasy mess on the tables in the dining room outside, to be restored yet again to gleaming perfection in the machine.

He saw the cook fighting his way through never–ending dinner orders, muttering, swearing, and wielding knives like a deranged samurai warrior. Under the pressure of the holiday season the cook buckled and began to come to work late, with whiskey on his breath. Luís imperturbably turned him out. His place was taken by another man from the rotating supply of Mexican and Central American cooks who travel the highways and byways of the San Joaquin Valley.

On one occasion Anton watched Nestor eyeing the smoking and sizzling stove as he stacked and straightened plates and dishes. "What's the matter, Nestor?" he asked.

Nestor shook his head as if to toss off an old thought or image. "Oh, nothing, my friend. Just an old memory. My papa used to tell me that Sicily sits on a great hollow cavern, with the ground under your feet being nothing more than a thin shell over a bottomless pit of fire. He said it was a very old tale, and did not know where it came from. I was very young when I heard it, maybe five years old. Sometimes my papa would take me for walks up in the foothills around Etna. He would go looking for water where it came out of the ground. When he would find a spring he would tell me that I could drink from it. Then he would say, 'Be careful or you might fall in,'—into the big underground cavern that the legends say are rivers of boiling water and fire. That was very frightening for a little boy. I would take one gulp of water then back up. I was thinking of that when I was looking at the stove so near the water."[44]

With the celebrations of Las Posadas and Christmas fast approaching, Anton became aware of the crushing pressures on the hostess. On this Saturday afternoon the restaurant was already half–full by five o'clock. Luís cancelled all days off, and told his workers to get rest when they could. Nestor, who was planning to stay up to two o'clock the next morning to scrub grease from the stove flue, was taking a longer rest than usual. In the kitchen the pile of dishes had not yet reached its peak, so María asked Anton to fill water glasses and to clear and set tables. With a clean apron he walked among the tables with a pitcher of ice water. Never before had he literally "carried water" for others. Customers usually ignored him. Some smiled, but most people looked right through him. He tried to adjust himself to the feeling of being invisible. Once a professor, he was now nothing but a broke dishwasher in an obscure Mexican restaurant. He consoled himself with an adage from Dorothy Day that "the closer one is to the bottom, the shorter the distance one has to fall."

Back in the kitchen, Anton resumed scraping, rinsing and loading dishes like a veteran. María came quickly through the swinging doors, said something indistinctly to the new cook, then returned to the dining room. The doors emitted a low mumble of customers' voices as she came and went. Ten minutes later she reappeared, flushed and anxious. She seized a handful of clean rags and strode rapidly back through the doors to clean a spill from one of the tables. The mutter from the crowd was louder now. The heat of the kitchen was rising. The stove had become a clicking, banging and bubbling factory of spicy delicacies. The cook sweated and sang pop tunes and called out completed orders. Waiters and waitresses hustled back and forth, the door letting in the noise of the crowd like the disordered low notes of an orchestra tuning itself for a performance.

María reappeared, almost at a run. Tears stood in her eyes. "We can't keep up!" she said through clinched teeth. "We're missing one of our bus boys. Anton, get Nestor, then come back to the dining room. Hurry!"

Anton threw off his rubber gloves and soaked apron. Grabbing a dry apron, he turned to stride around the stove, throwing the apron over his head as he went. He did not watch his step. His foot slid on some stove grease where it met a puddle of water. He felt himself spinning and falling. He reached out blindly for a handhold, and wrenched a pot of bubbling oil off the stove and onto the back of his hand and arm. He crashed to the ground with the cook's shout in his ear, "¡Madre de Dios!"

Anton lay on the floor, staring up at the cook. María came into view, biting her lips white, her face ashen. He could hear nothing except the far-off ebb and flow of sound, punctuated by discordant bleating from the trumpet of the mariache band.

Then, the pain. The pain scraped its way through his consciousness, burning away every thought, every image, every memory. Someone pulled him up and guided him to the worker's dining room table. There he lay down. He stared at the ceiling and into the collapsing darkness. He then felt himself carried outside and saw flashing red lights. During the bouncing ride he heard the voice of a stranger, perhaps an emergency medical technician, beside him. The ambulance stopped and he was lifted out, abruptly, with the wheels of the stretcher jouncing his back as they hit the sidewalk. He felt cool ice on his lips, then nothing at all.

O Lord, do not rebuke me in your anger;
Do not punish me in your wrath,
For your arrows have already pierced me,
And your hand presses hard upon me…
My loins are filled with searing pain;
There is no health in my body.
I am utterly numb and crushed;
I wail, because of the groaning of my heart.

                                        Psalm 38

Your Hand Presses Hard Upon Me

An indeterminate time later, the thought rose in him, Where am I? He wanted to say the words, but heard no sound. He drifted off. Later, he wondered, What is this place? Then he heard the words, "You are okay, Anton. Just rest," and he slipped away again.

When he finally opened his eyes, he saw a clean and white room. He was alone. He felt the light pressure of a sheet over his body. Trying to move, he felt restraining bonds around his upper arms. He felt a strange aching tingle on his left hand and arm. Then, he remembered the kitchen, the horrified face of the cook and María's frozen stare. He felt fear. Be calm, wait, he told himself; I think I am alive. He drifted off again. From time to time he felt gentle hands on his shoulder and the cool air on his body as the sheet was lifted off and changed. He heard a woman's voice, "Everything is fine, Anton." He did not know what that meant, but the calm words told him that he was alive, and not alone.

People filled his dreams. He dreamed that he was in a hospital. He entered an elevator on the third floor with other people. He pressed the button for the first floor. As the first floor approached he prepared to step out. Instead, the elevator began accelerating faster and faster, going down and down for hundreds of yards. No one seemed surprised or afraid. When the door opened he stepped out into an open patio. A crowd of people was gathered before him. Many were in wheelchairs; these had attendants behind them. Then, as if his arrival signaled their departure, the crowd began to walk or wheel themselves slowly forward along a concrete path. Anton wondered where he was and what had happened. He stepped off the path onto a deep green lawn. He walked a ways, then paused. Behind him at a fair distance he saw two young student friends walking listlessly along, heads down, kicking at the earth. He stared at them. A shadow appeared beside him and he sensed someone nearby.

Then he knew that he was dead. He fell to his knees on the lawn and surrendered to wracking sobs. At that moment, he learned that those who have died, not only those who survive, often carry overwhelming grief with them. Those many people who had accompanied his present—more, who had shaped his present life in all its meaning and texture—now were trailing behind on the path. Only memory and sadness connected them, and that too was waning away. His dream faded in oblivion.

Later, a doctor arrived. "You have burned your arm, but you are going to be all right. You must stay here for a few days so we can take care of you. Let yourself rest, and tell us if you feel any pain."

Anton let himself rest. The pain in his arm intruded like an unwelcome houseguest, an ugly presence that did not know when to leave. On the second day the doctor came again and told him that he had not had to do any skin grafts, but that the wounds needed to be cleaned every day. "The nurses will help you. Just rest," he said.

That afternoon two nurses came into his room and introduced themselves. "Anton, my name is Maggie. This is Carl. You are very fortunate. You've had the best doctor in the city. We need to wash your wound. Is that okay with you?"

Anton did not know what to say. Could he say that "It was not okay"? But no: he had surrendered to the care being offered to him. He nodded. They gave him a white pill and a glass of water, then left for fifteen minutes. During that time Anton slipped back into a drowsy state. When they returned, Carl set a sponge and a bottle of phisohex skin cleanser on the bed table. Then Maggie put one hand on Anton's right shoulder. "Relax," she said. She put her other hand on his left leg and leaned in with her weight. At Carl's first touch, pain wrenched through Anton's arm and squeezed his chest in a relentless grip. A low groan escaped from his clenched teeth.

"Try to relax. Breathe deep," Maggie said.

Anton found that by holding onto the bed frame with his good hand, and pushing against the bottom of the bed with his feet, and by holding Maggie's face in his sight, he could contain the scream of anguish that coursed around in his chest. He learned that by breathing deeply he could weep, and the tears flowed down his cheeks as he lay quietly beneath Carl's gently scrubbing hands. As if to balance the scalding invasion of necessary pain Maggie ended the cleaning work by touching Anton's eyebrows and temples while he looked up into her face, and his tears flowed no more.

Maggie also came to him in the darkness of night. The door would open and he would see her silhouette in the doorway. She rubbed his back with a cool and pleasant-smelling lotion. In this he experienced a pleasure that was both exquisite and comforting. He relaxed again into sleep.

Three days later, Luís and María came to visit. They were very sorry about what had happened. They hoped that he could be okay. "Do you want to come back to work?" they asked.

Anton said, "No, I am not a good dishwasher. And do not worry about anything. Maybe I could have my paycheck."

Luís smiled, "Of course. I'll bring it tomorrow. And everything here at the hospital is covered by 'workman's comp.' You may come back to our bunkhouse to rest when you leave here."

When she was not too busy, Maggie came and sat down on the edge of Anton's bed. Anton learned that she had gone through nursing school, but had gotten married before she was able to practice her profession, which was delayed further with the arrival of her new baby. "I'm very happy here," she said. "I was getting very restless at home. Now that my boy is in school, I can do this. I've wanted to be a nurse for a long time."

"You feel like you are making a difference," Anton ventured.

"Yes. I was so bored at home that my relationship with my husband was disappearing. It is very good now. I enjoy working with Carl, too."

"I was surprised to have a male nurse working with me. That was a first."

"He is my preceptor. I work with him every day for three months. He is the best nurse I have ever known—not that he lets you know it by talking about it. He is a master of the understatement."

"He teaches by example?" Anton asked.

"Yes. But what he doesn't do is sometimes as important as what he does."

"What do you mean?"

"Well, for example, in medicine there is a compulsion to do something, to fix something that's wrong or broken. People come in, injured like you or sick and weak, and we go right to work fixing you up without knowing much more than your name and blood type. If we can't fix you, we say you are getting worse, that things are getting bad, and so on."

"But that's what I would expect," Anton protested. "I came in here pretty broken up. I guess I still need the scrub-down and some patching up," he added wistfully.

"Well, that's right. But some of our social graces do go out the window. And the short stays of most people don't allow us to really get acquainted. If I have a chance to talk to someone, then I feel like I am really helping them. Then I can go home at night knowing that I've made a difference in someone's life."

"I guess I never saw myself as needing fixing," Anton said on reflection. "And I am grateful for your help. But I still feel a kind of imbalance, like it's you who is doing all the giving."

"You asked how Carl is teaching me. Medicine I am learning by doing. The books and instructors have given me know–how and technique. The patient teaches my hands and sense of timing. Carl shows me something different: how to be at the bedside. He just drops into a patient's room sometimes, and does this perfunctory little thing with his stethoscope, almost to distract people. Then plops down in a chair and really goes to work. Sometimes he spends the whole time joking with the patient or talking about their families or work."

The conversation paused for a moment as the nurse and the patient pondered Carl's example. Then Anton said, "It seems that Carl reminds them that there is something beyond this place, that they have something to hope for."

"That's what I mean. He serves something in them—their hopes and dreams. He sits with them, not looking down on them from a position of power and authority, but sometimes even below their eye level. You can feel the patient relax. He will do this with people for whom there is no fixing, no cure. It makes no difference to him. They sometimes laugh and tell stories. It is a sight to behold."

Later Maggie asked Anton about his life, and why he was in Bakersfield. "I am looking for something, or for someone. I am not sure, right now."

"But don't you have anyone back home?"

"Not now. I almost did, once. But she had other plans."

As Maggie gazed at him, Anton felt different under her eyes. He did not feel observed and distanced, as he sometimes did with his female colleagues, nor appraised, as he did from time to time with female students. Instead, Maggie's eyes were unveiled like mirrors, or like windows that asked to be seen through as well. She said nothing. For a timeless instant, another image—a fleeting female form—rose in his mind, then disappeared.

"You have been very good to me, Maggie."

"Where to now?"

"I have not begun to think about that...I just want to rest," Anton said.

On his last day, Carl helped Anton to shave and shower. "You are a new man," is all he said. Maggie came into his room and said, "Today is your last day. But you are not strong enough to go anywhere, and you must keep your wound clean. Do you know how to do that?"

He nodded.

"Here are bandages and some scrubbing medicine and some pain pills. You will be better each day. You have decided to return to Luís's place?"

"For now."

"Very well. The hospital will give you a taxi ride there, and one of our nurses will visit you."

Maggie wheeled Anton down to the entrance of the hospital and to the waiting taxi. He stood up unsteadily and looked into her eyes. I must remember this face, this moment, he said to himself. I may not have made an iota of difference in her life, but she has come into my heart forever.

"Maggie, you and Carl have been a blessing to me. I will miss you, and think of you often. I wish you and your family well."

Maggie placed her hand beside Anton's face and forehead one last time. "Thank you," she said quietly. Then she was gone.

A special gospel, a treasury of insights into the Beauty of the world, belongs to the poor. It has been bestowed by Providence on poverty alone, but which, in our uprooted world, the alienated and oppressed can no longer decipher for themselves.

> Simone Weil (1909–1943),
> *Waiting For God*

A Special Gospel, for the Poor Alone

Anton crawled into his bed at Luís's bunkhouse. On the first day, the hours drifted and he slept and awakened into formless twilight. While awake his mind wandered like a vagrant photographer. He saw classrooms of students milling and talking, frightening people with malicious eyes, a snake winding its way into the corner of a hospital room, where it looked around with baleful eyes. He dreamed of Maggie and Carl and Anita and Juan Carlos' little girl playing with raggedy dolls. When the dry cold seeped into the bunkhouse, he pulled the blankets closer and wondered where sunlight would fall after the longest night of winter.

The visiting nurse came on the second day to inspect his wound. She said it was healing nicely and nodded her approval of his surroundings. After urging him to rest and to eat well, she released him from hospital care and departed. María and sometimes Nestor brought him meals and gave him company. On the third day, the pain surrendered its central place in his awareness and began to recede, leaving a tenderness that Anton felt in his whole being. He ventured outside and down the sidewalk. The chill in the air and in the city neighborhood made him shiver. What next? he wondered. I cannot go back. I cannot stay here. He opened the door to a pawnshop, which jangled a warning at his entrance. He meandered up and down the aisles. Old radios and sporting goods gathered dust along with green and brown flower vases and tarnished school band instruments, pots, pans and appliances. Their uselessness offended him. Am I filled with such detritus of daily living? he wondered. He returned to his bunk and his rest. He did not return to the kitchen.

On the next day, Anton joined Luís for coffee at one of the dining room tables. "Luís," he said, "I am ready to go."

"Do you have enough to get by?"

"I've got two hundred dollars and my clothes and backpack. That's more than I had two weeks ago."

"I had less than that when I came here," Luís said. "I had my clothes, my canteen, and María, two years old. Nothing more."

Remembering what Juan Carlos had said weeks before, Anton asked, "Her mother is gone?"

Luís looked out the window. "She was the daughter of a leading family in San Salvador and was kidnapped and killed by the death squads." A far–off and unquenched glimmer of pain focused in his eyes. Anton could hear the breath sighing in and out of Luís's chest.

"I cannot conceive this, Luís."

"No, it is impossible to imagine. When my wife died, I took all my money and my little María and went north. I walked as far as the border. It was summer and very hot. It was better to walk because I could stop and hide when I was afraid. Sometimes the guerrillas or the National Guard shot up the buses, you know. It was not much better in Honduras. Once we got to Mexico, I took a bus all the way to Tijuana. It took three days. The bus was packed with people and even chickens and little pigs. Sometimes at a bus stop I would climb up on the roof with my baby and we would lie on the luggage, and that was better. At least we could breathe.

"When we got to Tijuana we got off the bus into pure craziness, just like the thousands before us. *Coyotes* came at us from every direction, making those great promises about how good they were at crossing the border. How can you tell a good guide from a thief? I had just enough money to pay a *coyote* for advice and an escort to the border, but nothing more.

"I'll never forget that day and night. Migrants going through Tijuana stay in *la ciudad de los perdidos,* 'the city of the lost ones.' There were lots of kids who were separated from their parents and who live off the city traffic. You see them with their squirt bottles and rags begging the tourists to let them clean their windshields at the border crossing. The *coyote* met us at nightfall. He had big plastic trash bags, and he walked us toward the open sewer that flows from San Ysidro on the U.S. side of the border. We were on our own from there. I wrapped the bags around my legs, one for each leg, and taped it tight. Then I put María on my back, and walked the forty feet across the sewer. The stench of the *mierda* nearly killed me, but we were not going to die there!

"When we got across, we hid in the brush and watched the border police and timed their truck patrols. After the third truck, I had the timing figured out, and after the fourth, I threw María on my back again and ran like a jackrabbit across the open stretch, and into the bushes. From there on we stayed in the brush and the hills. We stayed in a camp for awhile but that was an ungodly mess. Then some people gave me a ride to Corona near Riverside. I was broke and scared, but I got a job with a picking crew for a few weeks, and made enough money to get me and María up here to my people in Bakersfield. From there it was starting all over. That was twenty–five years ago. The '86 amnesty came and we got our papers. María is now a woman, and I have a restaurant. Many people coming north have stayed in the bunk house like you, Anton."

"Where are your people now?" Anton asked.

"Some are here in Bakersfield, others have moved up into the valley. My wife's brother, Gustavo, lives in the town of Armona in Tulare County. He is lucky to be alive. He was a Franciscan priest in El Salvador and a professor of theology at the university in the capital. He talked very openly about how it made no sense for the Church to be sitting down at the table with the *ricos* and the *generales*. That made him a marked man, and the Church too was very uncomfortable with him. He now lives with the farmworkers in a camp and gets around the country on an old motorcycle. He moves with the people when the seasons change. People find him when they need him."

"He has continued as a priest?" Anton asked.

"That never changes."

"Maybe he could receive a guest for a while?"

"That is possible," Luís replied. "I can't call him directly because he has no telephone. But the farm owner has one and could get him the message. I know that he'll be home. It is Advent before the Nativity, you know, and he's always with the people at Christmas."

"I would like to go," Anton said.

"Then I'll call him."

Later that afternoon, Luís returned to tell Anton that he would be welcome to come to Gustavo's community near Armona. Anton did not want to spend $40 for a bus ticket, and remembered that the young man Rusty drove up the Great Valley every week. With a telephone call he learned that Rusty would be coming to Bakersfield the next day, and could give Anton a ride.

When the great truck creaked to a stop outside the restaurant at midmorning, Anton came into the dining room to say goodbye to the people with whom he had worked. Nestor leaned against the door to the kitchen, but offered his hand and said, *"Arrivederci,* friend. Good luck." The cook said, "I am very sorry about what happened." Anton smiled and nodded. María said, "Come back and see us, Anton," and kissed him on the cheek.

Looking at the big truck, Luís said, "Are you sure, Anton? I can buy you a ticket for the Greyhound if you wish."

"No, this way is good," Anton replied. He boarded the truck and waved goodbye.

The San Joaquin Valley flows and ripples north from the Tehachapis, and is bounded by the foothills of the Sierras on the east and the Los Padres on the west. The huge garden glimmers with the splendor and variety of the legendary coat of Joseph, son of Jacob. Within the steady hum and gentle rocking of the truck Anton felt secure and purposeful and gazed far across the valley. He told Rusty about his injury and said, "This has to be the end of my bad luck." As he shaped his jacket into a pillow and lay back, he added, "Someone once said, 'By his wounds we are healed.'[45] I will see how that is true."

The young man looked at him with sympathy. He put some quiet music in the truck tape deck. Anton balanced his arm on his lap, where its tenderness made a persistent and wordless statement, "May my pain remind me of the gentleness of those who cared for me." He then slipped into sleep.

When he awoke, Anton watched the passing scenes from the window. Looking out over the fields he saw the fecundity of the earth contained in towering grain silos and storage sheds. Every mile or so they passed barns with tractors and farm equipment, and skyscrapers of crates and pallets. The agricultural machines looked like outlandish mechanical insects, all carapace and utility, accomplishing the same function as their smaller cousins, the grasshopper and preying mantis. Individual human forms appeared tiny against the grand profiles along the highway. Bare, brown fields, utterly purged of weeds or anything greening in nature, stretched for miles and miles with little or no sign of human activity. Fertilizer tanks loomed in the distance, and irrigation canals and pipes marked the boundaries of huge tracts of bare, pristine earth. Occasionally Anton would spy a John Deere tractor with wheels eight feet high, silently plowing rows and furrows for a winter planting.

They passed sprawling cattle yards where steers had been gathered from invisible inland reaches, only to jostle slowly along the food conveyor belt, an alluvium of industrialized life awaiting the slaughter. A lone pickup truck bounded here and there along earthen roads, carrying men to unknown tasks. The San Joaquin Valley gave the overwhelming impression of vast, clinical, and effortless productivity.

The truck pulled into a roadside station at Delano at noon. "Care for lunch?" Rusty asked. Inside the café they ate hamburgers and milkshakes and rested their ears from the thundering of the diesel engine. Back on the road again, Anton asked Rusty where his route was taking him this day.

"I have to swing through Visalia, then on east to Exeter. Day after tomorrow I'll come through Grangeville, a little north of Armona. I'm driving home on the 25th."

Examining a map, Anton said, "Tell you what: drop me off at the intersection of the 99 and 198. I'll catch the bus from there. I am staying with a family in Armona, and you can come by on your way home if you want." Anton gave Rusty the directions to the ranch where the Salvadoran priest lived.

By the mid-afternoon they had passed through Tulare. At the intersection of the major highways, Anton bade goodbye to Rusty and transferred to a local bus for the westward leg to Armona. The bus was filled with Latino workers traveling out of the larger city for the rural encampments. Across from Anton a middle-aged Latino couple spoke vociferously for a while, then quieted. At one point the man created a little hide from newspapers, behind which he gave his wife a passionate kiss.

By four o'clock the bus had reached Armona. Descending the steps Anton felt the heaviness of winter. The darkening sky was clear and clean and cold. Anton pulled on his cap and thrust his right hand deep in his jeans to keep warm, and sheltered his left arm under his sweater. Using Luís' directions he left the main highway and walked down an old asphalt road away from the small village. As the homes of the outlying neighborhoods receded behind him, the asphalt of the road gave way to gravel and ruts. Within fifteen minutes Anton had arrived at his destination.

Jesus said: "For the kingdom of heaven is like a landowner who went out early in the morning to hire men to work in his vineyard. He agreed to pay them a denarius for the day and sent them into his vineyard. About the third hour he went out and saw others standing in the marketplace doing nothing. He told them, 'You also go and work in my vineyard, and I will pay you whatever is right.' So they went. He went out again about the sixth hour and the ninth hour and did the same thing. About the eleventh hour he went out and found still others standing around.

"The landowner asked them, 'Why have you been standing here all day long doing nothing?' 'Because no one has hired us,' they answered. He said to them, 'You also go and work in my vineyard.'

"When evening came, the owner of the vineyard said to his foreman, 'Call the workers and pay them their wages, beginning with the last ones hired and going on to the first.' The workers who were hired about the eleventh hour came and each received a denarius. So when those came who were hired first, they expected to receive more. But each one of them also received a denarius. When they received it, they began to grumble against the landowner.

"'These men who were hired last worked only one hour,' they said, 'and you have made them equal to us who have borne the burden of the work and the heat of the day.'

"But he answered one of them, 'Friend, I am not being unfair to you. Didn't you agree to work for a denarius? Take your pay and go. I give to the man who was hired last the same as I gave you. Don't I have the right to do what I want with my own money? Or are you envious because I am generous?'

"So the last will be first, and the first will be last."

Matthew 20:1-16

THE BREAD OF HOSPITALITY

THE FARMWORKER CAMP LAY on an acre of flat earth at the corner of two country dirt roads. A flowing aqueduct paralleled one of the roads, and had to be crossed by a wooden bridge to reach the camp itself. Ten well–traveled house trailers lined the aqueduct like a row of postage stamps. A single electrical power line descended from a telephone pole to one of the trailers, then stretched from house to house. Fluttering shirts and trousers draped clotheslines that ran from one corner of a house to another. An old car with a grimacing front grill huddled at the end of the row. Hen houses and a rabbit run lay a few yards from the main path between the trailers. A large porcelain sink supported by a wooden frame and complete with a drain pipe served for the communal laundry. The trailers had hitches for hauling by tractor or truck from field to field to follow the harvest.

On the first trailer Anton noticed a sign, *"Barcas en el océano de Tranquilidad."* A soft medley of sounds greeted his ear: the rapid chatter of children, a mother's brisk command, the uneasy clucking of chickens scurrying away from the dogs who idled around the front steps of the trailers, a staccato mix of Latin voices and commercial jingles from a radio, the clang of pots and pans, and the tired whimper of a hungry baby. Down the road Anton noticed the outdoor latrines, and a bit further yet, a tangle of pumps, pipes and tanks that distributed irrigation water and fertilizer to the acreage around the little village.

"Estoy buscando el padre Gustavo," Anton said to a woman gathering shirts from one of the clotheslines. I am looking for Father Gustavo.

"¿Cuál es su nombre?" came the reply. What is your name?

Anton explained that he was being sent by Luís, Gustavo's brother–in–law in Bakersfield. This was satisfactory, and the woman disappeared around the corner toward another house trailer. Moments later, a man emerged from one of the trailers and approached Anton.

Gustavo appeared to be in his sixties, strong and assured in robust masculinity.[46] He had a shock of silvering grey–black hair, thick and swept back off his brow. His face bore deep creases from squinting in the sun, and a thin white mustache adorned his upper lip. A distinct limp marked his progress toward Anton. *"¡Bienvenido!* Welcome! You must be Anton. Luís told me to expect you. How was your trip?" Gustavo extended his hand, then hesitated when he saw Anton's bandaged left hand. "I am very sorry about your accident. It is a terrible thing to be burned. How does it go for you?"

"I am well," Anton replied. "A bit weary from the bus ride and the walk. But it's good to be here. Are you sure that I am not imposing on you and your family?"

"It is not an imposition in the least," Gustavo replied firmly. "I have no family here, and I have my own place. You will stay with me, all right? Come."

Gustavo showed Anton his trailer, which was bruised on the outside and needing paint like all the others. Inside, however, every available wall space carried a bookshelf. Anton paused to browse fondly at the titles of works from South America and Africa, Mexico, the United States and Europe. Works in contemporary fiction were tightly packed with books on theology and philosophy. A photograph of a young Gustavo being ordained a priest by a bishop sat on the shelf next to the dining table, along with a photograph of a young woman in a green dress. An old manual typewriter sat on the table. A register for a butane heater was fastened into a wall. "My little place," Gustavo said simply. "I do nothing here except rest and read and sometimes write. This bench becomes a bed. I have some extra sleeping bags, and my little heater keeps me warm in the winter. Let me show you." With a few quick moves a bed and lamp had been arranged for the guest.

At that moment, a dinner bell rang. "Come, it is six o'clock and dinner time." Gustavo led Anton toward a larger trailer. Along the way he introduced Anton to Juan the foreman, a burly forty year old in jeans, a denim shirt and a jean jacket. People poured out from neighboring trailers. Inside the *"comedor,"* a large trailer with no interior walls, Anton was enveloped in an explosion of smells. He could pick out individual scents: fried onions and meat soaked and fried in spices and salt; heated lard of fresh tortillas; sharp, incisive chilies and black and red peppers; and everywhere the warm, savory smell of freshly turned dirt moistened with sweat. Several people, young and old, were bringing bowls of beans and rice to the tables. Dolores the cook was wiping down the formica countertop while hurriedly pushing back strands of hair that had fallen out from her bandana. Little children prattled and giggled as they pulled back table benches with much scraping and banging. Soon all sat shoulder to shoulder before their glazed ceramic bowls and plates, scratched and dented spoon and fork, and paper napkin.

"*Amigos,*" Gustavo rose from his place. "We have a guest with us, Anton Reisen, a professor from a college in Los Angeles, sent to us by my brother–in–law Luís in Bakersfield. Please help him feel at home. Now, let us thank God for the blessing of our dinner."

The room quieted and became indeed a warm, tranquil vessel amid the ocean of fields stretching for miles in every direction. The aroma of dinner was carried aloft and spread around the room from the steaming bowls and covered baskets containing rare delicacies—*tortillas hechas en casa.*[47]

In hospitality to his guest, Gustavo departed from his native language to offer the following plea –

> God of abundance, we end this day of work in your fields and your barns in the company of your son, *nuestro hermano Jesús*. We are all well, and we have had no injuries, and for this we are grateful. We are tired and hungry, and we bring our needs and cares before you as we sit together at our table. You have blessed the earth with abundance, and for this we give thanks. May our community bless our guest Anton. Be with us now as we nourish our bodies, and nourish our souls with your tender love, that we may work today, tomorrow, and always to prepare your kingdom for others, especially those who lack these blessings tonight. For this we pray. *Amen.*

With an echo of *Amen,* the men, women and children began their dinners with exclamations of pleasure. Anton shared their appetite after his long day and walk. Happy voices of children chattering about Las Posadas and the Nativity in two days blended into the laughter and eager conversation of the adults and the scrapping of dishes and pots and pans. A young couple, Rosa and Miguel, announcing that they were with child, basked under eyes of approval. The hubbub subsided during the main course, then reached a crescendo as Dolores produced a large plate of custard–like *flan*, in recognition of Las Posadas. Within fifteen minutes the commotion settled to contentment as the adults drank coffee and rested and the youngsters snuggled against their parents or grandparents.

Juan rose to speak. *"Amigos,"* he said. "The *patrón* has told me that we should expect cold tonight. He says that one of his neighbors up the hill may need help with his orchard. I will listen to the frost report at 7:30 and I'll bang on your door if we need to go out. Keep your jackets and gloves handy." Then he sat down.

Anton thought that Juan's announcement meant that dinner was over, but he was mistaken. Conversation resumed and Anton heard snatches of commentary on the hourly wages and piece rates, a relative in the hospital in Visalia, the activities of *"la Migra,"* a daughter who had not been home for weeks, and someone's plans to go north to pick apples in Washington State. For the most part the workers tried to include Anton in the conversation, and tried their best to explain their concerns in English. For his part, Anton assured them that he was able to follow most of their dialogue.

At 6:45, a young woman picked up a guitar and tuned the strings deftly. "Zanita," Gustavo whispered in Anton's ear, "Juan's wife." The room quieted, and children turned with large, brown eyes, attentive and eager. Zanita sang in a simple but sure voice –

Tú has venido a la orilla,
No has buscado ni a sabios ni a ricos;
Tan sólo quieres que yo te siga.

"Can you follow it, Anton?" Gustavo asked. Anton shook his head. Gustavo then translated softly between verses –

Lord, you have come to the seashore,
Searching neither for the rich nor the wise,
Desiring only that I should follow you.

Everyone joined in the refrain –

Señor, me has mirado a los ojos,
Sonriendo has dicho mi nombre,
En la arena he dejado me barca,
Junto a tí buscaré otro mar.

O Lord, you have looked into my eyes,

Smiling, you have spoken my name;
In the sand I have left my little boat,
Near to you I will seek other seas.

Other verses told the people's story about their faith and work—

Tú sabes bien lo que tengo;
En mi barca no hay oro ni espadas,
Tan sólo redes y mi trabajo.

Lord, you know well what I have;
In my boat there is neither gold nor swords,
Only nets and my labor.

Tú necesitas mis manos,
Mi cansancio que a otros descanse,
Amor que quiera seguir amando.

You need my hands,
My fatigue, that others might rest,
The love that wants to follow, lovingly.

Tú pescador de otros lagos,
Ansia eterna de almas que esperan
Amigo bueno, que así me llamas.

You, fisherman of other lakes,
For souls in eternal anguish who wait,
Good friend, so thus you call me.[48]

As Zanita sang the verses and the young and old joined in the refrain, Anton felt the same emotion heave in his chest that he had felt when Juan Carlos' wife had set hot cereal before him after his desolate night in the Tehachapis. He felt tears gathering in his eyes. Maybe this is what I seek, he thought. He looked around him, and saw the tired but peaceful faces of the workers, the far-away look in Gustavo's eyes, Juan watching his wife with affection, the pots and pans on the stove, the happy disarray of the tables. Maybe this is it, he said to himself again.

When the song ended, everyone carried dishes and utensils to the sink. Two men went to work with a will scrubbing the plates and pots.

Other workers departed for their own trailers. When Anton offered to wash his own plate, he was graciously smiled off as the guest of honor. So, he said to Dolores, "A delicious meal. The best."

"A mi me encanta cocinar por mis amigos," she replied. I am delighted to cook for my friends.

Some of the workers lingered outside in twos or threes to continue talking or to smoke a cigarette. Anton could hear the words *"Buenas noches,"* and *"Que sus sueñes dulces hecho realidad."* Good night, may your dreams become reality. *"Hasta luego, no lo dudo."* See you soon, no doubt—with a laugh from someone expecting the early night rise. Juan remained at the table with his coffee. Anton sat, too, wondering what dreams awaited him, as early as this night.

We all have a realm, a private paradise, in our mind, where dwell deathless memories of persons who brought some divine light to our life's experience, who may not be known to others, and whose names have no place in the pages of history.

Rabindranath Tagore (1861–1941),
East and West

Fire burns brightest at night

When the kitchen trailer had almost emptied, Gustavo reached up to a shelf and turned on an antique and dilapidated radio. "It's 7:15. We have a few minutes before the frost report…I am glad you are here, Anton. You were able to hear our song, and it's a very good song. It goes with the name of our camp, a steady boat in the midst of the turbulent sea of life. These trailers are like houseboats. They are pulled all over the countryside, and we feel close to the fishermen who are alone in their boats on the sea. So we sing that song."

By now the radio tubes had warmed up and were producing a scratchy and warbling static. Gustavo paused to finish tuning the radio, then turned it down low. "There are not many of us here right now. It is not the picking season and we don't start pruning for a few days. A lot of people from other camps have gone to Salinas, or up to Washington State to work in the apple orchards."

"A quieting time," Anton offered.

"Ah, yes. It is not very often we have a teacher here. We take care of our own that way. We have never before had a college professor. It is a good thing."

"Just so you know, I am the last thing from being a member of the dreamy-eyed intelligentsia. I come with empty hands, nothing more, really. Nothing but some time on my hands."

"On your hands, not in your hand. Up here, time is not something we measure or hold onto. Up here the shadows of the sun are our main timepiece. The sun tells us when it is time to go out, and when it is time to come back home."

"And your kitchen bell tells the time for dinner. That dinner was perfect. Not just the food, either. The people enjoy each other so much. No one was rushing off to be alone, or to hide in front of a TV."

"Night time is time to be all together, women and men and kids. During the day we are separated a lot, like everybody. Night time is now safe time. Everybody is at home. After the sun has gone down, we talk about what we do all day in the fields and in the village. Some of our women work in the motels in Visalia. At night they are home, too. It is risky for them to work over there, because of the temptation or pressure to prostitution. Fortunately the *Migra* does not follow the women home anymore, and we have not seen the terror of a night raid on the camps like we did ten or fifteen years ago. Then, it was pretty easy to get away at night. In the daytime it was impossible to hide in the wide open fields. That has all stopped now, and our trust has increased again. We feel more confident talking to the boss, and we go to town without worrying about not coming back."

"Funny, in my old life," Anton reminisced, "I always took getting home at night for granted. That seems like a long time ago."

"You know that I taught theology and philosophy in San Salvador, Anton? Being a professor was a good day job, No? As my city became a war zone, it made less and less sense. I was spending more time taking shelter from the chaos than sitting with students. Academic philosophy had to go. Old Pascal said all the scholarly work in the world is not worth one hour of living. Of course, he was kicking at the intellectual maze of the medieval Aristotelians, the Scholastics and the like. And the kind of living Pascal had in mind would set your hair on fire!"

"So you don't miss your theological studies, Gustavo?"

"Oh, the old love is still there," he shrugged. "It's a good night job. I'm not talking about academic theology, you know, the stuff people write in journal articles and books. When it is dark outside you cannot see to write, but you can feel the inside fire sear the night! That is what I mean."

"Sounds almost subversive—lighting fires at night!"

"Exactly," Gustavo laughed. "That is why nice, middle class people say you should not discuss politics and religion in polite company! It starts fires burning! Can theology free us? You remember what Marx said of philosophy: do it in the streets, in broad daylight, and let it turn the world upside down! Please God, may we do theology at night, and may it turn the world right–side up! Nighttime is story time. At night we tell stories about our day, and about how we find God in our day, or how we do not find him, or how we fear he has jilted us or has fed us with the food of love, or has kept us clear and clean like running water. These stories help us make sense of the world. That's theology, I think..."

"*Theo–mythos,* 'God stories,'" Anton said. "A great place to start: telling stories about God might help us resolve that old quarrel between theology and philosophy."

At that moment, Gustavo interrupted, "*Momentito.* Just a second. Here's the frost report."

Beginning with Merced, Chowcilla and Madera, the weather announcer worked his way down Interstate 99 calling off minimum temperatures for towns large and small. Hanford was 28 degrees, Tulare 28, Earlimart 28.5, and on down the valley. Anton envisioned little groups of men and women all up and down the San Joaquin Valley sitting at kitchen tables, listening, marking the temperatures with pencils, consulting one another, culling the wisdom of their experience with the cold and its insistent demands. Armona 28 degrees, and a high dew point.

When the litany of temperatures moved into the southern part of the state, they turned off the radio and began walking back to Gustavo's trailer. "We go right to bed now. I'll be up soon," he said. "We have to keep the groves from freezing, or they will lose their new fruit buds. I would rather tell stories with you, but there will be another time, soon. The boss will probably be coming for Juan in the middle of the night and sending the bus over for the people. Do you want to join us when we go out?"

Anton's wound was tender but not painful. He was curious about this night work. "Yes, roust me out," he said.

"Then I'll need to write your name logbook. That way the boss will know your name. He always knows everyone in the camp, whether they work in his vineyards or in other people's groves.[49] Your name will always be in the book, even if you become discontented in the long winter months and disperse to other regions, or if you should leave us before the harvest is fully in."

Back in the trailer, Anton prepared to sleep. As he pulled the blankets up to his chin he noticed a rustling over his head. "What's that?" he asked.

"Just a family of sparrows nesting above the heater flue," came Gustavo's muffled, sleepy voice. "They enjoy the warmth from the trailer."[50]

With the sounds of the quiet stirrings above his head, Anton drifted off to sleep. It seemed but a moment before he heard the creaking and gasping of the old bus pulling into the camp. He heard Juan knocking on house doors with *"¡Levántense, amigos!"* Anton rose, looked at his watch: thirty minutes past midnight.

Gustavo was already dressed. "I heard the bus coming down the road," he smiled. "You learn to sleep light in winter." Soon the men were aboard the chilly bus with jackets wrapped tight, wool caps pulled down over their ears and cotton gloves on their hands.

The hours that followed left dancing images in Anton's mind. After a bumpy ride back to Highway 198 and west to King County, which lay on higher, cooler terrain, the bus pulled into a barnyard. The barn itself looked like a crippled giant leaning on teetering crutches. Behind the barn stood two old tank trucks, a weathered tractor with a soil fumigation tank, three or four tilling and plowing tools lying rusty and prostrate on the ground, and an abandoned pickup resting from its labors on a bed of weeds growing up underneath and around the tires. The moment the bus arrived an elderly man in faded jeans and a heavy denim jacket appeared with a rolled–up plot map. He gave instructions to Juan, who in turn spoke to the farmworkers.

"Not too bad. Only 60 acres. Most of the growers just use water on the orchard floor, but this one uses orchard heaters,—good, old 'smudge pots.'" Juan said. "We must hurry. The landowner says that he is seeing frost on the buds already."

"Go with Juan," Gustavo said to Anton. "I cannot carry the torch because I fell over on my motorcycle a few years ago. Not that that knocked any sense in me...I'll go with the old man and check the thermometers."

Within seconds the workers had each picked up a torch and were trotting down the outside of a nearby orchard. Anton picked up his torch gingerly and tipped it against Juan's to light the wick. With the torch sending a soft gleam of light before him and a black ribbon of smoke trailing behind, he followed Juan to a row of smudge pots.

"Here's how you do it, Anton," Juan said. "Knock the lid off the top of the smudge pot. Swing upward with the edge of your torch tank to knock it off. Then open and lift off the swivel door on the pot with your shoe. Be careful or you will bend it; or you can use a stick. Pour a shot of fire down into the bowl, then a short stream down the stack. Don't worry about the flame flashing back at you: this farmer knows how to mix the juice. It's not too sweet."

"What do you mean, 'not too sweet'?"

"It doesn't have too much gasoline. It's fifty–fifty, gas and oil. You'll hear the pot take a deep breath, sucking the fire down, then begin to blow up the stack like a big furnace. That means it's going. Close the swivel door again. The boss says leave one hole in the door for a strong fire. You can do all of this with your good hand, I think."

Anton was acutely aware of the dangerous mix of gasoline and oil in his torch. Holding the flaming torch far from his body, he knocked the lid off a pot, opened the lower door and poured in the flaming stream, then down the stack as he had been instructed. He heard sounds of gasping and crackling as old ash and crust burst into flame, then the deep surge of air pouring through the vents in the side of the stack. He lit the next pot and said, "I have it, Juan."

"*Bueno.* Then keep going right down the line. Lap back when you get to the end. Six groves, sixty acres. Don't let the branches hit you in the face." Juan disappeared into the shadows.

Alone now, Anton began walking down the rutted and tree–sheltered boulevard. His breath steamed out before him. As he walked his small circle of glowing, dancing light pushed the obscurity before him. A distant wind machine hummed and stirred the air weighing heavily on the earth. A blast of wind sent by the propeller enveloped him and shook the trees eerily, then galloped off into the distance. Minute by minute, rank upon rank down the grove, the regiment of lights grew larger. Each heater seemed like a sentinel who had drifted to sleep in the calm night, only to summoned to fevered attention by a shadowy figure who sent streams of liquid fire cascading down its dark throat. Nor was the action all silent, for accompanying the night liturgy were shouts of laughter and encouragement, the clanging of metal lids near and far, the ever approaching and retreating shiver of windy leaves. Anton could almost hear the deep throbbing of his own heart as he trotted along amid the furrows and branches. The scene reminded him of the passing of candlelight amid the smoky incense of the Easter Vigil service. With his own torch he tapped the sleeping, frozen metal figures into life, and worked with a will down the long row.

Within an hour the group emerged from their mile–long tramp back and forth through the groves, and walked back to the barnyard. There they settled in a bunk room in the old barn, lit a fire in a stove made from a forty gallon barrel, and sipped cocoa heated in an old coffee pot. The farmer came in from checking the thermometers, and told them that the temperature in the groves had already risen half a degree. Gustavo brought a box of donuts and said that all would be well. He would go back out with the farm owner to watch the thermometers and would call them if needed. The men lay back on the bunks, and, with musty blankets drawn close, dozed until dawn.

When the sun was peaking over the horizon the men rose slowly from their fitful sleep, stretched, and gathered outside. Once the sun was half above the horizon, they were back into the groves, this time trotting down their row of pots, slamming the top lid shut and closing off the air hole in the lower door. The pots crackled with annoyance until the flames died in a puff of grey smoke. Returning to the barnyard in half an hour, Anton felt weariness descending into his bones. A pall of soot hung over the orchards. In the light of the grey–brown dawn, the farm owner replenished torches while Juan maneuvered an indeterminately old, open–cabined tank truck into position at the corner of his orchards. Without needing instructions the men each took two short and squat, five gallon buckets and began filling the pots as they cooled. As Anton reached for his own bucket, Juan said, *"Ya basta.* Enough for one day. Ride along in the truck with me and take care of your hand."

Sitting beside Juan Anton marveled at the endurance of the men who had worked all the previous day. In his mind he calculated that they had been allowed three hours of night rest before being awakened for the bus ride to this orchard; then they had worked three hours during the darkest hours of the night; and were now each toting forty pounds of oil across the uneven terrain of the orchards. When the filling was done, everyone had rings of black smudge under their eyes, ashes in their hair, and splashes of oil on their jackets and jeans.

The men slept on the bus back to the camp, then arose as the bus creaked to a stop alongside the *Campo Tranquilo.* "We go to wash up and rest now. We have the rest of the day off," Gustavo said. "Tomorrow is Christmas Eve. It is a day off, too, we hope, if it is not cold. The people like to go into Visalia to see friends and buy presents. Then we will have Midnight Mass."

The people who walk in darkness will see a great light. Those who live in a dark land, the light will shine on them. Thou shalt multiply the nation, Thou shalt increase their gladness. They will be glad in Thy presence as with the gladness of harvest...for Thou shalt break the yoke of their burden and the staff on their shoulders.

Isaiah 9:2

AND THE YOKE SHALL BE BROKEN

ON THE MORNING of Christmas Eve Señor Kirkpatrick,[51] the owner of the ranch, arrived in a pickup. From Gustavo's trailer Anton watched as Gustavo and Juan greeted him alongside the water canal. Dolores came out of the kitchen with a heaping tray covered with tin foil, gave it to the farm owner, then returned to the kitchen. Anton could see laughter and smiles, then conversation as the three men stood beside the road with their hands thrust in their pockets against the cold. Sr. Kirkpatrick reached into the pickup truck and handed a packet of envelopes to Juan. He then waved and drove away.

Juan walked over to the kitchen trailer and rang the bell vigorously. Men emerged from trailers or from underneath cars that they had been servicing. Women left their laundry and chores, and children dashed ahead of their parents, almost tripping over dogs and chickens, who scattered under the trailers with squawks of alarm. Anton learned that Sr. Kirkpatrick brought bonus checks for his workers at Christmas time when the harvest had been bountiful and the market kind. In turn, Dolores or one of the other women invariably gave the farmer and his family fresh tamales ready for steaming.

Anton was astounded when Juan handed him a check as well. "But I just got here," he protested to Gustavo. His elder friend smiled and said nothing. Anton felt himself on the fringes of a mysterious ritual whose meaning had not yet been disclosed to him, and he was silent.[52]

Soon the bus was loaded and with Juan at the wheel, they set off for Visalia. The group was in happy spirits. "This is a special time for us, Anton," Gustavo said. "Almost all of our money goes back to our families in El Salvador or Mexico. This bonus check is about all we have for Christmas presents. It allows us to do something for the children and for each other.

"We have a good *patrón,* Anton. He trusts us, and we trust him. He gives us his bus for the drive to town. At picking time his crews always fill up early, because everyone knows that Sr. Kirkpatrick tells the truth and does not play games with his workers."

"What do you mean, 'play games?'"

"Well, let me tell you. Not all of the farmers in the San Joaquin have heart. Sometimes a rancher will tell a worker that a box of grapes is paying a dollar…That's high wages for a worker, you know. The worker works himself ragged to fill as many boxes as possible. At the end of the day, the owner will come up to him and say that he had been mistaken, and that a box is worth only fifty cents…There you have it. And sometimes a boss will hire workers who have no papers. He puts them onto the worst jobs, like digging fence holes all day or picking rock, then calls the INS who rounds them up and ships them back to Mexico.[53] He gets a day's work on the most thankless jobs, and does not have to pay anything. Nothing! That violates the old law, and justice cries out to heaven![54] Our *patrón* would never do that. No games. So we work hard and we can take care of our families with no anxiety."

Anton found himself speechless at the spectacle of injustice reported so simply by Gustavo. Looking down the ordered furrows he saw them leading to a deception as grand in scope as the national and international markets they served. The terrible secret lay mute like the soil, hidden from public view by method and science, yet known to those who defined the property markers and to those who stooped along the brown lines that rose and fell until they disappeared into the horizon.

When they reached Visalia, Juan stopped the bus at a small store. He and Gustavo entered the store, then emerged, the younger man lugging a sack of rice under one arm and a sack of dried pinto beans under the other. Gustavo carried a bag of onions and a fifteen pound bag of flour. As he set the bags on a seat, Gustavo said, "Further up the road I am going to visit an old friend in a care center. Want to come, Anton? We can catch up with the group later on."

Juan dropped Gustavo and Anton off at the St. Jude Senior Center run by Catholic Charities, and continued down the main street of town. Now with Anton's help, Gustavo carried the bags of food to the kitchen, then returned to the reception desk to ask for a resident named Elena. As they were walking down the hallway Gustavo said, "Zanita found Elena a couple of years ago outside of Hanford. The old woman was sitting beside a *descanso,* one of those little, nameless roadside shrines where people who have lost somebody in a car crash put up crosses. It seemed that someone she knew died out there in a *'pega y corre,'* a 'hit–and–run.' It was in winter like right now. She had no coat and was extremely cold. I put her in the bus and brought her to the hospital. She seemed a little *loca* to the people at the hospital, and couldn't tell us anything about herself. The hospital couldn't keep her, nor could the county. Nobody would claim her. But Catholic Charities didn't think twice about it, and St. Jude's took her in. St. Jude is the advocate of lost causes, you know. So we bring some things here, groceries or vegetables from our gardens during the growing season whenever we come to Visalia. It is okay with our *patrón*. Here at St. Jude's we named her Elena Vasquez to complete the registry, believing that she must have been very beautiful when she was young, like Helen of Troy. It's nice to think so. You know, we must always think the good of each other. Elena is mostly quiet or mumbles sometimes, but she looks at you very clearly so I believe that she understands."

Inside the day room, Gustavo stopped and nodded toward an ancient, wizened woman, sitting looking out the window. She wore a sweater and had a shawl over her knees. "The doctors at the hospital said she has dementia. You tell me what you think."

Approaching Elena, Gustavo said, *"Buenas días, Elena."* The woman sat perfectly still, ignoring the greeting.

"Pull up a chair, Anton," Gustavo said. The three sat quietly for ten minutes. Elena stared out the window. People came and went, Latino and Anglo, some in wheelchairs, others with walkers or canes. Younger attendants busied themselves with small tasks or updating medical charts at the nurses' station. Anton allowed his mind to wander and he began to doze in the quiet, warm hum of activity.

"¿Qué es lo que estás mirando, ancienita?" Gustavo asked. What are you looking at, little old one? The question woke Anton, and he saw Elena turn toward her friend with the clear, transparent gaze of a very young child. With utter clarity she said, *"Es mi angel, mi hermano."*[55]

Anton saw Gustavo's face move closer to Elena's, looking deeply into her eyes. He gazed at her with the rapt expression of a young lover beholding his beloved, a wondering, inquiring gaze of someone beholding another person's very soul. After a long moment he whispered in her ear, *"Es la gloria de la Navidad, Elena."* It is the glory of Christmas.

"Yo lo sé," she responded. I know it.

"Feliz Navidad," he said. Merry Christmas. She did not reply, but looked back out the window, far away.

Back in the village in the early afternoon, Gustavo said he needed to work on his homily and disappeared into his trailer. Anton went into the kitchen. Tamales and frijoles were boiling in large pots, and Dolores was flipping and searing the last of a stack of fresh tortillas. She gratefully accepted his offer to help setting the table and preparing vegetables for the evening dinner. She excused herself to tend to her family.[56]

While he was working he noticed a piece of paper thumb–tacked to one of the cabinets next to the sink. The words on the paper read,

> *Gracias, Señor –*
> *Por mis brazos buenos, cuando hay tantos mutilados,*
> *Por mis ojos, cuando hay tantos sin luz,*
> *Por mis manos que trabajan, cuando hay tantos que mendigan,*
> *Por mi voz que canta cuando otros están enmudecidos,*
> *Por conservarme siempre con buena salud,*
> *Por el pan nuestro de cada día,*
> *Por guiarme siempre por el buen camino.*
> *Es maravilloso, Señor, tener un hogar a donde volver,*
> *Cuando hay tanta gente que no tiene donde ir.*
> *Es maravilloso, Señor, amar, soñar, sonreír,*
> *Cuando hay tanta gente que llora, que odia,*
> *que se revuelve en pesadilla; y tantos que mueren antes de nacer.*
> *Es maravilloso, Señor, sobre todo,*
> *Tener tan poco que pedirte y tanto que agradecerte.*
> *Por todo esto, alabado seas, Señor.*[57]

Translated, it read –

> Thank you, Lord,
> For my strong arms, when there are so many who have been mutilated,
> For my eyes, when there are so many without light,
> For my hands that can work, when there are so many who beg,
> For my voice that sings, when others have been silenced,
> For keeping me always in good health,
> For our daily bread,
> For guiding me always on the good path.
> It is marvelous, Lord, to have a place to return to,
> When so many people have no where to go.
> It is marvelous, Lord, to love, to dream, to smile,

When there are so many who weep,
Who hate, who are disturbed by nightmares,
And so many who die before having lived.
It is marvelous, Lord, in spite of everything,
To have so little to ask for and so much to thank you for.
For all of this, we praise you, Lord.

Gustavo reappeared and said, "Come, Anton. Would you listen to some of my ideas for the service tonight? I am lucky to have someone here who can help me think through my homily. The Mass will last until late. Back home we called it *la misa de los pollos,* having Mass with the chickens and roosters. They would be waking up about the time when we went to bed. When the whole village comes to the table, it can take hours to serve everyone. I was always surprised, but not really, that there was enough for everyone, every time."[58]

Gustavo filled two cups with coffee and sat down at one of the tables. Taking a sip, he said, "You know, Anton, one's whole life is a preparation for the Mass, for receiving the gift. We are never ready for what it offers us, yet the gift is always there. Think about what has happened in the last few days: You have come to us, a good man certainly, wise enough with your hands empty and open, someone seeking for what you think you do not have. We read about such people in Matthew. The story of the Magi is one of my favorite Gospel fantasy stories. They were seekers, too, looking for something that held great promise. They might have been looking for a great monument or important personage, but they found a baby. They had to travel a long way to find something or someone they were not expecting. They might just as well gone around the corner of their own neighborhood to find a baby sleeping under a star. May you not have to travel so far, Anton."

Anton received this encouragement gratefully. "That reminds me of what a Salvadoran man down south told me, Gustavo. He said that I was 'searching for Aguilares'."

Gustavo's eyes widened. "I have not heard that expression for a long time. It was new when I was in El Salvador."

"I have thought about it ever since," Anton mused. "It has a kind of hold on me. I wrack my brain to see if there is anything like it in American culture today. It is a saying that troubles you or irritates when you think about it. The man who told me about it implied that it was a slogan, a call to insurrection like a slave working–song in the South."

"It is like that, Anton," Gustavo said emphatically. "The most powerful sayings act like a lever underneath a heavy, oppressive building. Think of the story of the Gerasene swine in Mark.[59] Jesus knows the Jewish people are going mad under the Roman occupation; so he exorcises the demons—the Romans, that is—and inflicts them on the pigs, who were anathema to the Jewish people, and the pigs gallop over a cliff. It's hilarious. The meaning of it had to be quite obvious to the people who heard it.

"But Aguilares is a different story. The symbol does not deal with land animals like pigs, but with creatures of the air, the *águila,* the eagle. Aguilares is total paradox, a place named after a dream...It is a place like the smelly, dirty town of Quayaquil in Ecuador, which they call *La Perla de la Pacifica,* 'The Pearl of the Pacific.' Or it is the City of Los Angeles, where angels walk on the sidewalks with you in South Central, disguised as community organizers and even as gang members.[60] Paradox, right? Like the man told you, 'Aguilares' is not a place; it is nowhere. You can't create it with institutions. We know all too well that there is no final political solution to the human problem.[61] Because it is an image in the spirit, the *águila* calls us back from the false gods of distraction and comfort. It rises above the gravity and downward pull of entertainment and complacency that people live in. And, because it floats and flows and drifts and moves above us in circles, always out of reach, it implies that spiritual purposefulness and ambition can make fools even of wise men, perhaps even the Magi themselves."

"I think I understand," Anton said. "Aguilares feels like another word for *freedom;* politics in the ancient sense—gatherings of free people, open debate and discussion, taking turns ruling and being ruled."

"That's the key thing, Anton. Free citizens taking turns. Everybody has to take their turn, all the way down to the local level. When you are free and you know it, and when people depend on you, you stay connected. Everybody has a stake in you, and you have a stake in everybody else. That is what people wanted in El Salvador, and that is what they found in the small communities. It felt good. People danced. It felt like a blessing, so people worshipped."

Anton whistled. "What an image! People queuing up to vote, processing to communion, dancing and praying, all in the same place!"

"There you go...That's *Aguilares.* When the *campesinos* came to vote, they also came to be with one another, to eat together and tell stories and sing songs. They did not just drop in their ballot and go home. Often they stayed for the celebration of the Mass, too. Always under the threat of reprisals and repression. So the expression, *'Buscando Aguilares'* is politically charged for a people who hunger for freedom. Gathering for the bread and wine of Jesus tells us that politics points beyond itself. It points up to the sky where the eagle flies, to the eternal dimension. And it reminds the people that although they may be trampled and feel the boot on the neck, they will be like the eagle in Isaiah (and here Gustavo spoke the words in his native language) –

Los mancebos se fatigan y se cansan,
los mozos flaquean y caen:
Mas los que esperan en Jehová tendrán nuevas fuerzas;
levantarán las alas como águilas,
correrán, y no se cansarán, caminarán, y no se fatigarán.

"You know the words, Anton, 'Even youths grow tired and weary, and young men stumble and fall, but those who hope in the Lord will renew their strength. They will soar on wings like eagles, they will run and not grow weary, they will walk and not be faint.'[62]

"So, Anton," he concluded, "you're no different than anyone else in this way. You will figure out what 'searching for Aguilares' might mean for your life."

Silence settled in the warm and well–worn trailer as the two men pondered their memories. Anton saw Juan Carlos with his children and diligent wife. He saw people gathered on the street corners in Los Angeles and huddled under the bus stops on rainy days; and Latino men, determined to hold onto their own ways, as they walked along Santa Monica Boulevard with their Stetson cowboy hats and boots, proud in their identity even in the long walk to their labor.

"So: Here *we* are. Today. Right now. Everything is happening right now." Gustavo continued, "Señor Kirkpatrick brought a bonus check. It is his way of saying, we are in this together. These are great gifts. Sometimes the farm owners do not care and we get hurt or sick and get fired from our jobs. But not by this farmer. He is just, and has mercy.

"We are from all over Mexico and Central America, but we stand together and we bring our songs. These days the Arctic wind brings cold weather, and we work hard to preserve our food from damage. We brought back Christmas presents from Visalia, some sweaters, perfumes for the women, toys for the kids. We know that life is an uncertain, difficult thing, and that people sometimes end up naked in the street like Elena."

"It is a different thing to experience Christmas here with you and your people, Gustavo. A long way from the world I knew."

"Very true," Gustavo agreed. "I wonder sometimes if people who have everything, who never feel what it means to be poor, who never feel the gnawing of hunger in the belly, can really appreciate Christmas. One thing seems clear to me: if you are not hungry you will not see the connection between the birth of Jesus and justice. You see, when we come to the Mass, we believe that our hunger and restlessness—and all of the hardships and difficulties and even indignities—have been embraced by the God of Love. The baby lying there is beautiful and cared for, yet living in near squalor, warmed only by a rugged blanket, the warmth of animals, and his mother's milk, just like so many babies today. Could I say that Jesus is poor? Never! But I will say that he, like many babies born in the camps at this very moment, are among *los apobrecidos,* those impoverished by the political and economic system; although many babies along the border tonight don't even have the warmth of animals."[63]

Gustavo drew a deep breath as the memories of the border camps gathered to his mind's eye.

"Then as a man Jesus will suffer much and experience loneliness and longing. Those who know him—and many Latinos know his loneliness and longing and identify with his suffering—they will be transformed. It is so hard to find the words to say what this is, this transformation. We understand it in our hearts when we are together, and know that our love does not need words to be shared. That, my friend, is the ultimate paradox, the scandal to our orderly minds: Because no tongue can soil this mystery with words, we take it into our mouths in silence, or with no more than an *Amen*. And we do this together. The gift of each other is so precious...yet love incarnate is as fragile as a piece of bread that we put into our mouth and wash down with a sip of wine. This is what the Christmas story makes me think about. What the facts are, we do not need to know. The reality, the truth of the story is greater than the facts..."

Gustavo brows furrowed. "What troubles me is how religion has become for many an activity set apart from the whole of life. Religion that is powerful is unpredictable. Jesus strides into your village and stands beside someone about to die under a rain of stones thrown by the self–righteous. He draws a line in the sand, and says, 'Let the one without sin cast the first stone!' When Jesus does this, his message is not about himself, but about justice. Our fascination with this great human being distracts us from his message. In reality, most of the great givers bring their offering and disappear from the stage of history. They say nothing of themselves...that is why Jesus asked his friends not to talk about him. Their refusal to hold themselves up, to display themselves, their silence about themselves, only adds to the eloquence of their service to the poor and their tribute to justice. Jesus does this so that we might live and live abundantly. At his trial, that shameful travesty of justice, he does not harangue his persecutors. Rather his silence allows them to hear their own words, to sense their own souls. Nothing else can penetrate the thick walls of their power and position. That is why Pilate is so amazed by the whole affair. He is implicated by Jesus' silence. The silence of the birth scene compliments the silence of Jesus' passion and trial.[64]

"So. Thank you for listening, Anton," Gustavo concluded. "You have helped me think about what is important. We celebrate the Mass tonight at ten o'clock."

As Gustavo finished speaking Dolores returned to the kitchen. With her was Guadalupe, an older woman with her dark graying hair covered with a bandana. They were accompanied by a little girl of eight or nine years of age. The women began pulling flour down from the shelves. They gathered the flour, water and powdered milk, salt and yeast and honey in a large wooden bowl while the child stirred the slushy mixture until it became stiff.

"*Abuelita,* may I taste it now?" the little girl said in an eager voice.

The grandmother nodded as she stirred the thickening dough with a wooden spoon and reminisced about the trip to Visalia and the family back home. The little girl ran her finger around the bowl and tasted the sweet, salty stuff.

"*Tan sabrosa, abuelita,*" So delicious, grandmother.

Anton watched the women scrape the dough onto a floured board and knead it with their strong hands. Sweat formed on the women's brows and dripped into the bread. They dug into the dough and pulled and pressed and molded it into two round loaves. Then, laying the dough on two smudge pot lids that had been scrubbed, hammered flat and tempered in fire, they placed the bread in the oven to bake with the ham.

As Anton and Gustavo were walking back to their trailer they saw a large tank truck driving slowly down the dirt road in the direction of the camp, its lights shining through the gathering twilight. Rusty had arrived.

"When I was coming north I met a young man who gave me a ride to Bakersfield, then later on up the Valley," Anton explained to Gustavo.

"He is a college student and has stepped out of school for a while. I told him how he could find me. I hope that this is all right with you."

"He is welcome," Gustavo replied.

When Rusty descended from the truck he moved stiffly and looked strained with fatigue. Gustavo welcomed him and invited him to stay, just as he had done for Anton.

As they were waiting for the dinner bell Rusty said, "Anton, I had to get up at four this morning to finish dropping off my load around Goshen. It was so beautiful. I saw a field of lights, and little groups of people gathered around campfires along the roadside. I have never seen anything like it, and would travel a long way to see it."[65]

"I know," Anton replied. "I was out night before last. These are some of the people who take care of the orchards."

When the dinner bell rang again at six o'clock, the excited throng gathered in the *comedor*. Before offering the blessing, Gustavo welcomed Rusty, who sat down next to Anton and opposite Guadalupe. As Anton took the first bite of the ham and sweet potatoes he felt that he had never tasted anything so delicious. His eyes feasted on the now-familiar faces of the small community. There was Gustavo with his round, smooth cheeks and mustache; the foreman Juan and his wife Zanita with the lovely voice; Carlos the middle-aged man who was an expert in fertilizers, his two young children at his side; Guillermo the young man who could use his ox-like strength to carry two oil cans in each hand; Henrique his father who was still sending money home for his own father who lived in Oaxaca; Yesenia the school teacher from Guatemala who taught the children how to read; Guadalupe, the most ancient one; Pedro and José and Pancho and their wives and children; and Dolores who faithfully prepared meals for twenty people twice a day.

As he was finishing his meal Carlos looked over to Rusty and asked, "*Joven* Rusty, what are you hauling on your big truck?"

"I brought malathion and gibberellin up from Los Angeles, you know, insect spray and growth hormone. The tanks are empty now and I'm on my way home."

A slight hush fell on the happy hubbub of the table. Rusty paused, his fork half-way to his mouth, and sent an inquiring glance at Anton. Anton himself was at a loss, although he knew something was very wrong. Carlos was looking at the grey-haired grandmother sitting opposite Rusty.

"May I tell him, *abuelita* Guadalupe?" Carlos asked.

Looking at her plate, she shook her head. *"No ahorita."* Not now.

After dinner Anton helped with clearing the table while Rusty offered to help with the dishes.

"How have I upset Guadalupe?" Rusty asked.

"You have to understand," Dolores replied. "She misses her daughter, Marguerita, and will always miss her. She was born to Guadalupe in the fields of Imperial Valley thirty years ago. The little girl with us is her grand–daughter, and was more fortunate: she was born in a clinic in Visalia a few years back. Marguerita was pruning in the vineyards near Earlimart last March in a field that had been sprayed with malathion only two days before. The law says that farmworkers must be kept out for at least two weeks and that the area must be posted. It was not posted. It was a sixty acre vineyard, and Marguerita got sick out there. She collapsed into a coma in the field. We got her to the hospital in Visalia, Rusty, but she died there, the same place where her daughter had been born."

Rusty drew a deep breath and stammered, "I–, I'm very sorry. My God, I wish I had known."

"It was excruciating for her, and for us. *Abuelita* Guadalupe fought God, raged at him, for many days during this time. She cried and cried, and walked around saying, *'¡Devuélvanme a mi hija!'* 'Give me back my daughter!' She asked me once why her insides felt so terrible when she felt nothing on the outside. I could say nothing to her at the time, but she showed me that people are not sticks: we are soft inside, not hard and brittle. We need to remember that when we talk to each other. She was so hard on God because he too sometimes gets shut away inside the tough shells we put around him. Yet he aches in his guts for us, like Guadalupe feels agony for the child of her womb. Her suffering has withdrawn into silence. Could it be that way with God, too?

"Watch tonight, Rusty. You will see Guadalupe lighting the candles for the Mass. She will be saying *'Cha–Cha,'* the name she used to call her daughter, you know, *'Muchacha.'* You may speak to her if you wish." Rusty nodded and stepped outside and disappeared in the direction of his truck. It was evident that he needed to be alone with his thoughts.

At seven o'clock Juan and Gustavo again listened to the frost report. Temperatures would be above freezing in the central valley. When the *comedor* was clean and tidy after dinner Gustavo began to rearrange the room for the Christmas Mass. The four tables were joined into a long rectangle. Small candles used when electricity failed were placed down the middle. Gustavo placed a Bible, a simple chalice and a carafe of wine and one of the fresh loaves from Dolores' stove on the table. With these simple preparations completed, the two men sat and waited.

A few minutes before ten o'clock, headlights flashed in the window and a truck rolled to a stop next to the camp. "That's Señor Kirkpatrick," Gustavo said. He went outside and returned with the farm owner, who entered the large trailer with his arms piled high with presents. The farm owner was in his early seventies, with clear blue eyes, a frame as lean as a post, a high forehead with thinning hair, simple clothes with a heavy jacket and boots. When Rusty returned from his solitude in his truck, Anton introduced him to Sr. Kirkpatrick. "I know your company, Rusty," the farm owner said. "I sometimes buy material from them. Welcome to Armona. Too bad you have to be away from home on Christmas Eve." To Gustavo he then said, "I'm on my way home now. Christmas blessings."

At ten o'clock Gustavo again went outside, this time to ring a small bell. He stood by the door as the farmworkers entered the trailer, saying *"Feliz Navidad"* to each person as they climbed the low stairs. Inside once again, with the small community standing around the long table, Gustavo gave a lighted taper candle to the grandmother, Guadalupe, who made her way down the room lighting the candles. As Dolores had said, Guadalupe's mouth was moving as she leaned over to light the small candles. Rusty watched her intently, and tried to swallow the lump in his throat. With Zanita playing her guitar, the assembled people sang a hymn familiar to Latinos all over the hemisphere.

Thus began the Christmas liturgy. As the people sat on the benches around the table, Carlos read the great prophecy in Isaiah 9 –

> And the people who walk in darkness will see a great light. Those who live in a dark land, the light will shine on them. Thou shalt multiply the nation, Thou shalt increase their gladness; they will be glad in Thy presence as with the gladness of harvest, as people rejoice when they divide the spoil. For Thou shalt break the yoke of their burden and the staff on their shoulders. For a child will be born to us, a son will be given to us; and the government will rest on his shoulders, and His name will be called Wonderful Counselor, Mighty God, Eternal Father, Prince of Peace. And there will be no end to the increase of his government or of peace, on the throne of David and over his kingdom, to establish it and to uphold it with justice and

righteousness from then on and forevermore. The zeal of the Lord of Hosts will accomplish this.

After a jubilant refrain from Psalm 96, the people then listened as one of Yesenia's children read from the Book of Titus. Here the message spoke of God's desire to reclaim a people that they might live in a manner after His own heart.

Then Gustavo rose to read the story of Jesus' humble birth in the Gospel of Luke. He told how the child had been acclaimed by the shepherds, the humblest of people, and by angels, the most sublime of God's creatures. Then he said,

"Friends, on this holy night *Jesús* is born. Having a baby is work both difficult and sweet. We who have traveled far from our homes, from Mexico, El Salvador, Guatemala and other places, can feel the fatigue and anxiety of Mary and Joseph who have traveled far and must prepare for the baby, who will wait no longer. The baby is born into a dangerous world, with Romans occupying the Holy Land, governing its sacred temples, pillaging the land for tribute to a city of people given to spectacles and circuses, and suppressing the slightest movement to freedom. We who know how dangerous the world can be, who are grateful for the safe refuge and good work offered to us by Señor Kirkpatrick, know Joseph and Mary as our brother and sister who travel under the direction of the dominating power, the emperor in Rome. We who have had babies in the field clinics or crossing the border know something of the unspeakable stress and fear of Mary and Joseph who must go into a stable of animals to give birth to their child.

"Yes, when we meet Mary and Joseph and Jesus tonight we meet ourselves in our humanity. That is where our faith begins—in living out our own humanity. We who have been uprooted, exiled, forced to flee into exile; we who have known what the world has done to so many people in pressing them down in the garbage dumps of the big cities to a life unfit even for animals; we who have chosen to leave a way of life that bound us in untruth and in the inertia of enslavement; we who are seeking to find the way to abundant life, for ourselves and others, even as we flee through the night: may never lose sight of this simple scene, this little family gathered around the child in love and peace and protection.

"So, we who have so much in our families, our work, our kitchen here and our warm homes must fasten our eyes on the infant Jesus, his parents, the simplicity and precariousness of their existence, and yet, always the joy and inner freedom with which this family lived. We do so that our homes and lives might be like warm inns, generous places for people to come and live and bring new life.

"Keep this scene in front of your eyes, my friends. When the day grows long, when we become fatigued, when we grieve the loss of someone we love, especially Marguerita and our families and loved ones back home, then look upon this scene of new beginnings and great hope. Keep also in sight the image of this child grown to be a man, who loved with complete abandon, whose loving stopped people in their tracks, whose loving transgressed and transcended social and political systems, whose loving resurrected oppressed spirits, whose *Yes* to life gave them the hope and energy to grow and flourish, whose loving became the redemption of our humanity.

"From this scene we know that this is possible, that God reaches into our hidden lives and draws forth joy. We also know that this work is too great for us alone. We work in the fields and vineyards. We prepare the soil. We plant the vines, too, and we go out and prune back the old growth. We make the vine good, that it may bring forth good wine. But we cannot provide the growth: that is the work of sun and water. So it is with our human hearts: we can prepare ourselves, but we must simply wait while the love of God works inside us to bring us to our deep humanity as promised in Jesus.

"To sustain us in patience and the joy of life itself, brothers and sisters, we gather to share the bread and wine of Jesus' life, the food that he gives us because he knows how long our journey must be, and how much we need him and his example to stay before us."

Anton was mesmerized by the ineffable warmth that radiated from Gustavo's calm countenance, his hands raising the fresh bread, then laying it again into the basket. The priest then closed his eyes for a moment and stood motionless in the silence. At this point he invited the people to offer prayers for themselves and one another and the whole people of God. When the last word was murmured from the workers, Gustavo offered a prayer for peace. As young and old moved and jostled one another with *embrazos* in the small space Rusty reached over to Guadalupe, the old grandmother, and said, "I am sorry about what happened to Marguerita, *abuela.*"

Guadalupe took both of Rusty's hands and nodded with a dignified calm. "Your saying so means that she did not die in vain, Rusty. Thank you. *Gracias a Jesús.*"

Dolores prepared a late breakfast for the camp the next day, Christmas. Everyone brought presents which they placed under the benches as they ate *chili rellenos* and toast and drank coffee. Once the tables were cleared presents were passed around and were opened with explosive rustlings and whistles and cries of delight. Gustavo gave Anton a small wooden cross wrapped with copper wire and with a small, simple river stone in the center. Anton placed it in his pocket with gratitude.

Rusty stood up to leave for his return trip to Southern California. "I have a long way to go, and my family is having dinner together tonight," he said. With a little cry Dolores hastened to her feet, and returned quickly with another helping of *chili rellenos* wrapped in tinfoil. This she gave to the young man. With an embarrassed expression on his face, he said, "Thank you, everyone, for taking me in and for telling me about your lives. *Feliz Navidad.*" He shook Juan's hand, and gave Dolores a hug. He looked steadily at Guadalupe. Drawing a deep breath, he turned to Gustavo and said quietly, "Ask her if she could come outside with me."

Outside with Anton and Gustavo and Guadalupe, Rusty stood next to his truck. The air was hushed under the wide, blue sky. Rusty looked at his big tank truck and the irrigation pipes at the edge of the camp, and at the broad, furrowed fields that fled away as far as the eye could see.

"Amigos," he said, "I have been thinking. I have driven all over the valley for the last few days. I have seen difficult and beautiful things. I have been lonely in my truck. I have wondered what I am supposed to be doing. Last night during communion I remembered something that Anton said when I picked him up in Bakersfield a few days ago. 'By his wounds we are healed.' Then I thought: *medicine*. Something about being with wounded people and their healing. I don't know what that means, except this is something I am supposed to look at, to explore. I did well in the sciences in high school, and biology was the one course I enjoyed this year. I need to think more about this."

"You have a great heart, Rusty," Gustavo said. "There is room for much love there. Maybe you shall share this through medicine."

Rusty gave Gustavo and Anton a hug and turned and looked into Guadalupe's aged eyes and face. "I take your story with me, *abuela.*"

"It is now our story, *muchacho,*" she said. *"Vaya con Dios."*

For six years you are to sow your fields and harvest the crops, but during the seventh year let the land lie unplowed and unused. Then the poor among your people may get food from it, and the wild animals may eat what they leave. Do the same with your vineyard and your olive grove. Six days do your work, but on the seventh day do not work, so that your ox and your donkey may rest and the slave born in your household, and the alien as well, may be refreshed.

Exodus 23:10-12

TOOLS AND LIFE

LATER ON THAT CHRISTMAS AFTERNOON Anton retreated to Gustavo's trailer to rest. Gustavo had bundled himself up with a sweater and a big jacket and had sped off to town on his Norton Villiers motorcycle; he had said that he was going to visit Elena and other friends. As Anton lay looking up at the books on the shelves in the little trailer, his mind drifted back to the stately libraries of his college. He saw himself as a young student walking with awe across the hallowed thresholds into the sanctuary of intellect and feeling; the hush and the comfortable arm chairs that wooed undergraduates to sleep; the fireplace in the reading room with racks of newspapers from all of the capitals of the great nations. He thought of himself learning, writing, gleaning, gathering, page after page, step after step into remote corners of history and culture. He also remembered the regularities of his academic life, which ranged from an ever–available meal–line, to mail and materials, to the easy schedules of summer and the comforts of tenure.

Looking at the scattered titles on Gustavo's shelf he felt surrounded by an august company: titles by St. John of the Cross in the original Spanish and books in English translations by the contemporary giants of ecclesial reform, Küng and Rahner. He saw Gutierrez and Boff, voices for the dispossessed; Simone Weil, the bad conscience of comfortable religion; and Luther, the zealous monk and pivotal figure of the Reformation. Some titles evoked faint images of battles and controversies: Spinoza, the "God–intoxicated philosopher" who escaped the religious oppressors of his time and experienced divinity in a spider descending in his web; and Bonhoeffer, who chose to return to the furnace of oppression and wrote his subdued yet passionate lament from the Buchenwald prison. Anton beheld the dialogues of Plato, whose encompassing genius earned him the sobriquet of "divine"; works of his respectful but contentious student, Aristotle; and the Peripatetic's intellectual heir, Aquinas, who melded Christian thought and classical philosophy into the concrete of medieval and modern Catholicism. Joining them on the bookshelf lay Erasmus, who spoofed the whole lot in *The Praise of Folly*.

Anton saw the books of firebrands who were always searching for readers with the internal mettle to wrestle with them: Friedrich Nietzsche, who thought of himself as dynamite and a destiny and who pined for disciples and authentic readers[66]; Sorën Kierkegaard, who believed that he had to think his way through every riddle and paradox of the spiritual life; Goethe, the greatest myth–maker of the modern age and the last of the Renaissance type; and Rousseau, the bohemian–genius who scandalized polite society, inspired French revolutionaries and the romantic movement. There were the collected lays of Shelley and the wanton yearnings of Byron and the mystical acclamations of Blake; the longings for free expression and dreamy voyages of the spirit in Wordsworth and Tennyson; the purifications and self–confrontations of Tolstoy, that nobleman and literary giant who scrabbled among his peasants. Karl Marx stood there as well, the one who gave the modern world a vocabulary and conceptual weapon, but who hated religion and tainted his affirmations of humanity with contempt for simple people and the simple life.[67]

Here, Anton thought, one holds onto a book like a starving man holds onto a cup of water and bowl of rice. How does one read these books in the boundless fields of the Great Valley of Central California? But they live even here, subtle footnotes in the great *liber mundi* being composed by persons whose stories will never be written down.[68] Nor would Gustavo ever commit the sin of arrogance in speaking eloquently about people for whom he had a secret contempt, or with whom he would refuse to live.

One book in particular caught Anton's eye, a collection of essays by Seneca, the Roman Stoic. Opening to a marked page in *Letter CIV*, he read,

> No sooner had I left behind the oppressive atmosphere of Rome and that reek of smoking cookers which pour out, along with a cloud of ashes, all the poisonous fumes that have accumulated in their interiors whenever they are started up, then I noticed the change in my condition at once. You can imagine how much stronger I felt after reaching my vineyards! I fairly waded into my food. Talk about animals just turned out to spring grass! So, by now I am quite my old self again. That feeling of

listlessness, being bodily ill at ease and mentally inefficient, did not last. I'm beginning to get down to some whole-hearted work.

Anton rose to his feet and opened the door of the trailer. He sat on the steps and looked out onto the fields whose smooth ground rippled away in the perfect furrows of modern farming. Across the road the bare vineyards lay leafless and grey, awaiting the first pruning of the new year. The camp was tranquil as though in a *siesta,* a time of rest after the late night and the excitement of Christmas. A rangy dog wandered by, nosing casually around the kitchen trailer for some morsel. Anton flexed his left hand. The skin was smooth and pink, and the pain was nearly gone. What am I to do?, he wondered.

The sound of grinding came to his ear, a clinking of metal and whisking of a file. Rising from the steps, Anton followed the sound around the trailers toward the road. Juan sat on the front fender of his old car. He was holding a tool in one hand, and in the other hand a file with which he brushed the blade with small circles. "*¡Hola, Juan! Qué tal?*" How's it going?

"*¡Pura vida!*"[69] Juan replied, pausing to waggle his thumb in an upward motion. "Tomorrow we start our pruning. Señor Kirkpatrick has 200 acres of grapes, burgundy, rosé, merlot. When we talked yesterday we agreed that it is time to begin." He laid aside the small shears that he had been sharpening and picked up a hoe. Bracing the hoe against his body he began filing the blade. Sparks darted to the earth as he sharpened the tool.

"Your hoe hasn't seen work for awhile," Anton ventured after a minute.

"No, not during the rainy spells unless we have flooding." Juan paused for a moment to catch his breath. "But my hoe and clippers are welcome friends. Our tools help us work. There's life in them. Our bodies have their shape, you know, thick shoulders and backs as sturdy as a burro's, hands like leather, because of our tools or the loads we carry. My hoe belonged to a woman who got too old to work in the fields. Her sweat and the dirt have made the handle smooth for my hands. We hoe weeds while we prune. It gives our bodies a rest. The pruning is very careful work, while the hoeing we can do with less attention." He resumed his sharpening.

Tools…, Anton thought. Tools and work. Long rows and long days. Yet the people stay together. They work in a line so they can talk. The simple in all its splendor…Unlike Hesiod's bucolic peasants who justly grumbled in their hardships, these people blend their songs with the wind.[70] They eat grapes when they are ripe and have lunch together. They prepare the vine for its fruit, which is delicious and produces the wine we had only last night.

"Do you think I could work with you, Juan?" he asked.

Juan stopped his filing and rested his warm eyes on Anton. "Oh, Anton, you have asked the big question. We have a saying about some people: *'Ellos buscan trabajo pidiendo a Dios no encontrarlo.'* They are looking for work, praying to God they do not find it. If you really want work there is always work."

"I really want work, Juan. Not a job. To be useful."

"It is hard work, Anton. We have another saying in the fields: 'When you work in the vineyard, you don't look up.' Of course we look up. It just that when you look up, the rows of the vineyard seem to go on forever."

Juan continued to file his tool. *"No estoy seguro...un gringo,"* he said doubtfully, almost to himself. Then aloud to Anton he said, "But you are not like some gringos. *Ellos sonreien mucho, sin sentir nada.* Humpf!" he wrinkled his nose. "You know, the people who 'smile a lot and feel nothing.' You can't trust them...But I saw how hard you worked in the orchard that night, even though you were feeling pain. Holding the torch after your burn accident was no small matter. And your hands were soft..."

He paused, then said, "I am not trying to talk you out of it. You may try it if you wish. I will speak with Señor Kirkpatrick."

The farm owner approved the idea. He brought new clippers, pruning shears and a hoe. He said, "Anton, you came here freely and you may leave freely. All work is a gift. I give my new workers their own tools if they don't have their own. They're yours to keep. Follow Juan's instructions and stay beside him until he says you may have your own vines. Someday, when you drink of the fruit of the vine, you will know that your sweat and blood have added to its flavor."

Juan offered Anton some sturdy canvas gloves with the fingers cut off, thin cotton gloves to cover his fingers, and a faded jean jacket with metal buttons. Someone else in the camp had an extra pair of boots which fit well. He was ready to apply his unlearned hands to the vineyard.

On the day after Christmas the workers had Dolores's egg and biscuit breakfast and began work at six–thirty in the morning. With his breath steaming and his nose red and runny in the cold morning air,

Anton joined the ten other men and women at the beginning of the long vine rows. Everyone carried the basic tools: clipper, shears and hoe; a canteen and sometimes a thermos of hot coffee and a snack.

Juan instructed him about one–year, two–year and three–year growth. He explained the subtle difference in texture and appearance in the wood, and explained that only one–year wood should be cut; otherwise the branches would produce rich foliage but no grapes. He watched Anton carefully as he developed his skill. Anton in turn asked questions and proceeded methodically and slowly. He was glad he was with Juan, because he knew that he would have been left lagging behind the more expert members of the farmworker team.

The group stopped at ten o'clock. Anton sat on the ground to rest. The group then resumed and continued working until noon. The blast of a truck horn signaled a stop, and the workers left their big tools, pocketed their pruning clippers, and walked out to the road. There a large catering truck was parked, its driver rolling up the side panels.

"*Taqueria,*" Juan chuckled. Anton learned that these catering trucks crisscrossed the entire San Joaquin Valley, indeed the whole California–Oregon cornucopia, taking lunch and refreshment to the workers in the fields.

"Don't worry," Juan assured him. "The food is *muy sabrosa,* and people very rarely get sick." He was right. Anton bought four tacos and a large orange drink for three dollars. He devoured them with gusto. He also bought a muffin for a snack later in the day.

The group returned to the field. Anton now had his own plants to prune, but knew that the foreman's eyes were on him. They worked until three o'clock, when Juan said, *"Vamos a la casa.* Let's go home. Enough for today. People get hurt when they work too long." Along the way, he said, "You worked well today, Anton. I watched. We cannot say of you, *'Te mueves mucho pero no haces nada.'* That is, 'You moved a lot, but did nothing.' The *patrón* will be pleased with your work. See you at dinner."

It was only a short walk back to the camp, and Anton removed his boots, his jacket and gloves, and collapsed onto his bed. Fatigue shot like lightning across his shoulders and back. He felt every muscle in his upper body. His hands tingled and his lower back ached from bending. He drifted into a dreamless sleep, and was awakened by the dinner bell at six. As he walked to the *comedor,* he remembered the ache after his long night in the Tehachapis, but now he felt rested in mind and spirit.

The one who finds God does not perceive separated lives and actions more clearly than the total life, for the total life has suddenly displayed its sources. His joy is to be nothing, to do nothing, to think nothing, but to permit the total life, expressed in its humanity, to flow in upon him and to express itself through his actions and thoughts.

W. B. Yeats (1865–1939),
The Vision

Yesterday is a tree with great spreading branches, and I lie in its shade, remembering.

Pablo Neruda (1904–1973),
Passions and Impressions

Companions in memory

Thus began Anton's work in the fields. Soon he adapted to the rhythm of the day: an early rise and hot breakfast. A walk to the fields and the first contact with the waiting vine as the sun showed itself full above the mist and fog of the early morning. Steady clipping and hoeing, hoeing and clipping, the cluster of workers moved down the field. A ten o'clock rest break; lunch, perhaps with a short nap; then back to work. His pain declined, then disappeared. His hands grew leathery from the dirt and sap of the vine and the handles of his tools. He saw his hoe bring forth sparks from rocks and movement from thick and fleshy earthworms in the rich soil. Vine by vine, hour by hour, day by day the weeks of early winter passed. The workers finished thirty acres before January gave way to February. As the days lengthened the work of pruning became more urgent. Already they could see the first hints of the new buds that would ripen into fruit later in the summer.

In the first week of February, Anton almost laughed out loud at the memory of his feelings in the dean's office, when he would have said with Hamlet, 'Weary, stale, flat and unprofitable seem to me all the uses of this world!/ Fie on't, an unweeded garden that grows to seed!'[71] Serves me right to be hoeing and weeding in an ocean of vines. All shall be well, he thought. He learned to lean on the main trunk of the vine and let the branches embrace him, to husband his own energies as he husbanded the plant. He knew that he stood on invisible roots that descended many feet below the surface. The rich, brown soil under his feet had been created by the cuttings and clippings and washings of the ages. They were all living things that had long since died into the earth so that they might support new life.

His Spanish improved as well, and he became more comfortable talking with other workers. They encouraged him and supplied the language of the tools and field, the weather, the aching parts of his body, the best curses when he was poked in the eye by a branch or drew blood with his sharp clippers. When Anton struggled to find a word they looked up in his face with sparkling eyes, and with suggestions and gestures coaxed the word from his limited vocabulary. He saw in their labor and their spirit the divine injunction to work well and hard, but to leave the fields fallow for the gleanings by the poor every seventh year.[72]

Amid the long hours and long rows Anton fed his memory. He had heard how prisoners of war or conscience reconstructed their lives often back to their second or third year of childhood, and how they painstakingly recalled every memory, every color, corner and cranny of their lives in the long hours of their confinement. This remembering was unusual for Anton, so accustomed was he to recalling the ideas and insights of learned authorities, but rarely inviting his own memories and their joys and sorrows. Here, free in the open fields, Anton felt no compulsion, but allowed the memories to swim to the surface of his mind to be beheld again.

One afternoon as he parted the vines to trim and clip he let his mind penetrate the darker corners of his life that had long lain behind him. 1980. Fifteen years ago…graduate school, that Elysian place where students gathered with teachers to remember and dream and dispute and write, to study and learn far beyond the confines of this time and place. Two years of course work lay behind him, with still a mountain of research yet to ascend; and beyond that, the comprehensive exams, the dissertation and defense, and finally, the degree. And, oh, happy leisure!—sweet original sense of the Greek *schole* or "school"—genuine leisure that allowed Anton to grow his beard, rise in still darkened hours of the morning and wander through the days as a true contemplative.

As was his wont, Anton remembered again the incomparable pleasures of his life as a student: Thucydides, Plato, Montaigne; an occasional stolen hour with the Romantic poets; music, pen and paper to pin down and frame those ephemeral entities called "Ideas." Oh, it had felt so complete! Though the future was daunting, the abundance of his previous years had created a myth which ran, "Challenge always; every year surpassing the one that went before." Friends, fellow students, passionate teachers. Great texts, and time to read and allow his imagination to soar into the dark spaces of the library where it could loft and curl around the stacks of ancient books. Did not Wordsworth hit the mark when he said, "T'was sweet to be alive, and youth was very heaven"?

To refresh his energies after the ardors of his first year in graduate school, Anton packed his bike into a cardboard crate and flew to Europe to spend the summer cycling through the countryside. For challenge he aspired to the Alps, those brilliant peaks looming beyond the clouds, glowing still in his memory like earthbound suns. What more pleasant training for the final ascent could there be than peddling through hundreds of miles of French countryside, along the rolling meadows in southern England, north through Wales and around Mt. Snowden also wrapped in clouds? He could still see the Rhine, calm and winding, carrying the *Dusseldorf,* the white steamer decked out with flags as it chugged alongside him for the one hundred miles from Cologne to Wiesbaden. The honored names of Freiburg, Tubingen and Heidelberg rose to his mind, those sober centers of learning and paradox in southern Germany that became the nursery of revolt in the thought of Melancthon, Feuerbach and Heidegger—theirs the calm voices for radical ideas fomented in the streets and trenches by ideologues and adventurers and ordinary citizens alike. Anton remembered gathering his strength for the Alpine climb, a winding, steady ascent from Zurich into the hinterland, zigzagging back and forth, back and forth, up and up into the drizzle of the Furka Pass and Blue Glacier; warming himself in the kitchens of village inns lost in the cloud lines; carving narrow, slippery tracks in the fresh highland snow of August, yet always warm from the exertion and exhilaration of the high places...

Anton's doctoral program had called for competence in two foreign languages. From four years of high school study, colloquial French had come easily and bore fruit in conversations with Frenchmen pushing their grocery–laden bicycles along country roads in Burgundy and in little cafés off the Champs–Elysées in Paris. And then there was German. Anton felt encouraged to undertake that mighty tongue through his love for Goethe and Thomas Mann, and by the promise of the earlier German Romantic poets, whose 18th century voices sang sweetly in the Schwartzwald, the Black Forest, before being swallowed in the deepening gloom and grandiosity of Wagner's music and Bismarck's cult of iron and blood. After all, had not one of Anton's primary missions been to travel to Messkirch in the rolling, sub–Alpine mountains of southern Germany, to find the gravesite of Martin Heidegger, who had died so recently? From his earlier studies Anton knew enough German to stir up the *burgermeister* of Messkirch, a rotund little man in a black double–breasted suit and starched white collar who gazed impassively at Anton from his civil servant's chair, but then bounded to his feet and rocked back and forth on his heels at the name of his village's finest son. German was the key to the ambiguous soul of that proud people, and Anton was not disappointed when the mayor, now thrilled and eager, guided him to the philosopher's gravesite. So there it lay, alongside that of grandmother Heidegger, in a small family plot in a nondescript Catholic cemetery outside of Messkirch. Perhaps irony is the pivot point in the world's scale of justice: Heidegger, Nietzsche's greatest apostle, his reputation darkened by his willing apology for National Socialism and never repudiated before his death, finding his perpetual rest with a Christian cross at his head in an obscure grave in the Black Forest!

Upon his return to his graduate studies, Anton resumed his research in earnest. Trips to the rare texts collection at the Huntington Library in Pasadena and the Honnold Library in Claremont swept him into the legion of scholars who had shared his passion for Homer over the centuries. But by the end of a year of musing among ancient books and modern journals, Anton felt a strange ennui descending, as though his passion were running out like the ink of an empty pen. Months dwelling in the stuffy bowels of huge libraries made him ready again for the clarity and open air of Europe. Through the school's international student office he arranged to lead a group of less-traveled students on a study trip to include Greece and Turkey. Their route would include Athens and environs, and conclude with a weeklong trip to Istanbul and down the Ionian coast of Turkey.

For Anton as he worked amid the vines and open spaces of the Central Valley these reveries raised warm and secure feelings in his resting mind. His nostalgia was arrested, however, when he thought of the main event of that second European summer.

After arriving in Athens and registering at their hotel in the Sounion district, the group agreed that everyone could sleep late to recover from the long flight. Wide awake before dawn, however, Anton arose and walked out into the still-sleeping streets. He wanted to watch the sun rise over the Parthenon on the hill of the Acropolis. Continuing up the sloping road, he crested the hill on the west side and aligned himself with a far western corner of the temple as the sun edged over the horizon. The first glimmer of dawn dressed the grey-white colonnades in a soft pink hue. Thus was initiated the atmosphere of worship that prevails there all the daylong. The optics of the early light magnified the temple, giving it a floating effect, creating a phantasmagoric allure that both intoxicated and invited. More than any other hard-earned pleasure from the previous year of study and research, this sight touched his soul: it sealed him with the assurance that Beauty indeed lies at the heart of the *agon*. Even in the slaughter and clash of arms in the *Iliad* one could see how anguish and exertion could be carried by the spirit of reverence to a new height of expression, thus producing classical culture as inaugurated by Homer. The sense of rightness in his studies in Homer's proto–psychology felt confirmed.[73] Anton walked around the building, pausing to gaze at the frieze with its solemn Panathenaic procession, viewed the Erechtheion with its somber Vestal Virgins, then continued around the perimeter of the hill on the eastern side.

Here he encountered Connie, kneeling on the floor of the portico, painstakingly measuring the circumference of the base of one of the columns.

Until now Connie had simply been a participant in the travel group. Anton knew little more about her than that she haled from Monterey where she lived with her mother. She had distinctively Latin ancestry, with shoulder–length, loosely curled dark brown hair against light–brown skin and remarkable blue–grey eyes. She had completed her master's degree and had intended the trip to be both a personal reward for her accomplishment and a transitional step to a doctoral program at another school. In the haste to board the airplane from Los Angeles to New York and Athens, Anton had only exchanged greetings and noticed a copy of Diogenes Laertius' *Lives of Eminent Philosophers* in her possession. Beyond that he had given her no thought beyond the regularities of his role as guide. Asked to describe her he would have been at a loss, for Anton was wont to avoid intimacy and preferred retreating into his well–ordered intellectual realm. To find her now in this odd, even comical position, crab–walking around the base of a marble column, struck him as bizarre. Hidden in the bright light of the morning sun, Anton approached unnoticed.

After completing the circle at the lower elevations, Connie reached up as high as she could to hold the tape against the column to measure its higher circumference, and resumed her awkward side–step. At this point, Anton greeted her.

"Good morning!"

She started and squinted in the morning light. "Would you mind not standing in my sun?"

"Oh, sorry..." He moved aside, surprised by her brusque tone. He watched as she moved around the column, holding the tape and letting it dangle as she measured the circumference as high above her head as she could reach.

Studying the tape measure she said conclusively, "Just as I thought: it bulges out."

"How's that?" The unusual comment baffled him. Connie's expression bored into him as if she were expecting an intelligent reply to a perceptive observation.

"I thought that 'straight' means 'straight.' I've been looking at this column for the last fifteen minutes, and it looks straight, but I have found otherwise."

"Maybe the Greeks did not have the technology to create perfectly straight columns with flutings and all," Anton shot back with heavy irony.

"Oh, whatever! Of course, I understand that. I have never thrown a perfect pot. Beauty will always be beyond the reach of our clumsy hands." With this peculiar and sententious piety, Connie gathered her backpack and strode off. Anton could not have known the meaning of his own thoughts even had he been conscious of them. He shook off the moment and resumed his morning walk.

But Connie had claimed his attention, to say the least. Her natural attractiveness dawned on him during the remainder of the day, especially her wavy hair and vivid eyes under dark eyebrows. She wore her beauty lightly and moved with the energy and economy of a *bolero*. Her intelligence and vitality impressed her whole person on him. In conversation with other students she seemed detached without being aloof. Her well-stocked mind ranged easily amid whole constellations of ideas, while her emotions seemed self-protective and reserved. She illumined her cryptic comments about "throwing pots" by mentioning that she frequented the college ceramics studio, and sent newly fired works to her mother, who reportedly used them in some kind of herbal healing profession. She conveyed to Anton the impression of another soul strangely kin, a choleric counterpart to his more phlegmatic nature. Still, there was something resistant, steely about her. He sensed in her a capacity for violence on an emotional, if not physical plane—and an uneasy resistance to this inner tendency as well. And her eyes could convey a chilling coldness on command.

Moreover, in his mind Connie's image seemed fleeting, ever in motion. She was restless and discontented. She talked little of her recent experience in graduate studies, and held her hopes and dreams in silent reserve. She arose early and walked throughout the city, usually alone. One exception occurred in the middle of the week when Anton walked with her to the ruins of Pericles' Long Walls. As they neared their hotel on their return Anton learned that she was dating a third–year medical student who was busily engaged at the same large university towards which she was moving for the fall term. Her elusive manner of speaking suggested that some serious intentions lay beyond that. Anton also learned that her field of study was the sociology of religions.

Energized by the exertion of the walk, he felt free to probe. "I think I understand what the sociology of religion is. What draws you to it?"

Matching his condescension with the tone of someone irritated by the question of a young child, she answered, "Freud demonstrated that religion is 'collective neurosis.' You would agree with that, I am sure. So, shed some light on the irrational behavior of religious experience, and you will understand something of peoples' fears and all irrational tendencies. We live in a time of mass movements, which sociologists love. Put the two together, and you will then understand the irrationality of mass movements; hence the sociology of religion."

The detachment and objectivity of her answer galled him. Anton felt that she was giving him permission to dislike her. Abandoning all caution, he retorted, "So what? Maybe irrationality is not such a bad thing; maybe it lurks even in this sunny climate!"

She unsheathed her nails. "Oh, brother! Even here light can penetrate only so deep! We remain in our benighted tutelage!"[74] Turning on her heel, she left him.

Anton was wounded to the quick by this exchange, and avoided Connie's company that evening. After dinner he retreated with some other students into the central hotel patio, a small, tiled, open–aired plaza with a fountain in the center and bougainvillea flowers in planters around the edges. As he was nursing a blistering hot cup of Turkish coffee, he was immediately put on guard when she approached him and said, "Anton, may I talk with you for a moment?"

"Very well…Let's sit over there," he said warily, pointing to a bench in a more private place behind the fountain. As they walked Anton could not help noticing the sway of her figure, and the smooth line of her back, shoulder and neck, this last graced by a slender gold necklace.

Sitting, she said, "I want to apologize for the way I have talked to you." Her voice was low, deep, husky, with an almost imperceptible hint of a Latino accent. Anton leaned forward, placed his cup on the patio floor and focused on her face. Her eyes had nothing of the chill of their earlier encounters. He kept his face blandly even as she said,

"First, up on the Acropolis, I was horrible. I was so concentrated on my research that I blurted out something stupidly."

"There's no need to apologize."

"Anton!" —Her voice tightened, grew tense, almost angry. "I am going to say something and will probably regret it: Do you realize that you minimize almost everything I say? Please don't do that!"

At this Anton felt himself perspiring in the warm evening. She continued, "It was mindless of me. I did not even realize what I said, and how I said it. I jabbed at you with a quip from an ancient Cynic and thought it cute![75] Later in the day, I was down at the Museum trying to figure out why Pheidias, you know, the architect of the Parthenon, could allow a bulge in the middle of a column. I learned that perfectly straight geometric lines create a sense of coldness, sterility. A curve ever so slight gives a sense of lightness. Softness, too. It makes the whole thing beautiful. I was absorbed in just one thing, one column. One shouldn't see one column by itself, but all of them together. After looking at them that way, I could appreciate how the curve in each column accents the whole. It is the secret of its grandeur. It also helped me appreciate the beauty of the one, individual column. Do you see? Did you know this?"

"Actually, I didn't."

Hardly waiting for his answer, she plunged on, "Then I had this horrible thought: that my own efforts to keep everything lined up, perfectly straight, you know, were warping my own perspective. I went back up the hill for another look that afternoon. I didn't take my tape measure. I just looked. And then I remembered how I spoke to you." With a catch in her throat, she concluded, "I am sorry for what I said and how it sounded to you."

Anton continued to gaze into Connie's eyes, which contained strain and regret. He was still tender from her bristling comment but the brilliance of her eyes was dispelling his resentment. Even then his ineptitude clouded his mind as he said, "Do you believe you have to be perfect?"

"What? I can't believe it! How can you be so obtuse?"

As Connie's anger flared again Anton half–stood as if to flee the charges against him, but had a fleeting recollection of his image as group leader, and kept his seat.

"Look, Anton, this is not about me, and not even about you. It's almost about something else; but it just doesn't hang together in my mind...Let me think about it...I had thought that Beauty was everything in order, nothing out of place. You know, *perfection*...But when I was standing next to the Parthenon, even the rubble became a mirror of truth."

"Pretty humbling, I would say." Anton ventured to speak again.

"Why should truth only push us into humility? That could be false modesty. Who are we to think that truth can be measured by our own limited capacity? But this is too abstract, drat it!" Connie's passion showed on her face as she racked her mind for an elusive meaning.

"Try it this way," she continued. "You know of the 'vanishing point,' don't you? How all the lines in a three–dimensional perspective seem to come together in a distant focal point? Very mathematical, very abstract, of course. It makes you feel agog, goofy, bedazzled when you first see it in early Renaissance art. What a discovery, and it's been right there in front of us the whole time! I am thinking about something like this, only different: Beauty, the mirror of truth, seems to send lines from some invisible source right into me: the lines intersect in my own soul, not in some distant point. That's the mirroring effect in what we understand to be Beauty."

"I think I see," Anton said, his hands pressing on his temples in concentration.

"So then, heaven knows why, but I attacked you right there, in the presence of something that I cannot name, and right at the home of where you want to be, in Athens. I warped the very thing I am trying to see, in my own self. I may never understand what I am looking at, but that gives me no excuse to lash out. I am very sorry. Please believe me."

"What you said did hurt, Connie. But I wasn't very kind either. I don't understand why I say things sometimes."

"Me, neither," she sighed. "Maybe it was envy for your being an older student, so well–traveled and self–assured, nearly finished with your degree. You seem so 'buttoned–down' and neat and tidy—even with a beard (and here Connie's eyes twinkled). And I really don't know where I am going. Something seems to be missing in my life. That's pretty obvious, isn't it? That's why your 'So what' hit home. And I lashed out. I'm sorry."

"Think nothing of it." With this bromide that begged for release from the emotional whirlpool that was claiming him, Anton picked up his cup of coffee and said, "Let's see what the others are doing."

Connie looked at him and demurred, her thoughts remaining unspoken. She excused herself, and departed for her hotel room. Anton heaved a sigh of relief.

But her words melded in his mind and underwent a strange alchemy: from an abstract Form, Beauty was becoming as complete and substantial as a Person, reflected and even embodied in a particular human being. She at the same moment was revealing the nature of art, and through her own feminine nature was transforming his masculine soul into both an agent of truth and a mirror for Beauty itself. Anton dimly perceived a triangle of conscious awareness in which the experience of Beauty depended on both personal and abstract elements. He felt a growing gratitude for Connie's having directed his attention toward something that he could scarcely imagine. Unknowingly she was birthing the romantic in him.

Though she might have felt ambiguity in her academic vision, Connie devoted unstinting energy and devotion to it. On a bus ride to view the memorial mound from the battle of Marathon[76] she told him that her undergraduate work had already included anthropology and the cultures of tribal peoples; fleeting glances at the world religions; and finer subjects like the marriage ceremonies of Aryan peoples and the burial rites of ancient Etruscans. Her academic interests, she explained, seemed to be a surprising distillation of her father's and mother's heritage: her father, whom she never knew, had been a seaman of Greek and Norwegian descent who had a brief *alliance* with her young mother in Monterey and then disappeared. Her mother, she said, had never married and had spent her whole life raising and educating her daughter; she was a practicing *curandera* or indigenous healer who delivered babies or prayed with the dying and was generally available to ailing people in the Monterey Bay area. For the blending of the natural and the spiritual, Connie allowed, her mother was the most gifted person she had ever known.

"But your name: 'Connie' is very English–sounding," Anton wondered.

"Short for 'Constanza,' which seemed to be my mother's hope, her challenge to my wayward father."

"She must be pleased that you are dating a medical student. There may be some stability in that." Anton instantly regretted the irony loading his words.

"I am not sure of that. She keeps her thoughts to herself."

Anton took the cue.

Connie went on to charm Anton with little anecdotes such as, "My mother once told me that she learned from the wayfaring Greek—the man who became my father—that Apollo's name came from the peony plant in the Near East. So: the God of light is first the God of healing. And we are the most heliotropic of creatures, just as the gods are. Why, look at the Vedas: linguistically the Sanskrit *diva* or 'shining one' later became the Greek Zeus and the Latin *deus*. Today the only thing left is the *diva* who craves the spot light and becomes the *prima dona* to be suffered by all lesser mortals."

She also vexed him with more challenging propositions, such as: "What would happen if we suspended all world religions that were not jointly conceived and sustained by men and women together? Give all the religions and their adherents a long–term Sabbath, a year–long holiday for all religious obligations. Don't the Greeks provoke us to that question? In our own case, how can we think of a creator God who does not unite the masculine and feminine principles? Even the Greeks may have felt that there was too much there to contain in a monotheistic principle." Anton could only meet her provocation by citing Aristophanes' suggestion that women might withhold their charms until all fighting and internecine warfare between men had ended.[77] To this *in apropos* remark she shot back, "Far be it from me to ask if this would make any difference with some men I know." Thus she silenced him. He had ill bodings about the seriousness of her relationship with the unnamed medical student.

This strange mix of seriousness and irreverence both attracted Anton and discouraged him. In his own youthfulness, he did not know how to engage a woman in friendship in the first place, and Connie's complex soul confounded him. If pressed he would have asserted that such friendship depended on the niceties of common interests and intellectual compatibility. Pretending to great thoughts allowed him to believe in his own high–mindedness, but he was becoming painfully aware that "the heart has its reasons which reason does not know."[78] For he was oblivious of the deeper movements of his own heart, whose churnings were so unsettling his mind. For Connie's part, she could not explain herself or her own doings or her ambitions; no, the meaning of her aspirations and her underlying hunger eluded even her.

Still, she intrigued him. Later that evening Anton raised a question with the group. With her in mind he said, "Connie has been helping me think that Greece balances between the poles of Athena and Apollo. We are living in Athena's shadow here in the city. Would anyone like to go to Apollo's shrines at Delphi or Delos? I'll take anyone who wants to go on the boat to Delos, and there is a public bus up to Delphi."[79]

All but Connie elected for the bus to Delphi. Anton was curiously pleased but bemused with the thought of a whole day with her alone. The next morning they rode the bus down from Athens to the seaport town of Piraeus. Making their way along the tarred and splintered waterfront at

Kantharos, they boarded a small cargo ship that carried tourists and people of Greek, Turkish and Albanian ancestry between the local islands of the Cyclades chain. The lower levels of the ship were rustling with families and babies, farmers and small landowners with their chickens and goats; and it was ever so fragrant with the smells of animal feed, manure and olive oil simmering on small charcoal–fired stoves. For fresher air, Anton and Connie climbed up to the top deck and placed folding chairs near the railing. From there they could see little flying fish banking off ocean waves and watch the wake of the boat burble and smooth the ocean for a few moments as it plowed through the water. So enchanted, they talked the hours away.

On the waterfront at Platis Gialos on the island of Mykonos, Anton looked dubiously at the small boat that was to take them across the open sea to the small island of Delos. The swarthy Greek sailor assured them with gestures and laughter that they were perfectly safe. Connie jumped in the boat and urged him in with happy banter. "Oh, if my father could see this, wherever he is! Come on, hurry up!"

As they arrived at the small dock on the sacred island, Anton reached down to offer Connie his hand to help her step up to the wharf. He was acutely conscious of the feeling of her hand in his and the blue of the Mediterranean reflecting in her eyes. They regained their land–legs during the ascent to the bluff and the walk down the Boulevard of the Lions. Though the avenue was wide and spacious they walked with shoulders only inches apart.

At the end of the avenue, they sat near the ruins of a sunken mosaic figure of a springing lion. Graceful and rich with meaning though the mosaic was, Anton could not take his eyes off Connie. An elusive hint of chamomile rose from her hair. Every tint and tone of her almond skin, the shadows cast by her hair across her face, the sea and sky gathering into the living faience of her eyes—all took his breath away.[80] Even the timeless mosaic at their feet seemed but an illumination and background to the beauty he beheld in her face.

"What is it about the light here? You should see your face," Connie said, then paused.

"It's not just the light," Anton replied, his heart sticking in his throat.

"I think that I'd like to go for a little walk," she said abruptly. "Why don't I meet you in an hour or so?"

"Okay, Connie." As before, Anton could see something of her detachment and inner withdrawal. They parted company for a while, Anton walking to the *Hieros* shrine and theatre, while Connie departed toward the summit of Mount Kynthos. When she returned from her hike, she was unusually silent and preoccupied. Late in the afternoon they returned the way they had come, by way of the open boat and the same cargo ship on its return route to Athens. When they arrived at their hotel in Sounion the group on the Delphi trip had not yet returned.

As they approached the bronze and glass doors of their hotel, Anton asked, "Would you like to have dinner together, Connie?"

"That would be lovely," she responded, "A perfect end to a perfect day."

"See you in an hour, then."

When Connie appeared at the outdoor table in the hotel patio, Anton was mesmerized by her appearance. She wore a light yellow dress of a chiffon fabric, its apparent simplicity highlighted by the gentle line it drew around one shoulder. For jewelry she wore a delicate bracelet on her right wrist. Her face glowed with the light burnish of sunshine and saltwater. Anton's earlier convictions about strictly intellectual friendships were now forgotten. Once wine was served, their conversation resumed.

"Connie, how was Delos for you?"

"I loved it. I felt bad we had to leave Mykonos so soon. I wanted to go for a long walk along the rock walls between the fields, or just explore the seaport. I have never seen a whole village whitewashed like that. Delos was very special: the light itself was the temple to Apollo."

"How was the view from Mt. Kynthos?"

"Great. Wide open…Something happened to me up there, Anton."

"Did you fall?"

"No, it was safe. I just got the feeling that I was missing something. That something is out of place, that what I most needed was right at my feet…I can't explain it." She evaded the perplexities in her own experience. "How was it for you?"

"I'm glad we survived the crossing on that little boat. It would have been very embarrassing to get sick."

"No one would have minded." Connie's eyes spoke gentle feelings. "But you don't like being brought to your knees, I am sure. That would spoil your fine academic dignity." She laughed to soften the gibe. "Being on your knees is where we find followers of Dionysios. It's okay, Anton, the boat ride kind–of got to me, too."

Anton laughed as well. He was finding Connie's teasing spirit refreshing. "Now on to Istanbul. What do you hope to see there?"

"I don't really know. Maybe just to see some of Asia."

"Will it help your studies?"

"Well, of course. At least I hope so. That was the idea."

"I think we will be definitely off the familiar ground. Byzantine Christianity. The Ottomans and Islam: names that struck fear into the heart of Europe. The Blue Mosque sitting right beside the Saint Sophia. The West and the East rubbing shoulders."

"Well, it's a start. I am glad you are our guide," she answered with a hint of flattery.

"Well, then. Where would you find a really sharp contrast between East and West?"

"Not in Istanbul, I think. Maybe in India. But I can't imagine going there. I wouldn't know how to survive."

"Nor I," Anton agreed. "But it is mostly in our minds, where East collides with West."

"What do you mean, Anton?"

"Well, for example in the Christian scriptures...Galatians, the second chapter, I think...Paul can say, 'Not I, but the Christ liveth in me.' The Buddhist *sutra* says otherwise: 'From enlightenment you will know that you are the Buddha.' The psychology of the East is very different."

"I think I see. I guess that I am in some kind of no–man's land, in neither East nor West."

"That's very honest of you. We are a long way from home. The winds of Turkey and the Holy Land blow right over us here. Let's see... Paul said a little later in Galatians that 'in Christ there is neither East nor West.' Somehow I think that he and the Buddha and you too are making the same confession. Is there any difference between them? I doubt any amount of thinking will show us how to close the gap between all of this. I have the hunch that only going to someplace like India can do that."

So went their conversation in the balmy patio of the Athenian hotel as it drifted back to Anton's mind, many years later in the vineyards of central California. He also remembered fleeting images, reports only, about Connie's medical student friend. Like her, he was a zealot for his chosen profession. Due to the imperatives of their education and the rigors of their schedules, they had been able to see one another only three or four times in the previous year. Anton was careful to avoid direct questions about the man's purposes, but he gained a sense of someone motivated by financial gain and the prestige of the medical profession. Connie expressed vague hopes about becoming engaged once she arrived at his university; she hoped to get married even before her fiancé had completed his residency training.

"What about you, Anton? What lies beyond graduate school?"

"You know, Connie, I hardly think about it. That may be a sorry failing on my part, but I am just savoring each day too much to make great plans and to hold myself to them."

"But you don't seem to be drifting."

"No, not at all," he assured her. "I know some students spend a whole year preparing for the comprehensives, which last only three days. Then they get so terrified that they walk away from all their course work out of fear of facing their professors in the dissertation defense. Life certainly must hold greater terrors than that! I'll stay with it. The day will surely come when I have to find work; until then, I am having altogether too much fun."

At this point their conversation ended with the noisy arrival of the remainder of the student group returning from Delphi, and Anton retired to his rest with a mix of delight and peace and strange sadness.

The next day the group made the long journey up the Anatolian Sea, past Aristotle's birthplace in Stagira, and on to Istanbul. To assure themselves of safe food and water, they stayed in an expensive "Four Star" hotel. Anton remembered the striking smells of his first Asian city, a blend of ocean mist, bunker oil riding on the ocean itself, rotting fish, spiced foods cooking on an open flame, raw sewage, and truck exhaust that was sulfurous yet vaguely aromatic. They visited the great centers of Byzantine Islam and Christianity and felt diminished by the size and the weight of their antiquity. He also remembered taking public transportation down the Ionian coast, through Canakkale, to Troy. There he talked of the soul of the ancient city lying beneath seven layers of civilization, the ten-year battle between the Trojans and the "large-greaved" Achaeans, and Alexander's altar raised to their memory. He encouraged his group to claim the memory for themselves through the *Iliad* and *Odyssey* and Plutarch's *Life of Alexander* after they returned home. The group then continued further south into Ephesus.

Ephesus. At the memory of the word, Anton's conscious mind gave way to a host of inchoate feelings. As he passed the hours in his work in the vineyard he allowed this glad memory to regain flesh and substance. He remembered the moment at the top of the amphitheater built into the hill overlooking the ancient city. The larger part of his group had remained at the footings of the Library while he and Connie progressed further up the Sacred Way toward the theater. It was a rare moment in the early afternoon when no one else was exploring the ruins. The pair had climbed up the smooth limestone steps together, stepping up and through the broken pieces and carved seats. Initially Anton offered his hand to Connie for assistance, then releasing her hand, and finally holding it lightly yet firmly and without any resistance from her as they reached the last row of seats. As they stood looking down into the theater, with its invisible audiences from untold centuries coming and going and watching the action on stage with thrill and horror and amazement, Anton felt himself in a sacred place like none other. Connie stood beside him, unusually quiet, looking out over the plain as it spread away toward the coast. He felt himself torn by impossible conflicts. In a few short days, he realized, they would part company, and she would be gone. He could not allow himself to believe that he might never see her again.

Suddenly, he said, "Connie, I have something to tell you. I want to say something for all to hear."

"But there is no one else here," she protested.

"I know. Wait here. Tell me if you can hear what I say." With that, he stepped and bounded down the steps again and stood on the flat, empty stage. He turned toward where she stood, high above and away from him, and said *sotto voce,* yet with passion,

"Connie, I love you."

He saw her head lift, and her hands came up as though to embrace him from the distance; then they fell to her sides. He bounded up the steps and approached her.

"Anton, I heard you perfectly. And not just today. You have allowed me to come close. But, I don't know, I don't know." Her voice was strained, troubled.

"I understand, Connie. And I wanted you to know that however far away from me you might be, no matter what happens or what the distance, or what day it is, this is my thought of you."

At these words, Connie took his head in her hands, ran her fingers around through his hair and down his neck, and kissed him on the lips.

Shortly after their return to the United States, Connie left as she had planned. Into Anton's heart swept an emptiness that was inexpressibly bleak. When he wanted nothing so much as to hear the sound of her voice, he felt oppressed by a heartless silence that scratched into his contemplative realm like a persistent and irritating noise. Unhorsed by her departure, he fell into spells of dazed disbelief punctuated by spasms of remorse that almost embarrassed him. He alternatively castigated himself for the lost opportunity to savor their moments together, and then extended himself mercy at his fundamental decency and reverent posture toward the female species, who embodied mysteries beyond his ken. Clearly he did not feel himself to be that fine sort of man who runs from snub to snub until favorably accepted by a woman, any woman. He did not seek the company of "any woman": such a thought offended him to the core. Connie had revealed to him, in the poet's words,

> ...the requisite chords to be set in vibration. With the key of art, he has entered into that land which is on the borders of Heaven and within sight of the City of Love. There he sits awhile to hatch delightful hopes and perilous illusions.[81]

In the years that followed, Connie's memory waned like a meteor's white scar across the night sky. Anton cherished this image, which suggests that one's serenity must be split asunder before the possibility of personal wholeness can be conceived. And he gained a new measure of compassion, for others and for himself. He had learned that there are obstacles in the path of life over which no amount of personal effort may prevail, and before which one can only hope to avoid a fatal collision. So humbled, he gained a lesson for a life–time: when it came to a woman who has claimed his heart, he would never again affect that veneer of autonomy and indifference that would surely dampen the ardor of her passionate soul.

Samson went down to Timnah together with his father and mother. As they approached the vineyards of Timnah, suddenly a young lion came roaring toward him.

The Spirit of the Lord came upon him in power so that he tore the lion apart with his bare hands as he might have torn a young goat. But he told neither his father nor his mother what he had done. Then he went down and talked with the woman, and he liked her.

Some time later, when he went back to marry her, he turned aside to look at the lion's carcass. In it was a swarm of bees and some honey, which he scooped out with his hands and ate as he went along. When he rejoined his parents, he gave them some, and they too ate it. But he did not tell them that he had taken the honey from the lion's carcass.

Now his father went down to see the woman. And Samson made a feast there, as was customary for bridegrooms. When he appeared, he was given thirty companions.

"Let me tell you a riddle," Samson said to them. "If you can give me the answer within the seven days of the feast, I will give you thirty linen garments and thirty sets of clothes. If you can't tell me the answer, you must give me thirty linen garments and thirty sets of clothes."

"Tell us your riddle," they said. "Let's hear it."

He replied, "Out of the eater, something to eat; out of the strong, something sweet."

Judges 14

OUT OF THE STRONG, SOMETHING SWEET

DURING THESE WEEKS in the fields, Anton heard the stories of his companions. Antonio, he learned, had lost his parents when they were deported back to Mexico by the *Migra*. He had been adopted and raised by another Mexican couple, and had worked and played in the vineyards in three different states by the time he was five years old.

Philippe had secured papers through his parents who had come north in the *bracero* programs of the 1950s. He had spent twenty years in the citrus ranches of Ventura, and now did the less arduous work of pruning vines. He told Anton that the night work in the groves made him very tired, and his leg would ache, never having completely healed from an injury inflicted by a box of fruit that slipped off a flatbed truck. Philippe said that if Anton wanted to see real strength, he should watch Guillermo dead–lift three crates of fresh grapes to the side of the truck, hop up to the bed from a standing position, then loft the boxes six feet further to the top of the stack.

As for Pedro, he confessed to having been a *coyote* himself when he was younger and was able to run through the brush and hills of Encinitas at night. He even spoke of braving the 805 Freeway south of Chula Vista, scampering across four lanes and throwing himself against the freeway divider as trucks and cars roared by. After he had seen people die in the desert from lack of water or snake bites or the attacks of thieves he quit smuggling and began to work in an orchard spray business in Imperial Valley. When the heat and humidity there became too heavy he left for the north, and had found his way to Armona.

José was a thirty–five year old who had simply ridden a bus across the border at San Ysidro in 1986. Later rounded up in an immigration raid in Oxnard he returned to his mother in Cuernavaca. After she died he returned to the U.S., but through the difficult route under the border fence and across the hills. He now had his green card and sent money back to his old papa through Western Union. He told Anton that times had become easier again and that the "Hundred Foot Rule" prevailed with the Immigration Services: "If the green card (which was no longer officially green) looks legitimate from a hundred feet, the *Migra* does not question you or round you up."

Pancho came from Oaxaca through the Baja–Imperial Valley route and had worked in the orange groves of Mecca in Southern California. He told Anton about picking oranges in the sweltering valley to the west of the Colorado River, in 95 degree heat with almost total humidity. There in the green groves abuzz with bees, with heat shimmering off the ground, young men on small scooters raced up and down the rows pulling hoses with sprinklers that kept the ground moist. "At lunch time," Pancho said, "we ate a whole bottle of chilies while sitting under the trees. It opened our pores, so we sweated more and cooled down." He described the teams working, loading the flatbed high with fifty pound boxes, then hauling them out to the dirt road and alongside a huge truck and trailer that lay nestled in a broad trench below the flatbed. Pancho's stories came alive and Anton could almost hear the lifting and dumping, crashing, sliding, grating and grunting as the crew lifted the fruit from one truck and sent it cascading into the other. Pancho told Anton to enjoy the cool days of winter, because when summer came he would sweat all the way through to his shoelaces.

Anton grew accustomed to waking early when the dawn was only a faint tint of dark blue on the eastern hills. As he lay on the simple bed in Gustavo's trailer, he felt his humanity, his inner life. His body felt healthy and alive and he loved the long stretching which raked his hardening muscles with friendly pains. He thought of his companions dreaming their dreams, sleeping husband or wife at their sides, and the children resting from their work in the fields as well. He thought about students and close friends from the college and his earlier years. He felt himself among the myriad of people who seek meaning by looking around, and up, and within. He thought about the many people who die peacefully, unknowing but believing, filled with hope to the full measure of their surrender; or torn with torment and anxiety, fighting lonely battles against jealous and wrathful gods.

One evening, resting in the trailer with Gustavo, Anton mentioned that he was beginning to feel strong, "like a lion."

Gustavo joked with him. "First a lion, then bees and honey, Anton? I was wondering when you would begin to sense the coming spring. *Mas vale tarde que nunca.* Better late than never! Your dream is an omen. You're in for a big fight or a woman might be appearing in your life."

"How's that?" Anton asked.

"'He who has ears to hear, let him hear,'" Gustavo laughed again. "There is a very strange story in the Book of Judges in the Hebrew Scriptures, the 14th chapter, where Samson gathers honey from the body of a lion and asks a riddle of his companions. They become outraged at him and demand that his new bride find the answer. The woman rails at Samson until he tells her, and he then goes berserk and kills the men and gives his bride away." Gustavo then surrendered himself to gales of laughter, in the midst of which Anton said, "Thanks for the warning!"

Regaining his breath, Gustavo said, "The whole story is a riddle, as are all things when a woman is involved. God gave us women to remind us perpetually that we are no better than the brute Samson if we do not receive the instruction of the Spirit, which comes in riddles."

"Did that young woman in the green dress teach you that?"

"You have sharp eyes, Anton. But these things are not easy to talk about..." Gustavo's voice deepened as he gazed across the table at the picture. Anton could hardly imagine the thoughts and memories that were rising to the older man's consciousness. Gustavo then continued at a slower pace, "Real life is more mysterious than Samson's riddles. Many barriers lie between me and her, the one whose picture is with me always...There's the ring of my priest's collar, my own nuptial ring which I rarely wear, but which I always feel. There is the *machismo* culture that I grew up with and which I saw in my papa...Thank Heaven I emerged from that...There was the civil war and my flight from El Salvador. Most of all, sadly so, there is time, too much and too long, ever so fleeting."

"May I?" Anton reached toward the shelf where stood the framed photograph of the woman. Gustavo nodded. In the picture the young woman stood next to a barn made from discarded construction wood and corrugated tin, its faded red façade blending into coffee or banana trees in the background—the outlines were indistinct; behind her in a corral outside the barn a sway backed, grey–white horse with Arab lines appeared to be nuzzling some hay. The woman was looking at the camera with a sweet and alert expression, utterly unprepossessed. Anton said nothing for a moment, then added, "I cannot believe that this picture is only decoration. You keep it here beside the picture of your ordination. This person dwells with you."

Gustavo measured his friend, then rubbed his hands vigorously over his face and through his hair. "Yes, her memory lives. I rarely speak of her. But she is alive in me, and always will be." He took the picture from Anton's hands and held it for a long, loving moment. "So, you want a story." Then, as in prayer, he said, "May the stories we tell bring the truth we need from the past to serve the present...May they redeem us...

"Here is how I met her: Back in 1960, a 'very good year' as they say in the song, September, I think, I was home from the University for a couple of days. I was with my papa and another man and his son Tomás who was my age, twenty–two. We were going to a *campesino* organizing meeting in the outskirts of our little town. My dad was a civil servant and was active in the seed groups that later became part of the liberation movement, and unfortunately the armed guerrillas, although that was not his way. Economically it was a disastrous time, as the big farms and the government were taking over the small peasant plots; and who could stand up to them, Anton? Work became harder and harder to find and people were flocking into the city to find work. El Salvador was not alone in this. While this was happening in our country, the idea of the *communidades de base* was growing up from groups in Nicaragua and Panama and Brazil.

"So, we were on our way to one of those meetings. We had to stop for some gas at the corner store. This store had only a few things, no privately owned village shop was very big, and the owner made shelves out of bricks and boards for the stuff he peddled. The shop also had the only telephone in town, other than the one in the police station. The owner was new in the neighborhood, and this was the first time I had been in his place. He had been a teacher in Managua, Nicaragua, but rumor had it that he had fled the Somozistas.[82] Now that he was in our country he was trying to set up a small business. He offered small loans at fair rates, and tried to keep his kids in school.

"My papa got to talking with the owner. We hung around the car while we put a few gallons of gas in. As we were standing there, a most amazing thing happened. Two young women with their mother came out of the house, minding their own business, going for a walk or something. I remember the older daughter wore a plain old cotton dress, and the mother had a strong and sure look about her. I hardly noticed the younger daughter. When the mother saw us, or really, when she saw Tomás, she put her hands on the older daughter's shoulders and whirled her right around, back into the house. I didn't think much of it, it happened so fast! In no more than five minutes the young woman and her mother came back out. She now had on a dress with cheery colors and had a ribbon in her hair. The mother too had put on a bright clean apron, and the two of them sat on a bench outside the store, and looked at us, while trying not to look at us. The younger daughter stood in the shadows in the doorway. She had changed into a green dress, but she looked despondent.

"Now I began to get a good idea of what was going on. Really, Anton, these women were astounding! The mother had become a little stocky, but you could still see the beauty of her Spanish and *mestizo* ancestry.

"We got back in the car, Tomás and I in the back seat. He looked over at me and whispered, 'Did you see that, Gustavo? My God, she looked magnificent!' I jabbed him in the ribs and said I was no idiot. Of course I had seen her!

"Later that evening, when we had a chance to talk, my dad told me that the store owner and his family had left the city of San Salvador because things were more unsettled there than they had been back in Managua, more dangerous for his family. Some of the National Guard had started hanging around their apartment, and one of them had tried to grab his daughter, the one who was standing back in the doorway, after classes at the secondary school. That was really frightening. The parents were in no position to call the police *commandante* to get rid of the thug and his paladins, since the National Guard *was* the police. It was dangerous and very frightening. So they moved from the big city, San Salvador, to our village, where we met them.

"Tomás never took up a lasting interest in the older daughter, and other things drew him away. But I became very interested in the younger daughter. The fact that she was hoping to go to college meant a lot, because very few people in El Salvador were able to go to school. But most of all, the fact that she was a young woman in some danger gripped my attention, and made her extremely important to me. I was finishing my philosophy and theology studies, and was already deep in conversation with the Franciscans to become a priest. But that did not blind me to who she was.

"I thought a lot about her over the next few weeks. No, that's not true. I thought about her all the time. I worried for her and wondered about her. I saw images of the Guardsman in his uniform, and felt the fear that swept her when facing his demands and his weapons. While my studies were very demanding as I prepared for my exams, that one memory of her standing in the doorway refreshed my spirits. In her vulnerability she became more alive, and mysteriously attractive.

"When I came back home for *Las Posadas* in December, I sent her a note to ask if I could visit. I didn't even know if she knew who I was. But she said Yes, maybe because her papa knew my own dad and felt safe.

"So, I arrived at her door with some flowers from the countryside, and she greeted me at the door. The sight of her was overwhelming! She was radiant, welcoming, gentle, and she wore that simple green dress. My life changed instantly and forever. I beheld in her a glimpse of the divine that is always suggested in our worship and scripture, yet had been hidden from me by lack of experience. The best part of me was born, I became a man, available for service, useful for life. I was being prepared to endure the sorrow of life's losses, for in love they became bearable and meaningful; I gave my heart away and never sought its return.

"In time it became clear that she grew to love me, too, with a kind of simplicity and eagerness that dissolved all barriers. For weeks we wrote letters and called each other on the telephone, which was hard because everybody in the store could hear us. I visited whenever I could break away from school. After many months later, with us the happiest of friends, she told me her story about life in the city. I also told her about what I felt to be my calling to life in Franciscan community. All of this was like a revelation, a way of her saying 'Here I am. Know me. Allow me to know you.' When we became honest like this, clear and true like fine wine, our love became complete. We were bonded in truth and transparent to one another. The best part of me, my capacity to love, became wider and deeper than all my plans and projects, and even grew big enough to contain the inevitable separations and differences we find in one another. While it may be vain for me to say so, she blessed my life like Clare blessed Francis. I learned that God had been saying the same thing all along: 'Know me. Allow me to know you.'

"Although our parting was in some way necessary, and we had to continue on our separate paths, I began to know how to love another person. Yes, I now know that it was only a beginning. But without her help in that beginning, I would be a complete failure; worse, a fraud in my life and ministry."

As Gustavo's words concluded, Anton pondered the story which was both unique and universal. "A lovely tale," he said. "I understand why you keep her picture close. I met a priest not so long ago who was afraid of even being seen with a woman. You're being truthful with feelings that must be shared by many."

"The church is a big family. I belong to it, and most closely to a little part of it, my brothers in the Order and this workers community. Some families are healthy about these feelings, powerful and uncontrollable as they are. My abbot always told me, 'To your own self be true.'[83] So, later in community with the other postulants, he did not censor my letters or read my mail; he simply accompanied me, and asked me to think about my whole life and the whole community we belonged to. He told me to trust God to reconcile what seems irreconcilable. Strangely, Anton, my experience with this lovely woman moved him, too. He shared with me that he knew his very life as a priest to be a riddle. He knew that a heaven awaits us all. But his priesthood was a recognition of his restlessness, his suffering. My love for this woman had awakened me to the possibility that I too would live in paradox: that the open and insoluble riddle of my life, whether as papa with children or as a priest, would help awaken the world from its spiritual lethargy.

"For a long time, waiting for something to happen, I felt the anguish keenly. Then, ever so gradually, I came to know that the separate worlds we had constructed—my relationship with her, and my life in community—were really one world into which my heart was growing. If you try to think your way through these things, Anton, then you realize that the choice is blind and the situation is absurd. But if you simply trust and wait and wait, all the while living with all the love of which you are capable, then the way becomes clear. Strong as my feelings were for her, and hers for me, I was bound for a life of simplicity and contemplation, not for marriage and fulfillment with her and *niños*.

"But I keep her picture close at hand. Here, let me show you something." Gustavo twisted back the staples that held the backing of the frame, and gently slid out a small piece of faded brown paper.

"I sent her flowers at our last Christmas before my ordination. Here is what I wrote," and Gustavo read the following words,

Estos capullos ofrecen la gratitud y alegría
que las palabras no pueden expresar,
Los pétales revelan la dulce fragancia
y el gozo de la amistad eternal,
Los pinceles de color que matizan cada pétalo
son los tiernos momentos que vivimos en años transcurridos,
Las hojas proclaman mi asombro y admiración

Cuando veo tu nombre y tu rostro.
El ramo entero dice lo que mi corazón anhela para ti:
¡La felicidad que trae la Navidad!

"Can you translate this for me?" Anton asked.

"If poetry were simply the voice of the heart, it would be excellent." Gustavo said, "But love knows no craft. Here's what it means:

These blossoms offer my speechless words of gratitude and gladness,
The petals peal back to reveal the sweetness in enduring friendship,
The tints hint at those tender moments we shared in years gone by,
The leaves proclaim my wonder when I see your face and name,
The whole setting says what my heart wishes for you:
The blessings of Christmas Day!

"You hold her memory like a bouquet of blessings," Anton sighed.

"So true, Anton. In a way, the bishop and the ordination are only a recognition of what had come to life in my heart through her. I will always see her as one of my greatest teachers. Were she to come through the door of my little trailer, I would recognize myself in her. If she would write me a letter some day, I would respond with words of tenderness and love as real today as then."

As these stories settled in Anton's mind he found himself quailing again before the ambiguity of his own calling. How, he asked himself, can I pretend to make a living by exploring questions of value, meaning and faith? How can I accept sinecure and status from this project? Had not the jury of common sense been outraged and offended by old Socrates' ironic suggestion that he be rewarded for his annoying questions by being given free meals at the city center?[84] Only his irony acquits him. Were not his dialectical victories over well-meaning fellow citizens simply too easy, and corrosive of public trust itself? And what of the airs of exclusiveness and prestige that surround my own Socratic profession, making it the object of secret envy and even the perverse fear that is heard in the contemptuous words, "ivory tower"?

On the one hand, people seem to do quite well when they pretend, against James Thurber's wisdom, "to have none of the questions and all of the answers," and thus go on about their business at the office, in the classroom, or the boardroom. They become unsettled and agitated when the questions come up, and prefer to go on about their lives as citizens, consumers, workers, teachers, physicians,...maybe even as church people and missionaries. Is this why our civilization has created the protected class of the professoriate?

On the other hand, Anton continued to puzzle, look at what we so–called professors have become! With the warm aplomb that comes from the habit of dazzling others, we weave together brave phrases such as "speaking truth to power," "the hunger for justice," "the virtuous poor." Truth to be told, do we not spend as many hours loading our precious rhetoric with lofty and awe–inspiring terms as do the great captains of empire before they launch new conquests? My meal with Juan Carlos taught me that our guilty consciences allow us to talk about "justice," but only after a good dinner takes away the hunger in our bellies. Is that all that a good conscience is, a garnish to the pieties that divert our attention from our deeper knowing? Priest John preaches with fervor, but only after adjusting the climate controls of his comfortable church. Then he can rail at his audience in their Sunday best about "the spirituality of universal compassion" without the heat of troubled conscience forcing them all from the room. This brew of words from which we sip is not the same as a cup of coffee carried by a cocaine–dependent woman in Los Angeles to a depressed, homeless man leaning against a wall. Perhaps we professional teachers, paid for our questioning, admired for our rhetoric and fattened on research grants, are simply one more head in the modern hydra of social and technological complexity that consumes us.

So Anton's mind moiled into disquieting thoughts, well outside the stable categories of organizations and institutions. Why is it, he wondered, that educated people stop with the questions about God inspired by Darwin, Einstein, Chardin or any other intellectual? Why borrow from others the work that belongs to them alone? Even the Buddha said that each of us has to work out our own salvation. My companions in the fields know nothing of those luminaries. Where do they find God? I see the bread being made in the kitchen oven and being offered during the Eucharist. I see the children sitting alongside their parents at the table. I see Zanita and Juan, Rosa and Miguel, and all these loving relationships. "Where there is love, there God is..."

But, Anton wondered, what about the formless and the void, the seething nothingness into which I fear to fall at my death? Or my dream of dropping into a crowd of the deceased, a Hades of two–dimensional and placid shadows? That's not so easy. Indeed it is frightening...

Still, he thought, I refuse to be the Epicurean who retires to his garden and its comforts and pleasures, intellectual or otherwise. Nor will

I be a sentimentalist who is clever with words and who organizes his own emotions for public propriety and effect. No. God is sweeping all of that away, himself departing with the words, "I will disappear so that you may long for me." No more fairy tales, miracles, unlikely stories from fervid imaginations, no more strained interpretations and dogmatism from mine or any other profession. No more retrenching behind the fortress mentalities of ignorance and bigotry. *Ecrasez l'enfame!*[85] I am finally ready to hear it: the battle cry of the Bastille echoes in the emptying chambers of my mind, until the last vestige of my arrogance vanishes and I am no longer safe from our dangerous God.

Only in our doing can we grasp you.
Only with our hands can we illumine you.
The mind is but a visitor:
It thinks us out of our world.

Each mind fabricates itself.
We sense its limits, for we have made them.
And just when we would flee them,
you come and make of yourself an offering.

I don't want to think a place for you.
Speak to me from everywhere.
Your Gospel can be comprehended
without looking for its source.

When I go toward you
It is with my whole life.

Rainier Rilke (1875–1926),
Du wirst nur mit der Tat erfast[86]

Spoken from Everywhere and a Dream

IN THE FIELDS Anton felt the circle of the community grow close. Here there was no sea of faces. Each person was as prominent and unique and irreplaceable as a peak on a mountain range. With them from day to day and vine to vine, Anton walked and worked the rows. From time to time one of the workers would begin to whistle a popular ballad. A voice or two would join in. Soon a choir of ten was sending *a cappella* the laments of the displaced peoples across the vineyards. The sounds rose and settled like the birds that moved along the vineyard rows ahead of the slow–moving company.

One Friday morning when the crew was well into the fourth ten–acre vineyard Anton heard Gustavo's motorcycle on the road and the feeble beep of its horn. "Anton...," he heard his name called.

With a wave and a shout in return Anton made his way back to the road where Gustavo waited. Underneath a heavy winter jacket Anton could see Gustavo's collar of his priesthood. *"¿Qué pasa, amigo?"* he asked.

"We need to be with Elena. Her time is near."

"OK," Anton replied. With a shout to Juan and a gesture of hoeing to ask the foreman to bring in his tools from the field, Anton bundled up his thick jacket, pulled his cap down over his ears, and swung his leg over the back of Gustavo's Norton. Gunning the throttle, Gustavo guided the motorcycle down the dirt road into Armona, then onto Highway 198 toward Visalia.

Anton had not been to Visalia for several weeks. His last trip had been a few days after Christmas. He had driven with Gustavo in Juan's old car to spend the morning with Rosa and Miguel, the young couple who had announced their hopes only a week before Christmas, but who were now suffering the loss of their pregnancy. Rosa was facing a difficult medical procedure and was frightened and sad. But *abuela* Guadalupe and Yesenia who cared for the young children were close by and consoled her continuously. Miguel, on the other hand, seemed ill at ease and sat in the clinic waiting room away from his wife and the other women. Anton joined him and encouraged him to talk about his family, the hopes he had held for his baby, and his sadness. The next day, when the couple returned to the camp, Miguel chose to work on the row next to Anton. Noticing this, Gustavo had said, "You have lifted the young man's spirits, Anton."

Arriving at the St. Jude Care Center, Anton was glad to dismount the motorcycle. The ride had been bouncy and the wind from the trucks had made Gustavo lean over close to their huge, whirling wheels. Anton felt cold, but exhilarated nevertheless.

"Come, we will go to Elena's room," Gustavo said.

Elena seemed to be sleeping deeply when they arrived. *"Elena, somos Gustavo y Anton. Estamos aquí."* Gustavo and Anton are here. She focused on Gustavo with the haggard eyes of the very old and very tired. He brought out a small book of prayers and Psalms, and a small vial of oil. As he anointed Elena's forehead and hands with the oil he said quiet prayers and the *Padre Nuestro*. Tears shone in his soft brown eyes, and Elena's own eyes closed again.

As Gustavo began to recite Psalm 139, Anton saw a most remarkable thing. With *"Tú me has examinado y conocido."* —"Lord, you have searched me and you know me," —Elena's lips began moving. When the priest said, *"Tú has conocido mi sentarme y mi levantarme."* "You know when I sit and when I rise…," she too began to speak the words in a quiet, strained voice. As her voice gained momentum and strength, Gustavo's own voice quieted and became a whisper. *"Has entendido desde lejos mis pensamientos. Mi senda y mi acostarme has rodeado, y estás impuesto en todos mis caminos."* "You perceive my thoughts from afar. You discern my going out and my lying down, you are familiar with all my ways…"

Then the words became Elena's own, and she completed the Psalm with Gustavo's voice echoing low and quiet beside her. *"Y guíame en el camino eterno."* "And you guide me in the way everlasting."

With eyes closed and with the softest whisper between her lengthening breaths Elena offered the poetry of the dying. *"No necessito vagar mas, mi hermano…Tu cruz al lado del camino no me detendrá…La señal me muestra el camino."* I need wander no more, my brother. Your cross at the side of the road does not hold me back. The sign has shown me the way.

"You have heard her word, Anton," Gustavo said. "'Poetry begins where death is robbed of the last word.'[87] Remember this well."

Gustavo and Anton remained in vigil with the old woman. Gustavo's last words to her were, *"No ten miedo. Sigue Jesús."* Do not be afraid. Follow Jesus. Her breathing quieted further and still further, and became no more.

The next morning, the funeral liturgy was offered for Elena Vasquez in the small chapel in the St. Jude Care Center. A small knot of people gathered, including members of the camp community brought by the bus, residents in their wheelchairs, a cleaning woman and the orderly from Elena's unit. For the community who had surrounded Elena and who were now losing her, the Gustavo said,

> Elena, like you, has known hunger. Towards the end she had no home. She may never have been to school. She was a woman and had to overcome oppression. She had to struggle for basic rights. Yet there is more. She is more. A wise Rabbi said that whenever someone dies, the world dies as well. It is especially so with the poor. For she, being among you, having nothing—no power, no big name, no money—*made the world nonetheless!*... She did so through her way of feeling, knowing, making friends with you, loving, believing, suffering, celebrating, and praying. You, my friends, have embraced Elena, Christ among you in distressing disguise. You gave her a place to remember her brother, who died in misery along the highway. Living with Elena here in St. Jude's Care Center in the little city of Visalia means sharing Elena's universe. Your fidelity to her and to one another bears witness to the Good News that is available to all human beings. With this, she has been loved into heaven. May it be so for all of us.[88]

Elena's ashes were carried back to Armona. "We know very little about this woman, Anton," the priest said. "We do know that she is a child of God, and that she must have known and loved many people. We know that she was loved until the end. We know that she walked in the garden of the Lord and heard his voice. We will return Elena's ashes to the earth." Together Gustavo, Anton, Guadalupe, Juan and Zanita walked deep into the vineyard. The buds of first year growth were appearing, and the tips of leaves could be seen in the second and third year growth. There, sheltered by the sky, accompanied by song, Elena's ashes were smoothed into the soil for the ages.

Early the next morning, well before daybreak, Anton dreamed he was standing staring up at a mountain. The mountain was huge and dark and grey and spanned the whole horizon. Thick clouds filled the sky, hiding the mountain's peak from sight. Anton could see a thin road winding up the mountain, and near the clouds, a small village, and the road continuing up beyond the village until it was lost from sight. The steepness of the mountain felt daunting. His dream took him to the sea. He was in the water. The warm water surged up to his chest, not with the mighty energy of ocean breakers, but with the calm of a lake. Anton could see the ocean spreading and blending without bound into the sky, which carried the sun and radiated its light in the ripples and foam of the water in countless flakes and dancing sparks. In his dream he felt something brush against his leg. Looking down, he saw a fish. Then he awoke.

In the fields later that morning Anton felt a wideness in his spirit. He looked back over the fifty acres of vines that he and the others had pruned in the last seven weeks. He looked at his friends bending over the plants. He could hear them breathing and talking quietly. He moved from vine to vine. One of the workers lifted his voice in song. Another joined and the melody floated above the vineyard, adding invisible color to the deep brown and fresh green of the buds and new one–year growth.

He remembered how Gustavo had said, "We plant the vines and prune back the twigs and branches that can give no grapes. We prune, but it is sun and water that gives the growth." I have been well pruned in this monastery of renewal, Anton thought. I have sharpened my tools every day. It is time to end my sojourn here, and bring forth sparks from my own life. It is the appointed time.

That evening Anton sat with Gustavo, Juan and Zanita in the kitchen trailer after dinner. "I think it's time for me to be on my way," he said. They looked at him with sweet and concerned expressions.

"Are you going back to your school?" Zanita asked.

"Not yet," Anton responded. "Last night I dreamt about mountains and the ocean. The mountains did not invite me, but they had a road going up, and they did not resist. I will not go to the top of the mountain: that is not necessary. I think that I must travel west through the mountains to the ocean. Simply to go to the ocean is enough...I think that I will go to Carmel perhaps, or Monterey."

The workers understood arrivals and leavings; their whole lives had been governed by the movements of nature and political fortune and misfortune. "Your dream carries you toward a new field, Anton," Gustavo said. "You are not ready to rest here. God is not done with you...nor are you done with God. The quiet has been good for you, but I don't sense that you have yet confronted the God who fashions the field upon which we live."

"Confronted, Gustavo?"

"Oh, yes, Anton, even raged at him! Think about it...Your response to the wilderness of your life was to taste despair—thankfully you did not drink deeply—but you certainly did not grumble, nor complain. You probably even have harbored a secret contempt for those who do. Am I right? You don't have to answer...But it does raise the question, Anton, of what has become of us, when we forget how to scream our anger and distress, when we are too proud to release our laments. We will send you off, well and whole in body and mind. Listen now, and watch and learn from those who have learned how to scream with shrillness to the Almighty. And, Anton, praising is the other side of complaining. Both are impolite, so do not be surprised if you feel uncomfortable...but when you begin to cry out with praises, then you will know that you are really praying."[89]

When Gustavo was done, Zanita said simply, *"Que te vaya bien, Anton."* May things go well for you.

"Thank you, Zanita. Say, Juan, could you give my tools to another worker? And please thank the landowner for my stay here?"

"Por su puesto, as you wish," Juan answered as he shook Anton's hand with the gentle strength of his calling.

"Gustavo," Anton asked later, back in the trailer, "How would you like to sell your motorcycle to me?"

Gustavo's eyes widened with amazement. "Anton, are you *loco*? I was not suggesting that you search for God in the metaphysics of an old 1957 motorcycle.[90] She is cranky and the battery is always dead. She sometimes bucks like a spooked *caballo*. What do you know about motorcycles? They are dangerous and everyone has a party trying to run you over. Buy a car, take the bus, but why ride a motorcycle?"

"Why do *you* ride a motorcycle?" Anton asked.

Gustavo sighed, then laughed. "Not fair! Oh, I wish you had not asked me that question. Really, what else is there? I love my old motorcycle not because she is faithful and safe, but because she is like my hidden self, uncertain, sometimes faithless, a risky business, noisy in low gear, just like me now that I am an old man. She is like me, like the philosopher Seneca said of himself, 'A youth inside an old frame.' Her tires may be bald, but she has not lost her teeth, so watch out! She takes a swift kick to get going, and runs slow when she is cold, but once you get the engine singing, she just flies through the air! She wants to go twice as fast, but I am not strong enough to hold on. You want to take her from me? What kind of *compañero* are you, anyway?"

He laughed again. "But then, I have saved some money and there is a '67 Triumph in the store in Tulare I saw a couple of weeks ago..."

So, it was decided that Anton would buy Gustavo's motorcycle for $300. The next day was Sunday and Gustavo showed Anton how to kick over the engine without gouging his calf, and how to work his way through the gears. When he moved from second to third to the accelerating snare drum of the engine he understood why Gustavo loved the old Norton.

By noon Anton was ready to go. His bedroll and blanket were wrapped in a poncho and bound tightly to the seat with his few other belongings. To his friends he said, "There are no words that I can leave with you that thank you adequately. Your generosity has given me life and a ground to stand on. You will always be with me."

Gustavo put his hands on Anton's shoulders. "Yes, Anton. Remember, we are your people. Remember we are here. If you are ever lonely, think upon us intensely and recall us to your presence. We will always be with you. And remember that Easter always comes."

Guadalupe brought him some fresh and flavorful *pañuelitos de queso* from Dolores' kitchen, "Just in case," she said. The whole community gathered on the road to say goodbye. Zanita brought out her guitar and everyone sang, *"Señor, me has mirado a los ojos, sonriendo has dicho mi nombre...En la arena he dejado me barca, Junto a tí buscaré otro mar."* O Lord, you have looked into my eyes; smiling, you have spoken my name; in the sand I have left my little boat, near to you I will seek other seas.

With one last wave and the sun high overhead, Anton set his course for the west.

How wonderful these human beings are
Who read the words which never have been written,
Who bind like masters tangled skeins of things,
And still trace paths in the eternal dusk.

> Hugo von Hofmannsthal (1874–1929),
> *Der Tor und der Tot*

Tyger, Tyger, burning bright,
In the forests of the night;
What immortal hand or eye,
Could frame thy fearful symmetry?

> William Blake (1757–1827),
> *Songs of Experience*

THEIR EYES WERE UPON ME

THE NORTON FLUNG ITSELF at the road like an arrow shot from a longbow. Clean, narrow, and running true, the motorcycle knifed through the air. The road was open; Anton was open to what awaited him. On his right he could see the tracks of the Southern Pacific railroad, and beyond, the fields of the Central Valley. Moving the machine up to sixty–five or seventy miles per hour wracked him with buffets, just as Gustavo had said. He also was jarred by an occasional pothole that appeared too suddenly for decision.[91] So he tightened the torque screw on the handlebars to give himself a firm steer, and loped along at an easy fifty miles per hour.

After riding for thirty minutes Anton saw a large, slow moving military aircraft with a radar disk on top descending to the north with its landing gear down. A sign with "Lemoore Naval Air Station" passed by. Anton recalled that his older brother Warren like to travel down from Fresno to watch his son fly Navy fighters out of the training base there. On this trip he gave no thought to stopping himself, what with the ocean beyond Monterey beckoning him. Soon he was slowing into the outskirts of Lemoore, a small town much like Armona with a hardware store, grocery store, a restaurant and tavern, a single-story professional building, and warehouses and granaries near the railroad line.

Gustavo had said that he should fill up his gas tank close to every hour, especially in the open country between towns. Anton pulled into a small gas station with one pump and a car with its hood up in the garage. A pickup truck with a gun rack was parked beside a telephone booth; a rifle was visible through the back window. Anton filled his tank, avoiding drips on the tank or hot exhaust pipes, paid the attendant, and looked at his map. One hundred miles to Coalinga. I can make that easily today, he thought. He kicked the motorcycle into life again, and idled up to the street.

There were hardly any cars on Highway 198 on a Sunday mid-afternoon, and Anton gently eased out the clutch and rolled on the throttle, pulling onto the street. At that instant a screech of tires shocked him as the pickup accelerated out of the station behind him. The truck was approaching from behind, its motor roaring and horn blasting. Without hesitation Anton jerked the throttle of the Norton open to the stop. The motorcycle engine erupted in an angry bellow. With his arms straining to hold on, Anton jumped ahead and out of the way of the racing truck. As the truck roared by with another blast of its horn, Anton heard a crash of metal beneath his seat. He lurched forward against the handlebars as the motorcycle decelerated. The engine under full throttle shrieked in protest as the chain to the rear wheel split, flapped once around the sprocket and clattered onto the street.

Anton quickly cut the engine and rolled off the street and onto the shoulder. Heart pounding, he dismounted and looked at the motorcycle as it stood motionless, crackling with cooling metal, the blue of its hot tailpipes giving way to warm brown. He looked at the rear wheel. It was soaked with oil. Picking up the chain, he saw that it was broken and wrapped back on itself. Oh, Rozinante, see what I get for flailing you![92] he thought to himself. He pushed the motorcycle back to the gas station where the attendant had hastened out of his office.

"Seems like I wasn't treating it right," Anton gasped as he pulled the machine back on its stand. "Didn't even see that guy coming."

"That 'guy' was a woman. She hates motorcyclists with a mean hatred," the attendant said. "Says she would soon as kill them as look at them."

"But wh—why in the world..." Anton stammered.

"Hey, for us folks who live out here, motorcycles only add to the racket of jet takeoff. If we can't have enough from the air, we get it on the ground. I didn't think to warn you. She has a farm out in Grangeville, and that's where she tends to stay, raising her pigs and keeping them cool in the barn in the summer. I see her in here from time to time, kind of serious, but Jesus!, I never thought she would blow off like that."

"What ever came over her?" Anton appealed. "I didn't cut her off or even look at her!"

The attendant pulled his cap off his head and wiped his brow. "Her father bought a ranch outside of Lemoore after the Second World War. He was a sullen type, no use for people after what he had seen in combat.

Said anybody who wanted war should have a tour of Hades first. He died shortly after his daughter was born. Shrapnel wounds from one of the European tank battles, I think."

"My dad had a heavy dose of that, too," Anton commiserated. "Strange how difficult it is to talk with them about it."

"Who knows? It might betray how much they miss the battle. But not in the case of this old farmer. He just died, bitter through and through. So the mother and daughter have struggled to keep the farm going. It has been hard because the soil is poor from oily run-off from the airbase and she can't get enough water from the corporate ranches to set her corn in the spring. The woman says she hates Navy fliers because they burn her land and make her pigs miscarry. Told me once some hotrod in a jet flew so low over her cornfield that she thought it would be scorched or flattened from the blast. She had been sitting on the porch with her old ma, and it terrified them both."

"Well, she sure scared the hell out of me," Anton said.

"Springtime never seems to come for her." The attendant shook his head. "Always grim...Lots of hardship in life. The earth simply does not yield to her...and she does not yield to the world. An angry type, but I never seen her try to run somebody off the road. Maybe the motorcycle makes you look like a flyboy."[93]

Anton's own anger and fear were replaced by a feeling of defeat. "Now I'm stuck."

"Maybe not. Let's take a look at that chain."

With the attendant's help, the broken link was removed and the chain was strung around the rear sprocket as before. With a few adjustments and fresh chain oil the motorcycle was ready to go. Gladly offering his benefactor twenty dollars for the assistance, Anton bade farewell. Looking carefully down both streets, he motored quietly out of town, and resumed his ride to the west.

The day filled fresh in anticipation of spring. The low-pitched vibration of the Norton's large twin cylinders massaged away remaining toxins from the encounter with the angry woman. Along the way the brown of the broad fields lifted a garland of lettuce green, cabbage purple, and radish red. A bi-plane flitted among the trees and power lines laying down chemical mists on the fields. Mile after mile fell behind as Anton drew a straight course along Highway 198 from Armona, below Lemoore and Huron and over the main artery of Interstate 5. He then banked north along Highway 33 and into Coalinga.

After filling his fuel tank Anton rested and consulted his map: an hour to King City, another two hours to Carmel, then a half hour to Monterey. On the other hand, the fork in the road south along Highway 33 stood before him as a question mark. What is it that drives me onward? he wondered. Certainly not habit. Nor does necessity compel me to change directions. The western mountains hold no terrors for me, nor do the declining hours in my day. I am feeling fresh and relaxed. With a sandwich to fortify me, and by keeping my speed under fifty and the handlebar torque snug on the long straight stretches, weariness will lag far behind. When the curves come, I relax the torque and suffer no strain in my arms.

The rolling hills suited the motorcycle as it ran up and down the gears, exhaust noise echoing against the juniper and oak trees bordering the highway. In King City, Anton fueled up again and continued north-west and parallel to the San Andreas fault line. The rugged fault, which emerged as an insistent reminder of the great and moving ocean of earth beneath the deceptively calm surface, bound the soil and ridge line like a hawser running the length of a weathered sailing vessel. At Metz, he turned west again, crossing over the Camino Real. The sun was low in the sky now and Anton hastened his pace.

Crossing over the first ridge of the Los Tularcitos range to begin the descent into Carmel Valley, Anton realized his headlight was off. He jiggled the switch and peered ahead for some illumination of the dark road ahead of him. From time to time a passing car blinked its headlights, and Anton realized that he was traveling in the dark. Lacking a guiding light, he felt danger gaining on him with every passing mile. He slowed, looking for a way off the road. Finally spying a dirt track leading away from the highway and into the oak trees, Anton departed the highway. He bounced and wrestled the motorcycle in first gear along the bumpy, indistinct path for a half-mile, emerged from the grove of oaks into an open meadow, and stopped.

As the rumble of the engine receded into the trees and chaparral, Anton felt deafened by the silence. Slowly, burbling sounds of the Chupines Creek reached his ear. The low sawing of crickets and katydids lifted from the background. A hundred yards behind him he could see a large oak tree a hundred yards away, standing alone in the meadow, the axis of its massive trunk ramifying into muscular branches and a canopy of leaves that held up the dark eastern sky.[94] The meadow spread around him, its flowers giving up even the faint pastel of color in the deepening twilight. An aging fence, crutching itself on thick branches or an occasional post, ran along the dirt track and disappeared.

With the quiet came speckled darkness. The evening star, Venus, hugged the western sky, bright and poignant, undimmed by any earthly haze. Slowly, almost unnoticeably, a widening bevy of heavenly lights began to accent the darkening night. Close by, an owl hooted. Anton felt the bird's eyes upon him, and shivered with the memory of a winter night when he had been thrown off his path. But I choose this path, he thought to himself without words. He pulled out his bedding, and laid his poncho over the Norton to hold the heat of its engine near his body for a few minutes. He lay down and looked up at the night sky. Here I am, wide awake, alone on a perfectly dark and quiet night. In the past I would gaze up at the night sky for a short time and then doze off, my mind weary and craving the oblivion of sleep. Tonight, not so.

He gazed into the night's starry face, freckling with bright dimples. The remote pinpricks became a misty torrent that coursed up the sky from south to north in a diaphanous, translucent abundance of light. Like the silver tip of an invisible paint brush, meteors drew lines across the dark canvas of night, leaving a shower of sparks that flickered and cooled into ashes. The little bursts of liquid fire reminded Anton of his own life. *I too hurtle through the darkness and leave my sparks behind.*

As Anton's eyes bathed in the darkness, Pascal's dismal lament framed a question in his mind: *"Effraient–moi la silence de ces espaces?"*[95] Does the silence of these infinite spaces frighten me? No, but it imposes on me the relentless question: Distant though we are, are we not related to these stars revealed in their intimate light? Our human ethics of obligation and mercy cannot bear the burden of this infinity of matter and space, so far is it beyond good and evil. Still, nothing is futile "up there," where galaxies and clusters of galaxies give weight and shape to the universe like a vast, fluttering drapery of fate and necessity. We hear the imperceptible whispers of their movements in the silent music of mathematics. Time gallops on, indefatigable. Apollo sweeps up auroral energies into thin beams of light, laces them under sagging space, and shares the burden of his mighty brother, Atlas. Motion, the fundament of physics, flows; things large and small dash and hurtle by or swing into the waltz of the orbits, here and everywhere. Comets streak effortlessly through measureless distances, containing in their crystals the sparks cast by momentary bursts of cosmic candles whose luminescence exceeds our own sun's brightness by a billion times. And yes: our living planet may have kindred worlds that harbor life and consciousness. If nothing can be counted for vanity "up there," Anton thought, then so too "down here" in our own brief lives. "Out, out, brief candle..."? No: MacBeth's were counsels of despair. These heavens contain me, Anton thought, and I weigh upon them too, though imperceptibly, and draw my life from them.

As Anton lay watching, beauty was revealed to his mind like the pulling aside of a bridal veil. What other response to beauty is possible than to open one's arms, to draw close, to embrace for but a moment? The encounter with beauty opens the door to self–discovery, an experience of the unity of the Self. It leads to the sacred wedding of souls, as in Jesus and his friends in the hymnic procession to his consummation as the Christ.[96] Nowhere do the heavens bequeath their truth and beauty to me as my possession. Beauty invites us not to grasp, or worse, to consume—, but to behold, to feel its glow unhardening our hearts. Such subtle power invites the human person to strain every nerve and every faculty to participate in its alchemical transformations. It insinuates itself in the soul so wondrously that even ugliness is no longer a reproach, but an invitation to heal and ennoble.[97] And these skies feel no limitation, though their boundary is lost in the oak trees and in the path whose twists and curves I cannot discern. What of them do I embody? Am I strong enough to comprehend that even in the order realm of Heaven, hot and chaotic energy swirls? As I look within and without, may my mind's eye be as clear as the owl's, for whom even the dim light from the stars turns the night into day. Even if I see less than he, may I accept with gratitude the brief flickers and sparks of the understanding given to me. And yes, as Gustavo urged, may I entrust my soul to this flight through the dark night.

Anton pulled his bedding close. His thoughts flowed into dreams, and he slept and rested from the day.

He emerged from his slumber sometime before sunrise. He gazed into the night. All was quiet but for the furtive scurrying of nocturnal creatures in the nearby meadow and the running water in the creek. Out of the corner of his eye to the east Anton sensed a growing light in the hatchery of stars. Turning his head he saw the crescent of a new moon revealed through the branches of the great oak tree. The curve of brilliant light, so sparing, so perfect, so fragile, shaped her dark wholeness into a question mark. He gazed in wonder. Slowly, like a lover leading her betrothed to the promises of the day, the moon rose through the branches of the tree until she disappeared in the broadening glow of the advancing sun.

Anton felt an acute pain in his side. He rubbed his hands over the rough earth, searching for an intrusive and jutting rock. Finding none, Anton shifted into a more comfortable position and drifted back to sleep.[98]

He awoke again when the dawn's mother of pearl was dispelled with the first beam of direct sunlight. Rising on an elbow and looking further down the valley, he could see gauzy mist clinging to the low places and watercourses, vaguely white and evanescent like the stars of the Milky Way during the night. With the first gleams of golden light battening on the hills and trees, Anton could see the silvery rays of a spider web reaching from a nearby shrub to the handlebars of the motorcycle. How is this possible?, he wondered. How could that creature span this space in the middle of the night? With a closer look Anton could see nearly a dozen other silver strands and cross–connections, and within the pattern, the master worker in the web. The spider paused her work. Anton could see her huge eyes staring directly at him. He looked back into the creature's eyes. We may see, he thought, but we may not touch. Nature reclaims our artifacts, stepping lightly as a spider's tiptoe while pulling with invisible threads.

With the broadening glance of sunlight the first note of the dawn chorus piped across the meadow. Within seconds the forest came alive with a symphony hastening towards its climax as the full orb of the sun burst over the living scene. Music rollicked from trees, birds erupted from bushes to begin their eager flight for food, and quail catapulted out of the grass and across the meadow. Trills sounded from rocky cliff to sylvan barricade, from bluing tree canopy to the meadow with its medley of spring colors. Anton's heart ached under the cascade of sound and the deluge of light.

Beside him, the many–legged weaver drew her flawless pattern, reaching and stretching and dangling, her smallness only magnifying the earth below. Anton recalled several lines of Walt Whitman's poem –

> Till the bridge you will need be form'd, till the ductile anchor hold,
> Till the gossamer thread you fling catch somewhere, O my soul.
> Surrounded, detached, in measureless oceans of space.[99]

Rising stiffly from his uneven bed, Anton stretched. His side still ached, and his blood ran slowly. The sound of the Chupines beckoned, and he walked to the edge of the meadow. As he swale the creek in a calm place a small flock of goslings darted away, leaving delicate V's as they vied for their mother. Anton found the water cold, bracing and pure. He filled his canteen and, returning to his campsite, rolled up his blankets, and prepared to mount the Norton for his continued journey.

Suddenly, he started in dismay and stared in disbelief and consternation. The front tire of the motorcycle was flat. After several seconds he became conscious of the enormity of his situation. Can I push this back to the road? Can I remove the wheel and carry it back, and hitchhike to town? Neither option seemed feasible. Finally, Anton decided to hide the motorcycle and walk. As he raised the kickstand the spider dropped to the earth and scurried for cover. Anton pushed the wobbly machine behind the oak tree. Under the tree its tires sank into damp leaves and became immovable. He covered the machine with his poncho and walked away.

Anton struck off with a steady pace along the country road. The road wandered in a westerly direction, bordered on both sides by gentle slopes that fed the winding Chupines River. Closest to the clarity of the sky were the oak and pine and an occasional madrone with its limbs clad in scanty bark. Nesting Western bluetailed butterflies flashed their wings at the sound of his footsteps and fluttered from flower to swaying flower. Early spring flooding had cleared away the earth, leaving granite boulders tangled with roots and branches. Here and there the creek rushed over sheer rocky falls, crashing this way and that, spuming into a thousand drops and dribbles and gurgling in eager haste to reach quiet places again.

Our thinking flows together, jumbled like this river, he mused, gathering water from the sky, washing the earth, revealing the bedrock of our psyches. Seen as movements of nature, our thoughts seek calm resolution like a swollen stream seeks the sea. And, like this riverbed, our Selves are fragile, wandering veins of color and stratum moving across the surface of life. We spend decades forming and informing the mind, and forgetting with more alacrity and far less effort than learning. Is this why the ancients pitied those who spend their lives learning and re-learning, never to truly know? It is as futile as building floodwalls and dams that are only overwhelmed by the torrents when they come.

Overhead a hawk flew silently. It flowed in an effortless gyre above a meadow pocked with gopher mounds. Watching near the edge of the meadow, Anton saw the hawk's prey, an indiscreet gopher shoveling out his hole with little bursts of dirt. The shower of dirt became predictable as the gopher trudged back and forth in his underground tunnel. The hawk narrowed his circle, then poised himself in the air with dancing wings. A puff of dirt, a flash of a wing, a brief, high pitched cry, a flapping retreat, and silence descended again on the meadow.

Who is watching me in timeless circles, his eternal medium, waiting to descend with fluttering wings and a relentless grip?, Anton wondered. He is like the hawk above, not flying through time from one prey to the next, but rather descending into time to seize us in shock and surprise and to carry us up to a higher view.

Soon the dirt road parted from the meadow and began a gradual ascent into the oak and pine forest. The early din of the dawn chorus was muted now. Small swallows flitted from branch to branch, flying black shadows that disappeared instantly into the camouflage of leaves. Monarchs and ruddy copper butterflies climbed the air around him, as black and orange-tipped butterflies flitted from branch to branch and rested with wings waving lazily in the warm air. Mating moths chased one another in churning madcap around fallen logs. Occasionally Anton saw birds jousting or pairing in a furiously flapping, vibrating sphere of feathers. He knew that he was being watched by a hundred eyes. All was quiet except for the imperceptible humming of bees and the rustle of leaves as small animals moved deeper into cover at the sound of his footsteps. Near the creek where it swelled with spring runoff, his steps disturbed a cloud of ladybugs that erupted like golden sunlight over the sparkling water. Otherwise, he walked in nature's silence. He knew that it was silent only to his ears, for the sprouting and greening everywhere was trumpeting the arrival of primavera.

The road became indistinct and disappeared. He was now walking along the wandering byways of the forest denizen. Once he startled a threesome of white-tailed deer, who bounded away in giant leaps that brushed the earth as gently as a swipe of a hand on a leather drum. An occasional clearing allowed him to see for a hundred feet or more, but more often his vision was limited to twenty or thirty feet. Even those spaces were dappled and smattered with light and dark as the bolts and blankets of light divided the shadows cast by the dark oak canopy. A woodpecker knocked a hollow tocsin on a log in unseen reaches of the forest.

Coming into a clearing, Anton encountered the mountain lion. He froze. The animal was three feet at the shoulder, tan-colored, taut and motionless in a small stand of madrone, ears pointing forward. His hooded, tawny-brown eyes were riveted on the alien who had stumbled uninvited onto the wooded stage. The woodpecker too paused his uneven drum-roll to watch the unfolding drama. Only the bees continued their aerial acrobatics around the glade and in and out of the shafts of sunlight. The lion stood and stared, immortal in the moment, measuring the man. Anton imagined neither fleeing the creature, whose claws could sink into his shoulders in two long leaps; nor flinging something at him, a pathetic and futile effort that would only make the stately animal angry; nor shouting and waving his arms, the indignity of which would have been despicable. Instead, he remained very still. Complete, serious, fearsome in his unleashed power, the lion completed his scrutiny. After a long moment he glided soundlessly away into the trees.

Anton breathed again. He felt awkward, like an intruder who had invaded someone's private garden. He walked on, heart pounding. He looked over his shoulder frequently. The woodpecker resumed his rhythmic accompaniment as well.[100]

Ah, who'll heal his afflictions,
To whom balsam was poison,
Who, from love's fullness,
Drank in misanthropy only?
First despised, and now a despiser,
He, in secret, wasteth
All that he is worth
In a selfishness vain.
If there be, on thy psaltery,
Father of Love, but one tone
That to his ear may be pleasing,
Oh, then, quicken his heart!
Clear his cloud–enveloped eyes
Over the thousand fountains
Close by the thirsty one
In the desert...

Wolfgang von Goethe (1749–1832),
Die Hartz Reise (1777)[101]

The Quickening Heart

WITHIN TWO HOURS Anton crested the highest hill above the Carmel Valley. The bank of trees fell away, freeing the broad expanse of sky into ever more stunning blue. Around the smooth hilltop summit lay another meadow covered with delicate white and blue flowers on a bed of brown and green grasses and foliage. A cool breeze lifted off the slopes toward the open sky. From the crest of the hill, Anton saw the far-off Pacific Ocean spread out in the distance, glittering like blue diamonds in the noon-day sun. *Thalassa!*, he whispered to himself. Like the Greeks of Xenophon's army of Ten Thousand who, when finally spying the sea after their long trek through an alien land, cheered and ran as one man toward their beloved element, Anton thrilled to the sight of the familiar element after so many weeks and months.[102] On the summit he stopped to eat the last of his bread and cheese and reveled in the warmth of the day and the invitation of the distant waters. He then resumed his walk down the ridgeline and into the meadows, leaving spiders with their looms, woodpeckers poised on their logs, lions at the hunt, and bees gathering their nectar.

By late in the afternoon, Anton had emerged from the hills and onto the gradual slopes of the Carmel Valley. The basin of the valley became a patchwork of alfalfa fields and forest outcroppings and open grazing meadows. Here and there cattle dozed under the trees, large brown and black clods mulling over their cud. Anton felt very tired. The encounters of the day remained fresh in his memory, but he felt the weight of his legs and the cutting of the straps of his backpack into his shoulders. The dirt road soon joined a broad field of freshly turned soil. A simple and well-maintained wooden fence ran along the field, within whose center a majestic oak held sway. Around the tree flowed fresh furrows like ripples sent from a pebble dropped into a calm pond. Near the edge of the field,

Anton could see a slow–moving tractor pulling a large farm implement with shining steel discs as large as cymbals, which churned the wild grey–green winter grass into the warm, brown soil. As the tractor approached the edge of the field, Anton waved his hand. The driver stopped the clanking and huffing machine, and turned off the motor.

"Hello there," Anton called. "I'm in a bit of a bind. My motorcycle broke down a ways up the road. I need to find someone who can help me take it into town."

The man on the tractor responded, "There's a garage in Carmel Valley village, about four miles up the road." He glanced at his watch. "But you probably won't get there before dark."

Anton's discouragement must have shown on his face. The man gazed at the traveler for a moment. "Tell you what: I have to get some material for the farm in Monterey and maybe I could drop you off in Carmel. How would that be for you?"

Anton accepted the offer, much relieved.

"See that barn over there? Two more trips around the field, and I'm done. Why don't I meet you over there?"

The tractor resumed its slow labors around the field. Anton waved his thanks and walked toward the barn. The grey and mottled hulk maintained an uneasy dignity while bowing longingly toward the ground. A pepper tree, green leafed and red berried, presided over the yard. At his approach, a flock of pigeons abandoned the berries on the ground and rushed with a whirling clatter to the barn roof. Splotches of white and grey on the aging shingles, they peeked at him from under their wings as if preparing for further flight. In the shade of the pepper tree Anton slung off his pack, removed his boots to cool his feet, and sat on a wooden crate to rest his weary muscles.

Eventually the tractor completed its slow wheeling around the hub of an oak tree and departed from the freshly manicured field. Outside the fence, the driver detached the discing tool from the chassis with a few powerful kicks and much wrenching, then drove the tractor into the barn, where the roar of its engine ceased. The man emerged and hauled the large door shut. Approaching Anton he appeared to be in his early thirties, with wearied eyes, thinning blond hair, and a stride that pushed against some invisible resistance. His clothes were spattered with dirt and grease from the day's work.[103]

"My name is Gene," he said, pulling off a work glove and offering his hand. "Why don't you come in for a moment?"

"Thank you. My name's Anton."

Behind the large barn was a smaller shed where Anton could see farm tools and outdoor racks for galvanized pipes, lumber and block and tackle. Two forty-gallon barrels, presumably containing wood-preserving oil, held a collection of eight-foot fence posts stacked upright like toothpicks. An old pickup truck was parked nearby. A large eucalyptus tree sheltered old farm equipment and a pile of stove wood under a tarpaulin. Across the barnyard lay Gene's house. A vegetable garden was laid out in front of the house. Inside a sturdy metal fence that kept whitetail deer from grazing, new shoots were beginning to show. A wisteria shrub heavy with purple blossoms clambered up the side of the house. The house itself was a weathered structure with a mossy roof and tongue-in-groove siding painted green at one time. On the porch a swing of aged and fog-mottled wooden slats hung from rusting chains. Dusty glass panes in the windows sagged and distorted the view to the inner room. The front door screen was rumpled and torn from careless use, and inside, the aging carpet completed the sense of ramshackle. The interior was less disordered than simply aged and bereft of any ornament. The overall sense was of dishevelment, dust, and disinterest. A large, featureless fireplace occupied one wall, before which sat a large couch and armchair with folded blankets and shawls. No pictures adorned the walls or low table in front of the hearth. The house contained an indefinable chill of sadness.

"Sorry about the mess," Gene said. "I rarely have visitors." Pointing to a side room, he added, "You can wash up in there. I need to change out of these clothes."

In the bathroom, Anton took a little longer than usual to wash the dirt from his neck, face, arms and hands. When he returned, Gene was already setting a fire. "Maybe you would like some dinner before we go?" he asked.

"I would be very grateful, if it is no trouble for you."

"No trouble. Let me get this fire going and I'll see what I can put together. It takes quite a blaze to lift the cold air that sits in the chimney." As he crumbled paper and laced together light kindling wood, Gene asked further, "You're traveling?"

"I'm a teacher on leave from my school," Anton said.

"What's your subject?"

"Literature. The classics. Ancient philosophy. I've been teaching college students for about twenty years."

"That's a far-away world." The laconic comment was immediately tempered with, "But I am familiar with it."

"Far away and strange," Anton agreed as he sat down on an overstuffed couch. "It's like living in a land of perpetual daylight."

"How odd," Gene said. "Who could stand to live in perpetual daylight?"

"You get used to it. For me while I was there, it felt like home. No, not really...Rather, it felt like the front porch of my true home. But about five months ago I got tired of sitting outside myself, and had to come in. Too much sun exposure is not good for you."

"You didn't know whether you were inside or out?" Gene queried further.

"I don't want to press the metaphor too far. I simply felt that I had been teetering on a threshold for years, for most of my adult life. I had been peering at reality from a great distance, but it had been so long since I had actually experienced it, I became afraid that what I thought was 'real' was nothing but hallucinations. All the patterns and relationships that I had lived with fell apart. There are no words for it: it's like the whole deck of cards was being reshuffled."

"Oh, the proverbial crisis."

"Yes, it was a crisis, but what's that? I sensed that my scene in the play had ended a long time before, only that no one had bothered to tell me. I felt like the fool who keeps swaggering about on the stage when the curtain is down. Even modern theater can't tolerate such stupidity. For tradition's sake and charity we put up with simpletons—ourselves and others—under academic robes and stoles. But when the clock strikes the hour, it is time to leave, and leave gracefully. The hour descended on me very hard and very fast, and I had to leave. I needed a break. I needed to break out. I certainly didn't need a sabbatical for more study and research."

During the discourse, Gene had stopped setting the kindling and firewood in the fireplace and gazed at Anton intently. "If you are alone in that world, that realm of perpetual daylight, it might be hard to know if you are crazy or not."

"Oh, I had plenty of people who insisted I was not crazy. The only thing is, we all lived together and had believed in the same conceits, and even then, no one could abide to hear about the images and ideas that were flooding me from a place well away from our enlightened institutions. I was suddenly deluged by the sense that I may have been living a lie, or maybe my earlier calling had become a false life while I was in a sleep state. First, it felt like I was being found out, but no one was acting differently toward me. Then, I started to listen to myself with other teachers, in the gym or at lunch or in faculty meetings. I asked myself, 'How in the world did I ever come to believe this?' Then, the weirdness spread downward, from my head to my heart, so to speak. I began to feel choked, smothered in unfreedom. As time went on—and I did not realize this until much later—I began to feel more and more lost. I was surrounded by people who seemed to know me better than I did. I felt like a stranger, like someone shipwrecked among intelligent aliens who expected some meaningful words or actions from me, but I didn't know what to do! To keep on going that way became impossible. Even my teaching was like eating sawdust, a precious kind of rhetoric. I would not have been able to convince myself that I was not a crank or a fool. When the old thinkers said that the happy person knows no regrets, I wonder if they knew that from experience or whether it just seemed like a reasonable thing to say.[104] I needed to know that for myself. At that point I knew I had to stop, to leave. The incongruity had become intolerable. Great minds and spirits had sacrificed their lives, their serenity, to live into their truth and to share it with others in their speaking and writing. Now all I was doing was doling it out in teaspoons, pre-masticated, to people who had paid enormous tuition sums to allow themselves to be force–fed with something they could hardly care about. My spirit took its revenge on me by turning my teaching into tired rote."

Anton paused to catch his breath. His words had spilled from his mouth. The silence of the day and the previous evening had been the preface to his utterance. Gene scratched a wooden match, which exploded with a brilliant blue flame, then settled into a bright, warm yellow. The flames crept in and out of the kindling, flickering and spreading. Sap boiled and popped, and soon the dark, chilly room was filled with warmth and light.

Gene arose and opened a large can of beef stew. To this he added fresh tomatoes, carrots and onions. "So how did you deal with this?" he asked.

"I began to travel," Anton said. "Some people leave for foreign countries to find their roots. I wasn't ready to look for my roots, like my ancestors or history or culture. I had to begin with myself. If 'wondering about your roots' is enough to get you started, so be it. For all I knew, I would be worse off if I found my roots! Jesus says something about that: you have to leave your family to find the truth about yourself. I needed to find myself, which, for all I knew, could be right down the street, or over the hills.

"This feels like my first journey in consciousness in a long time, Gene. Really, I began to live right where I was. And that changed my life. In five months I've traveled five hundred miles, no more." Anton shrugged and smiled wryly. "My hard shell of settled beliefs melted away, or was burned away. I've met a few demons. I've tasted food. I have felt sweat and its cooling on my face. The mystics talk about the plunge into ashes. I even got a bit of that as a bus boy in a kitchen. I sat with an old woman as she lay dying. I listened to stories and the colors on my canvas have begun to appear again, strong and bright, no longer grey on grey."

Occasionally while Anton spoke his host would stop and gaze intently at his guest. Anton finished his account of his travels, including the encounter with the mountain lion earlier that day. Gene moved between setting the low table before the fireplace and preparing dinner. He placed glasses of water and a loaf of bread on the table. The pot on the stove bubbled and sizzled and steamed. Within a few minutes Gene set two large bowls of stew on the table and the two men ate with relish.

When they finished, Anton said with a contented sigh, "That was delicious! 'My heart is sick with grief, yet my hunger insists that I shall eat and drink. It makes me forget all I have suffered and forces me to take my fill.'"[105]

"I take that as a compliment," Gene said.

"Homer. Odysseus in Alcinous' palace," Anton laughed. "But the comparison ends there. I told my story before dinner; he told his afterwards. So now it's your turn."

"A good story as dessert...I like that idea. Perhaps that is why I usually feel hungry after eating alone. But first, tell me what 'renewal,' as you call it, feels like. Having an appetite looks like a good sign."

"Well, to be honest, Gene, it's being able to *feel* again. The numbness is gone, just gone. It was a great discovery for me to learn that our thinking self is grounded in our stomach—the whole level of heart and gut. People in the East have it organized into chakras; I do not have that much insight, far from it, but I have a glimmer of understanding of what they are talking about. So, being renewed means being connected *within* myself again, from head to foot. My stomach weeping in joy; my heart petrified in fear; my mind shocked into simplicity...all this an awareness gained from living itself."

"That's what you mean by living right where you are," Gene said.

"There's more: it's trying to see consciously. To pay attention, not idly observing, but holding everything in a kind of tension. To accept what Einstein said from his experience: he complained that it took him two years to recover his imagination after completing his Ph.D! With imagination, he could see beneath the visible. His genius discovered a whole other dimension through the sheer force of his imagination. That's paying attention. For me, paying attention is being aware of both gifts and losses and celebrating and grieving. Whoever wrote the words in Ecclesiastes, 'There's a time to be born and a time to die,' was a completely renewed human being, in my opinion."

"So, where to now?"

"I'm not thinking much beyond Monterey. I know it sounds short-sighted, but I had a dream about the ocean not long ago, so I am heading there for a while. This is my year apart, it seems, and it's only March. A few days by the ocean would serve me well."

Quiet settled into the room as the burning logs settled and shifted on the grate. Gene leaned over and added a piece of dried oak wood. The embers glowed and sent sparks swirling around the fireplace and up the chimney.

"What about you, Gene? What brought you out here?"

Gene sat back in his chair. "It's a long story. But look, before we go any further, would you like to stay the night here? It's late, and I don't know of any place you can stay at the village."

"That's kind of you. Are you sure that I won't get in the way?" Anton replied.

"Not a bit. You can sleep there on the couch. Tomorrow we can go into town."

"Thank you. I do appreciate it."

"So, my story," Gene said. "I've been out here for about three years, no, four. It feels like forever. I actually don't own this place, but just live here as part of my pay. This may have been a homestead or farm of its own a long time ago, but now it's part of a spread that takes over a thousand acres on both sides of the highway through the valley. My job is to plow the fields and to bring tack up from Salinas and feed the horses. Then there's odd jobs like mending fences and painting, and doing what needs to be done. A kid from Carmel Village helps out a couple of days a week. I don't see the owner very often. He lives in Palo Alto, so we talk by telephone. And I see him when he brings people in to look at the horses."

"You are happy out here?" Anton ventured.

"What is happiness? That's like asking, 'What is truth?'[106]...I am settled, I guess." Gene was silent, then said abruptly, "Did I say that?

Has it come to this?..." Anton could see him painfully working over his thoughts.

"Anyhow, that's how I came here. Way back when, I was a student at the University of California in Santa Cruz. I was into the humanities, like you. The humanities are the voice of the homesick. Who but an incorrigible romantic would choose to be homesick all the time?"

"I hadn't made that connection before. Come to think of it, German has a couple of words for homesickness: *heimlichkeit, heimweh,* for 'home sorrow'," Anton offered.

"How can one study the humanities, no, feel their heartbeat, if all he has known is a comfortable home? In my case, in the beginning, I plunged into literature, not because I was particularly capable, but because I was abysmal in math and the sciences and bored with logical thinking. I never thought of my education in terms of employment. Engineering, business, computer science and all of that were absolutely foreign to me. Santa Cruz beckoned. I was to learn only later why this was so."

Gene paused a moment to think. "Santa Cruz. So much happened there. I had great teachers. One of them was an old man. He seemed old, but he was probably no more than sixty–five or so. I have vivid memories of him. He was an anthropologist, a student of comparative religions and cultures. He came to class in khakis and a *campesino* shirt and a couple of sheets of paper for notes. People began packing his auditorium for fifteen minutes before class, just to get a seat. They would even sit in the aisles. I heard about him and I went too, though I was not even enrolled in his class. I couldn't understand half of what he was talking about. He would come in, put on his microphone, and take us on a journey of wonder and fascination, to the very edges of love and death and art and archetype. He dredged so far beneath the surface, that ordinary life became like a mother lode fed by invisible veins disappearing into the depths."

As Anton listened he warmed to the pleasure of Gene's account, and he felt a strange mixture of nostalgia and awe.

"One time when the old man came in," Gene continued. "the room was packed as usual, and he went up to the blackboard and wrote about ten lines in classical Greek, Attic symbols and all. The room became more and more quiet. You could hear people breathing, then holding their breath. They were bursting, sick with question. This is it!, a new revelation from the Delphic Oracle! Then he turned around, and everybody leaned forward to hear the new dispensation. He said,

'Loosely translated it means, 'Does anyone have a quarter for a Coke?' The room exploded in laughter."

Anton laughed as well. "What better use for the classical languages than asking for a stimulating drink before a symposium? What else do you remember of him?"

"Well, if it was late in the term and you had survived the spiritual culture shock of the weeks before, you learned about 'the mystery of all civilizations,' as he called it.[107] He saved the best for last. What I remember him saying went something like this (I mulled over it time after time and still have a sense of how it went): 'In his *Geographia,* Strabo reports the saying of Hegesias, a contemporary of Pheidias, the mind behind the Parthenon:

> I behold the Acropolis; there is the symbol of the great trident in the Erechtheion; I see Eleusis and I am initiated into the sacred mysteries; I see the Leocorion and the Theseion. To describe all of this is beyond my power, for Attica is the chosen residence of the Gods, and the possession of heroes its progenitors.[108]

"Or words to that effect, Anton. The Athenian citizen (my teacher said) was only one voice among all the votaries during the succession of religious holidays in the ancient world. The Athenian was silent about the pink hue of the Eleusinian marble, or the solemnity and electric intensity of the processional chant, or the gravity of the ancestral rites presided over by the hierophant, the chief priest. He was silent about the dignity of the Areopagus which housed spirits benign and malevolent. The ancient Athenian says nothing about aesthetics or taste or the provenance of these works of art. What looms out of his statement, what's at the very heart of it, are the Gods and heroes and the sacred awe of his experience. Every intersection, threshold, structure, grove, and meadow had its myth, its claim on the sacred sources. In his very utterance you could hear the Athenian's ecstasy. His heart is so full he cannot, and dares not find adjectives to convey the elevation and abjectness of his soul.

"My old teacher then went on to say that this in–spiriting is the radiant core of all collective renewal. It's the restoration and future of any human life worth living. He reminded us that the so–called 'pagans' were originally the *pagani,* the simple people in the Etruscan countryside who tended the Penates like everyone else.[109] He impressed us with the durability of the ancient faith by referring to Ficino in Florence, the Platonist and garden lover. Ficino invoked the God Dionysios, believed by the ancient tragedians to be the agent of ecstasy when they broke free from the limits of natural intelligence and became one with the divine, if only for a moment. This possession let itself go in bacchic frenzy, which for some was orgiastic, and for others was creativity itself, language in its outer reaches, poetry and chant needing interpretation.

"My teacher would explain that the act of interpreting—especially his own teaching—is a sad step away from the real thing. He would compare what he was doing to what people do in church, where liturgy is at best an echo of the on-going prayer of the communal soul. Rather than batter our brains with interpretation, he said, we should make music. That is, when words fail, music begins. We must surrender our insane belief that words themselves can crush the grape against the palate! Only real wine, dancing, and music itself can convey the language of the heart.

"My teacher said that this was the crucial part. Like Pheidias' friend who is standing and looking, what is experienced in the heart of hearts cannot be uttered. The Eleusinian mysteries and all mysteries must not be revealed."

"How well I know," Anton interrupted. "Whatever is published is a long step away from the source of energy and life. What is published is as accessible to fools as to savants and *literati*. No author worth his salt would reveal his secret hopes for his readers' experience. That almost seems indecent."

"We have lost so much," Gene agreed. "The public space has become filled with noise and sentimental professions of faith and honest intention. Information and messages everywhere; a psychic onslaught. What Strabo and the old man were talking about was essentially esoteric, and we moderns are suspicious of the esoteric."

"They say that neither Jesus nor Socrates left any writings; I don't know if the same could be said of the Buddha; Mohammed did not claim his writings were from him, but rather through him. But they all talked. I would guess that public writing is inferior, less revealing than private speech; speeches are still inferior to poetry; music transcends even poetry; and divine silence crowns it all. I can see how you would find yourself out here in this quiet valley."

"The compliment is undeserved," Gene protested. "First and foremost we want to be touched by the divine, not by glossy substitutes and propaganda. The object of contemplation needs to be a worthy one."

"No 'Orgy–Porgys' as in Huxley's *Brave New World*," Anton chuckled.

"No: part of the horror of that book is its imitation of what we do routinely. I think Huxley was telling us the same thing as Strabo, but from another point of view. He calls the higher power 'Ford,' obviously a new–fangled phenomenon of mass consumption. True worship must recall something very old and tried–and–true. But I think your little hierarchy of communication is right. Watch people at worship and the way they gather around the altar. That's very public, isn't it?, and so very hushed. The silence deepens and the senses heighten; so rises the mystery. Few words. Listening, rather than reading. Stories, not lectures. And the stories that are told take people right back to the original experience. Worship is an invitation to ecstasy, along with the wine and firelight and smoke and music. All thoughts of the world are transformed; people's thinking becomes prayer and invocation; barriers between people dissolve, which is the experience of radical community; the maenads revel and dance with Dionysios; people sing, echoing the harmony of the spheres.[110] All of this, so my teacher liked to say, renews civilization, the inner core energy of human life and society. If we do not preserve it, but leave it shattered like the rubble of an ancient work of art, we might fall back into barbarism."

"You learned well, but don't seemed to have become a devoté," Anton said. "How does this play out in your own life?"

"That's a big question. I was impressed by how profound it sounded, without really understanding it." Gene put his arms high over his head to stretch and relieve the tension that had arisen during his account. "It went right over me. I thought that he meant that one had to go looking for the mystery 'out there,' and that it might be found in all the obvious places. I'm not the first one to make that mistake. In fact whole industries are built on it: tourism and travel agencies, fashion, catalog sales of foreign curios and artifacts, all of that. My first error was to think that I could encounter the mystery in books, you know, other people's stories and discoveries. That's the whole idea of the University, which is not such a bad thing.

"Then, during one of my college summers, I went to Europe to get closer to what I was seeking. I tended to rush in everything I did. Now that I think about it, I committed greater blunders than the people who claim to 'do Paris,' or 'do Rome' when they have a two–week trip. I remember going to Chartres, which seems to float on the plains of France like the Taj Mahal appears to float on water. It was one of those rare days when they had exposed the labyrinth laid into the cathedral floor hundreds of years ago. They should have known better than to expose it, my teacher would have said...In any event, I joined other people in walking along the slow, back and forth path. You know how it goes: straight from the outside right to the center, almost, but turning away at the last minute, throwing yourself out to the margin for a long spell, then winding closer and closer, and being thrown out again. 'I thought, how tedious!' I was having to wait behind other people, or turn sideways to let them pass. I got used to some faces, and even enjoyed walking alongside someone for a few minutes before she disappeared out of the circle. Next thing you know, I was walking with somebody who had that 'tourist smell' after a long day. A big, heavy woman kept stopping to pray with her eyes shut and I had to go around her. A child was grumpy and complaining to his mother. In the end, I just got impatient and stepped off the path and right to the center. No one seemed to mind. In fact, no one noticed, and nothing happened. I just sat there, my mind blank. I had skipped to the center and missed it by a mile. When I left, I didn't feel quite right, but continued my trip and soon forgot about it.

"I guess," Gene concluded in a tone of self–disparagement, "that I was no more than a moth circling around the crown of man's culture, leaving nothing, taking nothing. Underneath the patina of culture, I was just another grimy, globe–trotting Yahoo. I do my penance regularly when I shovel out the stalls here at the ranch."[111]

"We mete out our own justice, but there will be no end to it once we begin to condemn our own past myopia," Anton said compassionately.

"You're right. Reliving the pain is part of recalling the pleasure. I do remember such a moment of truth. It was clairvoyance. I was at the museum at Delphi, where I saw the archaic Charioteer, you know, the sculpture of the young man standing still and straight. He almost dangles the reins and looks out beyond the horses as though he is curious about the outcome of the race in which he competes. Utterly classic, utterly serene in the *agon*, the struggle. As I stared at him I felt bitterly my lack of capacity for art. It was not until much later that I recognized this demon of doubt is also an agent of truth, which the Charioteer helped me see. He was saying, 'Struggle, but stay loose! Hold the reins lightly, tread gently. Overcome your self–doubt or be unworthy of your task!'

"There must have been something there, because back in school I started to get focused. I was a liberal arts major, taking literature and history. I didn't think a lot about getting a job after college. I worked hard. In fact, I spent all my time with the books, and have to say that I took my friends for granted. What became of most of them? We are all scattered to the winds. I never got interested in politics, and never did anything radical, or took risks. I justified my privacy and lack of adventure by saying I always had homework to do.

"One day, early in my senior year, my teacher invited me to help create a garden downtown. He said it was a garden refuge for homeless people. He had been going through a terrific battle trying to get the city fathers to support it. But they finally gave in—or he wore them down—and they offered him a couple of acres outside of the main part of town. His idea was that homeless people would come there to work and grow their food, to get in touch with the elements and eat the food they had grown."

"A man after my own heart," Anton said.

"The garden would be their garden, and we were there to help lend a hand up, not a hand–out. A lot of people thought that this was the hair-brained idea of an unreconstructed 'flower–child.' Why, they said, look how the city has excellent social services! All we have to do is get people in the churches below the campus to give some vouchers and put up the transients in motels on Main Street. Then, the city fathers thought, get the vagrants out of town with a bus ticket to Oakland. Hah! The old teacher said that it was not about moving people through the system, but about 'digging in' and 'growing where you're planted'—literally. I was in the midst of classes and had tests and papers, and just didn't take up the invitation. It's pretty obvious that I had never made the connection between homeless people and my own studies in the humanities."[112]

"Most of us don't," Anton agreed, then paused. "So…you were on your own and seemed to know what you were doing."

"So it seemed," Gene said. He was silent for a moment. The fire had settled and the glow in the room had changed from orange to shady brindle.

"Wait a minute. I'm going to get some more wood." Gene rose. As he went out through the front door he said almost inaudibly, "Would that I could fetch for Miranda…"

It was I who saved his life, unprying him
From the spar he came floating here on, sole survivor
Of the wreck Zeus made of his streamlined ship.
I loved him, I took care of him, I even told him
I would make him immortal and ageless all of his days.[113]

> The nymph Calypso in Homer,
> *Odyssey* V.130-135

How with this rage shall beauty hold a plea,
Whose action is no stronger than a flower?

> William Shakespeare,
> *Sonnet 65*[114]

Calypso's Mantle

IN A MOMENT Gene was back with an armload of firewood. He pulled back the fire screen and placed two pieces on the hot coals and settled in the armchair again.

"'Miranda'?" Anton asked.

"The woman of Shakespeare's *Tempest*. She gave Ferdinand a reason to live and strive. He carried wood at her father's behest to prove himself worthy of her. She had such feeling for him that she wanted to carry it herself. The very idea caused him great pain. Their love was amazement itself."[115]

"Do you have a Miranda?"

Gene's mood darkened. A long silence settled in the room. Anton pulled a shawl from the arm of the couch and wrapped it around his shoulders. Its light yellow, green and blue pastels seemed incongruous with the other worn and rugged features of the room. He felt Gene's eyes on him.

"I did, once. That shawl is about all I have left from that time," he said.

"Is this okay?" Anton asked, fearing that he might have inadvertently presumed on the good will of his host.

"Of course," Gene responded with a slight tremor in his cheeks. After another pause, he continued, "How do I talk about this? Funny how it is with strangers, you know, fellow travelers on a night passage." He sighed and looked into the fireplace. "Tonight we have sparks to look at, however…

"I was telling you about that time of my life, early in my senior year at the University. There had been a woman in our college from my first year. To be honest with you, Anton, she had that kind of beauty that overwhelms a man. I had never in my life seen such concentrated, healthy, feminine vitality in any woman, and it only grew during her years at school. She had lovely auburn locks, with deep brown and red tints, and brown eyes, and a stunning figure—which she did not flaunt. Yes, she could have launched a thousand ships, but I doubt she would have let that happen, because she was so un–self–absorbed.[116]

"The only time we saw her was during the noon hour when we all gathered in the college quadrangle. Try to imagine this: We had planters and gardens all around, with roses and iris and lilac blooming and ivy growing up the sides of the buildings.[117] The perfume from the flowers drifted along the patio and under the arch of the library, which contained the pleasures of the mind as much as the patio released the pleasures of the senses. There were redwoods between the dormitories, green–tipped in spring and heavy with those beautiful little cones later in the year, and aspen and alder and a few wild madrone. The birds loved the spaces, especially the robins and jays and swallows who flew about the trees, looking for food for their nests. Seagulls came up from the ocean and strode around on the lawns. Monarch butterflies and ladybugs and moths flitted among the leaves. Even the ground was stirring with sow bugs and worms and little beetles!

"At the entrance of the patio we had a trellis with grapevines that ran riot and reached from building to building and hung down. It became heavy with grapes later in the summer. A fountain flowed in the center of our patio, too, so we could hear water music all day long. Young people spent long hours of spring and summer languor in this Elysian place.

"When this woman came through the trellis and onto the patio from time to time, my God!, everything turned on her presence! My friends and I would just sigh so deep and try not to stare as she strode through the courtyard. Oh, we all wished that she would pause awhile. None of us had the temerity to speak to her. After eating lunch or just sitting in the sun, she would disappear, going off to her classes, I guess. We didn't really know. We didn't even know her name, and it did not occur to any of us to ask what her name was.

"I will never forget the day she actually sat nearby and smiled at me. She sat close enough for me to smell the fragrance of her clothing. I overheard her talking to a friend. She said something like 'at the fountain's sliding foot/ Or at some fruit–tree's mossy root,/ Casting the body's vest aside,/ My soul into the boughs does glide.'[118] Heavens, Anton! I thought I was going to give way! Then she went on to read a poem that pleased her. I learned it later and committed it to memory."

"Can you remember it now?" Anton asked.

"Oh, yes, forever. Listen. She said –

Once in the forest
I strolled content,
To look for nothing
My sole intent.

I saw a flower,
Shaded and shy,
Shining like starlight,
Bright as an eye.

I went to pluck it.
Gently it said:
Must I be broken,
Wilt and be dead?

Then Whole I dug it
Out of the loam
And to my garden
Carried it home.

There to replant it
Where no wind blows.
More bright than ever
It blooms and grows.[119]

"Listening to her I was transported to a seventh heaven!" Gene sighed again, and his eyes and face gleamed with emotion. "We called her 'The Aphrodite,' an expression of high esteem from us,— unlettered youth that we were. Wherever Aphrodite appears there is spontaneous laughter, joyousness, 'cheer,' as they call it in the old literature. Yet around this person I felt something austere…yet liberated, sacred and mysterious. She stirred up verses and dithyrambs in me, the messages of divine beings.[120] I wanted to listen to music more and more, and discovered Elgar's *Enigma Variations*. She was perfect, and perfectly unattainable. No: unrelatable, outside our conscious will, beyond reach of any mortal association. I hope you know what I am talking about."

"I think I do," Anton said. "Some people evoke such feelings of awe that you want to flee."

Gene's effort to regain his composure was visible on his face and posture. He stood for a moment to warm himself by the fire, then, rubbing the backs of his legs to spread the warmth, he continued,

"As it turned out, I loved to body surf. After a day in the books, I would hop on my bike and ride down the hill and along the coast to a beach where the waves were up. I would then go for a forty–five minute run on the sand to get really warm, because the water at Santa Cruz is so cold and I didn't have a body suit. If you didn't do this, you would turn pink in ten minutes and it would take an hour to get over the shakes when you got out. All of this exercise made me exceedingly fit and I was not afraid of the surf.

"This time in the early fall the waves were really good at Pleasure Point near Capitola, probably about five feet high, which was challenging for me, near my limit. I did my warm–up run, put on my fins and was out in the water. The cold was sharp, but no more than skin deep because I was so heated up inside. For about twenty minutes the waves were fairly good, but they were growing, and I noticed a strong undercurrent. That is where my judgment left me. I should have come in. I didn't. I went out again. What happened in the next fifteen minutes I'll never forget. The waves kept getting larger and larger, and pulling the water back out relentlessly. I was swept off my feet time after time and was thrashed by the breakers and was losing my ability to resist. I was afraid to take a wave because they had lost their form and were dropping straight down and I did not want to crash on the sand. So time after time I had to dive down, holding my breath for thirty seconds, forty seconds sometimes, while the waves thundered overhead and I had to power–kick to keep my hands on the sea floor.

"I knew that I was getting too cold, and had to make a decision to take a large wave in, or not come in at all. So, I caught a big one, perhaps eight or ten feet high, and rode down its face and into the foam. I felt like a gnat on the back of tiger. The wave threw me down and for the next five minutes I had to fight with everything I had to get in. I made it to the shore, and lay in the water where the waves played themselves out. I was freezing, too cold even to shake, completely exhausted, and could not even get up from the sand.

"Then I saw a shadow appear beside me, and felt a large towel cover my back. I looked up. It was her, 'the woman beyond all names.' My mind was numb; I was too cold even to feel surprise. She led me up to the warm sand, where I lay down on a large blanket and she covered me with another towel. 'Don't try to talk,' she said. I couldn't have if I had tried. For the next thirty minutes I went through trembling, shaking, and changing from blue to white, then pink. Finally I was warm enough to get goose–bumps.

"When I would not embarrass myself with my own teeth chattering, I thanked her, and told her my name. She told me her name was Callie, and that she knew me from the college, and had noticed me in my distress.[121] That is how I met her. She may not have saved my life, but she lifted me up in my weakness. She tended me like a survivor from a shipwreck, Anton, and transformed forever the way I understand what a woman is.

"I remember her suit was pink and very, very becoming. There were no other people around. To this day, I don't remember what we talked about. All I remember is our being together, feeling the sunshine, seeing the sand on her tanned arms and the white salt on her eyelashes. I remember the warmth all around and inside and out, and my head inches from hers as we talked. The hour was sublime.

"Over the next year we became very close. I stayed the course with my studies, not really looking beyond college very much. How could I, when the world was complete with her in my life? Callie was an art major. She began to introduce me to art history, and I shared my favorite authors. Who can resist sharing poetry with someone you love? We went to the local symphony and to college plays, sometimes just for walks. Anywhere with her was everywhere. I began writing prodigiously, poems and stories gushing up from my imagination, filling my journals. She always had that effect on me, Anton, the magic of Miranda."

Gene paused, and looked at his watch. "How are you holding up? I realize it has been getting late. I haven't spoken of these memories for a long time."

"Just fine. Go on," Anton responded.

"Well, I didn't realize at the time that this year, my last year in college, was the happiest year of my life. I was so in love with Callie. Our love was sealed, and in the spring I took her home to meet my parents. They became very fond of her. And I met her mom and pop and sister. They lived in San Diego. We had only been together for seven months, but it could have been seven years or seven days. And so we began that wondrous, sobering dreaming about what marriage might be like after we graduated.

"One day, coming back home from her folks' home in San Diego, Callie developed a cough. It started light, but became a rib–cracking cough that really worried us. She was up all night and we went to a doctor the next day in Santa Cruz. She had a slight fever, but no pneumonia as far as the doctor could tell. He took a blood test, and that is where he got worried. Her immunity was way down. We went home and I took her to the University clinic, and stayed with her. When she was sleeping I tried to do my homework. For now it was my turn to take care of her. She kept up this deep cough and got sicker and sicker. After another day, the University doctor called her parents, and they both came up by airplane that afternoon. We all took her back to town and to a respiratory specialist, who had her put immediately into the hospital in town.

"Anton, it turned out that Callie had lymphoma. Where this came from was a total mystery. Suddenly, the world stopped. Everything stopped. Nothing was important to us except Callie, and what happened in her hospital room. The word got back to the University, and friends started showing up. They were anxious, helpless, but they came. It made no sense: Callie, so wholesome, so lovely, so vibrant with her vivacious spirit and auburn hair, now weak, bed-bound, withdrawn. I sat up with her parents on the second night at the hospital and listened to the oncologist lay out our options. An intensive care nurse and a chaplain joined us.

"The one option not available to us was wishing it away. You know how it is: during a crisis your mind freezes and you do not hear or remember what people are saying, certainly not doctors talking about life–and–death alternatives. The chaplain must have known that, because after the doctor left, she stayed and asked us, 'What have you heard? What do you think your choices are?' That must have helped us focus, because Callie's parents said, 'We must not give up. We must do whatever it takes. Every arrow in our quiver.' The sad truth is, we did not have the faintest understanding of what this meant. The nurse did, and maybe the chaplain did.

"We returned to Callie's room. She could hardly talk. We just held her and kissed her and explained that she would need emergency surgery and therapy for the cancer. The nurse told her that she would not be uncomfortable, and that someone would always be with her. How right she was about that!

"The next six weeks went by in an absolute blur, Anton. Callie came through lung surgery, but she remained on a ventilator day after day, unconscious and sedated. The chemotherapy was the strongest they could give someone of her size and age. She was watched around the clock in intensive care, with either her mother or father or me in the room. I overheard a doctor say, 'This is too hard. I am glad she is not my patient.' But the nurses never said anything like that, and just kept coming in, massaging her in her sleep, talking to her, telling her how beautiful and loved she was, even as her auburn hair gave away and her skin began to turn dark from the chemotherapy.

"Sometimes I would come late at night and play some music she liked. The chaplain came by too, and sat with me and talked when I wanted to. Early on I collapsed once, but she just sat quietly next to me until I felt better. There was none of that theological claptrap about 'God giving you no more than you can bear,' 'God's will,' miracles, and so on."

"Maybe, Gene, that sort of talk is meant to spare people from some kind of fall into madness."

"Dammit, Anton, I was so full of guilt anyway! What right did I have to leave her tottering alone down some road to death? Those bed–side words! Saccharine at best, or at worst, little brushes of tar that smear the soul when it needs to be clear. I felt like we were killing her with every medical arrow at our disposal. I never even had a chance to be with her alone before she went under anesthesia!

"As the days passed, I knew somehow that my Callie was not going to make it. The numbers just slid down, down. She became so tiny and frail in bed, like air was holding up the sheet. She never awoke. Then, one night at about two in the morning, I was sleeping in the waiting room when her mother and father came and got me. 'It's time, Gene,' they said. We entered Callie's room. The same chaplain joined us again; the nurses on the floor must have called her. Callie was so quiet. We put our hands on her head and cheek and said, 'We love you, Callie...' Then she was gone. Her parents cried a long time. I did too, with my face in the sheets of her bed. The chaplain sat on the floor with her arm around Callie's sister's shoulders.

"At Callie's funeral at the University chapel late in the afternoon a few days later it seemed like the whole college came. There were nurses and respiratory therapists from the hospital and her doctors. The words on the program said it all: *Others Discovered their Beauty in the Light of Her Consciousness.* Her parents knew that she had many friends at the college, and brought pictures and photos from her life. The chaplain spoke briefly, saying that Callie had been surrounded by grace, and that the whole hospital grieved with her friends and family. She also read from Wordsworth's *Tintern Abbey,* which stays in my memory forever –

It is a beauteous Evening, calm and free;
The holy time is quiet as a Nun
Breathless with adoration; the broad sun
Is sinking down in its tranquility;
The gentleness of heaven broods o'er the Sea;
Listen! The mighty Being is awake
And doth with his eternal motion make
A sound like thunder, —everlastingly.
Dear Child! dear Girl! That walkest with me here,
If thou appear untouched by solemn thought,
Thy nature is not therefore less divine:
Thou liest in Abraham's bosom all the year;
And worshipp'st at the Temple's inner shrine,
God being with thee when we know it not.

"When they showed pictures of Callie at school in the garden patio, with the fountain and the trellis, with her sparkle and smile, I just collapsed in my seat and sobbed and sobbed. I remember many hands touching me on the back and shoulders as people came by. They knew and understood. Then I felt someone put something soft under my head: it was Callie's grandmother and the shawl that she had been knitting for our first child. That is what you have on your shoulders now, Anton." Gene's final, halting words broke apart in his grief. His lips closed, trembling, ravaged by the old sorrow. A long quiet settled in the room.

Gene went on to explain that he never felt a sense of direction after Callie's death. He graduated and left school to live with his family for a few months, then returned to Santa Cruz to find work. At night he retreated to the cold sand outside the Boardwalk; from there he could watch the roller coaster and hear the rush of its wheels rising and falling in their tracks like the surf behind him. In all of this he allowed the awful grittiness of his despair to scour his broken heart. Nor could he bear to visit his college on the hill: when he tried to walk onto the ivied patio he felt like he was swimming in molasses and the place was dangerous with pain. He found work on a landscaping crew for the homes on the outskirts of town and lived in a barn behind the home of an Episcopal vicar.

"That's how I got here about five years ago, in a roundabout way. I put the wind to my heels and drifted away. I learned about this place and wanted to get away from the city, so came down here and found this job. First I just painted the barns and repaired fences, and that grew into overseeing the operation of the ranch. Such has been my existence, once full, then empty, now simply secluded, out in this valley with little more than horses and books for my own Lares and Penates.

"That was what it was like to love her, Anton. I loved her so deeply that I have not been turned by the sight of a woman for all these years. Like the poet said, I remain –

> Forlorn! The very word is like a bell
> To toll me back from thee to my sole self.
> Was it a vision, or a waking dream?
> Fled is that music: Do I wake or sleep?[122]

"Now Callie's life is reserved for my dreams alone. I deal with my ache in tilling the fields or carrying hay to the horses."

"Have you tried writing?" Anton asked. "There may be some release in that, some balm."

"I once sent a couple of poems up to a writers' journal in Santa Cruz, where they were published. Juvenilia and nothing more.[123] Since then, nothing really. All dried up. I live alone out here, spending time with the horses. I have really become quite fond of them, and call them my 'Houyhnhnms,' after the intelligent and graceful animals in Swift's *Gulliver's Travels*.[124] I take care of the fields and go up to Salinas every week to buy oats or hardware. Monterey is another matter...so close to the ocean and its memories. I hike up into the back country every now and then, along the Chupines."

The conversation grew quiet as the embers of the fires deepened into red–black. Anton's mind turned back to his troubling dream in the Bakersfield hospital.

"You're not alone in your grief, Gene. She grieves, too."

"Do you think so?" Gene said with surprise. "I had never considered that."

"We can only wonder. I sense that death cannot break our strongest bonds. I once knew an old woman in the Valley who walked through death, freed from life to greet the brother she had missed for a long time."

The silence that had long blanketed the fields and forests pervaded the indoors and Gene's lonely living space.

"I am mindful of what you said about words that smear," Anton said. "I guess all I can say is that some things in life completely define what we should do."

"My time with Callie taught me what was really important. I wanted to hold onto it more than anything, but I could not. That is what is so awful: we will never be able to hold securely what we most want. I will always feel powerfully connected to her. My question is, what would she want for me now?"

"Always the best for your life, Gene. She laid her mantle over your shoulders and helped you build the vessel of your life's journey...[125] By loving her you learned how to weep. And you have felt the anguish of homesickness."

"So true."

"Now, what gift do you have that she was so drawn to? She loved you! What is that deep beauty that will always be at the core of your life's happiness?"

"I am wondering about that, too, Anton…Thank you for letting me tell you my story. I feel very tired, but peaceful, strangely enough. Good night. Sleep well."

Was this the face that launched a thousand ships?
And burnt the topless towers of Ilium?
Sweet Helen, make me immortal with a kiss.
Her lips seek forth my soul; see where it flies!—
Come Helen, come, give me my soul again.[126]

>Christopher Marlowe (1564–1593),
>*Dr. Faustus*

GIVE ME MY SOUL AGAIN

DAYBREAK DAWNED COOL AND MISTY like the day before. Overhead, the sky was brilliant and clear, while coming through the wooded meadows the colors blended together in the dark greens, browns and greys of an early country morning. From his couch by the fireplace Anton awoke from warm sleep and forgotten dreams feeling deeply refreshed. His mind was as clear as if he had just plunged into the Chupines Creek where it emerges from the winter springs.

In the kitchen Gene was preparing a breakfast of thick pancakes and bacon. After breakfast and with coffee mugs in hand, the two men went outside and sat on the steps of the old house. The conversation resumed, drifting thoughtfully now after the deluge of the night before.

"I have never told the story of Callie completely to anyone, Anton. It was very hard work. Am I wrong to hold on to her in this way?"

"I heard the story as an act of love and service to her. I cannot imagine crossing that river of fire and ice on my own. It took courage to tell it."

"Funny thing: I had a remarkable dream last night. I awoke very early and thought about it, then went back to sleep."

"Do you feel like sharing it?"

"I can try. The first part was very vague. I was with animals, cattle maybe, or llamas. One of the ranchers down the valley raises alpaca. I had to trim them or groom them or something. They were very resistant and would not stand still. I remember thinking, 'For all your bright eyes and big ears, you are really very stubborn and not very smart. This must be what happens from being kept in a corral all the time.'[127]

"I went inside the barn to get some rope to tie them, I think. When I came out, the animals were standing stock–still, staring toward the forest. Then they bolted and disappeared. I looked in the same direction. There stood a mountain lion near the fence. Your story last night must have given me that thought. The lion was not looking after the alpaca; he was looking at me. He then turned, and walked back into the trees. Unlike you, I followed him. I could see his tracks, but not him. He had disappeared. I went a ways inside the woods, but still in view of the house. When I looked back I saw a little boy on my porch. The sun was rising and haloed him with a beam of light. He began to sing, and his little voice grew to a crescendo like an orchestral chorus. The sound was scintillating, fresh, full like a gust of an ocean breeze. The wind in his voice caught the leaves on the ground and lifted them up. They swirled around me and were carried back into the trees. The leaves joined the branches and stayed in the trees, Anton! It was eerie, awe–inspiring. I started back. Then I awoke."[128]

Anton found himself strangely moved by the account with its enduring archetypes. "The child image, the Holy Child. Not, if I might say, the weary, older man I met yesterday. What were your feelings as you saw this? Were you afraid of the lion?"

"No, I never would have followed him if he were frightening."

"Clearly not a Job–like dream," Anton mused.[129] "You did not quall before the passing of a wraith. I was thinking for a moment of those awful, baleful dreams in the *Zarathustra,* where animals cry out in loneliness. Your lion was healthy, not limping or mangy?"

"No, far from it," Gene said. "He was strong and sure. I had feelings of sadness in watching him. He never came close. He was always walking away from me. It gave me the kind of feeling you have when you send someone a love letter and hope for something in return but never receive one. It also felt good to be free of the pack animals."

"Hmmm." Anton thought for a moment. "Those animals carry loads and they flee lions. Alpacas are smarter than we give them credit. They know that no lion will sit down with them. He would rather stand and rule them. But you do not flee the lion; you follow him. In ordinary, waking reality, that would be foolish; but not in a dream where we are instructed to become foolish. Then, instead of seeing the lion up close, you see a child.[130] Do you often dream like this, Gene?"

"Not often. This dream was different than anything I can remember."

"Well, beware!" Anton laughed. "You are pulling the plug on the wine barrel of your unconsciousness. It's a great fermenting vat down there that intoxicates and seethes with raw life that expands with explosive powers. For good reason, wine barrels are held together with iron straps. Whatever it means, the message of dream will come to you, if you are willing to listen."

After breakfast was finished, Gene told Anton that he needed to feed the horses, then turn them out to the larger corral. He would then take Anton to the village in Carmel Valley while he continued onto Monterey as he had planned the day before. Anton offered to help, but Gene explained that he liked to be alone with the horses in the morning, and had an old habit of holding conversation with them.

While Gene was gone, Anton stepped outside onto the porch and looked at the young garden still covered with morning dew and laced with spider webs. Ladybugs were already crawling slowly on the leaves of corn, tomatoes and squash. The wire netting on poles for fending off hungry deer appeared intact. Anton set off on a walk around the freshly turned field where he had met Gene the day before.

When he returned from walking around the field, Anton saw that Gene had already returned. Entering the kitchen, he said, "Gene, I have been thinking. I think my days with the Norton are over. I would like to let go of it, and go with you all the way to Monterey. Maybe I will find work there."

"You are just going to leave your motorcycle out there?"

"You can have it if you want, or tell somebody about it, and they can go find it on the road outside Tularcitos Ranch."

"You sure?" Gene asked.

"Sure enough. The man who sold her to me felt like he was losing a sweetheart. It's landed me into a good conversation, but I don't want to tempt my fate. For him selling his motorcycle was a spiritual event. For me, it is a breakdown waiting to happen. I'm ready to let go of it. I'll get around on foot or find an old bicycle." Anton gave directions to the resting place of the Norton as well as his memory of the obscure night allowed.

The two men set out in Gene's pickup truck. It was a rugged old Dodge, older than both of them, with collapsed seat springs and no creature comforts. The whine of the transmission became annoying over thirty-five miles per hour, so Gene drove slowly. Cows and an occasional solitary bull dotted the fields, over which hawks soared effortlessly in their search for prey. From time to time Gene would slow to look at horses cantering around training rinks or standing still like expensive statuary. "How could anything that beautiful be natural?" he mused at one point.

"I've been thinking about what we talked about at breakfast," Anton said. "Where do we learn the matters of the heart? Our parents? Life? Why are its lessons so hard? Does our culture have any competence at all in these matters?"

"Life in agriculture is like a refuge from popular culture," Gene said. "I think that human beings are attuned to beauty like the compass points to the North Pole. But what with everyone being guided by movies and TV, is it any wonder that we have no way to talk about it? Culture is supposed to fine tune us. There are subtleties in good and bad, right and wrong, you know. TV bludgeons us with everything trite and infantilizing. Movies fan your feelings just long enough to get you to the next commercial blitz. It is so unreal! The real language of the heart is the most subtle of voices. Even after Callie's voice has been silenced, I will hear her whispers my whole life."

"Looking at my life," Anton concurred, "someone might say that I learned to mouth the words, but never mastered the language. The language of the heart began in the wrong place, in my mind, in my reading and reflection, not in life experience itself. And from what you say, Gene, and from how you have lived with Callie especially, it is clear that the language can be learned only by surrendering to a heartfelt relationship of love."

"You said the right word," Gene agreed. "'Surrendering yourself.' Offering yourself. A living sacrifice. That means it could be a heart–breaking, painful affair…Now, you won't mind if I say something that sounds offensive, will you, Anton? I mean no offense."

"Please speak freely, my host."

"Don't people in your position deceive themselves into believing that if they can speak and write about these things, they are being authentic? Look how the intellectuals set themselves up as the barometers of taste and guardians of public morals. Who asked them to make the rules?"

"I don't think that it is that simple, Gene. The intellectuals for the most part are people of incredible passion. Like everybody they want to make a better world, yet they know that the better world already exists. They want to tell people about that and to suggest ways to create a harmony between this world and that."

"But then again, Anton, the people with no agenda, the real lovers, don't have a mania for social organizing and don't care all that much about appearances. The valley has taught me that the show of propriety is empty. It only makes me appear more ridiculous to myself. But in what I just said, I was not only offensive, I was unfair and ungenerous. Your reading and teaching must have exposed you to cases of genuine love."

"Of course, but the point seems to be that to learn the language of the heart, one must have lived it. Only then can you entrust it to literature. I have that on Goethe's authority."

"Give me an example," Gene urged.

"Let me think a minute." Anton looked out the window at the passing fields and stands of oaks. "Well, here we are: Faust is a case in point. He is never far from my thoughts. He is a man guided by his fancies. What happens in his real life places him on the knife edge. There he balances between salvation or perdition. Look how he behaves toward Helen.[131] First, the centaur Chiron brings Helen in on his back! In Homer Chiron is the one who revealed Achilles' humanity and fate to him. It takes a *chimera*, a freak of nature to do so! So, Chiron reveals Faust's mixed nature to him, his humanity and animality. When Faust sees Helen he experiences the full force of his *eros:* he grows faint with desire for her, and calls her the fairest of feminine beauty. Now Chiron tries to caution him—careful, careful!—telling him that true loveliness is not found in features. But Faust is so possessed with his fantasies that he practically grovels for the meeting with Helen. May Heaven spare you such madness! And me, too!"

"And spare the women, too! Oh, Heaven help us!" Gene groaned. "Faust sounds almost adolescent to me, a case of thwarted development! Pity the women who crossed his path…"

"They don't seem to share our dual nature, do they, Gene? But only a woman may speak for herself in these matters, and even then I know we men will be at a loss. Still, it is a teachable moment for Faust. Chiron tries to tell him that Helen is a creature of myth. She is bound to deceive him. As a creation of poetic imagination she comes into view ever young; she never ages; she always keeps her alluring shape, and she will even be courted by men in their old age."

"What's so bad about that?" Gene objected.

"Sounds like Chiron needs to work with you too, Gene!" Anton laughed. "Chiron says that Faust's mind appears unhinged, so he offers to take him to Manto, daughter of the father of all doctors, Asclepius. Manto is a Sybil, a wise woman who knows therapeutic roots and herbs. She believes she can cure him.[132] Faust rejects that as well. He believes that if he is cured of his ruling passion, he will be like other creatures, dragging himself around in the dirt of practicality. He wants to live in his poetic imagination and ideas. Life itself is the only kind of therapy, radical or otherwise, that will bring Faust to his eventual apotheosis."

"Well, is Manto right about curing him? You should know by now, after everything you have seen."

"I would probably welcome her magic, because I am far less intelligent than Faust, and much less dangerous," Anton jested. "And don't pass the buck! That's for you to say, too! We have both shoveled plenty of dirt, haven't we? It's not that bad. Where has practicality gotten you? For some, it could be feeding the horses; in your case, they fed you...In any event, Manto is charmed by Faust's passion. She says that she cherishes those who crave what is beyond their reach. Does this mean that some women—the Manto's of this world—can be demonically possessed with longing for the beautiful as well?"

"What do you mean, 'demonic'?" Gene asked. "Does that mean possessed by evil?"

"No, demonic simply means divine power or influence. The good influences, when all congealed in one continuous experience, is *eudaimonia,* which, incidentally, was the Greek word for happiness. Why not think of happiness, our greatest good, as something divine?"

"But 'possessed'?"

"There are unhealthy influences, we surely know: *cacodaimonia,* the Greeks called them. If you could be conscious of them, there is some chance that you could avoid being possessed, fully occupied by them. They were not necessarily evil, as much as unhealthy. Satan—who, by the way was a Persian concept brought into Judaism but not into Hellenism—congeals all imaginable bad influences with cosmic repercussions. He still belongs in the royal court of Yahweh. You can see that he holds place in the heavenly court, at least in the Hebrew Book of Job. In Goethe's *Faust* the demon Mephistopheles appears to be a synthesis of the great Tempter of Judaism, and the *daimon* of Greece. He has great intelligence, wit and sense of humor. He even seems able to learn and grow in personality."

"Sorry I got you off the subject. So what does Faust do next?"

"He goes down, way down. He descends into the world of Neolithic religion, which seems to hold the hidden roots of the modern mind, and he comes to the surface again in dialogue with pre-Socratic philosophers. Are your eyes glazing over, Gene? Sorry to be so long–winded: I get lost in these thoughts and forget someone is trying to listen to me. What's the point of all this? In asking to encounter Helen, the archetype of beauty, Faust surrenders to spiritual chaos. So, confronting the craziness of his feelings prepares him for his eventual meeting with her. I think that Goethe is telling us that life teaches the soul, and that feelings are the soul's truth made conscious to the mind."

"This is starting to make some sense," Gene said.

"Faust is a soul at risk. Marlow and Goethe and even Thomas Mann try to show us that the consequences of his actions have permanent effect. That is, they are universal feelings and impulses. He is forever seizing on this or that power or person. No self–restraint, poor fellow! He is willing to go beyond space and time to claim Helen. He refuses to experience the tragedy of his truth, the limits placed of his human nature. He is like Hamlet in some ways, willing to wallow in untruth for his misguided love. Oedipus goes at life in exactly the opposite way: he would sacrifice his love, even his own life, for his truth. Not Faust. He would change his nature, sacrifice the innocent blood of Gretchen,— anything, to achieve an impossible dream. When he grasps Helen herself, she disappears in a blaze of light! Can you imagine Faust's pain? It is indescribable. It is the price he pays for his rapacity. He asked for the deeper knowledge offered by experience, and he got it! Goethe's teaching seems clear enough: to crave complete knowledge is to strike a bargain with the devil. To lay claim to beauty is a demonic act. If this applies to knowledge and beauty, I suppose it could apply to anything. The very act of *claiming anything* may be demonic." As he said these words, Anton's felt a growing sense of astonishment sharpened with a vicarious sorrow for the pathos of masculine striving.

"But I asked you about self–sacrificing love, not claiming and seizing and all of that." Gene's words brought Anton back to the conversation at hand. "What I want to know is whether human beings can endure living with beauty and goodness?"

"The love of beauty is not for the meek of heart. 'For they too shall have their rewards.'"

"But, answer me this, Traveler: can you live with the tension, maybe even transform it into something sublime?"

"That's the question!" Anton replied. "When I think about Goethe, I also have to think about Charlotte Von Stein. Theirs was a powerful, enduring love outside the context of marriage, and completely human. Charlotte, when she first met Goethe, who was famous throughout the continent, thought him an arrogant rake, cocky and proud. While she was not particularly striking in appearance, so they say, she exercised a powerful magic over him, and he rushed into love for her. Early on, he was outrageous, stormy, out of control. Eventually she acknowledged him as well. Goethe and Charlotte became soul–mates. And their marriages remained intact. They corresponded and carried on a dialogue for ten years and wrote hundreds of letters. Unfortunately, I believe hers to him are lost. But his letters show vulnerability, adoration even, and passionate longing for her presence. Their intimacy was most soulful. How the relationship ended, I have no idea. But it is clear that Charlotte filled a part of Goethe's soul that was for her alone. He never could have created the Helen or Gretchen figures without empathy for the feminine soul. Experience alone would have given him that."

Gene was infected with the argument. "So, where's the torment? It all seems proper enough."

"Who can know?" Anton replied. "The Psalmist says, 'Only God knows the hearts of a human being.' Then, you probably already know the case of Regina Olson and Sorën Kierkegaard. You would have to look long and hard for a more complex soul than Kierkegaard's. For Sorën, Regina embodied a fundamental choice: the married, ethical life or the religious quest. Because Regina was so desirable, and because he was so charged with his calling to theology, I think he held himself in contempt for his love for her.[133] In his writings he talks about the 'aesthete' who would love only the 'lovable' one, meaning attractive, winsome, educated, and the like—someone like Regina. But Kierkegaard felt that the Christ, who loved the soul beneath the darksome exterior, or even beneath the beautiful exterior, had abolished this posturing as a form of vanity, as Christ shows by never grasping or swooning away around the beautiful and gifted. I think that this is what Regina's very *being* did in Kierkegaard: it stirred up a kind of religious psychosis of longing. I don't think that the love of God came as naturally to him as the love and attraction to her. In denying his longings for Regina, he spent his life trying to persuade himself that the God of Love had the greater claim. How can one resolve such a dilemma on this side of the grave?"

"That seems inhuman!" Gene interrupted in a shocked tone. "If all people felt like that, it would announce the end of the human race in one generation!"

"You're right, Gene. I wonder how many men present themselves as scoundrels for this reason alone: to give a woman no better excuse to dismiss them so that they, the man that is, can pursue what they think is a nobler course, a higher love—which may be a deeper delusion nonetheless! And the converse: to detach so as to uncomplicate the life of the beloved woman to allow her to pursue her greater work? Oh, the irony and confusion of it all! What man really knows what a truly noble calling is?...But none of these stories really applies to you. Your relationship with Callie was completely natural, so full of grace. You found your fulfillment in her. The stories I have told you are confusing because they involve spiritual hunger, the need for intimacy, the eternal attraction of beauty, the fences and boundaries of our *mores,* and so on. These cross currents flow back and forth and jumble up our lives. Some people just chalk it up as aberrations of the masculine psyche. I don't think so. Even the adamantine refusal to follow the longings of one's own heart may be the fair sacrifice to the claims of the soul. We need to be careful when we honor the heart and counsel others to follow it. The passions of the heart may drown out the quieter voice of the soul...That seems to be what Kierkegaard was trying to attend to."

"But Kierkegaard couldn't have it both ways? Marriage with growth in his spirit?"

"He didn't think so," Anton said. "Within Danish culture, the married life looked simply bourgeois to him. And the religious life meant combat with the complacency of the church. I think that this is crucial: Kierkegaard was a spiritual warrior, to the very end. In fact, a pitched battle between his followers and opponents almost erupted as he was being buried. He did not believe he could have it both ways."

"How did Regina get through all of this?" Gene asked.

"She was truly enthralled with him. All was very proper, of course, in Copenhagen in the 1840's, but their passion was obvious to them and their families. When Kierkegaard began to hear his calling as a commandment—you know, the call to theological studies—she fought his leaving like a tiger, so he wrote in his *Journal.* The only way he pulled it off was to appear like a scoundrel for a while, frequenting the taverns just long enough to create a scandal, then going home alone to collapse in his grief. He wanted Regina to feel right about rejecting him in order to spare her grief. He loved her! He did not want her to suffer. I doubt if he was successful. The whole thing made no sense to him, so it became the paradigm for the spiritual life: you have to choose, almost blindly, willfully."

"Listen to you! As old Chaucer said, 'It must encumber your wits to have thoughts about all these good women.'"[134]

The comment took Anton by surprise. "I guess that it does sound rather odd," he said. "as though these people existed only to create legends about themselves. Maybe that's all that's left in the best of cases. It has to be a very good thing to even hold onto one lesson from the life of another person. In Kierkegaard's case, it was the idea of 'the leap of faith.' Regina later let it be known that even if she couldn't take that leap and instead needed to marry a prosperous Danish civil servant, she still suffered a great deal. She kept Kierkegaard at the center of her heart for the rest of her days."

"What does that mean, the 'leap of faith'? I hear people use it all the time. They give a little consoling smile when they say that. It's like those other clichés that buzzed around me like flies for weeks after Callie died."

"I see it as a leap into the soul's solitude," Anton said. "It is like being invited or *compelled* to go to the top of a tower, being given a trapeze, then being told to swing. And you are not trained for such a thing, and may be old and sick or grieving some huge loss. And you are told, 'When you get to the highest point, you have to let go. Someone will catch you. In mid–air. And oh, by the way, there's no safety net.' That, Gene, would be a leap of faith."

Silence ensued. "This throws a whole other light on the personal sacrifice for one's calling," Gene said. "The cost can become infinite."

"So true!" Anton answered emphatically. "Do you know the story of the Bull of Phalaris?"

"No, I don't," Gene replied.

"Well, it speaks to this. In matters of the heart, there are no innocent by–standers. Kierkegaard tells the story in the *Philosophical Fragments.* Apparently there was a poet in Phalaris whose words were so musical and winsome that all the people were flocking to him and not staying busy nor paying respect to the tyrant of the city. So the tyrant had the poet entombed in a brass bull, which he placed over a fire. As the heat increased, the poet's screams were piped through the bull's mouth. But, Kierkegaard tells us, even then the dying poet's cries and groans sounded like mellifluous and entrancing music."

Anton could see the furrow in Gene's brow and the tight grip of his hands on the old steering wheel. A couple of slow miles passed in silence.

"Have I disturbed you?" Anton asked.

"Yes, you have…But in a good way…I am wondering how I could offer honor and tribute to my lost love, to really claim the heights my life achieved during that time, and admit to the banalities since that time. I plow my field over and over. Yet I continue to have eyes for beauty. Everything we have said is but a breath away from my reverence for the beautiful and its enchanting forms in word and idea and verse. But…" and here Gene's words came in a rush, "What I have been afraid of, is feeling the pain of the fire–music, of uttering the words of my passion…of heaving my heart into my mouth. When that happens it utters inarticulate sounds of grief and longing for what I can scarcely conceive."

"Better to throw everything to the winds than hoard anything in your heart," Anton said. "Remember Zorba the Greek: 'To have a passion, to amass pieces of gold, and suddenly to conquer one's passion and throw the treasure to the winds.'[135] This is your fate, is it not? If you don't embrace it, it will chase you all the way to Carmel Valley and even to your grave. Even this idyllic place contains the shadows of death."

Anton was astonished at his own boldness. Still, his own situation troubled him more deeply. Had he not responded to Gene's question about the authentic life by telling stories from the literary tradition? More than anything, did not these stories impale him on his own need and poverty of desire? And so his boldness was tempered by a wistfulness that penetrated to his deepest heart.

Sometimes I go about pitying myself, and all the time I am being carried on great winds across the sky.

Chippawa–Ojibway saying

God breathes out and we live. God breathes in and we go home.

Mechtilde of Magdeburg

Wind, sea and song

The conversation waned as Anton and Gene continued their drive down the valley with its meadows rippling with blue wildflowers. Gradually forest and dell surrendered their dominion to houses and small businesses and traffic. The valley road merged into the Cabrillo Highway, which carried them along the gentle curves and hills rising above the coast. The traveler and the recluse were lost in their thoughts and spoke little.

Monterey appeared at last, looking in the distance like a handful of river rock tossed on the edge of the pool of the Pacific. The ocean waters curved in lapis lazuli from the black line of the horizon, became an undulating turquoise nearer the seashore, and unraveled in the fine grey and white lace of coastal breakers. Where the waves had been the solemn statesmen in procession across the broad ocean, at the shore they became impatient athletes, jostling, sprinting, and flinging sheens of fine sea–salt hair behind them. Toward the north the coastline curved away and disappeared in the blue grey of sea and sand. A forested hill with a lighthouse rose on the south side of the city. Compared to the ocean in its wilds, the city appeared tiny, minute, a marooned settlement on a small clod of earth, a tiny and frail village of sandcastles holding out briefly against the tides.

Gene stopped the truck on Del Monte Street near the Embarcadero on the waterfront, and turned off the engine. As they opened the doors, the rush of ocean sound filled their ears. Wind, waves and sand collided, melded and moaned. The smell of saltwater and seaweed assaulted their noses. Breezes whipped up their shirts and hair. Above the foaming, blowing fleece, gulls teetered and tipped and spied down for the sparkle of fish scales beneath the surface. In the distance came the clanking of rope and tackle on the masts of sailing vessels and pleasure craft. Still further beyond the jetty that protected the marina they could hear the chortle and bark of harbor seals mixing in with the pounding of surf.

After satisfying their hunger with a basket of fish and chips they parted company, Gene to buy groceries and hardware, and Anton to explore the area for work opportunities. Along the way toward Fisherman's Wharf, Anton could almost see the dirt roads of the old Pacific capital leading up to Steinbeck's *Tortilla Flat*. The emaciated warehouses stood as relics of the day when the sardine catch was strong and the canneries thrived. The warm sun smiled memories of *hetaera* winsome and wise in the ways of the world, strolling in sleepy disarray in the early morning hours. Here and there stood rundown shops where the indolent and capering *nouveau riche* of the Big Gold Bonanza had bought provisions for their resort homes along the coast. Sturdy baskets once used by abalone divers now held cascading blooms of spring impatiens. Even the narrow strand along the waterline seemed to wait for the shades of fishermen to stretch out their nets or to rest from their labors.[136]

Here and there sturdy Latino men waited for day jobs. Approaching two men in restaurant aprons standing outside a ocean–front restaurant on the municipal dock, Anton asked, "Know any fisherman looking for a helper?"

They inspected him for a moment, then consulted one another. "What about old Ramón? I know his shoulders and knees hurt him these days. I heard him asking around for someone with some strength in his back for some kind of lifting job."[137]

"Maybe so…," the other said, gesturing toward the long pier. "Go on out and ask for Ramón. He is one of those out there."

The old man sat fishing near the end of the wharf, his long and bruised pole hanging motionless over the edge. Although advancing in years, he was still burly shouldered and thick in neck. He wore dungarees bleached from salt water and dyed with fish blood and entrails; his hair was salt–and–pepper grey under a baseball cap.

"So, you want to work? Can you lift?" he asked after Anton's inquiry.

Anton held out his hands, palms up. Their calluses and etchings spoke the language of the fields. "I can lift. But I don't know anything about fishing. I need someone to take me out there." He pointed to the open ocean.

Ramón hesitated, chewing the inside of his cheek. He looked down at his tackle box, then again at Anton as if trying to resolve some unknown quandary. "Ok, I could use some help. I am going out into the bay tomorrow. But no pay: we share what we catch. Maybe you come with me to Salinas this afternoon. Are you ready now?" Ramón wound in his line, threw the remains of the fish bait to the eager gulls, and walked slowly up the wharf. As he walked, bowing and rocking, he seemed to Anton to be another substantial shadow, a living afterglow of a people long dispersed.

"Here's my truck. Hop in." Ramón's truck was shot–through with salt rust. It sat against the curb where the old man could jump–start it if necessary. As they rolled down the hill it creaked in every joint and fitting. Anton explained that he needed to say goodbye to a friend. They found Gene sitting at a park table near the waterfront. He was looking out over the ocean breakers as they played their sonorous scales on the sand. He sighed and brushed off his pants. His eyes were downcast, his face bleak. Anton introduced him to Ramón.

"It's been a long time since I have been here," Gene said. "It brings back memories…So, you found work. That's good. I need to get back to bring in the horses. How can I stay in touch with you?"

Anton asked Ramón if he had a telephone; he did not, but said something about "the cathedral office," and gave Gene a telephone number.

"Alright," Gene concluded. "Here's my number. Call me if you need anything. I might come back to town in a few days to see how it goes." Then he was gone.

Ramón kept his truck in the slow lane on Highway 68 leading east to Salinas, twenty miles inland through the hills bordering Carmel Valley on the north side. He spoke little, but simply gazed up the road with the weathered eyes of the aged Latino, the whites of which had become as brown as his skin. They pulled up on the gravel driveway of a large nursery and drove slowly alongside an array of pots and bowls and displays of outdoor fountains and rockwork. Ramón stopped next to a large, dusty shed that housed an indoor kiln made of red brick.

With help from nursery workers they carefully wheeled out a large, thick and shallow bowl, freshly fired, four feet in diameter, and loaded it into the back of the truck. The edges and underside of the bowl was smooth and glistening from newly fired glaze, while the inside still showed bits of clay and uneven surfaces and veins ramifying across the surface. They packed and padded their cargo with gunnysacks. Money changed hands, and soon they were on the road back to Monterey.

As they descended off the shoreline hills, a bank of distant clouds lying on the horizon held the sun like a shrouded candle. Ramón invited Anton to sleep on a cot in his simple abode. "You won't mind the sounds of the sea all night? But first, dinner and rest."

"Do we leave the bowl in the truck?" Anton asked.

"Yes, it will be safe. We'll deliver it in a couple of days. Tomorrow we take the bus up to my boat at Moss Landing. We fish in the bay on the way back. You may come along."

Ramón's home was a storage room in an ancient warehouse built onto the wharf. A bed with a sleeping bag lay along the far side of his room. Ramón dragged a cot from underneath the bed and assembled it. An old stove with an oven and four tarnished burners sat along one wall; hoses connecting to an outdoor propane tank disappeared into the wall. Above the stove was strung a clothesline that held a drying denim shirt and long cotton underwear. A small refrigerator with a freezer, a table made from plywood and pallets and two–by–fours, a food cabinet, and a couple of beach chairs completed the furnishings. A small bathroom was built behind a half–wall in the corner. The overall effect was one of safety and coziness. Windows and walls offered shelter from all the elements save sound. Around and beneath them the warehouse on its sunken pilings quaked, creaked and groaned like a wooden trawler run aground on the shoals.

Ramón put vegetables and soup in a pan and lit the stove with a match. When the soup was heated he poured it into metal bowls and set one before Anton. Whole wheat bread and a bottle of beer completed the dinner. Slowly chewing his food, Ramón spoke little, other than to say, "No fog tonight. But weather comes in tomorrow."

After dinner, the two men walked down to the end of the pier with its warped boards and pilings smeared with tar and bird guano. Isolated figures, bundled against the approaching chill, stood along the edge with their fishing lines and tackle boxes. Gulls sailed above in tranquility, looking for bits of bait that had fallen from the hook. But for the continuous thundering of the breakers on the sand and rocks near the edge of the bay, no discordant sound reached their ears. Ramón leaned on one of the pilings and looked out at the sunset. He then lowered his head. During the long moment Anton marveled that though he had lived near the Pacific for years, its presence had only begun to claim him since the sighting at the summit of the Carmel Valley; only now was its meaning becoming revealed. He felt it coming alive through the old man at his side. Ramón seemed as solid as an old piling, durable as earth and water, and yet as free as the pelicans that cruised above the waves. After a while, they returned to the warehouse home. Anton retired to his rest with a spirit of wonder about the new day to come.

The small port of Moss Landing lies an hour's bus ride north from Monterey, a spot on the map north of the sprawling gunnery ranges of Fort Ord, and just south of the broad Salinas plain. Many travelers no doubt pass by the Landing without even noticing it, their eyes being drawn to the large cooling towers of the electrical utility as they strike their promethean pose above Elkhorn Slough. But for a few impoverished tourist shops along Highway 1, Moss Landing belongs to the fishermen. During the ride Ramón said nothing at all. At one point Anton asked him what was on his mind, to which came the laconic reply, "Only the fish."

Descending from the bus and crossing over the one–lane bridge onto the land spit around the harbor, they were surrounded on all sides by the tools and trade of ocean fishing. Anton pulled his jacket close and turned up his collar against the gathering wind. Fog hung heavily, pressing the briny, fishy reek close to the ground. Sunk in the mud near the edge of the harbor, rusting carcasses of once–confident boats made a silent witness to the fate of ships that had survived the seas, only to be forsaken by their human crew. Between warehouses forklifts pitched and yawed on their narrow axles and raced to and fro with the raucous monotone of their diesel engines. The quick machines picked up and tilted and slammed enormous metal boxes that had recently carried the ocean harvest from the fishing trawlers back to the landing. A forest of masts and poles and ropes and stanchions darkened the skyline. Alongside the largest ships lying in the oily ooze of the harbor shoreline, regiments of seagulls strutted and craned their necks for remnants of fish that were brushed and hosed off the boat decks above.

"There's my boat." Ramón pointed down to the row of sea craft below. "Wait here while I get some bait and ice." He disappeared into a small fisherman's shop.

Looking at the tightly packed boats Anton settled his hopes on a forty foot vessel with clean lines, radio and radar antenna, and an air of prowess for deep trawling. Ramón returned with a twenty–five pound bag of ice on his shoulder and a butcher–paper package of herring and anchovy bait in his free hand. When they reached the bottom of the ramp to the boat slips Anton was about to make an admiring comment about the muscled yacht lying beside them when Ramón surprised him with, "Here, help me take off the tarp."

Anton was made speechless at what lay before him. He had not even noticed the small boat nestled between the larger ships, as insignificant as a remora fish hanging off the side of a blue whale. He complied with an uncertain hand. The tarp removed, Ramón's craft was revealed as a sixteen–foot open shell, fiberglass on wood, vintage 1950 ski boat. Its once blue trim had faded to a washed–out turquoise. The dented steering wheel and scratched windshield, the bulky Evinrude motor, the rusting fittings and chipped paint all seemed to protest the boat's durability. A quick inspection showed that it contained three five–gallon gas tanks, life preservers, rain gear, some sturdy fishing poles, paddles, tackle, a net and gaffe, and an ice chest.

"Small boat," was all Anton managed to say.

"Huh, you worried? She's big enough for my fish. She's made this crossing many times." Ramón proceeded to stow the tarp under the bow. "I store her here at Moss Landing during the stormy season. The shore catch back at Monterey gets me through the winter. Today, we make the first trip of the new spring. Today, we go out for the First Salmon! He is waiting for us. I'm only sorry I didn't do a sweat yesterday."[138] As for himself, Anton held only vestiges of the dream in the valley that had prepared him for his arrival at the ocean and this embarking.

The wind had quickened in the eucalyptus trees and flags and sails on the boats lying in the harbor had begun to snap. "Come. We must go," the old fisherman said. "Last night's clouds means wind today. Untie the stern."

As he stooped to unwind the stern line, Anton noticed the words *En–stum Nyoom–neeng–on* painted across the transom.[139]

"What does this mean?"

"'Little Storm' in the old language. As long as the little storm in my motor continues, we can ride out the big storm. Come along, we need to go."

Ramón hefted the gas tanks to confirm they were full, and shook the contents to mix the oil and gasoline. Then he stood straight and still in the boat, and raised and lowered his hands toward the four points of the compass and the four winds. This rite concluded, he took his seat at the wheel and turned the ignition. The engine ground over a few times, then popped into life. As they motored out of the secure neighborhood of the harbor, Anton could see sandpipers darting back and forth and burrowing for tiny crabs in the wet sand. Further out, where the breakers rose along the quay, pelicans sailed in regal dignity, nicking the tips of their wings on the foamy crests. By now the little boat was rising and falling, steering a course of southwest on the simple compass, its engine strong and purposeful.

"How far out do we go, Ramón?"

"About three miles. Then we drop our line and go slow. How are you feeling?"

"Good enough, as long as I can see the land."

"Here, pull this slicker on. You look back. I look forward. You'll get used to it."

As he propped himself with his knees on the back of the seat, Anton asked above the roar of the motor, "What about your people, Ramón? Do they come from around here?"

"Everywhere, it seems. My grandfather was Tolowa from northern California, one of the last ones. He died in the Thirties, when I was about ten. His wife was a Mexican, but I never knew her. He married outside his tribe because so many women had been killed during the Rogue River Wars."[140]

"What about your own parents?"

"Their daughter, my mother, married an Irishman. His ancestors came here during the potato famine. You remember all the rumors of gold. They may have found some, but mostly they found useless glitter and breakdown. Many ended up in the sardine canneries of Monterey. That's what happened to my Irish grandfather, and my papa followed right along. When he met my mother it did not matter that she was *mestizo* because she had great heart. And she didn't mind that he smelled like the cannery. There was always work in the cannery. The machines thrash the fish, and the smell is like a smoke signal: it says, 'There's work in the factory.' That's all there is: work. People worked 18 or 24 hours a day. My papa died when a conveyor belt thrashed him. That was shortly after I was born. I never knew him."

"That's terrible! How sad for your mother...and for you too, not to know your own dad."

"Oh, true. My mother said my papa never liked the sea. It was like he had inherited bad memories of the ocean crossing from Ireland. The cannery was tolerable and paid some money. My mother kept a picture of him in our little house in Seaside where I grew up. It was a black and white picture, but his eyes seemed blue. That's what my mother said of him. But all that is long ago."

"Do you have your own family?"

"No wife, no children. I had a sister, Eva, but she's gone. Now I only have my niece. Only she carries my family memory. We had hoped otherwise, but it is not to be so..." His voice trailed off.

"I haven't heard of the Tolowa," Anton said.[141]

"They lived all along the northern California coast, especially near the river mouths. That's where the salmon ran, and were they ever strong and thick! You could almost walk on them. My people had redwood houses, and their ways didn't change for many ages."

"Where are they now?"

"The last of them was almost wiped out by the white settlers in Oregon in the 1800s. The survivors were marched off to camps. They forgot who they were, and forgot their stories."

"This is hard to imagine, Ramón."

"Our memory is almost wiped clean. You know, when a people dies, they take more than just their artifacts with them. They take the songs and the gestures, the how–to of things: how to fish, how to purify and preserve food, how to settle quarrels, how to find a wife. Everything important. Maybe because my father died when I was a little boy I never learned how to find a wife. It's another thing still to know how to keep her."

"What do you remember about your grandfather?"

"A great deal. I never go anywhere without my grandfather. With him I belong to the whole Tolowa people. He had a boat, a clinker–built with a good motor. He used to take me out in the bay to fish when I was little. He would let his trolling line go down deep, where the big fish lives. After a long wait he would say, 'The bait is tasty, but the big one does not feel like nibbling today. But when he does, I will pull gently.' Today, Anton, with so many fish dying with only explosions and factory noises around them, I ask myself why I am fishing every time I let down my line."

By now they were far out in the open ocean. One moment they were surrounded on all sides by heaving waves, then they were riding high with the sea spray and could see the land behind and the unbroken miles of the ocean before them.

"Did your people always fish this far out?"

"Oh, no. They didn't have to. They began to come out here when the white man showed up. *Dios mío,* we had to go no further than the breakers to bring in all the salmon smelt we could scoop up, sometimes forty or fifty pounds at a time! They were so thick they would make the white waves turn black, and shimmering, too, from their shiny skins. The fish was everything, the center of our lives. We also went harpoon fishing at night, and used a torch on an A-frame to show the fish swimming along the bottom or stopping for a rest during their return home.

"My grandfather also taught me the Tolowa code of the sea," Ramón continued. "Learning it out here with the waves licking at your boat like a huge and hungry being, it has power! I can teach a little of it to you, Anton. He said, 'Child, never point at the sea. You don't point at people; don't point at the sea. Nod your head toward the ocean. A small offering from small beings, we Tolowa, that is.' He made me understand that the ocean is a mystery that deepens all the way down, where things and forces move around that we will never comprehend. You are beginning to know that now, aren't you, Anton? 'You may bring up its fish, but do not play in it,' my grandfather said. 'It will not play with you. It will ignore you, welcome you, or take your life, like that, and all in the same minute,'" and Ramón clapped his hands three times.

The sound of the claps overcame the rumble of the waves for an instant, cut through the whipping wind and was gone. It seemed like a summons, an invocation to the fish below to rise from the deep silence of the depths to the swirl and grumble of the surface. What witchery of man and sea and fish would complete this invocation was far beyond Anton's ken as he rode on the waves with his stolid companion. For the next hour the ocean carried them with its tranquil *gravitas,* waves surging in imponderable strength and speaking in the short gasps of surface turbulence. The little boat moved in respectful concord with the irresistible forces below, its engine lowering in register as it pushed up the front of a wave, then rising as it descended down the back slope.

After an hour of steady chugging Ramón throttled back on the motor. The fog had completely disappeared, but had been replaced by heavy clouds and the stormy chop of the sea. The coastline had become invisible. They were now out in the boundless pelagic where the deeps sustain human trials of audacity and courage, and yet swallow up vanity and arrogance as nothing more than spume on the breaking point of a wave.

"Here, Anton, you steer. Stay lined up with the current." Ramón turned to his fishing pole, baited his line with fresh herring, and cast it out into the wake of the boat. "We'll see who is waiting down there."

"How do you know when to start your lines?" Anton asked.

"I don't know. The fish knows."

Mystified, Anton pressed further. "Is it your skill, your experience that tells you?"

"Skill isn't important. *You* don't have any, and yet you wanted to be out here. The big-shot scientists at the marine lab might say that it's good fishing out here because of the deep, cold water down below; and they count a lot to prove their point. But they miss the point. You will never see them fishing out here, not in a boat hardly bigger than a canoe...No, it's not skill. I have been thinking about the First Salmon for weeks. Just this fish, not me; no plan, no stake out, or anything like that. The more you have to think about what you do and what you bring, the further you are from what your deepest heart wants. I fish. That is what I do. That means I *think* about him. (At this Ramón's eyes began to blaze and his voice grew stronger still as he spoke in the old way.) I put a little bait on my line. His *whole being* is a lure. What word would the fish have for catching human beings? Our fishing and hunting songs speak those words for them. Fogs hide. Waves are what the water does. The sky catches the waves and carries them up and brings them to the land on the wind. We are all like the waves of this sea or sky, here for second, powerful, alive; yet only to disappear, to be swallowed up in what we came from. Now, watch your heading...we are shipping in water."

Anton corrected his course into the on-coming waves and baled out water that had gathered against the ribs of the boat. Ramón wedged the base of the pole against the floor and seat and held it firmly with both hands while letting the line run free. Minutes passed. The engine throbbed on amidst the battening of waves on the boat's sides.

"You see, Anton, we mustn't think that we are doing this for ourselves, for we're not alone."

Anton sent him an inquiring look.

"My grandfather and his Tolowa ancestors are with us, as much as I am with you. They now offer us every memory of their own days along the Klamath and on the Rogue, and in the open ocean. They are invisible to us because they are too many to see. Even if we forget them—which is most sad, especially in old age—they are still with us. They're with us even if we don't believe in them! In either case, forgetting them is like losing the rudder off your boat: she'll still float, but will never make it to the shore in one piece. Without memory and her stories, we just drift here and there until we are smashed. Then all the little trinkets and ballast that fills up our lives and makes us sluggish in the wind will go straight to the bottom. If we do our work and tell our stories, we carry out our ancestors' dreams. My father couldn't carry out the dream, because he died on the machine in the sardine factory. My mother's dreams were carried out by her daughter, my sister; and her daughter after her. So, our ancestors' hands are on the wheel with you, Anton, and my grandfather's are on the pole with me now, whether we make it home tonight or not. They untied the rope with you, and will tie up the rope again tonight, if they wish."

"You hardly know me at all, Ramón, but I venture from what you say that perhaps it was my ancestors who pulled up my anchor and brought me here."

"They've walked the whole path with you, my wandering man. I hope that you will see this. Then you will have discovered the meaning of life...But here, now, I feel his tug." Ramón's pole had suddenly arched and the muscles in his neck deepened against the strain. "Slow your speed more. Let him decide. He needs to be sure...he needs to want this."

Heavy with waiting, calm amid the lifting and rolling of the ocean, time passed. The fish below assented. He swallowed the bait whole, and felt the tearing of the hook into his gullet. Ramón pulled and wound, bowed and dipped and strained backward again and again. As the pain in his shoulders grew and stabbed like fire, he turned the pole over to Anton in order to rest; Anton pulled and wound the line as well. The line drew in, bringing the three creatures together. Now the men could see the flashing, writhing body of the three–foot salmon rising to the surface. With Anton on the line, Ramón reached for his net and his gaffe. Anton noticed that the old fisherman had donned a headband of bleached white shells strung on a red leather cord. He began to sing in a strong and rhythmic voice. When the great fish was within reach, Ramón swooped under him with the net. His voice rose above the waves. The wind, the sound of the voice, the flapping of the fish barely beneath the surface came to a climax as Ramón looked the fish directly in the eye, then plunged in the gaffe. Thus, without experiencing the terror of suffocation, the fish met his death. He was brought on board, where the light in his eye dimmed and was extinguished.

"What is he?" Anton asked between deep, panting breaths.

"Chinook," the old man responded, his face calm and radiant. "Look at the black spots on his back and tail fin and the black line along his gum. See the hooked nose? That makes him a male. He's a big and healthy one, 20 or 25 pounds, I think. Maybe five years old...Think of it, Anton, five years in the open ocean. Don't we do right in honoring him?"[142]

On his knees in the tossing boat Ramón placed the paddles across the seats, laid the noble fish upon them, and cleaned him. "A stormy day for our first catch, no? Oh, my friend, we have here an immortal being who willingly gave himself to us for our food. If he was pleased with my song and my greeting, his spirit will return to the sea and encourage other fish to offer themselves to the people. My grandfather said this is the way we receive a good harvest, and we could make it through the winter. Even now the animal can withdraw the favor, so we do not mistreat or harm him. When we get back home we will eat a little bit, and smoke his flesh, and take it to the altar. When my people was together as one, the rich man of the community did this for everyone. Now, I will do it for my people wherever they are. Tomorrow we will take it to the altar of the great man Jesus who was both fish and fisherman. Come now, let's go home."

For the next two hours the little boat *En–stum Nyoom–neeng–on* plied the teeming waves. Ramón changed the heading to a more southerly direction. Anton rested, and felt more at home even in the freak waves and gusts of the blustery afternoon. With the motion of the waves and the current the boat was pushed steadily towards the shore, so the seaman changed his heading again to a more southwesterly direction. On one occasion he asked Anton to steer for him again. Taking the old man's steadying hand, Anton felt the strong pulse, the salt water and life–blood of so many atavistic memories, sorrows and loves, so small and voiceless amidst the torrent of ocean; yet ever resolved, the engine of the old man's confidence and strength.

In time an eerie and regular sound came to them, first as a whisper, then as descending bass notes that grew in carrying power. It was the air horn at the end of the jetty outside the Monterey harbor. Giving the end of the jetty a wide berth, they skirted the waves as they ended their regal Pacific journey and hurled off their green and blue vesture against the rocky barrier. Now they could hear the barking of sea lions—"ocean deer," Ramón called them fondly—and then they could see the city and its wharves and bustle of commerce. Soon they had moored the small boat, bailed out the last of the seawater and cleaned and rinsed their tools and nets. The ground now heaving strangely, for Anton at least, they walked back up the wharf toward Ramón's home. Along the way they stopped for more ice at a fish shop, packed it around the salmon in the ice chest, then carried the chest between them. Once inside, Ramón said, "We eat dinner. Spaghetti. Then we prepare the salmon for smoking. Tomorrow we take it fresh to the priest and the people."

After dinner, Ramón told Anton to rest on his cot while he prepared the salmon. "I learned this recipe from my sister. She worked it out well. She said it pleased the fish who had no idea that he could taste so good. Tomorrow you will tell me what you think." First Ramón prepared a thick solution of salt, sugar and water, which he stirred vigorously for several minutes. He then pulled a bottle of rum from the cabinet and poured in a quick stream, added a squirt of lemon juice, diced a garlic, shook in some black pepper and added fresh bay leaves. This he stirred again, then flowed over several filets of fish lying in a glass dish. He wrapped the remainder in wax paper, covered it with ice, and placed it back in the ice chest.

"We are now done."

"A good day, Ramón," Anton said as he settled back.

"A very good day," the old man said with a contented sigh. "I can take the final sinking anytime for one good day on the open sea. We remember this as we welcome our dreams now." Then they slept.

With your beautiful eyes, I see a gentle light
My blind ones could never see;
On your feet, I bear a burden my lame ones could never bear.
With your wings, I fly though featherless;
By your mind I am lifted ever upward;
At your whim, I pale or blush,
Cold in the sun, warm in the cold of winter.
In your desire alone is my desire;
My thoughts are forged in your heart,
My words are breathed in your breath.
Alone, I am like the moon, itself alone;
Our eyes can see it in the heavens only as the sun enlightens it.

>   Michelangelo Buonarroti (1475–1564),
>   *Veggio co' be vostr'occhi*[143]

For a great awe of the divine stops the voice.

>   *The Homeric Hymn to Demeter*[144]

My Thoughts Are Forged in Your Heart

When Anton arose in the morning he found that Ramón had already been up for an hour. The fisherman had rinsed the brine off the salmon, and had prepared a low, smoldering fire in an outside smoking oven. Over the next two hours Ramón added hickory and alder chips, and thus completed the preparations for their offering. By the early afternoon the smoked salmon had cooled. They tasted a morsel and found the fish to be inexpressibly fresh and tasty. Ramón then wrapped it in fresh paper. When Anton asked how much he would keep for himself, Ramón responded, "Not much. The old ways tell me. I bring in the first catch. That makes me the rich man of the tribe. In the old days that was a very big thing, more important than having piles of little things. The rich man is the law–maker and law–keeper. If someone had tried to steal or cheat the rich man of his fish, even with a cut an inch too wide, he would have fought him to the last breath. He still gives most of it away to the village. Since I am a rich man, I give most of it away now." He then said, "Come. We go up to the cathedral."

As they walked up the bluff of Camino El Estero, Anton could see the lighthouse at the top of the hill and the hardy live oaks and the pine trees swathed with moss. Turning for a broadened view of the ocean, he was struck by how the land diminished before the blue grandeur that bathed even the sky. The waters are our true *terra firma,* he thought. At the lip of the ocean the land surrenders under its relentless onslaught; the rocky rubble of the shore dispels any sense of permanence.

From where they stood, Anton could also see the campanile of the San Carlos Borromeo Cathedral. Walking up Fremont Street and turning left on Church Street, they approached the small mission church. Ramón parted for a moment to take his offering to the rectory nearby. Although modeled on the Spanish patterns of Castile and Madrid, the Monterey cathedral felt proportioned to the human individual. It did not make a grand political statement, casting long shadows over the city. Nor did it feel like an anachronism in the city whose spirit was elsewhere. Rather it was balanced, small enough for intimacy, large enough to contain the wisdom of its tradition. It conveyed strength and endurance in its adobe walls along with an air of vitality and growth embodied in the planters of blooming lavender, rock rose, and Mexican sage.

When Ramón returned from the rectory, Anton held open one of the heavy entrance doors to allow his companion to enter before him. He then stepped across the threshold. As the door closed, the sound of the ocean rushed away as if pinched off behind thick wooden lips. Once out of the sunshine and ebullient air they were engulfed in the still darkness of the inner sanctuary.

As Ramón walked ahead, Anton paused to allow his eyes to adjust to the darkness. He could see several seated figures ahead of him. A bank of votive candles huddled in a small chapel on the far left side of the altar. Walking down the center aisle, Anton settled near his companion. He could feel the river stone of the small cross given to him by Gustavo pressing against his thigh. The old man next to him stirred, then descended into his own interior communion.

Although centuries old in every aspect of its brick walls and flaking plaster, Spanish tile floor and thick–beamed ceiling, the interior space of the church looked alive in the present. Leaded glass windows allowed a quiet light into the room. The altar was bare of all settings and at eye level with the seated worshippers. Chairs behind the altar awaited the choir. Above, a central crucifix on the wall was draped in the purple of Lent. A tabernacle candle in red glass and bronze flickered dimly in a corner, signifying the presence of the Eucharist that had been reserved for the sick and homebound. Ficas and other plants softened the corners. Two large stands on either side of the altar held rose bushes which cascaded to the floor in small, pink blooms. Anton remembered that Palm Sunday and the beginning of Holy Week was two days away. "Easter always comes." Gustavo's parting words seemed at home here. Anton's senses quieted as his gaze rested on the altar. Inhaling deeply, he filled his lungs with the sweet and tangy scent of centuries of incense, sweat and seaweed. Time flowed on in deepening silence.

Out of the corner of his eye he noticed a small movement. Twenty feet away in a small chapel on the left side of the church, a woman sat nearly motionless before votive candles and an icon of Christ. She was leaning forward with her head on her hands on the pew in front of her.

The candles flickered and cast shadows on the wall around the solemn, penetrating gaze of the Christ image.[145] Seconds and minutes became lost in the flow of silence. As Anton's eyes grew accustomed to the dark, he became conscious of the muffled sounds of waves washing the air around the church, then heard in them Ramón's breath rising and falling like the sea below.

The woman straightened and leaned back. Anton could see only her profile. Everything in her face blended, from her dark eyebrow, to her lips, chin and neck. Like a maiden in forward motion, a Greek still–life, she sat poised toward the icon, held in its gaze which both beckoned, and distanced.[146] The light from the candles rose and fell and crystallized in her eyes. They were shining with tears. Anton glanced at the old man at his side. With the woman's motion the old eyes had shifted in her direction as well, and became rapt, alive. Ramón drew a breath and sighed, long and quietly, saying under his breath, *"Hija de Eva, ¡Qué tristeza, qué belleza!..."*[147]

Anton leaned over and whispered, "Is she well?"

"You may ask her. Go and see." The old man stood up and walked slowly toward the door.

Anton rose and walked toward the woman. Reaching her pew, he faced the icon and bowed, then turned and faced her. He was about to ask, "Are you all right?" when she raised her face to him, tears still standing in her eyes. His breath seized in his chest. The words died away, unspoken.[148]

No, this is impossible! Not here. Why here?

It was Connie from so long ago.

For a brief, almost imperceptible moment, the woman's face became as timeless and iconic as the portrait behind the candles. She beheld his face, and said nothing. Her focused, concentrated expression, the shadows of sadness or some other unnamed feeling framing her eyes, conveyed a meaning that neither words nor concepts nor categories could express. Her hieratic silence veiled a reality that was immune to his curiosity and his concern. She turned back to the candles and the icon.

Released from her gaze, Anton turned, almost wheeling before the central altar, and in his bewilderment made his way unevenly up the aisle toward the door. Outside, he leaned against the corner of the building to catch his breath. He could feel his heart pounding. His eyes adjusted to the dazzling afternoon sun as the sound of the surf surged over him. Even the sky seemed to pulse with the brilliance reflected off the adobe walls.

He became conscious of the scent of chaparral and the faint odors of rose bushes.

Ramón was sitting on a wooden bench next to the patio. He had been watching Anton as he collected himself near the cathedral wall. "Come, sit. Did she speak to you?"

"No, nor could I speak to her." Anton dropped onto the low wall behind the old man. His eyes adjusted to the rich but gentle colors of the cathedral garden, the drooping trees and shrubs beneath the graceful arches of tan mission brick. He felt his heart calming.

Ramón studied Anton for a moment. "She had nothing to say," he shrugged.

"Who is she? She seems familiar to me." Anton felt shot through with anxious anticipation for the impending answer.

"She is many things." Ramón again scrutinized Anton closely. "She is the *catechista* of the cathedral. We bought the bowl for her, and will deliver it today."

"Her face is captivating." Anton's voice sounded muffled in his ears as though in a dream. He hoped that the old man would understand.

"Ah, yes...Cyntheia has great beauty. It is too great for most men to behold it."

"Cyntheia?" Anton asked..

"That is her name."[149]

"Oh..." Anton felt his bewilderment grow.

Ramón then said, "She is my niece."

Anton reeled under this revelation. He was speechless from shock upon shock. Unaware of the depth of distress in the younger man, Ramón continued to draw from the mystique of his masculine psyche. "Most men who can see such goodness grip their tackle to keep themselves safe. Otherwise, they would be gathered up like the fish we caught yesterday, only more helpless. They would become useless as fishermen. But enough: we should neither speak too well and never ill of any woman."

"*She* seems like the one who is lost at sea..."

Ramón sighed. "*Ai*, man! This is the hard time for her. It is hardest during the calm days before Holy Week."

"Why is that?"

"That is for her to say."

Anton pondered for a moment, then inquired, "What is the bowl for?"

"You know what a font is?" When Anton nodded, the old man continued, "She wants to make a baptismal font. She wants to make something for the church community here."

"A great gift," Anton said.

"Yes, a font is an important thing. It is the starting point before going out into the deep seas. It is a calm place like the harbor at Moss Landing. Once we come out of the font we become the First Salmon for the Great Fisherman. After we're caught we sometimes need to soak overnight, too, though it seems to be a lifetime; and a little salt and some spirits can't hurt. Our journey begins at the font and ends at the altar. My niece doesn't care for fishing, so she keeps her head clear by making things with her hands. She does fine work in ceramics and tile."

"Oh, yes..." Anton's heart was almost too full for expression as wave upon wave of memory rushed in on him. At that moment, the heavy doors of the church swung open, and the woman emerged into the daylight. She hesitated a moment to allow her eyes to adjust to the sunlight. A sea breeze blew the long locks of her dark brown and grey-flecked hair across her brow, shielding her eyes. She wore a flowing, full-length and sleeveless sundress, and sandals on her bare feet.[150] As she approached, Anton could see a necklace of small shells encircling her neck. He averted his face toward the bell tower. He felt helpless, powerless, barely able to move.

When Cyntheia neared the bench, she gave Ramón a gentle hug and a kiss. "How are you, my dear?," he asked her.

With hesitation and sorrow in her voice she replied, "Oh, *tío* Ramón, this is a sad time." To this he responded tenderly, "I know... Please let me introduce you to my *compañero*."

Anton turned his face toward her, and engaged her eyes, blue-grey like the ocean mist, soft and steady and containing the pain from an unknown sorrow.

Her voice gathered with a fervor that smote him. "Anton!..."

"Yes..."

"My God, what in the world are you doing here?" One hand had moved to her mouth, which was gaping in her surprise. Her face was flushed, her eyes shining with the tears that rise when all control is forgotten. "There is no sense in this! Why are you here?" Her feelings seemed to be a mixture of shock, confusion and wonder. While she seemed disoriented, nothing about her conveyed fear or repugnance.

Through all of this Ramón had sat impassively, his brown eyes turning from one face to the other in the heated exchange. Suddenly he said with a deep fierceness, "Is this man a danger to you, dear one?"

"Oh, no, no, Ramón!, no, nothing like that!..." She stopped, then laughed, almost as though she had begun to breathe again. The laughter released the tension, and allowed the woman and the man to find a fleeting moment to rest their eyes, to gaze upon one another. Low sounds of falling waves bounded up the street and echoed off the cathedral walls. Even the gusts of sea air were breaths of life tumbling up the hills from the ocean, only to be lost in the stirring trees above the Presidio. The directness of Cyntheia's gaze disarmed Anton, and he looked for something to say. Not even knowing how to address her, he simply said, "Hello, old friend."

"I'm sorry, Anton, I didn't recognize you at first. You used to have a beard," she said.

"That was long ago. Believe me, I'm as surprised as you. I had no idea you were here."

"How long has it been?" Her eyes became distant as though she were looking back through the years to their European summer. "Fifteen years?"

"A long time. A lifetime." Anton felt no hurry to speak. His feelings were in turmoil as he beheld the first woman who had ever awakened in him the high and honorable passion of reverent love.

A long moment passed. Cyntheia studied Anton, her gaze regaining the focus that he had seen earlier, before the candles and icon, and even further back to a time when she had asked his forgiveness in the patio of a Mediterranean hotel. She looked out to sea, then turned to him. "You are quite a ways from home, Anton. The last I heard you were living in Los Angeles."

He hesitated, searching for words. "At one time I would have said, 'traveling,' just to brush off the question. In the beginning I thought I was searching for something. Now it seems like something is searching for me. I met Ramón and helped him bring back the bowl. Then yesterday we went fishing in the bay. I think that I came closer to the reason I am here."

"Did he help you catch anything, *tío* Ramón?"

"Yes, he did. His arms are strong, and his hands are weathered. He steered the boat straight and knows how to listen. The day may come when he too can wear the necklace of shells and offer his song...The good salmon is now with the priest."

"I never would have known how to ask for what I was given, with Ramón, I mean," Anton said, looking at Cyntheia. "When you're seeking you have to give up asking. Not so long ago I would have thought it all to be a fool's quest..." As she eyed him curiously he shrugged at the paradox in his words and said, "You changed your name. Why is that?"

"A story for another day...You're in that story, Anton." Cyntheia straightened as she prepared to depart. "Duty calls now. Tell me, could you and Ramón bring the bowl up this afternoon? I would like to start work on it tomorrow. Maybe you would like to help?" At his nod, she smiled and turned away. As she walked, the sea breeze blew her hair back from her face and into the wind.[151]

Anton and the old man began walking down Camino El Estero. Ramón ambled with a slow, swaying gait, as if he were carrying a broad beam on his shoulders. "¡Híjole!, hombre...You looked like you lost your sea legs for a moment, like you were going to fall off the boat. You know my niece somehow?"

"Back in graduate school."

"You looked like you plunged in deep, way over your head. I was like that when I was younger. I would hear that the really good abalone were out beyond the breakers at Point Lobos. I wouldn't think twice about it, and would swim further out and deeper than I had ever gone before. I had only the sea otters out there for company, and I would lay on my back like them and be carried by the ocean when I grew tired."

"It seems so long ago. Her name was Connie then. She seemed like a mirage. I could never catch up to her. She would just disappear beyond the horizon when you reached out to her."

"Careful, my man..." Ramón chuckled. "As you Anglos say, be careful of what you pray for! Come along now. Let's get the truck and the font."

For the rest of the afternoon Anton assisted Ramón in unloading the bowl in the parking lot, and carrying it, carefully balanced on the gardener's wheelbarrow, back to a grassy place with a grotto–like enclosure and patio behind the cathedral. An aged copper–plated statue of St. Francis presided over the patio, which Anton noticed and pondered as a silent reminder of his original intention. They took measurements and purchased wood for a frame. This, Ramón explained, he had offered to construct for Cyntheia, confessing his lack of ability with ceramics and mosaic.

As he lined up wood and assisted in the measuring and cutting, Anton wondered, What have I done? I held my question safely in silence, and did not blurt it out in front of Connie, the woman—No, this lightning rod—who concentrated my energies in bygone times. Yet, given her heritage, she may know the meaning of this northern journey better than I. Gone from her is that edgy truthfulness that chiseled off my easy manners and blasted my serenity. Now I sense something new in her tears and surrender to natural feeling...How will our conversation be henceforth: saying so little to each other about so much? She returns to my life now like a visitation...Her name, "Cyntheia"...What can this mean? If a person can adopt a new name, then things and even truth seem mutable. Still, in the primal rites, a person invokes a tutelary spirit at a moment of confirmation. So: her name signifies a mystery which has not been disclosed to me...This feeling for her, this intuition, this epiphany...After all these years, a completely unique experience? My quest drew me here, unknowingly, step by step, day by day, moment to moment. Will it now revolve around her in an unimaginable way?...I entered into the darkness of an ancient Christian church and came face to face with someone whose beauty became visible, mirrored in a solemn icon...Sparkling tears transformed by flickering candles into little prism–making stars...Then I discovered I knew her all along. The inner obscurity of the sanctuary overcame the dazzling, distracting brilliance of the day. Silence and darkness allowed another world to fold into my own. The whole thing had the grandeur of the ocean and the simplicity of old Ramón in his blue jeans. The commonplace frames the extraordinary: the human face, the bare table, candlelight, the passionate sigh of my aged neighbor—ordinary, simple things, coming as hints of a never–to–be disclosed secret.

And this shocking encounter has freed an avalanche of meaning that will envelope me. Connie...or Cyntheia? Her name traces something hidden...*Beauty is momentary in the mind—/The fitful tracing of a portal...*[152] She did not invite me through those old wooden doors and over that threshold into her life. But she does not seem displeased. How far her soul seems to have flown since our sunny and windswept days in the Mediterranean! Is this how we reach into that deeper realm: through surprise and shocking memory, through recollection of a truth that rockets through us, yet with all the gentleness and fragility of a fleeting dream? We can hope for nothing more than this. We can stand before the veil, but we may not draw it aside: *that* is a spontaneous gift that can only come from the Other.

Our world of wild storms is kept tame with the music of beauty.

Rabindranath Tagore (1861–1941),
Stray Birds

Every breath, a thought of you

The next day, the Saturday before Palm Sunday, Anton awoke early. Cyntheia and the mystery of her presence were his first thought. He ate a light breakfast with Ramón, then decided to walk alone back up the hill to the cathedral. Along the way, remembering Ramón's admonition, he became attentive to an invisible assembly of long forgotten artisans who had built the cathedral, willingly or unwillingly, the natives of the area dragooned by the Spanish governor and his soldiers to build a place of worship for the God of love and wrath. What devotion came alive in them as they built this sacred space? How could its patterns, modeled after magnificent yet distant European antecedents, embody their hunger for immortality, these people who knew tides and volcanoes and boundless skies? Or was such a hunger alien to them before the arrival of the Europeans? Did their own native vistas become obscure in their souls as they gathered bricks and straw for the construction of temples that were so alien to them?[153]

Arriving at the Presidio chapel site, Anton walked past the ancient doors and around the corner to the secluded patio. There he settled to wait. Before long, Cyntheia emerged from a workroom with a bucket of brushes, cloths, rubbing stones and small chisels in hand. Her hair was loosely tied back, and with her simple skirt, cheery expression and sprightly gait, she looked the picture of health and vigor. A warm wave of gladness swept through Anton at the sight of her. She wore the same necklace of small shells from the day before; Anton now noticed that they were similar to those of Ramón's ceremonial headband. Mindful of Ramón's gentle suggestion from the day before, he felt a strange mix of uncertainty and anticipation.

"Did you rest well? Good breakfast?" she asked with a lilt in her voice. Then, looking down at the underside at the font, she said, "Oh, the glaze is perfect! See how it seems to reflect the earth below it!" She ran her fingers around the smooth outside and rough inner surface. She appeared deep in thought for a moment, then looked up and met Anton's eyes squarely. "Thank you, Anton. It was good of you to help my Uncle Ramón like this."

"It is a privilege. I have thoroughly enjoyed my time with him. He has shown me a great deal. I never would have known you were his niece."

"If you like him, you would have loved my mother," Cyntheia said.

"I seem to remember your telling me about her when we were in Greece."

"Yes, she had a thriving practice then with the migrant workers in the Salinas Valley. What Ramón does on the open ocean, trolling and all, fishing, my mother did on land, sifting herbs, feeling the pulse, watching the breath. They were very close, Ramón and my mother. Now I'm his only family."

"We talked about his parents and grandfather while we were out fishing. I never would have guessed..." His words fell away.

"I was just as surprised as you, Anton."

As in the encounters with friends and intimates of the deep past, old tones sometimes rise to the surface to be revealed either as lovely harmonics or as false echoes of an unrequited sacrifice of feeling. Where he had remembered her directness and even brusqueness, Anton was now struck by her honesty and gentleness, much as the petals of a rose are protected by its small barbs and thorns.

"Maybe I can watch you work on this?"

"Oh, I could even use your help, Anton. It's been bad planning on my part. This idea only came to me a little while ago, and I had to order it from the nursery and to find the right design. There is so much to do, and time before Easter sweeps me away. Ramón may have told you that this is to be a gift to the community here."

"Ramón did tell me. Let's see. Today is Saturday. Easter is a little more than a week away. Can it be done in time?"

"Actually, it needs to be done no later than next Wednesday evening. I'll explain that later. Thank heaven the Bishop celebrates the Chrism Mass on Thursday instead of Monday. But we have plenty of time."

"So you have a pattern in mind?"

"I do see the outlines. But I've never laid mosaics in anything this big before."

"Well, the day is young...Ramón said you are the director of religious education here. It must be busy right now."

"So true. Tomorrow brings Palm Sunday. Then the Chrism Mass and *Triduum* of Holy Thursday, Good Friday, and the Great Vigil with baptisms and confirmations; and Easter Day itself. Liturgies throughout in English and Spanish."

"So, a few days of quiet, then the pilgrimages. It makes me think of what Jerusalem must have been like during Passover week."

"I can hardly imagine. I also have a play planned for next week, a little thing, but meaningful to me...We'll have time to talk, and we can 'get acquainted,' if that's the right word." (She said this with a little laugh.) "Maybe you could tell me a little more about what brings you here as well."

Anton felt abashed for a moment. "I'll tell you, Cyntheia, if you want to hear it. It's a story I have not begun to figure out. There's disorder and sorrow in it, both early and late, and it may not make very good listening."[154]

"I would love to hear it, Anton. Then after we do our work here, Ramón will take care of the piping. His knees hurt too much for him to be bending down and helping for hours with the sanding."

Encouraged by this he offered the admission, "I've gotten used to being on my knees."

"Hmm, sounds intriguing. Here," she interrupted herself. "Let's start working. We can talk as the spirit beckons." At this, Cyntheia set out the tools and a bucket of water and a whiskbroom.

As for himself, Anton felt deeply pleased as his anticipations were becoming an antiphon to their renewed communion. On this balmy day he hoped that the hours with her would slow to an imperceptible movement, time moving to the rhythms of the heart.

Once the tools were arranged, Cyntheia continued, "So: what do you think about this bowl?"

"Handsome work. Even the mold must have demanded a lot of attention."

"And that's long gone. Funny how even out of the mold the bowl is pretty much raw material, raw nature; rough, but receptive. Now we only see its final pattern in our mind's eye."

"It seems like nature is a container for all the pure shapes, all hidden in various disguises," Anton ventured.

Cyntheia let out a low whistle and shook her head. "Oh, my God...A philosopher! I had almost forgotten. Hopefully you now have a sense of humor?"

Anton laughed easily enough. "I don't trip over what's right in front of my nose as much as I used to, if that's what you mean."[155]

"We will make an artist out of you yet, even a poet. Join me now, Anton, in thinking about what we are doing." She traced her finger around the periphery. "What does this geometry mean to you? Anything come to mind?"

Anton thought for a moment, then began tentatively, "A circle, certainly. It contains all symmetries. I am told that squares signify completeness, and triangles imply relationships; while the circle itself suggests wholeness."

"What else?" she pressed.

Slowly Anton began to remember old anecdotes. "They say that Plato had the words 'Let no one enter here who has not studied geometry' inscribed over the arches to the Academy.[156] It was the gateway to higher learning....Let's see...The Greeks did a lot of work with perfect squares, numbers like four and nine, and thirds. The old Hebrews and Kabbalah gave a number value to each letter of their alphabet, so that words themselves had numerical value. That gave a kind of heavenly weighting to the holy word. And Galileo said that mathematics is the language of nature, and that without it we are mute. That's all that comes to mind..."

"Whew! Good memory, Anton!" She laughed gaily, then rollicked on, "I'll have to be very careful not to poke fun at you like in the old times!"

"I wouldn't mind in the least, Cyntheia. I'm a little old to be a Parsifal, but still aspire to the holy fool."

"Thank goodness! You are well beyond being high–minded now," she chuckled. "Of course, of course! Let's keep it simple. Look at the circular shape. A fine symbol for the universe, the big world 'whose center is everywhere, its circumference nowhere.' Pascal. Some think that the world is God's body."[157]

"God's body..." Anton echoed the sibylline remark. "Caring for another person's body, even when it is run down and near the end, is like caring for the whole world."

"Exactly. Gentle hands even with this rough material, and an attuned spirit. We apply our hands to our work as through we are touching God's soft curves. This makes me think of Michelangelo's sculptures: all the chiseling of the rough material was for something smooth and living within."

"That's an astonishing thought. It makes me wonder why we whack away at nature."

"Ah, nature has become so dispirited and vulnerable. Every place and thing, every nook and cranny near and far is a sign of God's presence. I believe that the primal in you and me knows that. Uncle Ramón lives it, which is one reason I love him so much. I have learned to see so much through his old eyes, even at night. Seeing like he does is like looking into a really fine telescope, even as his eyes grow dim with age. Focus on one dark, tiny, black point in the night sky and leave the aperture open, and you see a blizzard of galaxies in illimitable space. It's astounding! At these moments, God is like a maiden dancing in the meadow, panting as she twirls, casting galaxies about like dandelion spores. Isn't that a thrilling notion?" Her inflected voice rang mellow and clear like a French horn.

"Oh, yes! It is such as pleasant reprieve from the grandiose vistas and equations that beggar our imagination."

"Then, on the same note, there's the other side: life on our winging planet is full of hazards, little everyday dangers, and even the big one, where God is like the great fish who pulls you down, or like a tiger or a lion hiding on a limb above waiting to pounce."

"I know a little about lions," Anton said, fresh with the memory of his intrusion into the lion's grotto in the Carmel Valley. "You and I walked among them at Delos. Just standing there as a statue or in the flesh, or even in a dream, a lion conveys indescribable power. He couldn't care less about our nice categories of thinking. Our zoology means no more to him than our theology means something to God." He picked up a pumice stone to begin sanding the bowl with its many surface cracks and fissures. "Now, where to begin? Shall we first polish out these ridges?"

Cyntheia reached over and stayed his hand. "Wait, wait...Easy does it. I know we have much to do...it makes it so much more important to slow down." She smiled at him, softening the shock of their first physical contact since the moment long ago, above the ruins of Ephesus. He took a deep breath to relax.

"My mother taught me that how we begin is as important as what we produce. 'The beginning is half the whole,' she used to say...If the world is God's body, then people and things are holy. I guess it's that simple. So too with our tasks, even hoeing a row of vegetables, or painting a wall, or here, polishing some clay. My mother taught me to bless the hammer before it strikes the nail, and thank the axe before you sink it into the wood. Caress even the stone before you begin to shape and polish what comes from the earth: simple rites that take you back to the beginnings."

Cyntheia took up a piece of pumice and balanced it lightly in her hand. She looked at it carefully, a spongy grey chunk of stone resembling a shaved and shriveled asteroid. "This is the end of the journey for this stone. Think of its story: being fired in some volcano like Parnassus or Shasta or Krakatoa, then blown up from the guts of our living planet; being blasted through with searing hot gases on its wild and frantic ride into the sky; then falling heaven knows where; and oh, so long ago. As we lift this rock, we honor its long story, and learn from it as it dies into fine dust. It will live on in the substance and shape of our bowl, our tiny container for the waters."

With that Cyntheia began rubbing the interior of the bowl in small, graceful circles, then across the circles with long sweeping strokes. With her head near Anton's, Cyntheia's breath became deep and steady. Sweat gathered on her brow, and she wiped her forehead with the back of her arm and her hair became streaked with red clay dust.

"Now, your turn."

Anton began working steadily in the large and small circular strokes that Cyntheia had shown him. The work proceeded easily. Soon, too, Anton's arms and shirt became a dusty red.

As he moved around the circle, Anton was grateful for the work, even if his whole mind was not on his task. Never had he worked so close, side–by–side with a woman whose femininity so blended with her sense of purpose. Was this the same woman who had galvanized his heart and mind in a distant past? Here she had such ease with him. The original purposefulness was still there, but now with no pretense, pushiness or demands, just natural grace and poise. How does she experience her own transformed soul? he wondered. Through what valley of shadows and light has she walked? How generous she has become with her inner life, so spirited and disciplined and enthusiastic! Here, in her, he was seeing inner and outer beauty converge like the un-geometric yet perfect lines of classical sculpture. She was as natural and unpretentious as the sunset, yet had an effect on him that was joyous and liberating. He wondered what she was feeling and thinking. He stopped working for a moment.

"Is Easter a time of celebration for you, Cyntheia?"

She appeared lost in thought for a moment. "In some ways, in some ways not. Would you permit me a small catechesis?"

Anton nodded. "Yes, I would like that."

"Easter has been celebrated for two thousand years," she said. "When you think about the hundreds of thousands of celebrations here and there every year, we have to believe that the earth is being transformed by it. It's a time for initiation, nourishment, honoring the sea–changes in people. It means incorporation, wholeness...and so it feels so good. But what lies beyond? That's what I wonder about, more and more. Usually everyone just disperses after the big party, you know, family times and Easter egg hunts. The whole meaning seems to dissipate. But really, to keep that from happening the tradition has whole weeks devoted to the aftermath of Easter, in *mystagogia*. It's rarely a success in big urban parishes or places like this, because everyone hustles back to their homes and big jobs on Monday. It gets very quiet around here again."

"What's 'mystagogia'?"

"It means being 'led into the mystery.' Our lives are supposed to be different after Easter. They *are* different. Easter is not just a process of socializing someone into a religion. I have departed from that path of thinking a long time ago. Easter is more. The mythic mind saw the resurrection of Jesus as a rift between the old cosmos and the new, a transformation of time itself. I am content to say that since the original Easter our consciousness has been different. Mystagogia is 'being led into that new mind,' which even suggests 'being led into a new Universe.' Somehow we need to realize that."

"How can one extrapolate from one individual human life, no matter how great and significant, even the life of Jesus, to the nature of the universe?" Anton asked.

"Easter *compels* us to do that. To say the least, Easter up–ended the old moral universe. The sword that pierced Jesus sliced through the old dualism. Look at it this way: in Israel people could reach out and touch the utmost sacred on one hand, and the abominable on the other: right over there stands the Temple; over there, in the same space, the crosses of the Romans' public executions. Similarly, in the temporal dimension, his life spans and unites the profane and the sacred. Christmas and Easter contain both. Jesus helps us experience the messy stories and awful contrasts, and make them new. If we do this in our living, and not just in our imagination and liturgy, we are transformed, made new. Our riches expose our poverty. The dying give us life. The poor bring gifts precious beyond price. The spare change that we hoard in our pockets and bank accounts place us on the scales of justice. Those in prison invite us to be free. Those shrieking with agonal grief or howling with madness compel us to question the mental and emotional health of our communities. Somehow we must all arrive in heaven on an equal footing, Anton, with the great souls leading the procession. That doesn't mean the most famous souls, either, or even the most educated, mind you. You know that from your reading of Flannery O'Connor. Isn't that where our Easter faith takes us?

"But you asked if Easter is a celebration for me. Let me ask you: How on earth can this make any sense if 'change' means 'going shopping,' 'transformation' is a 'make–over,' and it's against the municipal law to be poor?"

Noticing her rising color Anton said, "This makes you very angry."

"Yes, it does," she said. "It's not for me to say that the Easter celebrations scattered around a million altars, in all the high places and low places, amount to anything or not.[158] I *think* it does...But I don't think that our schedules and calendars have a lot to do with it. The change we are talking about brings *joy:* human joy renews the world, or transforms our perspective on the world. That's why we celebrate. Jesus was a man of seriousness and joyful play. The Quakers have a frolicking song about Jesus dancing. The little play we are working on is about the resurrection of each person's heart on any conceivable occasion. All of that is Easter. With Easter coming, everyone around here has been looking at the calendar, counting the days. My question, Anton, is not 'When is Easter? but 'Where is Easter?' It is not just a day on a calendar. We need to keep our eyes open. It might be around here somewhere. Or maybe not...But I have talked enough. Here, I want to give you something." She reached into her shoulder bag and produced a small bottle.

"This is olive oil. Rub it into your hands after you wash them, and whenever they feel chapped. Now, tell me about you. How have you found yourself here, Anton? And tell me about that lion."

Both charmed and challenged by the task, Anton set about culling the cream of recollection from the years that had separated them. He was conscious that he was not really telling Cyntheia about himself, his inner self to whom she had pointed; only hours and days of companionship and silent witness would reveal his true self to her; and this was a prospect that he could scarcely dare to conceive. But he warmed to the task, the more so as she seemed receptive and curious, even as she laughed at what was ludicrous in his experience. She did not flinch when he alluded to his despair, although the muscles in her jaw tensed during his account of the thieves of the winter night. Most consciously he sought to disentangle those common strands of memory that could meld their separate worlds into a shared landscape. At the same time he felt encouraged to point to the loose ends and tattered remnants of his experience that were the edges of new growth and discovery.

"And all of that is suggested in that one word, *Aguilares.*" he concluded. "The Salvadoran shared that with me back on the summit of the Tehachapis. It is a notion that stretches the whole length of the Great Valley."

When he had finished, she asked, "After all of that, Anton, how will you be able to go home again? Has homecoming become impossible? From now on will you always have to be shoving off from shore?"

"I don't know, Cyntheia. That question has come up for me time after time along the way. Only when I am home, someday, will I be able to know if I need to wander further. I have learned that travel for its own sake is illusory. I do know that I will need to go home, to attend to my family and our troubles and our affairs. But first, I need to walk this path until its end. Tennyson says it for me –

All experience is an arch where through
Gleams that untraveled world, whose margin fades
For ever and for ever when I move."[159]

Cyntheia thought for a moment. "How about a question, Anton?"
"Certainly."
"Is everything tending toward some good in your life? Have you come closer to happiness?"

"I really am happy, Cyntheia, although the ancient wise men would say that we need to leave that question unanswered as long as we are living. They must have known something about homecomings, about life in the broadest sense."[160]

"But do you really know where life is taking you?"

"Not really," he answered. "My old friend Gustavo in the workers' camp was the happiest man I've ever known; but never once did I see him insist on an answer to that question."

"Your Gustavo's happiness may have been due in some part to his having 'camped,' set down some roots," she said. "It seems that he is not forever on the go. Eternal migrating is for buffalo and butterflies, not for a man or a woman who has tasted happiness. I think a nomad in body or spirit must come to some infinite resignation: one day he will come to the river or the barren desert that he has crossed scores of times in his life with his flocks and family. He looks at his withered body. He has no more strength for the arduous swim or blistering walk, and he knows that this is his final day. He sits down on a rock or under a bush and dies there alone, his people of necessity leaving him behind as they move on with the herds."

"Is this something you learned in your studies?"

"No, Ramón and my mother taught this to me. Their old memory recalled the migrations of their ancestors across the Bering Strait, long, long before they settled along the river mouths. There they gained much heart for the fish who do the migrating. My mother's people have always pretty much stayed put, and they knew happiness."

"I have never thought of it this way, Cyntheia. In order to know happiness, stay put. No fuss. I could see it in Gustavo: every day he felt like he was being born anew. Staying with him and his community freed me from the tyranny of the mind and its plans. If you'll forgive me an awful image, our categories of reason are like prison cells of logic. Life batters them down, sure enough."

"Any mother will tell you that having children does the same thing, Anton. And you don't have to travel anywhere."

"Have you had children, Cyntheia?"

He instantly regretted his abrupt question. In that moment Anton saw a pained wistfulness cross over her face, a soundless sigh rising from her heart. The meaning and value of everything he had said to her suddenly became dubious for him. He sensed that he had uncovered an old wound.

"I have not, to my sorrow."

"I am sorry that my question troubled you."

"No, I am grateful you asked. My mother used to say that children are the answer to the riddle of life. We know that we are doing the right thing if we make our world a safe and nourishing place for children. *That* we can all agree upon. That means *home*. So, I hope that your adventure ends in a homecoming. Somehow I think that men must understand this, so that their wanderlust and restlessness are balanced by their love of their homes and their families. I wish my own father had known this, whoever he was. It would be a tragic world if life were only a riddle with no solution. Thankfully, children are a large part of the answer."

Ekam sat vipraha bahudha vadanti.

Truth is one, but the wise call it by many names.

The Rig Veda I.64.46,
(Sanskrit, ca. 1500 bce.)

Our trials, thy pathway

With these words, Cyntheia quietly gathered herself up and left Anton working with the bowl. Her final, strained words had silenced his learned sophisms. Alone, he continued the smoothing and polishing, the whisking of his pumice stone blending into the shiver of pine needles in the trees outside the cathedral courtyard. After the nubbins and ridges and dents were smoothed, he applied himself to the hairline cracks with a finer grade of stone and continued his progress around and around the bowl.

Early in the afternoon, with the sun just beginning to touch the trees on the Presidio hill, Cyntheia returned to the patio. She brought sandwiches and a tall glass of cool water with her. "I thought you might like this. Why don't you rest a while?" She then settled cross–legged by him, her skirt lying about her on the grass.

Anton thanked her, and joined her in the lunch. He then lay back on the lawn and rested his eyes on the blue sky and listened to the sound of the ocean, ever–present to his ears. The scent from the roses along the pathway wafted through the garden. From one of the cathedral arches he heard wind chimes played by the gathering sea breeze of the afternoon. A brief, clicking whir announced the presence of a hummingbird. The bird paused, its head and neck red and vibrant like a flame suspended in space. He drew nectar from a tiger lily, turned on a silver wing, and disappeared.

"Could you tell me what brought you here, Cyntheia? And why you decided to change your name?"

"The naming part is fairly simple. Do you remember the time we went out to the island of Delos?"

"How could I ever forget?" Anton sighed.

"I know, I know..." Cyntheia laughed. "Actually, I never told you about what happened out there, while I was walking around Mt. Kynthos. I didn't even know myself. That afternoon on the trail in the brown fields with the big, blue sea all around, out of nowhere I got this thought: 'You don't know who you are. You don't even know your own name.' I had not even been thinking about my name, but it suddenly became a question for me."

"You mean, 'Connie' didn't sound right any more?"

"Something like that. My mother gave me that name...hoping, I'm sure, that I might have a little of the Christian virtue of constancy. The sense I got up on that hill was that I am *not* 'constant.' Not that I don't care about constancy. I just didn't want that to be the label over my whole life. I thought about it for months as I was moving to my new school."

"All that was going on within you...I never would have known. I had really banished that time from my memory, I suppose, until earlier this year when I walked through it all again."

"Was I unkind to you, Anton?"

"No, not unkind, just always moving, you might say. I loved it when we really talked. But it often seemed like you were looking over my shoulder, like your mind was elsewhere. You had your sights set on the other school and your fiancé." Anton stayed on safe and superficial ground as he discerned her interest in exploring the memories more deeply. "But how did you find your new name?"

With a pained expression Cyntheia continued, "I read the *Odyssey* as you recommended. I discovered the Circe figure and was really struck by her power over Odysseus and his sailors.[161] Have you noticed how unconsciously she uses that power? She reduces the men in her life to pathetic and fawning animals without a moment's hesitation. Not that any woman has ever done that to you, of course! What intrigued me in the story was her transformation. She meets Odysseus and does not so much as greet him but tries to drug him on the spot. When she fails, she raises her wand and orders him into the pigsty—an image that has more power than our modern rationalism can ever comprehend. Then, quick as lightning, Odysseus subdues her with his sword and spirit. She is completely charmed and humbled by him. When she realizes that her own fate is being fulfilled, she becomes more than divine: she becomes human! She becomes conscious of herself. She restores his men, and they are more handsome and robust than ever. She helps build his boat, and teaches him rites that charm the spirits. She also tells him that he must travel into the underworld and how to survive there. Only Circe can navigate that space. Her nature, you see, was complex: I think that she could even be the female counterpart to Odysseus, at least in ingenuity and vision. She became my favorite Homeric figure.

"The mystery of who Circe is led me to discover her affiliation to Artemis, who was worshiped in Ephesus—do you remember our climb up the theater steps there, Anton? I learned that Artemis is closely associated with the Moon. I followed her further, and found her connection with some of the minor deities that inhabited the slopes below Mt. Kynthos. During all this, subconsciously I guess, I was thinking about the way Circe surrendered her powers when she met her match in Odysseus, how her humbling allowed her to become a savior, a pivotal person in the whole story. I suppose I was also thinking about my Greek father whom I never knew, but whom I imagine knew all of these islands. When I told my mother about my search, she just smiled and said, 'You have your father to thank. He is behind all of this.' That made it easy...I had found my name and adopted it when I began studies at my new school. That's where 'Cyntheia' came from, from the Artemis spirit of Mt. Kynthos."

"A charming tale. The name carries me back to the hills that I just traversed, above Carmel Valley. I like how it sounds, how it holds a meaning even in the saying."

"'Cyntheia' comes closer to who I am. It is hard to be named after a virtue or a saint. A name is a pointer. The Moon allusion in the name points to what I need: a sense of knowing what time it is and where I am in my own waxing and waning. You know the Circe legend continues on: she gets mixed up with Telemachus, Odysseus' son, and so forth. But for Homer, it was enough that Circe equip Odysseus and send him on his way home to Ithaca."

Anton remained silent at this elliptical comment.

"Now, you asked what brought me here. Funny thing, Anton: perhaps you did."

He waited for an explanation.

"You said long ago: go east, go to India. I went there. Somehow I came back."

"Tell me about it, Cyntheia. I can work and listen." He picked up a pumice stone to resume polishing.

She took a deep breath, as though to gather energy for a labor she knew to be daunting. Then she began the following account –

"After our trip to Europe, I went back east to begin the doctoral portion of my studies—remember, in the sociology of religion. When I got to my new school I was shocked by how expensive everything was, not just the tuition, but even simple living. To get by, I had to get a job. Being fairly prudent, I thought that working for the university would help me get tuition remission; I was right about that, and was fortunate to find work in the fundraising office. That's where it all started.

"My journey to India began in a white–tablecloth restaurant during the spring term of my first year. I sat with the founder of a large philanthropy *(that* made my head spin!) and the vice president for college advancement, and a trustee. They were including me in the conversation, politely of course, like I'm supposed to be some kind of maven for the moneyed circles these people ran in! Anyhow, we were eating lunch, talking about opportunities for college advancement: you know, thinking about ways to help other people spend their money; always with the greatest propriety; although, of course, the best way to avoid envy for people with money is to ask them to give it to your good cause! (Here Cyntheia's voice changed to a mix of silliness and resignation and she chuckled and shook her head at the odd notion.)

"Like everyone in the profession, I was learning how to be on the lookout for new opportunities. At one point, after a couple of drinks, I think, the trustee reminded the group that the board expected us to raise on the average about one hundred thousand dollars per week; he said we should not complain, because the presidents of the biggest colleges have to raise a half a million a week or more.

"In any event, in the course of the conversation one of us suggested a grand and ludicrous 'what if': 'What if Mother Teresa were to visit our college?' Who knows, maybe even I suggested it! Anton, a thousand thoughts must have boomeranged around in our brains: 'The greatest living saint...visiting our college! Why not? After all, we are a Catholic college. At least our title deeds say so. Think of the hoopla! Think of the spotlights and the announcements! Think of the *éclat*, the swooning delight of our major donors! Imagine the awe and excitement that would ripple through the student body, the thrill felt by our alums from decades upon decades past, who would flock back and boost our participation percentages! This the philanthropic foundations would find most telling, and reward us a hundred–fold for our excellence and our dedication!'

"'And, Oh, my!, let us revel in the proper and pompous piety that would possess us as we welcomed and made way for that humble and diminutive woman. The energy and renown that would flow to us would redound to our benefit for years, and our fundraising jobs would become easier and more pleasant! We would not cut down palm branches of course! Oh, no! No such imperial triumph for her. But we would trim and groom our noble campus gardens and sidewalks like never before! We would bedeck our avenues with tasteful welcomes and banners for the thousands who would come, and smile and bow to the deserving few who would have a private audience with our guest and receive her blessing. Hosanna! Blessed is she who comes in the name of the Lord! Hosanna! And how worthy of respect are we who thought of it!'"

At this point, Cyntheia stopped. Anton had started laughing, and began to dissolve in tears of hilarity as her preposterous vision emerged. Cyntheia looked at him strangely and picked up a masonry hammer and feigned to knock him on the head. "Sorry, sorry," he said through his gasps. "Please go on."

"Thank you, Anton," she said. "You are my comic chorus. Far be it for you to ever descend to such follies…Obviously no one was around to deflate our grand vision. The vice president (who had departed from his own reason as well) said, 'Well, how do we invite her?' To which, the trustee replied: 'Send Cyntheia to ask her! She can use my million frequent flier miles.' And that's where we left it. Having lost our common sense, only pragmatism was left in its place, and we turned our attention to opportunities closer to our grasp, the daily work of panning for other people's gold."

"I can hardly imagine how you must have felt, Cyntheia. No matter. I'm not laughing at you. In my more lucid moments I can hear a little Sancho Panza on my left shoulder, whispering caution, usually being overwhelmed by the Don Quixote on my right shouting, 'An adventure! Forward to the Cause!' It takes courage to confess our great illusions and possessions."

"My memory is all very flawed, Anton. I am sure that I remember only the parts that don't implicate me the most savagely. As they say in India, I wouldn't be willing 'to vouch for any of it with my hand in the fire.' As it was, I should have stopped right there. Frankly, I hadn't been the type of person to give a dollar to a fellow asking for a cup of coffee, and usually locked my car doors at intersections where people hold up signs saying 'Will work for food.' So, here's what happened –

"I had set a departure date for India and received a battery of vaccinations: diphtheria, tetanus, hepatitis, cholera; and picked up medicines for malaria, intestinal upset. I purchased water purification devices; cooking equipment just in case; insect repellent and bed netting; visa and passport and travelers cheques. Looking at this array of preparations, I was stunned and embarrassed. It all but shouted my anxiety and helplessness as I prepared to venture to an alien land. Ironically as well, I hardly talked with the fundraising leadership about the whole venture. I learned later that they thought the idea was absurd, but if there were any grace in it, it would cost them little or nothing.[162]

"Finally the departure day arrived. Soon I was on a flight that took me from Cincinnati to Frankfurt and onward, halfway around the world, all the way to Mumbai, the new name for Bombay. I arrived late at night. It was like being dropped into a pot of bubbling soup. The sights, the smells, the heat, the noise and traffic hit me from every direction. The city was noisy and cacophonous like a large, amateur orchestra tuning up before a screechy performance. I stayed in a hotel a few hours awaiting my next flight, feeling very much alone and a long way from home. I then boarded Air India for Calcutta.

"The view of India from 35,000 feet is like looking down at a tight mosaic of villages and fields with hairline highways connecting them. It is so dense with people and settlements! I sat next to a turbaned Bengali man, an oil company executive, I believe. When, at his request, I told him where I was going, he said, 'Please bless Mother's feet for me.' This was the highest of compliments. It reversed the customary deference in India of a woman for a man. It showed his profound reverence and respect for Teresa, the Old Woman whose name is known around the world.

"Oh, Calcutta, Calcutta...No other city stirs such discomfort and unease in me. At the airport terminal, I began to swelter the instant my feet hit the tarmac. I faced the usual customs officials, the slowly moving queues, the money changers, the inhuman restrooms with their heavy air, the echo of voices and crash of luggage, the rasp of auto exhaust and the whistles and honking of taxi drivers. It was overwhelming. I was alone. I was going by faith and viscera.

"I hailed a taxi—a small bug of a car with a toothless Bengali driver—and we began our careening drive toward the city center. I did not know if he was gouging me by asking ten rupees for the ride, because I didn't even know that a rupee was worth ten cents. We shrieked along at forty–five miles an hour on a shoulderless road,

past road workers squatting with heavy hammers breaking up the tired asphalt before a steam roller pulverized it into gravel,

past people pulling truckloads of merchandise by hand,
past children ambling along or guiding a cow with a stick,
past large, open settling ponds that catch the water of the Ganges during the flood season, and which serve as open sewers for the people who have no indoor plumbing,
past corroded stucco buildings with brown flood marks up to the second floor where the families move with all their belongings when the first floor is flooded,
past the indolent palm trees and mangy dogs and crowds upon crowds,
and dirt, dirt everywhere, the fine dust of the inlands brought by Mother Ganga to this suffering city.

"That short and wild drive was the pattern of my whole time in India, the last spiritual civilization on earth: I raced past everything, going too fast to meditate on anything.

"My driver took me to the Hindustan Hotel, a 'Ten Star' hotel by Indian standards. I paid him his $1 plus a tip for the twenty mile drive. A Sikh, turbaned and gracious, greeted me at the door. I checked into my room which had been fumigated with DDT for my arrival. I opened the windows, then closed them again to keep malaria mosquitoes out. I didn't even have the presence of mind to rest. I was an automaton, a waif drifting like a leaf on foreign waters.

"It was late in the afternoon but I remembered I was a woman with a mission. I asked the bellhop how far away Mother Teresa's convent was. He said, 'One quarter of a mile over on Lower Circular, but you will never make it on foot.' I understood. Already people were beginning to stake out their small squares for sleeping on the sidewalks. You may know, Anton, that Calcutta is a city of about twelve million people. Half of them sleep in the streets at night. As a Westerner, taller by a foot than most Indian people and many shades lighter in complexion, I would have stood out like a neon sign and would have been besieged by every child and poor person over that quarter of a mile. I took the taxi.

"Mother Teresa's center lies on a main thoroughfare in Calcutta. It is a large, two story former office building or agency, with faded yellow stucco paint, broken shutters, and a tile roof. It looks like any other faded and drooping building in Calcutta. Walking down the alley to the main entrance, I was scrutinized by a dozen weary Bengali people. They had seen many, many European or American women and men come down this alley before, and I was not in the least bit unusual. I knocked on the door that has been photographed so many times. The sliding sign with

'Mother Teresa' written on it was slid to the left, exposing the word 'In.' She was 'In' today.

"At the door I was greeted by a woman with a badly disfigured face. I learned later that she had survived one of the 'bride burnings' that still happen in some of the remote villages. At the Mother House, the surface, even one's face, does not count for much. In fact, in the days to come, I began to think of her as a bride's maid to the Queen of Heaven. Whenever I greet people at the door I think of her. She led me into a small room where an Irish Sister with brilliant and serene hazel eyes said, 'May I help you?' I told her that I came to volunteer. By now, that was the truth, Anton. By now I had realized that I too needed help. I was not there to propose a business trip to Mother Teresa. That false dream had been forgotten back in Bombay or before."

At the sound of his name, Anton set his stone down and rolled over on his side and cradled his head in his arm. "Cyntheia, you just gave me a most uncomfortable thought: Could this be the way we enter heaven? We knock on the door and present our business and whatever is worth bringing from our life work?"

"You might be on to something, Anton. I remember something in my studies from the *Hadith*...how Mohammed said somewhere that 'a person's true wealth hereafter is the good he does in this world to his fellows. He said that when a person dies other people will ask what property has he left behind him for their use, but the angels will ask what good deeds he has sent before him for his arrival in heaven. We are to care for this world as if we live in it forever, Mohammed said, and work for the other world as if we will die tomorrow.

"So there I was: I came to that city hoping to bring something back with me. By the time I got to the door, all the gilding was gone from that dream. I just wanted to bring something to the Sisters' work. As it turned out, I even had to leave that wish behind. Can you fathom that, Anton?"

"Hardly. Go on. Sorry to interrupt you."

"The Sister suggested I go upstairs where I might meet 'Mother.' I walked into the courtyard, up the stairs, and sat down on a bench outside a large chapel. An American priest in his sixties was there before me. He was a Sacred Heart Father, he told me, and had just been reassigned from his teaching order in Bangladesh. His community had given him $500 as a bonus. Since he did not need $500 he wanted to give it personally to Mother Teresa. I told him I thought that was a fine gesture.

"Sisters came and went, bowing or kneeling and genuflecting each time before the altar within. Sisters and a few volunteers were below in the courtyard hauling water up from a hydrant and carrying buckets to various places around the house. For her personal property, a Missionary of Charity has her two saris, her sandals, and her bucket. Buckets for water and food and the essentials are conveyances of life in India and all of Asia.

"As I sat, I saw Mother Teresa emerge from her apartment. She was very short, no higher than my chest. It was as if all the heavy burdens and dying bodies that she has carried had crushed her under their weight. She was surrounded by a Bengali family, two parents and two kids. She looked exhausted and might have been trying to return to her apartment. As the family moved away, the priest stood up and walked over to her. I heard him explain his intentions. She looked at him, shook her head and took the man to the railing and said, 'See that man down there?' A man was down below, one link in the bucket brigade toting water to the Sisters' laundry. Mother Teresa said, 'That man has the same problem with his money. Jesus doesn't want your money; Jesus wants you.' The old man walked back to the bench and sat down with a dazed look in his face.

"So. With that simple exchange, mercifully overheard, the entire purpose of my journey evaporated. The trustee's frequent flyer miles could have taken me around the planet a hundred times, and I would not be one inch closer to myself. There was nowhere to go but back to my hotel. The Sikh doorman asked me about my day. I was evasive, but said that I wanted to go out to one of the Missionary sites the next day. He said that he knew a man who had volunteered with Mother Teresa for seventeen years and who could go with me if I wanted. I thought that this would be a good idea.

"In the morning I descended from my room at 6:00. My guide was waiting for me. He was a late middle–aged man in slacks, a thin grey cotton shirt and sandals with no socks. He said we had better walk to the Mother House, and from there out to the worksite.

"Most of the millions of inhabitants of the city who had slept on the sidewalks that night were up and queuing at the public latrines or were trying to eat something before turning to their labors. Already the city was a roaring din. A group of twenty half–naked men were pulling a heavy wedge into the air with a bamboo derrick and dropping it into the ground to soften it for the picks and shovels of another group who were digging a trench. Further down the street a man was demolishing a building with a sledge hammer, with each blow giving off futile puffs of dust.

"Now the Mother House was full of people. At least seventy volunteers from all over the world joined the dozens of novice Sisters for morning Mass. Mother Teresa sat in the back with her Sisters, deep in repose. In her white and blue sari she looked like an aged Madonna immortalized by a Michelangelo. She was surrounded by her Sisters from many countries, and appeared to receive no special deference. Following Mass the Sisters gave us volunteers breakfast, which consisted of a tiny banana and two crackers and tea. We ate like they did, and they ate like the poor whom they served.

"Tagging along with my guide, I walked out into the city, into a world that I cannot comprehend nor banish from my memory.

"People were everywhere. A little girl, no more than thirteen years old, tired, and dirty and with a baby on her shoulder, pushed herself against me and said, 'Rupee, please, Lady, please.' Men lined the sidewalks, bathing from faucets and hydrants. Following their bath with water and soap, they faced the sun and prayed Vedic hymns. Women bathed discretely behind large tarpaulins. The streets screamed as four lanes of traffic interlaced, left on right, right on left and inched this way and that. Horns blared constantly as children, animals and old people wandered across the highway. Lepers and amputees, their teeth black from beetle juice, sold tobacco and other items on the sidewalks. Skinny men hauled rickshaws against the unfriendly tide of humanity.

"Watch out! A stream of garbage came catapulting out of a doorway. Ahead the street was littered from the first throw of the morning. Poorer people picked through the refuse looking for bits of food or other useful objects. Ribby dogs nosed around behind them. Birds on the buildings above surveyed the scene, waiting for their chance. Move aside! Around the fringes of the garbage piles, competing with the dogs and birds, were the *dalits* or Untouchables with their brush brooms: driven by their hunger, they would finish cleaning the streets until the next day's jettisons.

"Along the way I learned that my guide, whose name was Sacci,[163] slept under the veranda of the Hindustan Hotel. He was a *sannyasi*, a man of simplicity, but not a purist like the *sadhus*, because he wore trousers and a shirt and sandals instead of being dressed only with ashes and the open air and sky. When I told him what I had eaten for breakfast, he thought me fortunate. His one meal that day would be given to him by the Sisters. He had been a banker from his young adulthood until he turned fifty, and at that point had let it all go, and begun that way of withdrawal that was preparing him for eventual death.[164] All these years he had been working with 'Mother,' as he also called her. I asked him what he did for Mother Teresa, and he said that he mainly hugged the kids, especially the little ones at the train station, the ones abandoned due to poverty or leprosy, or those dealing with the loss of a limb that had been sliced off by a train wheel.

"At one point the sidewalk was blocked by a gaunt, meandering Brahma cow. We stood waiting for the cow to sleepwalk her way down the street. I asked Sacci how he felt about cows in general. 'We love them,' came his response, as though he were astonished by the question. His eyes grew luminous as he said, 'I feel for her like I feel for Mother, Mother Teresa, that is. I think of this sacred creature on the sidewalk with us, and I think of my Sister friends, and I think about the times when I poured the cow's sweet milk, mixed with rose blossoms, on the altar in my home, long ago.'

"After a half–hour walk we reached Prehm Dan, the home for the mentally disabled poor. It lies alongside the railroad tracks and is lined with low mud hovels no bigger than our closets, with naked children running around. We walked right into the dirty, old warehouse and into the far depths of the building. There we met our charges: old, rickety women, helpless, hungry and vacant. We picked them up from their steel cots, and walked them or wheeled them in rusty wheel chairs out to the concrete patio. There we gave them soap to wash with, and rinsed them with water from buckets. While they were unclothed they were treated for their physical pains with medicines from a nearby room. I witnessed massive untreated tumors, leprosy, and several forms of mental illness; I saw people in pain but never in anguish. Why is that? I would not hasten to say that people in our North American nursing homes are any better off. But no matter. After the women were rinsed, we took them to an open–air patio. There we gave them tea in their one personal possession, a small tin cup. They sat quietly or moved about. One old woman walked on her heels all morning singing a Hindu song in a high, thin voice. A similar scene was unfolding on the men's side of the warehouse.

"We gathered their soiled linen and waistcloths and threw them in a huge vat of boiling soapy water. From there they were flung onto the patio where we banged them with two–by–fours to remove stains and solids. Finally the clothes were dowsed in rinsing tanks and carried upstairs to be hung on wires and dried in the sun. Two Sisters worked the tanks, singing and sweating, stirring and throwing steaming bundles of sheets and saris and aprons. By the day's end the clothes would be cleaned, and dried, perhaps even sterilized by the boiling water and sun's rays, and folded and made ready for the next day.

"At ten o'clock we enjoyed a break. I was exhausted. We had two more crackers and tea for a snack. The Sisters gathered in the chapel and prayed and sang for thirty minutes. A Mass for men and women together was offered in the chapel between the two wings of the center. Anyone could receive the Eucharist without distinction of religion or caste. I was so tired, I just sat outside with the crows and flies.

"Lunchtime, the one major meal of the day, came at eleven. The Sisters brought out huge pots of rice and green curry and deep-fried crustacean-like creatures caught in the rictus of death as though they had been boiled alive in the curry soup. We carried food and water to the women. Then we carried or wheeled them back to the cool of their bunkroom for their afternoon rest. One woman got angry at me because I left her water cup behind. I hurried back for it.

"My last assignment for the day (I thought) was to clean the patio. Joining a Missionary Sister I carried water in my bucket from a slow moving faucet, flung it over the patio and swept bits of food and dirt with my brush broom. Bucket after bucket, we swept and swept until it was clean. Finally, I put my buckets away, took off my apron, and collapsed on a bench, numb with fatigue.

"No sooner had I sat down, than a Sister called to me, 'There's a woman in the bunkroom who needs you.' I arose, found the woman and changed her bedpan. Once done, she lay back and looked up at me, her bright eyes almost illuminating her gaunt frame and sunken cheeks. 'Thank you,' she said in English. I will hear this word until my dying day.

"Sacci helped me make it back to my hotel. I cannot remember how we got there, by foot or by car. He returned to spend the rest of the day at Prehm Dan. Back in my room, I dropped my clothes in a heap and showered. Then, lying back on my bed, I began to cry. Anton, I cried for two hours. I've never collapsed like that before or since. There is nothing worse than crying by yourself in a distant hotel in a foreign land: you are not even sure that God speaks your language there, or would understand why I was such a wreck. The only words that came to me were 'our trials, thy pathway' from the old Anglican hymn. They have echoed in me ever since. God was dropping a wedge into my fur-lined rut, transforming it, I can only hope, into a path for his footsteps. My own grief shocked me. My ignorance stared me in the face. I realized that I knew nothing about a whole world of human experience. I was too tired to blame myself for the arrogant fool that I was. I did not know what my path would be, but I knew that I needed to learn something for my whole life from this experience.

"A few days more of the same and I was back home. I had not done much—washed some clothes, carried rice in little pans and water in buckets, swept a patio, given a few women a drink in the shade. I had been gone ten days. I had not spoken to Mother Teresa, but she and her Sisters had revealed a hidden world to me."

To have a peaceful life is good; to have a life of pain in patience is better; but to have peace in a life of pain is best.

Meister Eckhart (1260–1328),
German Sermons[165]

Peace in a Life of Pain

At this point, Cyntheia leaned forward with her chin in her hands and looked at Anton with a gaze of peace that he had never seen in her before. The slowly declining sun cast soft shadows around her temples that accentuated the calm in her eyes. "Well, there you have it, old friend. It is okay to call you 'Friend,' isn't it? You once said that I might find something if I went further east. And you made some mention of the Christ within. By the time I had returned I did not know why I should study the sociology of religion or why it was even important. I didn't even know why I was at that particular university. I gave up any pretence of knowing anything really important. All I knew when I had returned and recovered from the trip, is that God is not stingy, revealing himself to one people, at one time and place, or in only one sacred scripture or tradition. Sacci was only one person who showed me how much I had to learn."

"How about your job, Cyntheia?"

"I hardly thought about it, due to my wedding plans. You know how those dates have a kind of tyranny over young couples. We were married as planned, and to make a short story even shorter, we were together for about four years. He was always gone, working the insane hours of an intern and then a resident, at the hospital one hundred hours of week, always defending his practice with a kind of noble–sounding, selfless rhetoric. I'm sorry, Anton, I know that sounds resentful; it's how I saw it at the time. For sure he was too tired for any kind of life. I came to a kind of crisis of loneliness and left my work in the fundraising job."

"What a rupture that must have been," Anton said with empathy.

"Sadly," Cyntheia replied, "I had little regret about any of it, and mostly kicked myself for waiting for so long. There was a period of several weeks when I spent a lot of time reflecting. Then, I found out I was pregnant. I knew I had to decide: whether to live with this man who was hardly ever around and then only cranky and exhausted or find my way home. There was really no alternative. I realized that I was being drawn into a world that creates its own Prehm Dans through lack of care for either healer or patient. Knowing that, and knowing my mother's rhythms lived in me, I knew I had to leave or become crazy myself. So, I packed up and came back to Monterey to be close to her."

Anton listened acutely to this account, and was trying to decide whether to ask how her husband had responded to her decision, when Cyntheia shocked him with,

"After all of that, Anton, the baby was never born."

He said nothing, but gazed on her.

"I lost him at six months, at this very time of year. Why, I will never know." Her eyes gathered a soft gleam of tears.

"That is terribly sad, Cyntheia."

"Oh, yes, Anton. It hurts the most when I think about it, and about other mothers who have lost their children…Holy Week is not an easy time for me. Jesus' disciples may have recovered from their desolation, but I am not so sure about Mary his mother. In any event, I was here now. My mother helped me recover, and I began helping her in her practice, and later, cared for her when she became ill. Old Ramón has always been like the father I never knew."

"I have no idea what it feels like to lose a baby, Cyntheia…It seems impossible to comprehend."

"One cannot understand it, Anton. What good is understanding in these situations, anyway? The wheel of loss seemed to be rolling faster and faster. Living with my mother ended the spinning of the wheel, but now, with her gone, I know that my journey is beginning to unfold again. Working here is like being in a big, comfortable yacht with a huge keel. It's certainly not Ramón's little boat; you know how light and tipsy that is! Religion is the boat to help us cross a river. We are not in the boat alone, and I would want to be the last one out at our destination. Hopefully I can be as steady in the boat as my old uncle. But at the other side of the river, you park the boat. We would be fools if we toted it along on our shoulders on the dry land of our destination…But you and I need to do some work here."

Even as she recalled their attention to the work at hand, gratitude gleamed in her eyes as she said further, "You have been a fine listener, Anton. That touches my heart…more than ever…I need to attend to our final rehearsal before Monday. Could you keep going without me? And perhaps you would like to come to the play…"

"I would, very much," Anton said. "I'll be done sanding by the time you get back."

By the middle of the afternoon the work of smoothing was complete. When Cyntheia returned she brought a simple string and pencil. "Hello! How are you doing?" she asked. "Getting tired?"

He smiled away her concern. "How was your rehearsal? What's your part in it?"

"You don't really want me to tell you, do you?" she laughed. "Better to be surprised. Let's go right ahead. It's time to draw the circle. I'll hold the center, and you draw a circle just inside the outer edge." That done, she shortened the line by an inch and said, "Now, make a circle within the circle. What does that suggest to you?"

"Frankly, Cyntheia, doing this reminds me of the moment I met you." She looked at him, puzzled, then laughed when he recalled their meeting at the foot of the Parthenon column. "I had forgotten all about that! It would have been much, much easier if I had asked you to help me measure that column. But no, I was too proud even to invite you into my folly."

Anton shared in her merriment. "Just like I said yesterday: fools finding solace in one another! Our wisdom now is knowing that our folly even has a place in life."

"I like that!" she responded. She then turned her attention to the font and ran her fingers around the sanded area. "This circle says to me that we never really have the big picture but we are gaining better hunches all the time. If this circle is an image of the whole, we admit from the start that we do not know whether the great font of the universe has the shape of a sphere, a donut or a saddle. Maybe the font of our own universe is just one among many floating on the sea of possibilities. The Hindus suggest this when they say that the world is shaped like an elephant or a monkey or Shiva with her many arms. Now, I like to think of it this way: the inner circle is like the boundary between us and the greater context that we do not know. What we don't know is represented by the larger, outside circle."

"That makes sense, as much sense as anything, I suppose. Even Plato tried to imagine the whole thing inside a special shape, the dodecahedron, I believe. He thought that meditating on it is seeing the Ideas, almost like a meeting of the human and divine minds."

"The font is also like the iris of the eye, isn't it? Looking into someone's eyes leads to a joining of hearts, you would agree?"

Anton nodded, wondering if he would ever be able to look into Cyntheia's eyes with such transparency.

"Now, let's try to see the whole font at once. Look at the whole thing," she said.

"It's hard to do that. I keep wanting to focus on this part or that."

"Just so," she agreed. "If we could see clearly, we would notice that God welcomes all. Imagine it this way: holy people, and venal men and women will step into this water. We will share communion with them at the altar, the virtuous and vicious alike, side–by–side. Some will taste the sweetness of the Lord; others will gag on his food in their hearts."

"Gathering for communion is like being with yourself at every point in life," Anton said, remembering the gathering of old and young, men and women and children in the workers' camp.

"We are on a common path," Cyntheia said. "If I feel proud and virtuous today, the suffering sinner next to me reminds me that my day of reckoning is coming. Same with a baptism. A strange sort of initiation, being soaked in front of a whole community of people. I have a bit of a problem with the way it happens, however."

"What's that?"

"The assembly is told in the rite to remember our own baptism. Words used like that time after time gradually empty of all meaning. We become just spectators, focusing on this one individual being baptized. Sprinkling a little water around the congregation doesn't help much. The old Baptist hymn had it right: 'Shall We Gather at the River.' Just think of the massive migrations to the Ganges for the sacred washings of Kumbha Mela: forty million people show up over a one month period, all in the same place, doing the same thing, washing their head and body with the water that has washed the mountains and valleys above them, and the millions of people all around them. An individual is everything and nothing. That's a real baptism. One should come out the waters of baptism delirious with joy, drunk, babbling in awe, careening off the walls, fired up, branded with light in one's memory. Heaven has become intercalated with our world like the mosaic on the hidden surface of our font! Language falls short of what I mean."

"Many paths to the shore and many to the peak...," Anton said, "I believe with Kazantzakis that the sacred mountain ends in a plateau that broadens as one approaches the summit. There is room there for all who arrive from countless paths. Many are unheralded, like your Sacci, and unlearned, like Baal Shem Tov.[166] I remember a Louisiana cleaning woman at a conference not so long ago who cheered me on every morning with a booming voice. 'Have a good day, Professor!' she would say. 'Come back wise!' Then she would laugh, deep and rich, like she knew that I was a lost cause. She's there too, ahead of me."

"Well, she may beat you to heaven, but may you always have a laugh at your side, Anton!" as she handed him a flexible straight edge and tape measure. "Now comes the hard part. You relax while I guide you. And let's take our time. Divide your circle into four parts with a line through the center. Now subdivide each quadrant and find the mid-point of the radius. I'll hold the tape measure for you."

When that was completed, she said, "Look at this. Look carefully." Then, "We are now touching the origin of the beauty in the design, and only you and I will see this. How are you feeling?"

"Tense," Anton responded, surprised at the word that rushed to his lips. "Stretched. Yet balanced, like the human figure Leonardo da Vinci drew inside a circle."

"That is how I feel too, when everything seems to be quiet and composed around me. My mother helped me learn to live with the tension when she spoke of inhaling and exhaling: effort, relaxation."

"It seems to be like an energy source," Anton said, looking carefully at the design. "It's not moving, but seems to be the origin of movement. If I could speak like a good Greek, it would be the *stasis* that produces the *kinesis,* the unmoved mover, the visible tension of the completed pattern."[167]

"Or think of it as the systole and diastole of our own heartbeat, or as the ebb and flow of the tides…always there, moving, murmuring. People will stand upon the pattern but not see it, Anton. And we may lose sight of it as well. Everything is a blank prior to it; without it, everything is chaos. The created world will turn around that still point at the center of our circle. After we are finished, it will be hidden from sight. But it will always be available to the mind and memory and the understanding. And as I said, what we will see is Beauty."

Anton was astounded by the enormity of Cyntheia's Platonic vision. So this is how the world is, he thought: so much beauty, so close, yet hidden behind our physics and logic that we might not be overwhelmed by its grandeur.

With Cyntheia's guidance, Anton drew out four conical circles in the four quadrants of the font. Each of the four circles launched an outward whorl from its own center that merged with the inner circle of the font.

Working with care, and patiently overcoming his confusion, Anton also completed four cross–bridges between the four quadrants. At one point Cyntheia reached over and stopped his hand and pointed to a paradox that he was creating. He corrected the disrupted symmetry and continued.

When he was done, he looked over the design. "There is no way I could have done this without you, simply following verbal instructions. I don't think words can convey what just happened here. Even when I look at it, it seems impossible." Anton felt very moved, exhilarated and even exhausted by his concentration.

"Well, my friend," she laughed, "we have worked very hard, and have created something very simple. This is how I understand faith. You cannot explain it to other people with words alone. It would be a complete jumble and lives would be all tangled up. The whole thing is an allegory. The font: a cleansing ocean. The two–dimensional geometry: a flat surface like an icon, pointing to the dimensions we cannot see. We could have had a three–pointed pattern: the 'three' is the symbol in the *Book of Revelation* of the spiritual order. But that is not our place. So, we will have the 'four' in the quadrants, which symbolizes the created order. *That* we have a hand in. The design with its texture and unities is a symbol that invites meaning and beauty to be disclosed in our ordinary experience. Let's stop here," she concluded. "In our own small way we are participating in God's work, and we need to rest more often than he."

This abrupt ending caught Anton by surprise. Deliberating for no more than a second, he said, "Cyntheia, could we talk a little this evening?"

"I would enjoy that, Anton. Tell you what: why don't we meet down on the waterfront tonight after dinner?"

At the agreed–upon hour, Anton awaited Cyntheia at the end of the open wharf. When she walked into view, he drew in a deep breath and exhaled slowly to calm his heart. Passing by the open door of Ramón's home she called in a greeting. There were passing words about the fish coming closer to the surface seeking the light of the growing Moon and about the approaching fog bank, and then, *"Buenas noches, Cyntheia,"* and *"Buenas noches, tío mio."* At her approach Anton could see that she wore blue jeans and a thick sweater and scarf, and that her face was flushed from the brisk walk down the hill. Greetings offered, they settled on Ramón's old beach chairs and listened to the tide as it leaned and labored on the heavy pilings beneath them. The sun had dropped deep into the distant clouds and the sky was transformed into a spectacle of blues, golds and purples.

"I like to come down here and sit with Ramón," Cyntheia mused. "Sometimes he stitches a sail or mends his nets or just plays with knots and hitches. I've heard some amazing yarns out here, and fish stories, and folk wisdom from the Tolowa."

Looking up at the stars that were beginning to dot the darkening sky, Anton said, "The whole sky seems like one vast net, doesn't it?"

"'God's net over all creatures.' Meister Eckhart. Find any one line, and you find God," Cyntheia agreed.

"Connections. Everywhere."

"So true. Look how people who love one another strive unceasingly, in song, poetry, actions, dreams or whatever, to see their loves as lines in God's great net. The lines are made of some kind of divine material. They endure the greatest tugging and stretching without snapping. Eckhart also said that serving God in love is good, but 'grasping the love in fear is best.'"

"Sounds desperate. Like hanging–on for dear life. What did he mean by that, Cyntheia?" As Anton asked the question, he directed his gaze away from the deepening grey of the water to Cyntheia's own blue–grey eyes, so focused and sparkling with life.

"'To grasp the love in fear…' I suppose that when the whole Kingdom appears, it will be unbounded love, the most frightening thing imaginable. There is an inverse proportion between complacency and zest for life in God's Kingdom."

"That's a different way of thinking about our little fears and cautions. Maybe they are less protections as preparations for that day."

"So it seems. To make matters worse, if that is the right word, Eckhart said, 'To have a peaceful life is good, but to have a life of pain in patience is better; but to have peace in a life of pain is best.'"[168]

Anton thought for a while. "The Kingdom is not yet here. Love— not yet complete. That may be why there's always so such pain in the company of love. Peace is absent…Hence the pain."

"That is one of the things I am getting to like about you, Anton," Cyntheia said, laying her hand on his arm. "You wrestle with your own dark truth."

At her closer touch, a hint of chamomile passed over him, bringing shades of memories, soft and warm, from an island moment so many years before. The conversation paused for a moment. What is she thinking?, he wondered. What is she feeling? She seems less austere than

I had thought. How could she simply sit there with such serenity, so close, and say these things that stir my heart and mind and wonder? Cyntheia's smile and gaze and use of his name were gathering around him like invisible, intangible, yet ever stronger lines of love and enchantment. He felt his mind growing blank, empty, yet alert. Is this what Ramón had meant when he had said that, for Cyntheia, a man would be "willingly gathered and made helpless like the fish of the sea"? Overhead the moon began its soft, gauzy statement as its light contended with the rising fog from the bay.

"Behold the Moon, Cyntheia."

"It's growing full. On a clear night it would be bright enough to read by."

"The Moon..." Anton pondered. "She has suffered from four hundred years of disenchantment. Yet she illumined my path and retreated from my sleepy eyes like a wordless question."

"I like the way you put that, Anton," Cyntheia smiled. "Where did you learn to talk like that?"

"Who knows? It just seems to be the way things come to me when you are around," he replied, nonplussed. They both sat quietly for a moment, conscious of so much left unsaid.

"The Moon...Sister Moon to Brother Sun. She also tells us when Easter is. Did you know that, Anton? Everything we do here is shaped and guided by the Moon: the tides, our calendar. And she lies in a bed of mystery immune to science. Looking up, I don't even know why her bed—I mean the night sky—is dark instead of purely sparkling with the light of all of those uncountable stars.[169]

"In the city with all its lights, we have nights that are dark only in name," Anton said thoughtfully.

"Yes, we need to thank God for darkness true and deep, and for the dark side of the Moon! My sense is that God is all of this, the dark and the light, plus passion beyond measure. Immense strength and utter weakness, not unlike that thirteen year old girl I told you about. I think that this is the view that Eckhart gives us, the view of the whole horizon from the mountain peak."

"I feel like we have made a little of that ascent today, Cyntheia."

"Yes, we have. God's net is wide. Now is the time to rest, Anton. Tomorrow is the Sabbath, even if it is Palm Sunday. Let's plan to meet on Monday." With a smile and again the lightest touch on his arm, she left him.

At her departure Anton felt a small shock of aloneness, a vacancy to his senses, almost as though a little death had occurred. He retrieved several sheets of paper from Ramón's home, and, returning to his sitting place, laid a fresh sheet across his knees. It rested calm and smooth like the ocean, awaiting his touch and his thoughts. For a long while he rested his eyes on the darkening sea. From where he sat he could barely see the campanile of the cathedral standing as a silent sentinel for another world. Memories of his travels, his slow days in the fields and the recent rapid turn of events flashed before his mind's eye. Cyntheia's face and voice rose again in his memory. He had been in her life for little more than a day. How could he begin to account for the strange and tumultuous feelings that welled up in him? Why account for them at all? Why not simply confess them, before returning to the darkness of the night? With several starts and pauses he wrote the following lines –

> One day far away you will sit beside me, my beloved, my friend;
> In your face will abide the beauty mirrored from the divine beyond,
> Fine lines will seat your eyes, the musical score of life's melodies.
> We will speak of works and nights and days,
> All begotten and bid forth and surrendered to laughter;
> Yes, all Loves received, yet waiting to be fulfilled.
> We will speak of dreams unfurling their hopes and wonders,
> For all hope points to the Love I have known through you.

When the words were before him, he looked at them with surprise. He felt that he had received a great and unmerited gift, with no demands for reciprocity, nor any claims. For this he felt simply sweet amazement at the day's end.

Her life was noble, although not widely visible. The effect of her being on those around her was incalculably diffusive; for the growing good of the world is partly dependent on unhistoric acts; and that things are not so ill with you and me as they might have been is half owing to the number who lived faithfully a hidden life, and rest in unvisited tombs.

Comment on the life of George Eliot (1819–1880),
Author unknown

What lovers love most is to see one another, and they prefer sight to all the other senses, because love exists and is generated by sight more than by any other sense.

Aristotle (384–322 bce),
Nicomachean Ethics IX.12

His ear to hearken to my need

Sunday offered rest to Anton. He slept in until the middle of the morning, rocked by the never–ending waves beneath the wharf. He attended a late morning Palm Sunday liturgy at the cathedral with scores of the faithful. He did not see Cyntheia. During the afternoon he walked around Monterey, visited the Robert Louis Stevenson museum and spoke with its gracious curators. He then spent the remainder of the afternoon with Ramón, alternately dozing in his fraying beach chair or holding a line over the railing.

In the evening while waiting for a fish to take his bait, Ramón wove leather around a strong, circular copper wire, and tied nylon lines in a complex, spider–like web leaving a hole in the center of the ring.

"What's that?" Anton asked.

"A 'dream–catcher,'" Ramón answered. "It nets bad dreams, and lets good dreams go through the center."

Anton studied the small object, with its dangling beads and smooth leather tails. It reminded him of Native American drums decorated with sacred animals; their mere presence in a room contributed to the healing of the spirit.

"Some dream–catchers don't have a hole," Ramón continued, "just cross–ties. They're for older people who welcome all their dreams. In fact, the old become the dream–makers. Just look at the lines on their faces…their eyes and their mouths release the dreams that are within them. Here, you keep this. I make them quickly."

That night, Anton retired early and slept well. When he emerged from Ramón's home on Monday morning he felt completely refreshed. The sea and sky were calm, and a low fog hung again over the bay. Looking over the edge of the wharf Anton could see sheets of water swirling through the pilings, glinting steely grey like the "Mohammed's ladder" of a fine Damascus sword.[170] A fine drizzle spread a morning veil over the immortal nakedness of the Pacific.

When he arrived at the cathedral patio, Cyntheia was nowhere to be seen. Boxes of tiles and a twenty pound bag of dry mortar covered by plastic lay beside the font, indicating that she had been there before him. Since the rain had ceased, Anton removed and folded up the covering. He sat beside the font and ran his hands and fingers around the bowl and rim, feeling its smoothness, and contemplating the geometric design that he knew was soon to disappear beneath their handiwork. He heard a door close and turned to see Cyntheia approaching. She was dressed in a skirt and cotton blouse as before, but also with a warm sweater. The sight of her, fresh and simple, gladdened him. She walked toward him with a long stride.

"Good morning!" he called to her.

"Good morning to you! The promise of a glorious day!" she exclaimed.

"Full of promise," he agreed. He was considering asking her about the previous day's celebration, but felt that the question "How was Palm Sunday?" would be a cliché unworthy of her. He was relieved when she settled beside him and said, "Let's see….I think we are ready to lay the tile."

"There are still many imperfections. They just didn't want to rub out," Anton said.

"Looks like a lot of them, doesn't it?" she smiled. "And they are so small! But who cares? Here, we laugh at perfectionism! Remember, this little bowl is a symbol of the Red Sea, and the whole ocean. John the Baptist would have been very rough with perfectionists. 'Lay straight the way of the Lord' does not mean that life is a straight line between two points.[171] Looking at his life, it would mean living with passion and value and meaning! Perfectionism keeps people living on the lowlands!

"Really, Anton," she continued, as she laid out rows of polished black and white mosaics and tile, "It's just so much bigger than our pet projects. The river and the ocean carve and gouge and polish whole cliffs and continents, and they do it with grains of sand. We need not get caught up in the details."

Anton laughed as well and said, "Only devils and no angels in the details!…Cyntheia, that reminds me of what I wrote a couple of nights ago."

"What was that?" she asked.

"Well..." Anton hesitated, then sighed, regretting his impulsive comment. Groping for words, he said, "I would like to—in the right place and time. Later, when our work is done. For now, I feel that there is some justice in my doing this grinding and sanding."

"And why is that?" she looked at him curiously.

Her question increased his confidence. "Beside you I feel tried and tested by life...the years of teaching flowing into each other, hundreds of students, the months in the vineyards; being weathered by wind and cold, the wandering. You seem so fresh, so..." he paused, searching, "so engaged in creating, I guess, and so vibrant and alive. I feel the ages, and ask what fruit I might still bear. At this point in my life I am less inclined to launch new projects than to behold the monuments of memory, to wonder..."[172]

"Yes," she said with a thoughtful smile. "But that is where your wisdom begins.[173] Only you must be careful not to live in your thoughts."

"With you beside me, that would be impossible." He stole a glance at her, and laughed again deep in his chest.

"And with you here, I am not left in lonely labor," she rejoined with the slightest blush on her cheeks. She addressed herself to the arranging of tiles. "Yes, I hear your wondering. Even these hills seem less like barriers than reminders of what lies beyond them. It is good to have a companion in wondering, and wandering, too." She also appeared to be nonplussed. "How we see what is around us, and hear, too, is the essence of creating. Don't be hard on yourself, and don't look too hard, either."

She paused and looked around the quiet garden as it gathered the light and shifted its shadows in the morning sun. A flash of silver blue caught her eye. "Look over there. When the butterfly or hummingbird visits us, we simply see it. The butterfly will flutter her wings slowly so you may experience yellow and balance with her on the stamen or pistil of a flower. That hummingbird keeps his family under the shade of the arches. The little thing will fling himself away from you should you try to reach for him. He will disappear even from our mind's eye should we try to turn his flutter into a sine wave and frequency. My mother, who never pushed her mind into the shapes of physics, could sit on one of those patio benches and open her hands and a hummingbird would settle into them like a nest." With that, Cyntheia cast a golden, sparkling smile on Anton.

"I would like to ask a favor of you, Cyntheia."

"What is that?"

"I would like to think of myself as your apprentice in this work."

"What do you mean?"

"I mean, this is the work you have done for years and years. It is completely new to me. I have the sense that if I do it, I might find a special kind of refreshment. It feels like a new beginning for me. If you show me the pattern, and show me the technique, and then let me do the work, then I would really know that I was present at its creation."

"Then, let it be so. We will begin together. Why don't you stir while I add water to the mortar?" Cyntheia began pouring water into a bucket while Anton stirred with a trowel. When the consistency was right, she showed him how to spread the mortar and fasten and align the small tiles. Through the morning hours she offered the following words like so many mosaics, sealing the verses into memory with long pauses of silence –

> I arise today
> Through the strength of Heaven,
> Light of sun
> Radiance of moon
> Splendour of fire
> Speed of lightning
> Swiftness of wind
> Depth of the sea
> Stability of earth
> Firmness of rock.
>
> I arise today
> Through God's strength to pilot me,
> God's eye to look before me
> His wisdom to guide me
> His way to lie before me
> His shield to protect me
> From all who shall wish me ill
> Afar and a'near
> Alone and in a multitude
> Against every cruel merciless power
> That may oppose my body and soul…

And the refrain –

> Christ with me, Christ before me,
> Christ behind me, Christ within me,

> Christ beneath me, Christ above me,
> Christ on my right, Christ on my left,
> Christ when I lie down, Christ when I sit down,
> Christ when I arise, Christ to shield me,
> Christ in the heart of everyone who thinks of me,
> Christ in the mouth of everyone who speaks of me
> I arise today.

Followed by additional verses —

> I bind this day to me forever,
> By power of faith, Christ's incarnation,
> His baptism in the Jordan River;
> His death on the Cross for my salvation,
> His bursting from the spiced tomb,
> His riding up the heavenly way,
> His coming at the day of doom,
> I bind unto myself today...

> I bind unto myself today
> The power of God to hold and lead,
> His eye to watch, His might to stay,
> His ear to hearken to my need.
> The wisdom of my God to teach,
> His hand to guide, his shield to ward,
> The word of God to give me speech,
> His heavenly host to be my guard...[174]

Anton held the silence during his tile laying. The mysterious verses reminded him of Ramón's sharp handclap above the high seas and the old man's song as the fish was brought fighting to the surface. In Cyntheia's chant he believed he also heard her mother's *curandera* spirit during birthing or healing ceremonies.

During the morning hours of silent working the shadows in the courtyard dwindled, and the pattern took shape. The repetitive motion and Cyntheia's quiet meditation calmed Anton's mind even as his heart was unsettled. Here in Monterey, where the fogs, storms and brilliant blue burst on one another, he was seized by feelings of ambiguity, of alluring possibilities that could become dashed hopes. When the work was done, would there be another moment like this, with her so close that he could hear every breath and feel every touch of the hand and brush of their shoulders? Anton became aware that he wanted to slow their work, and struggled inwardly against it. As she finished the last verse, he sighed long and deeply.

Cyntheia leaned toward him and said, "That was a deep sigh! A penny for your thoughts, Anton."

How could I tell her what I am thinking? he wondered. If the heart's joy could thunder, one could hear the booming! If prayers could clear clouds, the sun would be beaming! Elusively he said,

"The Christ of whom you speak is about love. The Jesus that proclaimed 'the Christ within' was a scandal. The more I think about it, the more its meaning dissolves in my mind. What is it about love, Cyntheia?...the Love that transcends family and tribe, even nation, even humanity itself, to become the fabric of the universe, the essence of God, as the prayer has it? Aren't we setting our unknowing in stone, in these very tiles?"

"I am right with you, Anton! What about the whole life that follows on this unbearable unknowing? How important is security and anonymity and normalcy to you, to me? What would happen if we walked away from it all, including the religion that refuses to deviate from the dominant culture of controlling, confining, buying, wasting, exploiting...and maybe even challenged it right down to the root, just like the witnesses and followers in Jesus' own time?"

"Well, Cyntheia, then we would know the truth about ourselves. Perhaps our bones would become a battleground, or more than likely we would simply live obscure, happy and loving lives with others."[175]

Quiet descended again. Then Cyntheia said in a lowered voice, "Anton, ordinarily I would avoid a conversation like this...feeling that I was mocking God with my false pieties, you know, words saying one thing, actions another. Precious principles don't claim me much any more."

"How well I know..."

"More than ever now, I value silence. 'For God is in heaven and we are on earth, therefore let our words be few.'[176] But I am grateful to you...We share a similar hunger. A question is real if it draws you forward in life."

She sat back, gazing at Anton steadily. Anton too returned her gaze. Between them lay images contained in indecipherable feelings. Then she said, "Duty calls...I'll be back in a little bit."

Anton continued working alone throughout the morning. Had he just spoken truth? Would his bones lie as a sacred destination for others? Would he live and die a beloved and cherished human being? He thought long and hard about the protections and comforts that he had erected to silence the real questions and to keep himself safe and secure. Salaries and tenure. Retirement plans and life insurance. Savings accounts and summer vacations. As he had discarded these conveniences, he felt like he was growing into a wealth of relatedness. True to the pattern that was emerging under his hands, where the whorls of the Breastplate led both to the edges and to each other, he felt closer to a center not of his own making.

Shortly before noon Cyntheia returned, bringing sandwiches and juice and fruit. As they were finishing their lunch, Anton pointed to his tile work and asked, "Cyntheia, how is this looking? It's not easy to line up the tiles up across the dark spaces. Any ideas?"

"You can use another tile for some alignment," she smiled, "but don't worry about being too precise. When it is all done, it will look right, not straight, but right in relationship to everything else. Also remember what happens to straight lines when they are under water."

Anton said, "So keep going the way I am?"

"Yes," she said, rubbing her hands across the small tile pieces, "It's just fine."

They sat and worked in the warm silence of the garden. The slow movements of the day brought the brightening hues to the darker sides of leaves, and a lone bird whistled or chirped from its nest. And always, always, rose the low murmurs of the ocean.

"Our little play is this afternoon. Would you like to come?"

"I would enjoy that." Anton's curiosity was piqued. "What's it about?"

"A little 'Oberammergau,' a 'passion play,' if you like. Not the great Passion that we all know, but simply the drama of an encounter, a day in the life of Jesus, but set in Holy Week."[177]

"Rather like setting the mundane within the sacred; not the other way around?"

"Exactly...one little moment that prepared everyone for the great Moment."

"What do you mean?"

"I'm not going to tell you the story. Only a hint: I have to believe that all the people around Jesus experienced something deeply shocking and uplifting in him. There are all kinds of people in the Gospel stories, of course, some you notice, others you don't: some scurrilous people; others who are too nice for their own good; some who claim your attention but seem offensive to Jesus; others who are leading characters and have some personality; and still others who have no name or lines in the drama. I think that Jesus affected them all. We try to tell part of that story."

"Did you write the script?" Anton asked.

"Hardly. It's from the Gospel of Luke, embellished, or maybe corrected with some ideas from Mark. There is some language from the Song of Songs that reminds us of that good, vital Hebrew energy that unfortunately was lost on later Christianity.[178] Our imagination supplies what the writing itself leaves out. That's the wonder of the Gospel: it's so austere it forces you to fill in the full human texture. I need to be going now, but I hope you come along. You might enjoy it."

"Where is it being performed?"

"In the sanctuary."

"Good. After it is over, I'll come back here and continue working. Can you entrust this to me?"

"Completely. No reservations, whatsoever."

"Thank you. I'll see you there."

Left alone now, Anton worked carefully and steadily for another two hours, placing and aligning and twisting the small tiles into place. He wondered what awaited him.

The Lord spoke to me saying, "Look at my heart, and see!" A beautiful rose with five petals covered his whole breast, and the Lord said: "Praise me in my five senses, which are indicated by this rose."

Mechthild of Magdeburg (1212?–1282),
Liber gratiae spiritualis[179]

THE RED ROSE OF CARMEL[180]

A FEW MINUTES before the drama was to begin Anton dusted off his shirt and trousers and washed his hands and rubbed in some of the oil that Cyntheia had given him when they had begun their work. He walked around the building and through the thick doors of the cathedral.

Inside, curtains were drawn across all but one of the windows, this last allowing a gentle light to settle on the front altar space. Hanging candelabra lit the way down the center aisle. The altar had been rolled back and all the chairs had been moved into a theater setting facing the altar. A single candle on the altar concentrated the light in the room around the space below. The transept and much of the audience space was lost in the shadows. A low couch was placed before the altar itself. A small table stood at the far end of the couch. It held a bowl of Mediterranean fruit, dates, figs, raisins and oranges, and a decanter of water or wine. There were no other props.

A player dressed as a household servant walked down the side aisle and lit additional candles on stands beside the altar. The rustle of the audience quieted in anticipation. Someone then rang a gong near the cathedral doors, which were opened by another servant. A group of men in traditional Hebrew clothing entered and jostled and pushed their way down to the stage area. They were clean and groomed and wore sandals; a few wore headdresses to ward off the sun. They were gesticulating and laughing and engaged in intense but garbled conversations. Political and religious words could sometimes be distinguished, with references to Caesar, the month of Omer, the celebrations of Shavuot and Pesach, and the success of the wheat harvest.[181] Another, older and jovial man with a prayer shawl and rope belt, the traditional clothing of the Pharisee and presumably the host of the house, entered from the wings and greeted every visitor with a handshake, smiles and a kiss on the cheek.

The gong sounded again and the host drew away from the group to open the door himself. He then led a man in his forties, presumably playing Jesus, down the aisle. With a gracious gesture of welcome and liberality, the host invited Jesus to settle on the couch. This time, however, the doors were left open, and the audience could see a motley group of people, young and old, gawking and engaged, milling outside the house of the wealthy Pharisee and even pushing themselves several yards into the aisle of the cathedral stage. For a moment, Anton wondered who the real audience was—those sitting like him in the cathedral chairs, or the men in costumes in front of the altar, or the nameless numbers near the doors. He then re-focused on the action of the play. By now Jesus had said words of greeting to the other men, and was reclining on the couch. In the candlelight the shadows sank deeply into his weathered and sun–burnished skin. A thin and threadbare cloak barely reached to his dusty feet.

At this point, a small scuffle took place in the crowd of villagers outside the door. Overcoming low cries of disapproval and restraining tugs, Cyntheia in a player's garb pulled away from other women and villagers. She was barefoot and dressed with the utmost simplicity in an ankle–length robe that was threadbare yet clean and free of wrinkles. One arm and hand was kept hidden beneath her cloak. The moment she entered she drew aside her veil with her free hand. Behind her the common people peered and gaped. Hands flew up and covered foreheads and mouths. Amazement and consternation abounded among the villagers long accustomed to standing outside the thresholds of privilege.

Cyntheia calmly and gracefully walked along the center aisle, yet remaining in the shadows. There was nothing furtive or unsure in her gait, nor any haste. Her hair was bound up and around her head, and she wore earrings. Her hair was also adorned with a single red rose. Anton was startled to see how lip balm and eye shadow had transformed her Latin beauty into a striking Palestinian motif. Passing unnoticed behind the group of chattering men, she mounted the altar steps from the side. The men standing below and to the sides of the altar continued to engage one another with the same energy and motion, although now with quieter voices. At her first words, they became perfectly still and motionless in postures of engagement. Thus the new arrival could share her thoughts with the audience, even before her presence was known by the other players. With a distant, searching expression she began her soliloquy[182] –

> Dark am I, yet lovely, O sons and daughters of Jerusalem,
> dark like the tents of Kedar,
> like the tent curtains of Solomon.
> Do not stare at me because I am dark,
> for I am darkened by the sun.
> My mother's sons were angry with me
> and made me take care of the vineyards;
> My own vineyard I have neglected.

At this point the woman knelt on the altar steps, still unseen by the guests. Her voice grew rich and clarion with emotion as she continued,

> Tell me, you whom I love, where you graze your flock
> and where you rest your sheep at midday.
> Why should I be like a veiled woman
> beside the flocks of your friends?

> All night long on my bed I looked for the one my heart loves;
> I looked for him but did not find him.
> I have gone about the city, through its streets and squares;
> I have searched for the one my heart loves.
> I looked for him but did not find him.
> The watchmen found me as they made their rounds in the city.
> "Have you seen the one my heart loves?"
> Scarcely had I passed them
> when I found the one whom my heart loves.

During the speech Anton again glanced around the audience. All eyes were rapt or perplexed, staring at the uninvited guest or shifting between the Jesus figure and the men in their mute postures. Jesus himself had fallen silent, and was looking away from the source of the voice and toward the one open window, whose light dressed his face in a warm glow.

At that point, with the last emphatic words, *"whom my heart loves,"* the woman stepped into the illumined circle, and knelt directly in front of the reclining Jesus. At her sudden intrusion, the men reacted with shocked and indignant emotion. One or two men uttered a guttural groan or explicative. Another half–shouted, "Swine!" Shouts of "Remove her!" and "Horror to my eyes!" were heard. The host appeared equally aghast and distraught.

But rather than seize her, the guests melted away, clearing more space for the woman and Jesus. The men then froze in figures of distress and anger, words unuttered, hands raised, faces contorted. The stage effect created a still–life of the reclining guest of honor, the kneeling woman, a bright–colored fruit basket, and brilliant points of light from the candles, an island of calm and serenity in the midst of anger and chaos. Anton could hear the audience gasp at the sight, as emotionally stark as a Caravaggio painting.[183] All the while Jesus remained silent, his eyes now resting on the face of the kneeling woman.

In a slow and deliberate way, with her face lowered, the woman drew her hidden hand out from beneath her cloak. She held an alabaster jar with a lid, and placed it on the floor. Another shock rippled through the audience and guests as they noticed her hand was riddled with leprosy. With both hands she withdrew the rose from her hair and placed it on the couch near Jesus' chest. She poured some oil on her hands, then lifted Jesus' weathered and dusty feet and rubbed the oil back and forth, around his toes, his heel, and the arch, first one foot, then the other. Lifting his feet ever so tenderly, she kissed his feet, tears bright on her face. As she rubbed his feet she said,

> While the king was at his table,
> my perfume spread its fragrance.
> My lover is to me a sachet of myrrh,
> a cluster of henna blossoms
> from the vineyards of En Gedi.
>
> Like an apple tree among the trees of the forest
> is my lover among the young men.
> I delight to sit in his shade.
> Strengthen me with raisins,
> refresh me with apples,
> for I am faint with love.

The woman now glanced up at Jesus as if to explore his emotions. Her action seemed to ask the question for the whole audience. How would Jesus respond to this? With queasiness at the touch of her diseased hand? With embarrassment and fear of doing something shameful? With anger as the codes and conventions of the purity culture crumbled? Instead, Jesus' face was calm, completely at peace, even blissful. He leaned toward the kneeling woman. With a shock the audience noticed that tears were gathering in Jesus' eyes as well. His mouth was slightly open. He swallowed and whispered words for her and the audience alone, words emanating from his mind as he sang his own love song,

> You have ravished my heart, my sister, my bride,
> You have ravished my heart with a glance of your eyes,
> With one jewel of your necklace.
> How sweet is your love, my sister, my bride!
> How much better is your love than wine,
> And the fragrance of your oils than any spice![184]

The woman stirred, looking for something with which to dry Jesus' feet. She felt the hem of her dress, reconsidered, then with her eyes meeting Jesus squarely, removed her scarf, unpinned her hair and shook it down around her shoulders. Gathering her hair, she wiped Jesus' feet and dried them of all the oil and dust and tears. At this very instant, the men in the crowd, who had been standing like anguished statues, came alive again and reeled as one at the sight before them; they then froze again into new expressions of animosity and condemnation. The audience gasped again at the rising threat of violence against the woman as her actions shocked the prejudices of the men. She then said,

> But to confess my love!
> To take your face in my hands,
> to kiss those parted lips
> that bring forth words of another world,
> another, greater truth!
>
> Your tears mingle with my own.
> 'Oh, turn your eyes from me.
> They overwhelm me.'[185]

Jesus said,

> Friend, with your oil I am anointed;
> with your perfume, all things even unto death
> are made beautiful.

He then arose and said,

John's baptism is completed in her anointing.
I tell you the truth,
wherever the great dream is shared throughout the world,
what she has done will also be told, in memory of her.
Make way for her, and hear her.[186]

He then stood aside. At this, the woman wrapped up her hair again, sending its earthy, damp perfume smelling like roses wafting around the room. She arose and walked, tall and strong, outside into the day and her community. Jesus remained standing in his place while the other players departed through side exits; he, too, then turned and departed through another side exit.

Anton departed with the audience to reflect upon what he had seen and heard in the drama. He imagined Cyntheia and the Jesus figure to be communing, almost the Great Mother of India engaging the Rabbi and Healer of Nazareth for purposes far wider than their own cultural and historical milieu. He mused over the interior and shared passion and desire expressed by the two figures in their roles, and the balanced image of their both standing to achieve a new point of view, a larger horizon. He saw the courageous feminine breaking herself loose to encounter the truth of her heart, yet returning to live again with her people, a whole woman in the human community, called to love greatly and acclaimed as prophet and annunciator of the Good News.

Cyntheia's invitation to the play had been an invitation into the very life of her spirit. Who was inviting whom? Who was the lover, who the beloved? Was he not being found by someone whom he had not been consciously seeking? He remembered the frequent use of the word *Friend* in the Gospels, and the rejection of any sense of slavery or servitude that obscured the self–surrender of love. Could the lesson from the play be that the Christ presence gathers all the loves of the human heart: its simple affections, solid and stable friendship, restless and ecstatic *eros,* and *agape* without conditions or constraints? Furthermore, could only the Christ live in or through these loves without the frailties, denials, obsessions, complexities and complaints that accompany most human experience of love?[187]

Back at work and guided by the pencil etchings, Anton laid tile after tile with a careful and steady touch. From time to time he added a little water to the mortar to keep it moist. Before long he had finished the two circles on one side of the font, then began laying the tiles between the two circles. As the tile was laid down, he noticed textures and contrasts that had been subtly present in the design itself. The first bridge between the two circles was accomplished without great effort. Then, before it was complete, he noticed that he had left out small black tiles which lay at angles on the path like so many hurdles; so he had to pull the pieces off and add in the black squares. When these pieces were in place, a whole new dimension of the pattern became apparent. He also noticed the contrasting black on either side of the cross–bridge, and how both light and dark revealed and complemented each other.

By late in the afternoon, Anton had covered the entire concave surface of the font. He was surprised by how quickly he had progressed. It had taken him a whole day to prepare the surface, and a little more than a few hours to create the pattern, and fewer still to complete it with the ceramic materials. He felt satisfied as he looked over his work and scraped and cleaned little pieces of residue from the tiles and sanded surface. He felt weary but pleased.

That evening after dinner, while Ramón settled near the railing and let down his line, Anton took one of the beach chairs and moved away to the leeward side of the wharf. He pulled out some paper and began to write –

Cyntheia,

> After what I have seen today I can only say with Dostoevsky, "Beauty will save the world." It is futile to try to describe beauty directly. But the need to do so has never waned, for we cannot but respond to its power.
>
> So, speaking to my future memories, I would describe you as freed from the tyranny of time. In your face you condense the miracle of human nature...What more can be said?...Your complexion is tanned, smooth, vivacious. Your blue–grey eyes and a smile radiate joy itself. Your hair, mid–shoulder in length, dark–brown with tints and traces of bleaching from the sun; a strong frame and shapely figure; a necklace of shells; skirt and sandals.
>
> Your mind conveys thoughtfulness without a trace of book-ishness or arrogance; a mind fully alive, with memories that illumine the present, but do not constrain the present to the formulas of the past. You see dignity in the distressing condition of the poor and abandoned and have compassion for

those who stagger under the burden of affluence. Not for an instant are you possessed by an ambition for doing or accomplishing. You respect your old uncle's wisdom and strength and, perhaps, a younger man's wordless longings and restlessness. You esteem yourself and your femininity and needs. You understand intuitively the role of art in clearing our minds to see and receive the spirit and to give voice to the heart...

Cyntheia, by your side, in your service of things that I can only remotely understand, I see the education of my desire. Your very nature beckons. Even when you are close at hand, by my very side, you invite me onward. It is as though you lie on the new side of the moon, moving ahead of me as you wait for the full light of the sun to shine on you, and thereupon me and all others.

All of these are words from my mind. Listening to my heart I feel something else...You are like a dream...a wondrous dream or an answer to wordless prayers. In my journeys, I have come to trust the truth of these feelings of delight, of adoration. Beside me, your beautiful and living soul shines through the sparkle of your eye. My soul is enlivened by your smile and laughter and intensity and thought...In all of this, the divine is disclosed to me, made close, passionate, desirable.

Anton

It was her voice that made
The sky acutest at its vanishing.
She measured to the hour its solitude.
She was the single artificer of the world
In which she sang. And when she sang, the sea,
Whatever self it had, became the self
That was her song, for she was the maker.
Then we, as we beheld her striding there alone,
Knew that there never was a world for her
Except the one she sang and, singing, made.

>From Wallace Stevens (1879–1955),
The Idea of Order at Key West

The Timbre of Her Voice, Nature's Music

On the Tuesday morning of Holy Week Anton worked alone. By noon he had finished all four of the whorls and cross–bridges and the dark background. The pattern was striking and mysterious. While the skin of his hands was cracking from the rubbing and drying of the mortar, he felt an immense satisfaction. Up close he could notice irregularities and even cracks in the small pieces; but from a standing position, the whole pattern was symmetrical, graceful and dynamic with suggested meanings.

Cyntheia arrived just as he was placing the last tiles. She had a walking stick and a small pack back. She smiled and laughed with excitement at the sight of the nearly completed work. "Oh, this is just so exciting! A masterpiece! What was to have been my gift is yours, Anton! Thank you, thank you! Now, before we can rest, we will do our grouting work. Then, I promise you a walk to a special place with a lovely view. I brought a picnic lunch for us. And by the way, there was a note in the office that your friend Gene called. I called him back."

"How is he?"

"Okay, I suppose. We don't know one another, but I did say that I knew you from college, and that we were getting acquainted again. That helped."

"And…?"

"None of your business," she laughed with mock sauciness. "We had a very nice talk, and not a little about you…Seriously, though, I learned that he had been to Monterey a few times, and had lived in Santa Cruz. He wanted to know if you were still here. I said Yes. He said that in that case he will be coming down out of the valley tomorrow."

"Is he all right?"

"Generally speaking, yes. He did not go into detail."

Pleased with the prospect of seeing the lonely younger man again, Anton turned his attention to the font. For the next hour, he and Cyntheia smoothed in the sand–colored grout between the tiles, and followed with strokes of damp sponge. They worked quickly while the grout hardened.

"There!" Cyntheia said as they finished wiping the last excess from the bowl. "It will be watertight in a couple of hours. Ramón will fit the piping later this afternoon, and our work is done! The community says that it may be used during the Vigil."

Anton gazed on the completed font with a sense of awe. From a rough bowl in the Salinas nursery to a completed, gleaming font in little less than a week! The shiny white and black tiles caught the afternoon sun like an emblazoned shield, a gigantic flower that claimed the attention of the patio garden.

Suddenly Cyntheia was on her feet, saying, "Come along! We must go down now to the ocean. We will bring back some of its water. I want to show you a special place, too. We will need to walk fast. We have a ways to go."

Instead of descending the now–familiar Camino El Estero, Cyntheia led Anton along side streets and along a trail near the edge of the forest between the Presidio and the town. The trail turned into the forest and soon all habitations were lost from sight. Silence dwelt beneath the whisper of the wind and the crunch of their steps and the incessant bass timpani of the waves below. They entered a clearing surrounded by second–growth redwood and pine. An invisible parliament of birds chortled and bantered in the shrubs and trees.

"This is one of my favorite places," Cyntheia said as they walked along a leaf–strewn path towards the center of the meadow. "I like to think that Robert Louis Stevenson wandered through here during his visits to Monterey. He came to our little village to tend to his sweetheart when she was ill, I believe. It's a good place for our lunch."

Anton whistled between his lips, then plopped down on a fallen log and absent–mindedly pulled up a long blade of grass to chew upon. "I learned about that down at the Stevenson House," he said. "Funny thing, I noticed a certain conspiracy of silence down there among the older women docents. I had heard that Stevenson had an old shack up in the Carmel Valley somewhere. But when I asked them how to find it, the ladies had only vague, round–about directions. They found themselves suddenly engaged with other visitors. When I just waited until they could talk with me, they said that you had to deal with construction and obstacles further down the valley, or that the path was obscure or overgrown. I can accept that. It just seemed rather strange."

As Anton spoke, Cyntheia spread a tablecloth on the leaves and wild grass and set out sandwiches and juice. The warmth and clarity of the whole space slowed time to the buzzing of ladybugs and glinting tilt of silvery leaves. "Stevenson is alive in those women," she said. "They have the map to his treasure! You expect them to part with it with just anyone?"

"Well, maybe not. On second thought, maybe I have already discovered Stevenson in Gene, my forlorn friend living in the gloom of the valley."

"Then all that is missing is his beloved Fanny Osbourne."

"There is more sad truth in that than you know, Cyntheia. But in the spirit of all that, if Stevenson tramped up here, it would be a good place for me to give you what I wrote the other night."

"Thank you, Anton. That sounds very sweet. But first, let's give this glade a name."

"And a place on our own treasure map. Any suggestions?"

"Hmm...I would call it *yotokut*. Uncle Ramón told me that this means 'center of the world,' where the first redwood grew. These young redwoods are timekeepers. They contain their memory in their growing rings, and the innermost ring holds the memory of the first beginning. Only thing is, if we called this *yotokut,* we would have to build a sweat lodge right here for the First Salmon rite every year. That means we would have to make a home in the village...What would you call it, Anton?"

Forcing himself to concentrate on the question after Cyntheia's astonishing off-hand comment, he ventured, "How about *perikalia?* That means 'beautiful–all–around.' Homer could think of no better word for the center of Circe's world in the *Odyssey*. The name is worthy of your patroness."[188]

"A man after my own heart!" she laughed. "Yes, look around! Isn't it stunning? Look at the sky up there, always blue or misty grey, the green trees waving their arms to the music of the ocean below or weeping with gladness for all the water that rains on them."

"The noble trees...," Anton said. "If we could only understand their language! Their only weakness is their inability to protest our misuse of them and their earth. But they do speak...Away up here in these hills, their branches sing and rumble as they twist. Listen..." He let his words die away into the surrounding silence. "The pine needles sound like,

like… I don't know, Cyntheia!, like some kind of baleen instrument that filters the air as it roves."[189]

"It does restore the soul," Cyntheia agreed. "I wonder what tales come home here. Probably every nook and cranny has a story about little sprites who hold court when we're not looking, and trolls scheming new night raids! Here's your sandwich. Better eat it before one of the little ones steals it."

After a few minutes, Cyntheia said, "I would enjoy reading what you wrote."

"Here it is." The intoxicating atmosphere of lightly floating seed spores and bees busy gathering pollen helped Anton to surrender his anxiety.

Cyntheia read quietly as they ate. When finished, she folded the paper and its verses and put it in her backpack. She then placed the pack under her head as a pillow. She gazed up into the trees, then took Anton into her eyes. "Your calling me beautiful, Anton, says a lot more about you than about me…"[190]

Anton did not hasten to respond. Ever so slowly he pieced together his words, "It is an experience beyond my ken, Cyntheia, that you would acknowledge your own beauty! I can only offer my tribute. But even now, I am filled with a sense of futility of doing justice to what is before my very eyes.[191] I have been your guest here. My work is nearly done, and I'll be going on. But I don't leave as I came. I have been living in the great valleys and dreamed of a great mountain peak; although," Anton paused wistfully, "not to be able to come back here with you on another day feels more like looking over a cliff."

"I think I know what you mean…Don't think you're alone in this," Cyntheia said. "But come on, this is today, and we're together and we have a ways to go."

They gathered up the remnants of their lunch and brushed the grass where they had lain back into its natural state. Anton's spirits were lifted with Cyntheia's confession echoing in his ears. Emerging from the forest, they slid their way down the sifted sand to the shore. They were wrapped in their own thoughts and embraced by the unending rush and lap of the ocean. The shoreline with its uneven cliffs and chasms showed the ravages of innumerable storms. Short junipers, standing stalwart and twisted, ran along the top of the sandy berm, along with grasses and succulents that huddled under the driving elements. Smooth and gnarled branches and logs littered the shoreline, along with clumps of tangled kelp and fragments of crab exoskeletons and the formless blobs of beached jellyfish. Seagulls marched along the embankment of sand, and sandpipers ran their free formations with the ebb and flow of waves.

"This is a good place. Let's sit a minute," Cyntheia said. Digging her hands into the cool sand, she continued, "Sometimes when I have time I walk down all the way down to the Tor House where Robinson Jeffers lived."

"Angry, lonely Jeffers…," Anton said.

"Oh, he belongs here as much as the harbor seals and the killer whales along the coast," Cyntheia said. "He gave a human voice to the tides and water spouts. And he is a master of demolition. Look around," she swept her hand from the horizon to the hills. "He was overwhelmed by the grandeur of it all, the whole cosmos. Standing before all this, humankind seems very small. He saw his little castle of sea stone in Carmel as a refuge and as a stubborn statement. Old Uncle Ramón says he expects to blow away like a cloud. Jeffers faces his chest against it all like a storm wall, only to crash like a wave. We need the angry poet to assure us that even our futilities are endearing. I try to read a little of his work every time I come down here."

"I remember feeling like I had come through a battle zone when I read his poetry."

"On a really stormy day out here, Anton, any language to describe the sea must be apocalyptic. As Luke said, 'There will be signs in the sun, the moon, and the stars, and on the earth distress among nations confused by the roaring of the sea and the waves.'[192] That's the perspective of a little sea creature like the sand crab, whose world below has been rocked by our footsteps. Why should we be surprised we are all caught up in the wailing, the squall, the torment of tortured nature?"

"Who are we then, *what* are we, who both suffer and tell the story?" Anton asked.

"Jeffers' answer is clear," Cyntheia responded. "He said in 'My Beloved Subjects,'

> My love, my loved subject: mountain and ocean, rock, water
>   and beasts and trees
> They are the protagonists; the human people are only symbolic
>   interpreters.'[193]

"If we are only the interpreters, what is the language?" Anton persisted.

"Feelings, my good man!" she said. "Our body's message to ourselves that we are fully alive!"

"And the noblest feelings, of awe, of wonder?"

"He said of beauty that it is the 'divinely superfluous.' He often associated it with the stupendous forces of nature, the forcefulness of things that stirs our sense of the sublime," Cyntheia responded.

"But the beauty that stirs me is quieter," Anton persisted. "As in Shelley's *Hymn to Intellectual Beauty* –

Thy light alone, like mist o'er mountains driven,
Or music by the night wind sent
Through strings of some still instrument,
Or moonlight on a midnight stream,
Gives grace and truth to life's unquiet dream.[194]

"That's the language of the spirit that has been echoing in me ever since my arrival here. When I first saw you, Cyntheia, everything in your face both drew me and pointed me toward something else. I was conscious of no feelings. Just direction. The icon there confused me, too. Instead of looking off in the distance, you were somehow looking into a mirror and seeing yourself. But without one bit of narcissism. It was like that holy triangle of Beauty that we knew long ago."

"Perhaps," she said. "Let's sit and listen…"

The water moved and raised a sea of sound above the ocean itself. Anton reveled in the grandeur of the moment. Cyntheia's calm countenance and half–smile spoke of her pleasure as well. Anton put his arm around her shoulders, watching her eyes carefully for signs of discomfort. There were none, and Anton was conscious of utterly sweet feelings.

"It's music out here, Cyntheia. Could music be nature's language then? I love the timbre of your voice, its music. It carries nature's message into my life."

"Maybe Adam was a musician first and foremost," Cyntheia said. "The first names for things would be a chord, a song…"[195]

"Then Eve was the voice. What was her song when Adam awoke to discover her gazing upon him with soft, wondering eyes? Would that the world could have known such a great peace…Perhaps we would never have been closed out of Paradise." Their voices grew quiet as they listened to the bassy boom of waves, accented by the flutings of seabirds.

"Come on, let's walk a bit." Cyntheia stood up and offered Anton her hand. They walked down closer to the waves as they spent themselves on the shore, and removed their shoes in order to walk along the water's edge. They settled into the pervasive, quieting sounds of the sea. After a while, Cyntheia spoke again.

"Speaking of music: listen...this whole seacoast is the greatest percussion and wind ensemble in the world."

"The melody is lost in the crescendos," Anton observed.

"'Our blessed rage for order'!"[196] Cyntheia laughed. "It is simply too big! Out here, God dances his ecstasy like a primitive tribesman. His chant slams into our consciousness. He is a prodigal in his vitality, a wild, swirling inferno of creativity. He sets the very water spirits alive so they climb ship masts in electric storms. You can reach out and wipe them off in your hands and smear them on your hair!"

"An amazing image," Anton said.

"We have to keep a sense of perspective. Out here, and under the stars at night and in the fields and forests and along the cliffs of Big Sur and the thousand year old redwoods, we waver like weak reeds."[197]

"But thinking reeds, and soft inside," Anton said, remembering his learning from the Great Valley.

"Yes!, and life is too short but to think on the greatest of things and to squint toward the great light." Cyntheia smiled at him. "And so we do! Come on, Friend, take my hand! Let us go deeper into the water." She offered Anton her hand. Their eyes met and reflected the sparkle of the ocean.

When the water was up to their knees, Cyntheia pulled a small glass vial from her pocket, and, leaning over, dipped it beneath the water and filled it half full. "Now, your turn," she said, handing the vial to Anton. Placing it beneath the water, he watched small bubbles come to the surface, and knew that the vessel was full. "It has been many months, too many months, since I set foot in the ocean. This is called the *aurum potabile,* the elixir of life, in the old dispensation."

"May it pour into us, then. This water is the essence of our blood. It is the lifeblood of our spirit," Cyntheia said. "The ocean is fed by all the sacred rivers: the Columbia...the Mississippi and Missouri...the Indus and Ganges...the Tigris and Euphrates...the Nile and the Yangtze and all the little trickles and torrents that wash the land. It is our great source and destination." She ran her hands back and forth in the foamy wavelets, then continued,

"The best we can do is to take a teaspoon from the waters. This ocean is our unknowing; the land, our familiar ground. The sands speak...Would we have the ears to detect the crashing grains below! The shore is the edge of what we know and what is safe. Why else do children love to stand in the waves and feel the sand disappear under their feet when the waves rush out? Such are our lives and our proud knowing."

The water ebbed and flowed, a toccata of timeless music, accompanied by the lonely cries of wheeling gulls in their descending tritones.

"Children do not stand on the shore alone," Anton said quietly. Nor will such beauty ever ebb and flow like the tide, he thought. "Cyntheia..." He opened his arms wide and she came into them and nestled her face on his chest.

"This is a great goodness," he said, his lips next to her temples.

She smiled up at him and placed her hand around his neck. "Yes. The same gift as of long ago," and her voice offered up the words of love. And then, as they stood on the rim of the Pacific with its living waters playing at their feet, their lips touched and time stood still and even the sound of the waves waned away...

After walking back up the bluff to the city and the Cathedral, Cyntheia and Anton found Ramón on the patio fastening a copper pipe and valve beneath the center drain of the font. To test the integrity of the tile work and piping, they filled the font to near brimming and allowed the water to become still. Then they sat and gazed into its quiet depths. They could see their faces reflected in the pool. But more apparent than their faces were the swirls and patterns of the tile design beneath, and even the flaws and fissures that gave the bowl its mortal texture.

"The seal is good, *maestra*," Ramón said.

Smiling at Anton, Cyntheia said, "We have the makings of a new *maestro* among us, my old uncle. Soon he will do his own work, and need no one's help...Now that the pool is calm, Anton, take your finger and write your name in the water."

Anton dipped his index finger in the center and paused. The ripples from his touch disturbed the whole pool until it became chaos. He waited until calm returned, then inscribed the letter "A," then an "N." By the time he had inscribed his name the pool had again become a tumult of waves bounding and rebounding in chaotic motion. When he had finished, the waters grew calm again.

"So much for that," he laughed ruefully. "The harder I wrote, the more turbulent the water. Even the pattern below disappears."

"At our first touch, the ripples flow to the very boundaries of the pool. It's not so much our name as our presence that is communicated throughout."

"Another lesson from the waters," Anton said.

"Yes. Even a drop creates waves and valleys of symmetry and proportion. Our heavy, clumsy hands stir up storms in even a small pool like this. As we knew when we began, the still, motionless center is now obscured from sight. Only a calm surface can suggest its very existence.[198]

Looking at Ramón she said, "Shall we take it inside?"

After draining the font, they lifted it onto the gardener's cart and wheeled it into the Cathedral. As they entered their eyes underwent the dazzling, disorienting effect of darkness after bright outdoor light. They unloaded the font onto its waiting frame just beyond the threshold of the Cathedral, near the entrance of the nave, then stood back to contemplate their work. It lay solid and graceful and inviting in elegant rondure.

"We will add the water tomorrow. I will slip in a bit of the ocean water, and the priest will add a few drops from the river Jordan. Thus, the first ritual action: baptism," Cyntheia mused. "From here into the community of belief and memory. Back again to listen to the story of freedom and salvation. Share the meal again and be filled with its strength. Then out again into the world for action. It is all so very simple."

Old Ramón smiled and took both of Cyntheia's hands. "We are done, with plenty of time before Easter."

"We were not so crazy after all, were we, *tío* Ramón? Come, let's light some candles."

Walking up to the side chapel, they took long matches and lit several rows of candles. Blank like an unthinking mind, the wall behind the shelf of candles came alive with shadows that moved and rose and toppled with the waving flames. The icon reigned in its sanctuary of darkness, a hint of the God who reveals nothingness to the hungering soul. Suggesting neither remorse nor commentary on the human condition, offering no invitation, extending no consolation or affirmation, the icon simply said: *Behold. Ponder. Balance the Yes and the No.*

When they were outside again, Anton said, "Let's sit for a moment" and walked to the low brick wall where he had first met Cyntheia.

Noticing a pensive expression on her face, he asked, "What's troubling you?"

With her focused gaze Cyntheia said, "It's what Ramón said, 'Time before Easter...' I've been thinking about it all week, but haven't given it a moment's real thought. I know that that sounds absurd. If Easter is something that we celebrate every year, it obviously has to be happening all the time, and right here, too. But, I hate to say it, nothing seems to be different from one year to the next. I still have a hard time seeing it. So I keep asking, 'Where is Easter?' I am thinking that this question is compelling me to free myself."

Cyntheia stood up and waved her hands across the arch of the sky as if to free herself from the unanswered question. "But our work is done and it is good!"

Then, dropping her hands, she looked at Anton again, intently, as though a question or an image had become etched in her mind. Surprised by her own sudden surge of passion, she turned her back and walked to the low brick wall that overlooked the bay.

Anton felt at a loss. He was startled by her next words,

"How would you both like to come to my home for dinner tonight?"

Anton and Ramón returned home and bathed and rested. Anton walked down to the shoreline and settled on a park bench with a view to the salty blue that always and never changed. He drew out a fresh piece of paper and wrote,

Cyntheia,

> How you call me to you! Often during these days I thought of kissing your exquisite lips, just once, or maybe more than once...thoughts stolen from my tile work, or perhaps etched in my heart by the work itself and your presence...
>
> Yet even as I thought this, I imagined taking you by the hand and drawing you down to the bluff where the ocean waves seethe. Yet it was you who drew me there! Has your heart been here with me, all along? The gift of a kiss in such a place!
>
> I came north, first escaping, then searching, surrendering, now finding. I have seen that what I seek lies just beyond my reach, beyond the threshold, in a paradise where serenity and the wilds dwell together. When I said, "Children do not stand

on the shore alone," I meant that I cannot cross that threshold by myself.

He did not complete the thought. After a few moments, he resumed –

> I have no words for what is occurring in my heart. And I am limited in my understanding and my freedom to speak. Yet what is all this meaning, this voiceless language that passes between us? Seeing must have its own language. Looking upon you is like a blind man seeing for the first time. He beholds his first flower, gazes with wonder upon a bird, a butterfly, a tree, a woman, all as they fully are. We are more than voice, more than language...We are creatures who delight in seeing...I needed to see you, because I could never have imagined you. You are one of those human persons whose mere existence awakens my awareness of a whole dimension, hitherto hidden.
>
> Only a few nights ago I looked up into the Milky Way, its lacy folds draped over the dark and quiet valley where I rested. I saw the Moon slip between my dreams and the dawn. In the glow of that memory I will give the vision a whispered name, your name.
>
> Now, as I go to join you for dinner, your home itself will be a feast for my eyes. Laugh at my helplessness... And I will laugh, too. But may my laughter be a blessing on you. I will offer thanks from my depths, my heart and mind that have been expanded by our time together. And may the future find us together.
>
> *Anton*

"Sleepers, wake! A voice astounds us,
The shout of rampart guards surrounds us:
Awake, Jerusalem, arise!"
Midnight's peace their cry has broken,
Their urgent summons clearly spoken:
The time has come, O maidens wise!
Rise up and give us light:
The Bridegroom is in sight. Alleluia!

> Philip Nicola (1556–1608),
> Adopted by J. S. Bach in
> Cantata 140, *Wachet auf!*[199]

    He has made everything beautiful in its time. He has also set eternity in the hearts of men; yet they cannot fathom what God has done from beginning to end.

> Ecclesiastes 3:10

A Feast as Mends All Length

The sun was still on the horizon when Anton and Ramón began the walk to Cyntheia's home. Ramón consulted his silence and tottered up the sidewalk as though he were balancing a long, invisible load on his shoulders. He had said that Cyntheia's home, formerly her mother's, lay well above the city and that by walking, rather than driving, they could extend the day. Anton felt suffused with peace. The stillness that he had experienced by the ocean with Cyntheia echoed in his unformed thoughts. They paused for a moment at the cathedral bench so that Ramón could rest his knees. Anton entered the garden, selected and cut a single long–stemmed rose. As they continued, he bent off the thorns and trimmed unneeded leaves, leaving the red and green of the flower to express their beauty with utmost poignancy. The final ascent did not take long, which pleased Ramón although he did not complain.

Cyntheia's house was the last one on the hill above the city. It was a small, shingled bungalow held against the hill with a low retaining wall of ocean–polished boulders that held ferns and mosses in the crevasses. A small, contoured garden with blooming rose bushes lay around the front of the house and disappeared to the side. A large window opened onto a wooden deck facing the sea, suggesting that many evening hours were spent watching the setting sun.

Ramón knocked on the door. In a moment, the door opened.

"Welcome, *tío mío*. Welcome, Anton. Come in."

Cyntheia's effect on Anton was profound. Her happy smile, the lift of her eyebrows and warmth and feeling in her voice, the sound of his name on her lips, startled him. Her hair was down about her shoulders and dusky. She wore a dinner apron over a simple skirt of pastel colors. He felt again that uncanny paradox of attraction and the desire to retreat. Every step forward was a willing surrender as scattered thoughts impinged on his sense of discretion. Were his clothes, faded by road, vineyard row, mountain and sea, fit for the occasion? Were his heart and mind clear? Was he able to receive, if never contain, the love that he heard in her voice and welcome? Thank heaven for the rose which sent the message that lay beyond his utterance!

Cyntheia's quick eyes must have sensed his hesitation before the entrance, and she reached out to receive his gift of the rose. Her voice said, "Oh, how lovely! Thank you!" while her eyes assured him of her pleasure and her welcome. The rose seemed to turn a deeper shade of red in her hands.

She took him by the hand and said again, "Please, come in." As he entered and she closed the door, the ocean waves receded again into the distance. She led them into her kitchen, and said, "Welcome to my home. You are my guests. Come, rest from your long day."[200]

Anton's first words were, "Thank you for inviting us to your home, Cyntheia. It is so good to be here." He listened to the strains of music from another room. "Bach," he said. *"Wachet auf."*[201]

"I knew you would like that," she said, and led them into her living room. "Please be comfortable. I have a few things yet to do in the kitchen."

Her living room was living warmth. Sounds and smells from the kitchen mingled with the *pizzicato* of boiling pine sap in the blazing fireplace and the baroque strains of Bach's cantata. A thick area rug covered the hardwood floor in front of the hearth. Large pillows lay piled up in a corner. Ramón stood near the large glass doors and looked out over the azure bay, his thoughts lost in the timeless gaze that reflected his years and his heritage.

This is Cyntheia, Anton thought as he wandered about the main room, portals and clues to her depth, the true and deep self that was unknown to me and even to her in our earlier years. This is the one I love, the one revealed to me under the sun and at the ocean's edge. Candles filled irregular places in the small room, bringing forth indefinable colors from the walls, a bit of buttery cream color here, soft blues, deeper shades of browns and greens there. Mirrors multiplied the candles and carried their gleam to every angle. The rooms were adjoined with arches framed with a oaken trim near the ceiling and deeply stained wainscoting at the floor. A short, darkened hallway led to her bedroom and place of rest. Above the fireplace an iron–wrought landscape of coast juniper conveyed the energy of the oceans below. Near a side window looking up the hill stood a reading table and a chair of aged wicker. A basket of yarn and needles rested on the floor.

Pictures in old frames sat in bookshelves, living memories for Cyntheia and silent statements of how little he knew her. And the books—scores of them! They disclosed how Cyntheia's curiosity ranged from Doric and Ionic temple design to Gothic cathedral architecture; delved into the correspondence of the "Souls" of the Transcendental Movement in 19th century Americana; Quaker theology and the practice of clearness; novels by Argentinean women and Nigerian post–colonial writers; and commentaries on the Catholic liturgy through the Jewish antecedents in the history of the Mass. Rabindranath Tagore's *Thoughts on the Free Life* kept company with the *Bemerton Poems* of George Herbert and novels by Robert Louis Stevenson. Museum books on Renaissance artists and Flemish painters were wedged into the taller shelves. Throughout the room there was no sense of clutter, but simply treasures meted out for sharing.

An old wooden desk occupied one corner, its bank of narrow shelves filled with letters and cards, pencils, and even crochet needles. A half–finished hand–written letter rested on an ink blotter, covered with an opened book as though Cyntheia had been corresponding with a friend only moments before, stopping only to prepare dinner. A bulging travel journal bound with a leather strap sat on the top shelf of the desk.

In the dining room, which adjoined the kitchen through an arched doorway, a circular oaken dinner table awaited them, simply–set with glasses and silver from a nearby hutch, four candle stands, and woven napkins folded and placed for three. Everything invited comfort and ease and the purest enjoyment of food and friendship.

In the midst of his musings, Cyntheia appeared with his flower in a tall glass vase, placed it on the table and, presumably with several ingredients converging in the kitchen at once, said in a cheery voice as she left, "It will only be another moment."

Anton could only reply, "We're very content. Let us know if we may help."

Looking further, he spied a framed poem facing the door. It read –

For what is happiness but growth in peace,
The timeless sense of time when furniture
Has stood a life's span in a single place,
And as the air moves, so the old dreams stir
The shining leaves of present happiness?

No one has heard, thought or listened to a mind,
But where people have lived in inwardness
The air is charged with blessing and does bless;
Windows look out on mountains and the walls are kind.

– May Sarton

How true, Anton thought. Cyntheia's durable and aging furniture appeared to have been given to her by her mother or other, more remote ancestors, and was arranged to allow guests to behold both the fireplace and the setting sun. Simple curtains hung down along the glass doors to the outside deck, reminding him of the gossamer in a cold, remote night in the Carmel Valley; he could imagine the curtains billowing in the summer breeze when the windows were thrown open.

At that moment, Cyntheia reappeared, stepping lightly into the room with a decanter of wine, and a tray of crystal glasses and a small plate of cheese and crackers. "Come, sit," she said. As she poured the wine its crimson accented her lips and brought to life the soft colors of her dress. "I drink to you, Ramón my uncle, and to you, Anton, Dear Heart, and to all paths laid down and found in the walking."

Conversation entered the room and added laughter and happy words to the crackling of the fire and dance of candlelight. Anton felt launched onto a sea of enjoyment, propelled by the gentle energy of delight and gratitude. Cyntheia came and went and in a few minutes announced that dinner was ready. She lit the candles and said, "Friends, let us thank God for the blessings of our table and our friendship –

Come, my Way, my Truth, My Life.
Such a way as gives us breath;
Such a truth as ends all strife;
Such a life as killeth death.

Come my Light, my Feast, my Strength:
Such a light as shows a feast;
Such a feast as mends all length;
Such a strength as makes his guest.[202]

Then Cyntheia began bringing in the dinner. The simplicity of the meal helped Anton to relax from his spellbound attention in the loveliness of the moment. Soon bowls of steamed vegetables, rice pilaf, homemade bread, onion soup, and fresh green salad graced the table. Wine flowed in modest courses, a savory complement to the spices and tangy flavors of oregano, curry and basil. Yet, for all the deliciousness of the food, itself an experience of soulfulness and overflowing delight, Anton knew that this event was but one more syllable in the question that haunts the very heart of human love.[203]

As dinner concluded, Cyntheia said, "Our dinner has been fine, friends, and all are deserving. We have lit four candles to include the one yet to be fed. Perhaps you will invite him to our table, Anton? The last verse of our blessing remains a prayer for the only food that can truly satisfy us –

> Come, my Joy, my Love, my Heart:
> Such a joy as none can move;
> Such a love as none can part;
> Such a heart that joys in love.

Within a few moments, Ramón pleaded fatigue. "My dear, I am honored by your hospitality," he offered from his ancient dignity. "I go home now to rest. I'll see you tomorrow. You can find your own way home, Anton?"

Gathering wordless assurance from a quick glance at Cyntheia, Anton said, "Yes, Ramón. *Hasta mañana.* Good night.*"*

When the door had closed Anton returned to the fireplace to receive its warmth. Cyntheia put a recording of Smetana's *Moldau* on her turntable and poured fresh wine in their glasses. The throaty tones of flutes and the deep strains of bass viol underscored the quiet of the evening surrounding them. Cyntheia walked to her desk. Anton could see her uncover the half–written note on the blotter, add a few words, then fold and seal the letter in an envelope.

"Here is my letter to you, Anton. You may read it later."

Anton gazed at the letter and his name written in Cyntheia's steady hand. He remembered another leave–taking and Gustavo's blessing in the Great Valley. "Thank you," he said. "I will read it at the appointed time. Even then, I may not understand it." He placed the envelope in his jacket pocket, and buttoned the flap for its safe–keeping.

Cyntheia stood near the window. He gazed on her profile as she looked over the bay. The curtains stirred, noiselessly, gently, as though responding to the oboes and flutes of the symphony.

"Some dinners are ended, Cyntheia, by the shattering of the wineglass."

She turned to him. "Yes, there is a time for some things to be broken off. I don't think that this is one of those times. Do you, Anton?" she asked, searching his eyes.

"No, no." Anton pulled two large pillows before the fireplace, took Cyntheia by the hand and drew her to him. She leaned against him, bathing him in her glance, then placed her head upon his chest. She closed her eyes. The warm light and shadows played upon her face. Then, looking into his eyes again, she said,

"Anton, I am afraid..."

"Tell me, Cyntheia."

"I don't want you to go."

At her words Anton felt an ache rising in his chest. "Then you know what I wrote was true?"

"Yes," she said. "As true a prayer as one could ever express...the sweet song that had only begun to arise in us in our earlier years."

After a pause, she continued, "When you came here, I was on my knees, grieving my old loss. You may not have seen it, but my sword was half–drawn against life itself! But instead of cursing my adversaries, God visited me in you! So, the sword must return to the lake, as the old romance would have it."[204]

"Of all the surprises in my life, this has been the sweetest," he replied.

"God is the One who presides over intersections of surprise. Your quest, my own wondering about what lies ahead...And now we have been brought together."

"I have felt like a blind man groping his way across this intersection, Cyntheia."

"Me, too. Over these days with you I feel like I have been drinking a potion that has been transforming me. It wasn't until the seashore this afternoon, with our feet in the water, that I felt that the ground could hold me. And when you said that about the sand slipping away, and holding one another, I knew I was no longer on my own...I wanted to tell you this in the best way I know how, with inviting you into my home, to have dinner with me."

As Anton listened to these words, he also felt as though he were stepping beneath an arch to a new heart and mind. Where he had been bracing himself for an end, he was finding himself with no defenses left. His ability to understand had been arrested, without regrets; his proud knowing had vanished, unlamented. This could not be the end! No, Life was right here, with her.

Slowly, hesitantly, the words came to him. "Your face. Your voice. I want you beside me. I have loved you from the beginning. From the earliest moment here you hinted at the promise of my journey. I want to walk the journey with you."

Her eyes on the fire, she smiled and moved against him in happy contentment.

"Could our journeys become one?" he continued, the sparking and muffled popping of the coals giving a quiet emphasis to his words.

She looked up into his face, and said, "'Easter.' You understand...It is bigger than our lifetime, bigger than our lives...Then we do have a tomorrow?"

His heart full, Anton said, "Yes. Do you remember how you put it, 'That a man should have peace in a life of pain is best.' Now I understand. I will feel the pain of longing while apart from you."

"Easter can never be far off, can it? I want you to seek it out for me, for us. It cannot be that hard to find."

"I will try, Cyntheia."

"When I talked with Gene earlier today, he gave me a precious clue. I want you to go up to Santa Cruz, the City of the Holy Cross. Gene talked about a community for homeless people, somewhere near the University. Would you look there for me? I think that he would take you."

"Yes. He told me about that as well. Everything in me believes that Easter is this close. For such a small, hidden thing we might have to look in a big, sprawling city.[205] If I find it and you come there, I will find peace."

Anton took a deep breath, then added, "Cyntheia, you have brought a beauty into my life that has changed me forever."[206] He brushed her brown curls away from her face and gathered her still closer in his arms. He closed his eyes and breathed deeply. He yearned that her scent blending with the perfume of roses from the open window, the contour of her face and brow, the feeling of her warmth and gentleness, would fill his memory and become etched into his soul. They sat in this way with the soft strains of music playing behind them.

After a long while, Cyntheia stirred. "Anton, please, take my necklace with you. It will remind you that you are not alone."

The backs of his fingers lightly brushing the smooth skin of her neck, Anton carefully removed the talisman of small shells that had graced her person each day. He placed it in her hand. She in turn placed it carefully around his neck and fastened it.

"A circle with no end," he said.

"Oh, you...Oh, Anton, please, come and dance with me."[207]

With the sounds of the cellos as they wove the deep rhythms of earth, river and ocean, the two embraced in the dance. Thus they forever impressed upon one another's soul the image of love which is the sublime message of the human face. With these promises and blessings to sustain them, they bade each other good night.

Clear away from your heads
The masses of impressive rubbish.
Rally the lost and trembling forces of the will.
Gather them up and let loose upon the Earth
'Til they construct at last a human justice.

> W. H. Auden (1907–1973),
> *Night Falls on China*

Through the City to Civilization

ANTON SLEPT SOUNDLY during the night. The waves below, lifted by the tides, rose and fell beneath the stilted home and his bed. When he awoke the little home was empty. He gathered his belongings and rummaged around for a simple breakfast. Then, with backpack slung over his shoulder he walked out to the end of the wharf to bid farewell to Ramón. With a firm handshake and warm smile, the old man urged him to embrace what awaited him. He then walked down to the Embarcadero to find Gene's truck parked on the street. As Anton approached, Gene got out of the truck and leaned against the fender with his foot on the bumper. His face looked eager yet peaceful, and he greeted Anton with a smile.

"You're back! Did you find the Norton?" Anton exclaimed.

"Nope. Not for want of looking, that's for sure."

"My directions weren't any good?"

"I have no idea. I got back to the ranch and took my truck back up to Tularcitos Ranch. I know the country, and have driven down the road you told me about, but it took me heaven knows how long to find the dirt road that you went down. Then I had to poke down the road, looking around every boulder and river bend. I didn't recognize anything at all, and you hadn't given me any details since you went down in the dark. I didn't want to give up, but it was beginning to look as if I had to buy the whole ranch just to find it! You see, beyond the paved road, none of the directions you gave me made any sense. I began to think that the backcountry was bewitched!"

"Too long since your last 'walk–about' from the sounds of it."[208]

"About right. I confess I spent a fair amount of time sitting by the creek. I would stop the truck and just walk for a while in the trees, then come back, and move the truck along for a bit. Sometime late in the day,

I think I found the meadow with the big oak, but I can't be sure. There were no bike tire marks off the path, nothing under the tree. It was rough going even for my pickup: I almost took out my oil pan getting along the road. The motorcycle wasn't there. It just seems to have vanished."

"Well, I could have been all turned around up there in the night as well. No great loss. It had a better master...Cyntheia told me that she talked to you and that you might be coming to town today. That's good. My work here is done."

"Just like that?" Gene looked quizzically at Anton.

"No! It's a new day. But first, what about you, Gene?"

"Let me tell you, Anton, something began to happen in my life after you came to visit. Going to Monterey was no small matter, to begin with. When I got back from looking for your motorcycle, I just went back to work. I spent the days driving in circles with the tractor and shoveling horse manure. A couple of times I had these thoughts—no, not thoughts—collisions of feeling and truth that almost flattened me. No great emotions or anything like that, just blasts of awareness, like a volcano erupting in my backyard. I tried to ignore them, but I just couldn't keep going. Driving the old tractor, I felt like a prisoner in a pit, way down underground, nursing my little resentments, poking at my insides to see if my liver were diseased, and trooping back and forth, back and forth in perfect monotony, never wearying of the path of sorrow.[209] Then I was out in the middle of the corral with a wheelbarrow and scoop shovel, sweaty, covered with manure, and out of nowhere came this wrenching shout, like a howl—'Enough, you contemptible, miserable, beast of burden! You must end this!' So I did."

Anton listened in astonishment. "Well–roared, Lion! Oh, my friend, do I ever understand this! So, the valley holds no poetry for you?"

"Are you kidding? It never did! I told you that. Life in that valley has been nothing but a wretched palinode. I've been alone too long. Not a hint or whisper of poetry in my empty lair. For all I know, the Muse has jilted me forever.[210] So, I packed it up. I put the tractor in the barn, called my helper and told him to feed the horses tonight. I called the boss in Palo Alto and said, 'I quit.' I got up early this morning and drove down here to Monterey."

Anton looked at him steadily. "Cyntheia has sent me on an errand. To Santa Cruz."

Gene caught his breath. Half to himself he said, "My ancient hillside…"

"Could you take me there?"

Without answering, Gene put his chin in his hands and leaned on the hood of the old truck. His eyes gazed far off toward the northwest where the sea, sand and salt blended in the indistinct horizon and the nub of land that bore the coastal city of Santa Cruz. He stood up again, "Perhaps it is time to walk back up the hill again...I have savings for a couple of months, and there's fresh oil in the truck. It's beautiful along the coast in spring. Why not? Let's be off."

Anton thanked him. "At least from there we'll always be able to see Monterey, if not the Valley..."

As they left the sea-side town of Monterey Anton felt like he had fallen into the interstices of time. When the curves of the road allowed, he gazed back at the roofs and boat masts and trees of the hill rising above the bay, and was acutely conscious of movement again in the realm of memory. The moving of minutes and the passing of the landscape around Seaside and Fort Ord and the country beyond did not so much as threaten his memories of who lay behind him as create the physical geography of prayer—prayer for Cyntheia, her safety and well-being, and for the collapse of time until he might be with her again. Fields of brussel sprouts, lettuce and cucumbers spread away as far the eye could see, a lake of agriculture connecting with the sea of fields that filled the central California valley. The road curved back to the coast, and eucalyptus trees began to appear. As the sea winds gathered, the trees stood full and strong, yet supple, swaying like *viola d'amore* under the direction of the invisible conductor of a gigantic orchestra.

A sign said, "Capitola Beach 2 miles." Anton reached across the seat and put his hand on Gene's shoulder.

"Could we stop there for a bit?" he asked. Gene nodded.

At the shoreline the waves rolled in and died quietly on the sand. Mist, fresh and motionless, blanketed the horizon, its grey softening the edges of the sharp cliffs carved by Nature's trembling hand. The ubiquitous gull charted his low course across the sky, casting a dark and archaic silhouette against the white and golden cirrus clouds far above. Here and there little family groups sat on blankets and towels while children ran back and forth with buckets of water and sand. Wordlessly, the two men knew that this was a time for silence. Gene sat down with his back against a log and looked out over the ocean that had nearly taken his life, but had granted him the beatific vision of Callie.

Anton left to walk along the shore by himself. He remembered the ancient Buddhist saying, "As the rain falls on the just and unjust alike, let your heart be untroubled by judgments and let your kindness rain down on all."[211] If so, he thought, then the ocean also receives and surrounds all. Finding words from his own journey, he joined them into the lyrical rhythms of the Breastplate:

> The priest's welcome, be thou with me;
> The dean's dark shadow, even within me,
> The thieves' cruel taunt echoing behind me,
> Children leading me forward,
> The prisoner still to win me,
> The *abuelita* to comfort me,
> Cyntheia's spirit ever beside me,
> And the gentle nurse to restore…

He felt that the moment had come to read Cyntheia's brief note from the night before. Opening the envelope, he read the words from George Herbert's prayer of the night before,

Dear Anton,

Come, my Joy, my Love, my Heart:
Such a joy as none can move;
Such a love as none can part;
Such a heart that joys in love.

Come, Dear Heart, let us live this together.

From me, to you.
Cyntheia

At these words, Anton's heart turned in tumult. He thought, Cyntheia, how Love unveils our hearts! See what is being revealed in my soul! I am infused with a frightening passion. Your attraction and your words, our hours together, those shelter moments in *yotokut* and the *Perikalia* of your home have shed a brilliant light into my being. My body is transfused with energy, my soul is fired with your allure. With you I became that tiny vessel at the seashore, filled with a drop of that divine vitality that shapes the cosmos. Oh, how it courses through my veins. Being away from you…the suffering of separation feels acute. Last night we said *Yes* to our futures—unequivocally. The only *No* was to the prospect of *no future*…

Then, Easter...You sent me to seek it. You trusted that I would have the eyes to see it. Knowing my blindness, I will see as through your own eyes. Your letter blesses me with the same word, the same refrain that invites everyone to the table. The impossible stretching of the lines of language—the motionless center revealed as joy, itself joying in love—ensnares me and the silent, motionless man or woman with no home, far from the center of joy signified by your table and its meal. I think that I am beginning to understand. Through these words I am beginning to see more of the whole of Life. These words are for all of us, for the homeless one within, for what in us dies incomplete, and for those who die along the path without reaching their summit or their center. What would it mean to love others with as much abandon and with as little discretion as suggested in these encompassing words? I simply send this prayer heavenward. My eyes cannot focus on that greater whole, but how well they focus on yours! My passion, my enchantment, birthed in the dim glow of candlelight and lifted by the breeze from the sea below, has been fanned into a great firestorm. Oh, be still, my soul. See with Cyntheia's eyes, and hold to her vision which has become your quest.

When he returned, he sat at a distance from Gene, respecting his silence. After a few minutes, Gene said, "Anton, you know how I love the ocean. I remember the warm waters of Southern California. Like these waves they would grow and grow while you were out with them. They too could be unforgiving and break and throw you directly onto the sand. But the waters down south are warm. They would hold you in a boiling and burbling embrace before releasing you into a long fall.

"I remember once choosing not to swim through the turbulence, and gave up any illusions that I could ride through it with any grace. Instead, I went further out, way out, where you begin to think about sea creatures being attracted to your kicking legs. I stayed out there for a long time, treading water, and even holding onto a buoy. It was the only thing out there for people who were being washed away. Eventually the waves lessened a little, and I swam back through them to land. The beach was so warm, a great heated bed. Its shape, texture, and contour owed everything to the powerful waves nearby. Rising in her waves so beautiful and mighty, Nature was speaking to me in deep sighs. Now, as I behold Nature and honor her, so grand, so fragile, I thank God for the people who place the buoys."

"Out there, in the elements, Gene, we find what we're really made of, where we're bound. The passions that pound in the human heart are only echoes of this ocean."

"A good thing is happening to you, Anton. After meeting Cyntheia, you are becoming poetry in a woman's hands. Pretty soon your mind will be putty." Gene laughed at the twist in the cliché. He then leaned forward off the log and pulled a sheet of paper from his shirt pocket. "While waiting for you I whittled a little something myself. It says something about the seasons in my own life. Want to hear it? Still rough around the edges. We could call it, 'From Winter to Spring.' Here goes –

As the fields and meadows end their rest,
I bend my bow, launch my quest.
Nearby, children clamor 'round and play.
"Drear' winter's past! Come out! Stay!"

Still, spring holds seeds, words unsaid,
Winter burrows down, that fruit may grow red.
Could I green in love proclaimed?
After long, cold nights, may my Love find her name?

Anton pondered the verses, then said with a smile, "A lovely hope! May you take a big bite out of that fruit, seeds and all! May something wonderful be born out of your long waiting!"[212]

"Since meeting you, Anton, I feel like I am no longer carried by that awful riptide. You have been that buoy for me."

By early afternoon they passed through Soquel and into the heart of Santa Cruz. Gene took an early opportunity to leave the busy main highway, and slowed to ten miles per hour as he wended his way along the bluffs, past the seaside roller coaster and theme park, past a very proper City Hall, and down Main Street into the city center. Unlike tourists who stared blankly at the sights, Gene gripped the wheel with great tension as memories flooded him from his University years and its unfulfilled hopes and longings.

"Let's stop for coffee," Anton suggested. Gene agreed. They continued their drive down the main part of town, passing the supermarket where middle–aged men in swimming trunks and sandals drank beer while lolling around their cars and past the boutiques, burrito shops and fast–food drive–throughs. Going was slow due to young families walking from the beach with sticky sand and salt adding to their irritation and fatigue. Soon they found a coffee shop, parked the truck and entered.

Although a commonplace in the affluent world of North America, the coffee shop was a palace of the palate that would have teased even a

Sardanapullus to new levels of excess. Its shelves conveyed impressions of sophistication and refinement. Connoisseur teas and trendy coffees; plastic–wrapped, German–engineered espresso grinders complete with alarm clocks; chocolates swaddled in tinsel, and packets of red–dyed pistachios all begged to be the final accoutrement in the completely commodious life. The line of customers inched along, accompanied by the mantra of orders and perfunctory "thank you's" from the unsmiling cashier. The names for this or that luxurious brew bantered back and forth with a clipped precision of a livestock auction. Newspapers in five languages lay in racks on the floor, offering the facts, but nothing of the feelings, of fortunes made and lost, battles engaged and surrendered; displaying the fashions that claim the attention of the moneyed everywhere on earth; and reporting on the "who loses and who wins; who's in and who's out" of politics.[213]

Anton bought his tea, and Gene his cup of coffee, and they settled in chairs near the window. As Anton stirred the drink its steamy scent evoked images of the highlands of Nepal that he had read about. He imagined shepherds descending from the uplands hidden in the Himalayan mist to the high valleys of curry and chili fields, a hardy people warmed by little ceramic pots next to their chests, hot coals within, all wrapped in blankets; finding shelter under smoky tents; water boiling in a pot hanging over a fire made from dried cow dung; hot milk and tablespoons of sugar warming the insides for the next leg of the journey...

A strident voice intruded on his reverie.

"Well, sell it! You're supposed to be ahead of this! That's what I pay you for!" A young man in a tailored suit entered the shop, speaking into a cell–phone, and oblivious of his surroundings.

"...I know, I know! We can't control these things," the speaker continued. "First it was the civil war, then the hurricane. That wiped out production. How could we buy then? Nothing's happening now and prices are dropping again. Here's what I want you to do: when the people down there get stirred up again, or you see the El Niño building, or there's talk of a cutback in foreign aid, then commodity futures will begin to move up. Just buy! Don't bother to call me and don't ask questions! We'll make a killing!...Remember my rule: 'Buy on rumors, sell on the news. Keep your capital fluid!' That's the essence of what I learned in my international business courses...Talk to you later." With casual deftness the man flipped the cover over his telephone and pocketed it. He then noticed another, older man in the coffee line ahead of him.

"Well, good morning, Judge. Going to the office?" the young man said in an ingratiating tone to the older man.

"After a game of handball," the Judge responded.

"How's things in the circuit court?" the younger man probed.

"Never a dull moment," the Judge said, barely hiding his annoyance and ordering his coffee. He looked imprisoned between his interrogator and the cashier stand. The pause gave the younger man a moment to consider his next move.

"What do you think about the Mayor's appointment of the city ombudsman?"

Anton could see people in line shifting their weight nervously, as though their feet were shackled to the floor. They tried to avoid eye contact with one another and feigned interest in the list of commodities and prices on the wall. The Judge did not respond, but moved away, coffee in hand.

"Well, have a good game," the young man said.

"I always do. I always win. I'm a lawyer," the Judge retorted over his shoulder, and departed through the swinging doors.

Anton's stomach clenched and he felt rising nausea. His eyes grew misty. An image of *campesinos* sweltering in the coffee plantations of Guatemala and El Salvador flashed across his mind's eye. Where's the justice in this?, he wondered. Would there ever be an end to troubles as long as moneyed meanness flourishes? The banality of the conversation had dampened out even the *faux* classical music drenching the upscale coffee shop.[214] "Ready to go?" he asked his companion. Gene concurred.

Outside, Anton said, "Young people come to college to ask 'Will I have new life here? Will I be transformed?' The answer is a strange concoction of the sublime and the humdrum. We can drink from either pool, the one deep and clear, the other shallow and murky. From the outside they can both look the same. Let's go. Do you know your way from here?"

"I think so," Gene responded. "Up High Street, left in front of the campus. From there, we will have to feel our way. Thankfully there is no fog today."

Gene drove his truck slowly past the well-appointed churches on High Street, his memories alive and pressing. He stopped for a moment in front of the Episcopal Church. "That is where I lived," he said, pointing to an old house across the street. "Maybe we can stay there with the vicar again. Let's see if we can get you to the Garden first."

With help from a couple of local residents, they arrived in front of a large open block nestled on the edge of the city neighborhoods. They had arrived. A bus sign and wheelchair ramp from the road to the sidewalk were silent signs of the city's blessing. They parked the truck and walked toward the Garden. At the entrance stood a graceful wooden gate crowded with ivy. Carved in wood and placed over the gate was the single word,

Προπψλαεον

On the left side of the gate were the carved words –

> He who stands on tiptoe
> Does not stand firm.
> He who rushes ahead
> Does not go far.
> He who tries to shine
> Dims his own light.[215]

On the right side another inscription read –

> Where persons make peace,
> Where human love meets human need,
> Where the oppressed are struggling free,
> At these points, however small,
> The Commonwealth of God is always
> Reclaiming the attention of humankind.

Inside the gate, a woman well beyond the midpoint in life and wearing a spattered painter's smock arose from her seat and easel. "Welcome!" she said.

"Thank you," Anton responded. He touched the Greek word and asked, "What's this? Why here?"

"What better name for a gate leading to nowhere?"[216] the painter responded. *"Propylaeon* was the name of the entrance to the Parthenon on the Acropolis, where reigned Athena, goddess of wisdom. It is a gate of welcome. We have no walls here before a temple of sacrifice." Then she laughed. "But we are not here to re-create Athens, nor fight the old battles between the ancients and moderns.[217] Simply to discover nature—our own and the world's—is enough, and all in freedom. The entrance is also the exit. Please come in."

Thus Anton and Gene, wanderers in their own fashion, passed through the gate. In doing so they stepped beyond the unstable world of trade and traffic and continual movement, for the gate itself, like a door to a home, opened to both settlement and civilization.

Socrates said: "It looks to me as though the investigation we are undertaking is no ordinary thing, but one for a person who sees sharply. Since we're not clever, in my opinion we should make this kind of investigation of it: if someone had, for example, ordered those who don't see very sharply to read little letters from afar and then someone had the thought that the same letters were somewhere else also, but bigger and in a bigger place, I suppose it would look like a godsend to be able to consider the littler ones after having read these first, if, of course, they do happen to be the same."

Plato (427?–347 bce),
Republic II. 368d[218]

To live again, an ancient ideal must pass through the living medium of a modern mind.

Wolfgang von Goethe (1749–1832),
Wahrheit und Dictung

A MEADOW FOR THE MUSES

ONCE INSIDE THE GATE, Anton explained that he had come to the Garden, not with some project in mind, but only to see it, to experience it, and, if possible, contribute something to it. Gene inquired about his professor from the University. The artist replied that he had gone up the coast into the hills of Ben Lomond. His return was expected in the near future.

"But come with me for now," she said. "We'll find Akamu, and he can show you around."

As they walked, Anton and Gene began to discern a sense of order in the efflorescence of growth around them. Rows of vines three–deep enclosed the whole acreage around. Inside the enclosure the garden spread out before them like a medieval commons, devoid of property lines and following the natural contours of the earth. In the distance it sloped upward and disappeared behind clusters of trees and an occasional grassy knoll, the reappearing and disappearing again behind forest outcroppings. From where they stood they could see several orchards, shining with newly greened leaves and white blossoms. At the furthest highland reaches, they could see a small farmhouse and a small barn. A small meadow lay between the two structures. From the thin plume of smoke rising from the barn, they could guess that it was a community center or a cookhouse. Between them and the outer boundary of the enclosure were several open meadows or greens, where people were working, sitting, or standing in pairs or in small groups or alone.

Near the Propylaeon Gate a group of people sat in intense conversation. Some had graying or balding pates, while others were obviously students from the University. Their bench encircled a slightly raised grassy lawn, and had an opening on one side. It was obviously unfinished. A stack of bricks lay nearby, partially covered with leaves and garden cuttings. Ferns and blooming rhododendrons surrounded the bench and lent it some privacy. Torches on stands stood ready to illumine night gatherings.

"This is our Circle for the Perplexed," the artist said.

"That's an odd name."

"It's a place to mull things over. We put the circle near the entrance so people could come or go."[219] She chuckled softly and reminisced. "Actually, in the beginning, I spent a lot of time hanging out here in this Circle. Down in the city I had been going from seminar to seminar, conference to conference, always taking in, looking for a new way of thinking, a new technique. So many presentations and workshops! If words are Trojan Horses for the mind, I was the first one to open the gates! Then a friend, a true friend, told me what I needed more was a swift kick in the pants. I needed to get on with things. So I went further in, beyond the Circle...Sometimes people just bolt out of the Circle, grumbling and resentful. Others walk out, clear about who they are and what they are about. Here you can learn to appreciate public places, dialogue, playful banter, whatever. The public space is a great teacher, you know, as long as it's not paved over with streets and parking lots."

"I see that there's still work to do on the bench," Anton said. "It doesn't look finished."

"Nor will it be...Here the questions are always more evident than the answers. If we finish the bench, we would just have to knock it down and start building it all over again."

"It also looks like a *cul de sac,* a place of dead–ends."

"Yes, or simply a container, a place to invite people and ideas together for a spell," the artist laughed. "It tends to the noisiest place in the whole garden. People who go beyond it are always struck by the silence all around. We give up being so wordy. After leaving the Circle I sometimes go all day without talking to anyone, even though I work and eat with people. They seem to understand. It's how I have found myself at home here."

Passing between sundry flowerbeds and neat rows of growing vegetables, they soon reached the edge of a spacious lawn surrounded by rhododendrons. Near the center of the green, a man of Polynesian ancestry was presiding over a springtime choral music fest. He was bare–foot and wore baggy pants and a brightly patterned cotton shirt over his generous midriff. His ears pointed through his thick, black hair, and he had a mischievous grin and puckish sparkle in his eye. He looked like a mellow and good–tempered satyr.

He greeted Anton and Gene with a smile and said, "Welcome! My name is Akamu. Did you come to sing?"[220]

Gene explained that he had heard about the Garden several years before, and had come to visit and introduce his friend to the one who had originally conceived the project.

"He's not here all the time, now," Akamu said. "He has other things calling him, and has left it in our care. We usually hear when he is on the move.[221] Why don't you have a seat for a few minutes until we finish with our rehearsal? Then I'll show you around."

The visitors learned that the weekly musical contests were underway. In the center of the green, a group of people were gathering and arranging themselves into musical sections. There was a disproportionate group of altos and basses. They were newcomers whose years of cigarette smoking had damaged their vocal chords, giving them deep, rasping voices. In many cases the women would begin in the alto section, and men in the bass section. This would commence the healing of their voices. As their voices recovered, some would move up into the soprano and tenor sections.

Pointing to one of the few tenors in the choir, Akamu said. "See that fellow over there? He's a new member of the choir. He came here a couple of weeks ago looking for his son from the college. He had on a starched white shirt and black wingtip shoes. He drove up in a shiny car and got out and stormed through the gate and yelled at his son who was planting peony flowers. [222] He hauled the boy away from the planter and cursed at him for wasting his tuition dollars. Then he laughed at us and said we were lazy and unproductive idiots. He got even more angry when he got mud on his pants! On his way out, I said to him, 'Can you sing?'—just recruiting likely candidates, you know. He didn't even bother to answer me. So I walked alongside him, just out of range of a swinging fist, mind you, and said, 'God has put a song in your heart. May you find it…It will sooth the sting of resentment.' He stomped off and slammed the door of his car.

"I thought a lot about him over the next few days, and realized that I hadn't been at all kind. His resentment was the painful surface of a heart perhaps repeatedly broken by his adolescent son. I imagined that many times that boy had bit the hand that fed him, yet the dad never gave up on him, and sent him off to college with undying hope. So, I appreciated his rage and frustration a little more.

"But lo and behold, the dad came back a few days later, and didn't say much to me other than, 'I need to learn to sing.' Why, only Heaven really knows. There he is, in the back row. That man next to him had a capital sentence at Folsom federal prison until the governor threw out the case against him for bad evidence and granted him clemency not long ago. All things considered, it would be an honor to sing in their choir." As Akamu concluded his little parable of the prodigal father, Anton could see the two men looking quizzically at the music sheets and humming together to find a good pitch.

"When our choir begins," Akamu said, "it is sheer cacophony. The singers don't seem to mind. For a lot of them it's like all the sound they've ever known. It reminds them of traveling in boxcars with the rhythm of the rails, or of camping under the overpasses or under the landing lights at airports—the only places left where they're not harassed. While we don't make a rule of it, almost everyone here feels called to be part of this. The music softens our natural roughness so we can sit down with one another at the table, or leave the garden to work in the world, or learn something new.

"And the setting is just right. Our space here is like the best opera houses: lots of defects and irregularities—some accidental, some on purpose. 'Diffusion,' they call it. Look around! With a lot of practice we eventually achieve some kind of harmony."[223]

Beyond the choir space on a tightly mowed green a form of lawn bowling was being played. Akamu said, "This is our Green of the Octaves. Let's watch this." Anton counted fifteen people sitting along the alley, with one receiver at the end, and one player at the beginning with several small bowling balls. The alley for the game was marked off with white and brown lines, so that the whole strip of lawn looked like two complete octaves on a keyboard, from a low C to a high B, with the brown lines representing the black keys or sharps and flats on the piano. A piece of steel tuned and pitched to a high C was placed in the center of the alley at the far end beyond the high B. When the ball came to a stop in the alley, the adjacent player would strike a tuned piece of steel made from a railroad spike or brake drum. The neighbors would then strike their notes in sequence, all the way up the octave.

"Stand clear!" Akamu called out. "You don't want to be near Calliope when she is on a rampage!" A large, heavy-set woman with curly black hair moved around the green with maenadic abandonment.[224] She cheered on the players with clapping and brisk commands and called out the name of the mode created by the musicians in their sequenced banging of steel. Sometimes a particular pitch and its accompaniment created a hanging effect, as though someone had been playing scale in a minor key and had stopped at the seventh note in the octave. When this happened, everyone would lean forward in agitation, awaiting the resolution of the mode. Calliope would protest, "Aaargh! Locrian! Quick, pitch again!" Thus, players gained in skill, both in counting and in hearing the notes and half and whole steps up the octave. When a ball struck an opponent's ball, several players leapt up and launched *rat–a–tats* and *thumps* and *boings* and *splats* on steel drums made from forty gallon barrels. In the rare event when a ball actually struck the hanging stake, the high C at the end of the green, another player would slam a gaudily painted oversized barrel covered with graffiti, and the other players played their tones at random. The thundering of the barrels and clanging of tempered steel spikes was greeted with cheers and clapping from workers around the heath and from children playing in the water and mud. The overall effect of bars and gongs, percussive steel drums and tinny rumbling, created a spontaneous metallic symphony, softened by giggles and laughter and cheers.

"I've never heard anything like it," Anton marveled. "There is something enchanting about it. It's like wind chimes for the whole hillside."

"The divinities will return when we re-enchant the world," Akamu agreed. "which means we must begin with the inner world. For that there is no better medium than music. That's the idea here. It's so simple. Our education begins in play, the never–ending game.[225] We play instruments, don't we? Out here the players learn all the modes and scales, which provide the rules of the game. Then they will be analyzing intervals and find themselves discovering fractions, ratios and other patterns. This takes them easily into geometry and the Pythagorean theorem for earth measurement. In winter we use what we learn by measuring out the furrows in the vegetable gardens with their lines, planes and angles. Lifting heavy shovels of dirt gives us appreciation for the weight and resistance of earth and the elemental physics of work and force and inertia, indeed all the matter in the cosmos and its embodied energy. Then, Anton, when we think about the moment of creation, the weight and magnitude of it all humbles us to the last iota. As spring approaches, we go up to the Meadow of the Stars by the cookhouse and elevate our gaze to the sun to measure its slow rise in the sky, and decide when to plant the first seeds. We figure out the arrival of Easter by timing the spring equinox and the second Sunday following the full moon. So, you see, music, math, the planting and harvest celebrations are all wrapped in one reality. On a cosmic scale, this little game helps locate our short lives in the grand scheme, and points our way to eternity."

Enthralled by Akamu's tale, Anton mused to himself—Cyntheia, Easter spreads across the cosmos carried on the glancing rays of the sun. "Where?" and "When?" occur simultaneously. You, my dear, need not look so far.

Akamu paused a moment as a Monarch butterfly gyrated from blossom to blossom in a bank of firefly heather, still ruddy red from the winter. "Look at that: the butterflies discover their path with such ease. They align themselves with our tilting planet and fly back from Mexico to the spring and summer flowers here, each year, year after year. We do the same sort of thing, but need much more thought. Yet, like them, we too bask in the sun that warms us from so far away. The sun gives us a sense of direction as we wing our way around the fringes of the Milky Way. We feel less like whirling Dervishes and more like partners in the waltz of stars. Now, that's real music! When we go out through the Propylaeon, we often find ourselves humming *solfeggio.*"[226]

At this point Akamu invited Anton and Gene to rest while he returned to another round of music and voices that were rising above the Garden. Anton thought back to another garden where a chorus of song was greeting new buds in the vineyards of the Great Valley.

Having come out through Necessity's throne, all made their way through terrible stifling heat to the plain of Oblivion. For it was barren of trees and all that naturally grows on earth. Then they made their camp, for evening was coming on, by the River of Forgetfulness whose waters no vessel can contain. Now it was a necessity for all to drink a certain measure of the water, but those who were not saved by prudence drank more than their measure. As he drank each forgot everything. And when they had gone to sleep and it was midnight, there came thunder and an earth-quake; and they were suddenly carried from there, each in a different way, up to their birth, shooting like stars.

Plato,
Republic 621a

LETHE'S ELIXIR[227]

Anton and Gene sat awhile, enjoying the colorful montage of rows and furrows, groves and meadows around them. When Akamu returned he said, "Let's go on up to the farmhouse. I want you to meet someone."

The walkway took them around the musical green and joined a brook that played among mossy boulders and shrubs. Graceful ferns, heavy with seeds, spread their fans, while tiny birds zoomed in and out of shady spots. A young couple in mismatched clothing sat quietly on a boulder, whispering to one another in soft tones. The boy's hair was bright yellow like a blooming dandelion, and the girl wore small metal rings in unusual places.

Stopping at a distance and discretely looking down at the ocean below, Akamu said, "They were kids who wandered into Santa Cruz in the early planting season. When they met in the chorus it was not long before they created their own competition in kissing, which they have certainly won, hands down!" Akamu's mirth was barely containable, and his laugh rumbled deep in his belly.

"Now they are shoulder to shoulder, and dreaming about what life might hold for them. I have seen it before, especially when Lady Moon rises beyond the Gate and draws young men and women back out, renewed for the world. Love does that, you know: it tames the hearts that may be as hard as iron. We gain a new kind of strength.[228] They leave, shoulder–to–shoulder, taking what they have learned here into their future. Happiness takes many forms, and can find its way into any soul."

They walked on, Akamu's words echoing in Anton's mind. He stopped and looked back at the musical green where the choir was forming and the game rolled on. Cyntheia…Her name came again to Anton like a whisper. Dear One, your memory is music. I am hearing that soundless note in the octave of our own communication... The echo of your name in my heart is as precious as the sound of your voice, as dulcet as the first drop of rain on a perfectly calm lake. Could we, sweet Cyntheia, save that one note for us, that note of ecstasy, whose slightest tone rings like a bell in the heart of Love? When all notes fall short, linger, and wane away, that one note will remain. May your very name be that note in my heart, uttered in my longing for you, held so close 'til that moment when I greet you again, and speak it with the softest and most sustained brush of my lips against yours. I will call to you when I have found where the sunny beams of Easter intersect in the human heart here in our world...

A few moments later Akamu stopped them again. "This is our Writing Circle," he said, and pointed to a large circle of flat stones with a small campfire circle within. A woman with muddy jeans sat alone on a rock, worrying the end of a pencil with tobacco–stained teeth. A piece of paper lay on the rock beside her. "We could call it our 'Poet's Circle,' but we don't want to frighten people off."

"Meaning?..." Gene asked.

"The homesick people who arrive here are pungent with poetry!, even the man in the shiny shoes who believes his life–blood is flowing out with his taxes and debts; or the battered youth who knows about beasts and blows; and yes, the student from the university above us who longs to know love and war first hand, beyond his books and illusions of security. That's what I mean."

"You make it sound like poetry isn't such a rare accomplishment. I find that comforting," Gene observed.

"Healthy people are not afraid of poetry," Anton said. "Only we 'recovering academics' are: we are Plato's revenge.[229] I think that real poets pull religious people and academics out from behind their prepared statements. They cut through our brightly colored but heartless concepts and blow them away in the wind like the petals of tired flowers."

"That's right," Akamu agreed. "That woman there: would she insist on the truth of her thinking? Why bother? She simply suggests it. That's poetry. It's for real people with real lives. Not many are here right now because it's time to be out in the fields, turning the soil."

"I guess that's a good sign, too."

Akamu spread his arms across the landscape. "You would be surprised what comes from a few hours of hoeing. No one should write if they have nothing to write about. Something weighs on that woman there, so she is unburdening by writing. Pretty soon, at noon, lots of people will gather here. Sometimes experienced writers do some coaching. Then, at night we gather around the fire and hear the stories and the poetry that has been written down."

Gene was looking at the woman in the Writer's Circle intently. "Akamu, ask her if we could talk." When asked, the woman shrugged and nodded. Gene then sat down on the stone next to her and engaged her in conversation. Then, in a moment, he turned and said to Anton, "You go on ahead. I'll catch up later."

Akamu led Anton further along the graveled path, and up a slight hill. The path wound its way up through a stroll garden of maples in early bloom, miniature pines and juniper shrubs, towering redwoods, mossy groundcovers, and early flowering hibiscus. Here the creek ran down the slope, scampering and falling and twisting and streaming with eager haste, all the while seeming to say, "Swish and slow, burble and flow, toss and tumble, all time, all time."

Beyond the clump of trees the path narrowed to cross a small, leaf-strewn bridge reaching from one side of the creek to the other. A pool lay above the bridge where it was fed by an underground spring with a strong and continuous flow of fresh water. A small sign at the foot of the bridge read –

Λnθης
Sweetly drink, but sparingly[230]

Beyond the creek lay a small open field. "Our 'Meadow of the Stars'," Akamu said. "We come up here anytime, but especially when there is a meteor shower or eclipse."[231] He paused for a moment, musing. "Someday we may have a total solar eclipse in these parts. Back in 1991 in Hawaii we had a total event. Have you ever seen that? We hiked up one of our peaks, where we could watch the dark appear from the west in the middle of the day. There were hundreds of us there. It was an uncanny thing, so completely unexpected. Sure, we knew it was coming. But as the day darkened, people huddled down and got real quiet. During the totality we moaned and held on to one another, our minds frozen over, feeling like we were being taken by cold, dark death. The corona of the sun was a bright, circular ring of light. Then, the moon broke away from the sun. The shadow swept over us like a knife blade, and galloped away to the east, rising and falling over the hills like a blanket being dragged over the earth. With the light raining down on us, we got up and jumped around and shouted and danced and it felt so good! What a rush!

That was an eclipse! Then too, during ordinary times, we come up here to the meadow when we want to be our best, to be fully human, to look at the stars and to think big."[232]

They approached the farmhouse, an aging and rustic home with a mossy roof that sloped into the hillside to ward off the winter gales and to provide shade in the summer. One whole room of the house embraced a huge oak tree whose main trunk and branches were framed by the roof, and whose canopy swayed over large portions of the whole house. The tree and its magnificent branches created the sense of a cathedral of nature. An old golden retriever snoozed on the porch of the house, and a cat sat impassively in the shade of the oak tree. The buzz of bees mixing in with the burbling of the creek added to the indolence of the afternoon.

"We have turned this house into a home for people nearing the end of their lives," Akamu said. "We call it our 'Caritas House.' Come on, let's find Penelope."[233]

Upon entering the house they found a clean and well–lit family area with adjoining rooms and hallways. To one side was an alcove where the dim flame of a tabernacle candle could be seen, gleaming red and veiled. Penelope emerged from one of the rooms and approached them. Her face was sculpted with smile wrinkles. She wore the work habit of a Catholic sister. With her blue eyes inches from Anton's face she said in an Irish brogue, "Welcome, lad. Staying awhile?"

"I am."

"Come and see. I want to share our dream with you."

"Go on ahead, Anton. I will see you in a few minutes," Akamu said, then seated himself in the sun next to the creek.

Sister Penelope led Anton from the sitting room into a small and simple kitchen. Overhead skylights and broad windows let in the spring sunshine. The bright light was tempered by earth–toned wallpaper, throw rugs on the floor, and knit blankets and crazy quilt coverings on the furniture. A green vine was finding its way up one wall and across the ceiling. A hallway led from the kitchen to three living spaces. The first two rooms were clean and neatly appointed for guests, while the third was clean but empty of any furniture.

"This is our dream, still in the making," she said. "You have come at a good time. Look, we are almost done with our construction. Before long we will have our first guest. The kitchen and plumbing are hooked up. The only thing we have yet to do is complete the far room, the one with the oak tree growing into it. The tree was part of the house when we got it, and we do not want to lose the room. So, we're just sitting tight until we figure out what to do with it."

Anton walked down the hall and into the room built around the oak tree. Huge branches ramified out from the trunk and passed through a large skylight. The floor had been completed and sealed around the trunk as well. But for the imposing presence of the tree and its branches, the room appeared quite ordinary and spacious.

"Whoever built this house liked trees," he said. "It reminds me of the baobab tree in *The Little Prince*. I also slept under a tree like this, not so long ago."

"Well, there it stands," Penelope said, and led him back to the porch. Outside the building she showed him a sand landscape, raked into undulating curves, with a little island of black rocks and earth with a bonsai tree rising serenely above. "This is a very special part of our hospice as well, Anton. It was built by an old Japanese gentleman and his wife who had endured the internments in the war. He also helped us design the Japanese landscape below the creek. In the summer months we'll be able to bring our guests out here and make a bed for them in the sand plot. They'll lie on their backs and look at the sky, or on their tummies and look at the sea. We'll just brush them off when they are ready to come back to bed. They will have their minds filled with sights of sea and sky.[234] I have to prepare dinner now. We prepare it over in the community kitchen, and bring it back here for our guests. Are you staying for a while?"

Anton informed her that he was making a long "retreat."

"Maybe a working retreat?" she asked.

"Yes, plenty of that," he replied.

"Well then, you belong here. *'Ora et laborans.'* Work and prayer. No better way to enjoy God's creation and the gift of life."

With that, Penelope spoke to Akamu quietly for a moment, then left to tend to her affairs. On the way she sang a stanza from an old English ballad,

Sumer is i–cumen in,
Lhude sing cuccu!
Groweth sed, and bloweth med,
And springth the wude nu,
Sing cuccu![235]

As the afternoon was slipping into evening, Anton rejoined Gene at the Writers Circle and together they walked back to the main gate.

"Let's go find the vicar," Gene said. They were pleased when the Episcopal rector remembered Gene and welcomed them to stay in the guesthouse in the backyard behind his home. During the night Anton dreamed of trees. The branches of all the trees of his recent journey—the palms of Southern California, the citrus of the Central Valley, the solitary oak in the Carmel Valley, the eucalyptus in the Aptos–Watsonville plain, even the little bonsai in the sand garden—all seemed to be sending a slow, silent semaphore which said: "Forget not your roots; you cannot grow upwards without growing downwards." Their leaves and branches translate dreams into guiding messages. That night he dreamed of the oak in the farmhouse, and saw a sleeping figure nestled in its girthy arms.

In the morning Anton said to Gene, "The tree in Penny's room: it could be made into a bed." Then, a new word arose in him: "We could call it the *Totenbaum.*"[236]

When they arrived back at the Garden, they proposed the idea to Penelope. She encouraged them to work on the project. "I thought we might put you to work," she said.

Both men quickly adjusted to the rhythms of the Garden. The food was excellent in the cookhouse, so each morning they walked up from the vicar's home to join the small group who gathered for a light breakfast. By 8:00 in the morning the first workers began to arrive on foot, or on bicycle, or the local city bus. Morning prayers were offered at 8:30. Throughout the day, the community engaged in a peaceful rhythm of gardening, pruning, weeding, picking produce and preparing food, practicing music, singing and resting.[237] Now well into springtime and especially during Holy Week, flower bouquets and arrangements were picked and sold in profuse quantities to individuals and groups from town. For the citizens of the garden community, talking, standing silently, playing with water and mud in the furrows, and working with hoe and trowel were the mundane complements to the grand seasons of time and space all around them. When the choir and musical game were not underway, the silence was profound, under-girded by the sound of waves crashing against the promontory of Natural Bridges in the distance.

Throughout the day additional people came up the hill from the city to engage their work with no fuss or fanfare. A Hindu man continued an old habit of walking up to the Garden every day to build birdfeeders. A lady pastor offered her stentorian voice to Calliope to help create short musical epics for the homeless people working in the Garden; she said that it was a better use now for her failing voice after years of night–watch ministry in Los Angeles where she had used the vocal power of Brunhilde to stop domestic quarrels or street fights before the shooting started. A carpenter came up after his day at work and showed people who had left the street how to carve profiles and masks in wood, and thus how to restore their sense of having a face. One of these was a Puerto Rican veteran of the Korean War. Come rain or shine, he would stand outside in the furrows and lift his lined face up to the sky and feel the rain washing down the wrinkles and ridges pinched into his cheeks by the harsh hand of life.[238]

The man who had founded the Garden returned from Ben Lomond and visited everyone and enjoyed a good dinner in the cookhouse. When he met Anton, he thanked him for offering of his time and skill in working on the *Totenbaum;* he also suggested that Anton could visit his class at the University when he was finished with the project.[239] Anton thanked him and let the invitation rest in his heart.

People came and went by themselves and in pairs. Two women with obvious and joyous affection for each other worked in the vegetable patch—"like two peas in a pod," the cook laughed. Another woman with manic eyes and bedraggled hair and a reputation for throwing rocks at people, was put in charge of the spice beds. She enjoyed a tea brewed from special herbs twice a day and sat in the sun and walked peacefully in the garden. The urge to fling stones, rooted in an unknown but malignant memory, died away as she received the therapy of sun, water, companionship and herbal medicine. The man who had been released from Folsom spent many hours in the open fields with a Buddhist elder telling the stories of his chaotic childhood and youth and quieting his Furies.[240] Eventually he volunteered to become the convener of morning prayer.

The picking of early spring vegetables took place in the morning, and cleaning and packing in the afternoon. After working in the earth, workers rinsed their tools of the mud and limestone grit and placed them in a shed behind the barn. A light meal was served at mid–day. Since workers ate freely from the crops as they ripened, the mealtime served primarily as an opportunity for conversation and refreshment.[241] People from the surrounding community arrived in the afternoon, buying produce for the various partnerships that had been created with families and homeless shelters. There was food enough for all, and little that was picked was left unconsumed; what remained was composted for future plantings. All was handled with great care and gratitude. After dinner, a fire was lit in the Writers Circle, and someone would share a newly crafted story. As the days lengthened, people stayed later into the evening, sometimes providing a chorus to comment on the stories that were told.[242]

For his own part Anton worked steadily on the bed in the oak tree in the farmhouse. Dubbed a "master craftsman" by Cyntheia, he found himself working with unconscious confidence with tools and materials. He fashioned legs for the bed out of four–by–fours and carved and sanded them into graceful shapes. Three of the legs rested squarely on the floor, and the fourth was braced by a large branch and the trunk. He cut wide slats to support a mattress and springs. From a reclining point of view, the patient would see the branches beyond the sky light in the ceiling, and feel a slow movement when the winds lifted off the coast and blew among the leaves and branches overhead.

Sanding and finishing the headboard were the final tasks. As Anton worked, he returned to the rhythms of his font polishing and vine pruning. Nonetheless, the hard, repetitive work wore down his energy, and he would step outside to rest and take a sip from the creek. On one occasion the elder cook from the cookhouse was sitting by herself on the bridge. Anton greeted her, and dipped his cup to take a sip from the creek.

"Ah, this is so good!" he sighed.

"You're paying attention to the sign, 'Sweetly drink, but sparingly'," the cook observed. "Most people don't read it when they're thirsty, or bother to ask what it means. They just gulp away."

"I am thirsty, but not so thirsty that I would forget everything for one cup of water," Anton responded. Thinking of Cyntheia, he added, "And I have things—or should I say *someone*—whom I need to remember. How's life for you?"

"Life is good. At this point in life, some things get easier, other things get harder."

"What do you mean?"

"It is easier to accept my own getting along in time, for one thing. It is even easier to accept the suffering of others. Living in a continuous sense of mystery is not so easy."

"I'm surprised to hear you say it's easier to live with the suffering of others. That sounds pretty clinical, but you don't seem dispassionate to me."

"Let me give you an example, Anton," the cook responded. "A little while ago a women came up from the fields to get a drink. I was here taking a break, too. She was tired, exhausted, even though she didn't look dirty and sweaty from work. She looked drawn, tense—signs of stress, emotional conflict were all over her face. She had brought a cup with her, and took a big cupful and was going to drink it down, but glanced at the sign with the word *Lethe* on it. I said to her, 'First, let us pour our libation together to Memory's daughters, the Muses.'[243] She followed my example and poured some out and sipped, just like you. She puzzled over the letters on the sign, then asked me what a 'libation' meant, thinking the water might be unhealthy or something. I told her that the water was perfectly healthy for her body and her soul, but she needed to offer some of it back. She needed go away a little thirsty in order to remember her thirst. She didn't follow that, and said she wished she could take a bucket down to the garden plots so people could just walk over any time and get a drink of water. I suggested the water would lose its sweetness if it stopped flowing, and that the walk up the hill to the source was refreshing, too.

"In any event, sitting there, the woman offered a libation from her very heart. In a nutshell, she comes from town to the Garden to take refuge from herself, 'her passions and obsessions,' as she called them. But even with all the hard work here it seemed she had not found peace. She told me that she had had three husbands—not quite the extreme case of the Samaritan woman at the well.[244] They were available and attractive at first. Then they became bland and boring, while she wanted fun, excitement. She wanted to relish life but was beginning to despair of ever finding happiness. Her passions were so powerful, she said, she couldn't understand them or tame them, and did not want to tame them.

"We talked a long time, Anton, and what we came up with was something like this…I used images from the kitchen, since that is what I know. I said that each person is like a container—saucepan size if you want, or even a big cauldron. You're a pot that sits right on the fire, even you, Anton. And each pot has a lid which is a perfect fit."

"I like this!" Anton laughed. "A kind of 'pot psychology.'"

"Very good! You're getting it. The fire under the pot is life–energy itself. And the pot can be made from all kinds of materials. First, there's gold, that warm and glowing metal that cannot take too much heat without going up in smoke. This one is the person for whom 'golden' is the only adjective you can think of. Or a pot is made mostly of bronze: he's the proud one, the container used to sitting on the top shelf, mostly as decoration, almost as though he's afraid of the stove itself. He is very easily tarnished. Or the pot is solid iron and insensitive to the greatest heat and pain; it can be heavy and brutal, as we know all too well. These are just a few images of different personalities and their composition.

"What do these pots look like? Low and squat, or flat and shallow, or tall and broad, you name it: these are the emotional mesomorphs and ectomorphs fashioned by the ethics of their culture. Their habits and prejudices and upbringing have stamped and impressed them; their biases have twisted them into outlandish shapes; their lifestyles and commitments and covenants have polished them, and dented and bruised a few as well. All of this works together to give them identity and personality.

"Now, what's in the pot? All the meat and potatoes in the alchemical brew of an individual human life. Encounters and events, surprises and plans, relationships, discoveries, learning…all mixed up into the unique stew of our lives. And spices: we cannot forget the flavoring…There's *eros,* the longing for beauty, dancing and heady wine, that lovely, ecstatic stuff. There's a pinch of salt for our sense of self–worth, and so on.

"And what about the lid? It fits, of course, all too perfectly. But strangely, it is we, not the cook, who choose when to put it on and when to take it off. A good stew needs a lid for a while, but if we leave it on too long or too tightly the pressure will turn everything to slosh. And because we are *living* containers, we take the lid off from time to time and let the rich aroma spill out and waft around."

Here the cook's voice changed from robust and wry to almost wistful. "And the whole purpose of Life is to be a good stew, seasoned and balanced with spices and substance, and shared and enjoyed with others. Sometimes we have to cool off a little so others can taste us without being burned. The woman really liked that, by the way; she wanted her passion to give joy, not harm. And our food can make others strong, or it can stick in their craw. We can fill them with energy, or we starve them emotionally and make them deathly ill."

"And is there a cook?" Anton asked.

"Of course there's a cook! Who adds wood to the fire? The cook is the master chef, an expert! Everything she does is her specialty. Every dish is her best work. No mass–production of here! She huddles and hurries around all in a sweat, tending to this or that fire, cooking up a storm. You remember how we were talking about bearing the sufferings of others a few minutes ago? We're to be like the cook, sweating and stirring and smelling the full spice of life, but not jumping into someone else's pot. You know how we are: we sometimes take from other pots to add to our own, usually without permission, and then bubble over into the fire itself. We even try to become the fodder for the fire itself, a martyr complex that usually leads to everybody around getting burned up."

"A whimsical parable about a polity of pots," Anton said. "Are you in it, too?"

"Ah, me," the elder sighed. "Someone needs to tell the story, and the cook is too busy flinging things around, creating her feast and making a future. I just tell the story after it's happened. That's enough. The woman seemed to like it. She had some choice comments about the Chief Cook who sets all of Nature ablaze instead of staying in the kitchen, then she went off laughing. One day I think that she will know herself as a bringer of grace as well as a woman of passion," the elder concluded.

What fills us with radical amazement is not the relations in which everything is embedded but the fact that even the minimum of perception is the maximum of enigma. The most incomprehensible fact is the fact that we comprehend at all.

Abraham Heschel (1907–1972),
Man is Not Alone[245]

Dreams, plays and sudden sight

While Anton spent most of the day in the Caritas House, Gene tended wander around the gardens in conversation with other people. He was clearly breaking out of his long isolation. He particularly enjoyed sitting with visitors and people from the Garden community in the Circle for the Perplexed. He commented to Anton that it could be a "theater in the round" for people to offer their wonderings about life; rather than create a niche of privilege and pride, its shape invited people to engage one another.

Gene also spent a whole morning with the woman whom they had initially seen sitting in the Writers Circle. "You have to hear this, Anton...She's been working on something for a couple of days, and wants to give it to her sweetheart this afternoon. She's had a hard–lot life, mostly on the streets, but her heart wants to belong to her man. Come and listen."

Anton and Gene sat themselves on the flat stones of the circle and waited. The writer was no more than forty years old and sun–burned. Her pants were stiff with dirt and held up with a nylon rope, and her tattered shoes were re-enforced by layers of duct tape.

"First," Gene said, "Let's hear what you wrote before you came here."

"Oh, it's horrible!"

"What you wrote about was horrible," Gene rejoined. *"How* you wrote about it took me right back to the boardwalk. Go ahead."

In a gravelly voice the woman began –

Crushed, jostled, caterwauling
drunk with broken waters
coated in the stench of orange rinds,

reeking with plankton rot and manure
feeding myself on sizzling grease
feeding myself to the wharfworms
wheeling over wharfknots, bottle in hand.

Through doors and around tables,
grinning, scratching, chiseling through metal music,
my old flowered self wilts on the bar,
my eyes blinded by tears.
Oh, were he with me!
Away with these filthy heroes of battling bottleships!
Away with their woody winebarrel breath!

Oh, could I find the door,
see sincere fresh sensual stars
breathe again clean air in a clean breeze.

When the woman's voice shuddered to a stop, Gene said, "Now, the 'He' you talk about is here, too, right?"
"Yes, down in the chorus."
"So, how about your second piece?"
"If you say so," and the woman continued in a new vein –

Nights, cold and black without end,
Until in this garden I began to mend.
Now I am rooted and render flowers;
From the dark earth, silent, striking colors.

For years I drifted alone,
Benches and bushes my lonely home.
But for my friend, I would drift in gloom,
Thanks to him, I am joy in bloom.

"I know, I know," the woman said in the sing–song voice of one who had swallowed whole the contempt of others. "Gene tells me to keep playing with the rhyme and meter. It sort of shuffles along, like my life."
"No, bravísimo!," Gene replied. "A pastiche worthy of Dos Passos. Too much schooling will drive the poet out of you. Keep picking and pruning. Soon enough even your effort will become invisible.[246] You have not hidden your talent nor promised too much. And your man is

here, too. Soon all we will hear will be your voice in harmony with his. It will be all grit, elements, and sheer contentment."

As the woman returned to the furrows, Gene said, "Who says that intelligence and grace are the exclusive privilege of the rich and educated? All she needs is an audience and a listening ear. It's as if she remembers who she really is and is born again."

"Here you are, Gene, back with your humanities teacher who praised silence, and had his doubts about writing. Do you think that she has found her voice through her writing?"

"There you go again, pummeling your brains, Anton! We are not allowed to ask the question. She had it all along! Who are we to say that the humanities make us more human? That's a tired question for the learned. Our poet declares her meaning to the world. She could have done that with a touch, or with a smile at the man she adores. But the word she has written reveals her meaning to her own mind."

Early one evening, Anton told Penelope that the bed in the oak tree was ready for use. She looked it over approvingly and said, "Come, let's go talk in the Meadow of the Stars." There she said, "Anton, tomorrow I want you to go find the first guest for the bed. Go look in Watsonville. One of my sisters will meet you." She gave him the name and address of a local clinic in the town that was served by her religious community.

Guided only by these words, Anton left the following morning in Gene's truck. Watsonville lay twenty miles to the east, a community of agricultural businesses, commuter neighborhoods, and barrios for farm and factory workers. Soon he found himself standing with Sr. Isabel in front of a collapsing house in a poor neighborhood near the railroad tracks that ran through the town.

"This is Leon's home," Isabel said to Anton. "I've been here before, and we're expected. They have heard about Caritas House and what it offers. They may say that moving Leon there is the best thing for him, but in their hearts they know it will be one of the hardest things in the long, hard road of his illness. In the end, it is his choice where to stay or leave."

They knocked on the door, which was opened tentatively by a middle–aged woman. They stepped over the mildewed threshold and into the hovel. Inside, wreckage was everywhere. The carpets were torn and thick with ashes and dirt from an aged oil furnace. Even the walls reeked of cigarette smoke. Small possessions and collectibles lay in heaps and shambles on shelves and dressers, on the floor, and under the furniture.

Dirty dishes filled a grimy sink. The floor showed tracks of mice and cockroach leavings. The room sank in the darkness created by pulled shutters. Anton almost reeled back in the onslaught to his senses.

Isabel introduced Anton to Shana, Leon's daughter. Shana in turn introduced them both to Innocenti, a burly, bearded Italian man in a tee–shirt and jean–jacket reduced to a vest. Anton noticed that the jacket had motorcycle insignia on it and that Innocenti's arms were covered with tattoos. He nodded at the newcomers, but said nothing. As Isabel had mentioned, Shana had already learned about the Caritas House and welcomed the idea of a refuge for her father. She led them to a room in the far back of the house. An old black man, late in his seventh decade, white haired and flaccid and covered with thrift store blankets, lay on a bed in the gloomy room. Anton's eyes caught sight of a revolver on the bedside; he noticed nothing else in the room and kept his back to the door.

"Hello, Leon," Isabel said. "Shana has found a place for you to help you feel better. She is coming with you, and Innocenti is coming, too."

"Will we be coming back?" the old man asked.

"I don't think so, Daddy dear," Shana said with resignation.

Leon accepted this with the silent stoicism of someone who had lost untold treasures through a long life. Anton moved furniture back to clear a path for a wheel chair. Shana and Innocenti lifted the old man onto the chair and covered his knees with a blanket. Outside, they tilted back the passenger's seat of Shana's station wagon and transferred Leon from the wheelchair into the car. Leon groaned when he was moved, and stared at them with eyes glassy and powerless. They covered him again and seatbelted him and positioned pillows under and around his neck.

As he was being settled, the old man said in a tired, halting voice, "Know what, Shana?"

"What's that, Pop?"

"My granddad was the son of a slave. He had a hard, hard life. Didn't do much more than tend the mule on another man's forty acre plot."[247]

"That's right, Pop."

"Me, I would rather drive the mule or even be the slave of that poor dirt farmer than be the king over all the thugs and pimps who have made my place a hell–hole. Even a poor mule or slave must have some place to call his own."[248] With this pronouncement Leon settled back and closed his eyes.

As she gathered Leon's few possessions, Shana expressed her relief at having assistance with her father. With the sole help of her taciturn partner, Innocenti, she had cared for Leon for nearly a year. Then, in a long, nearly incoherent ramble, she described the trauma of the last years: how she had to take her dad to the Veterans Administration hospital in San Jose for chemotherapy treatments that went on and on to no avail and to Leon's continuous misery; how her own husband had run out on her during her second pregnancy; how one of her teenage sons hung around all day, then went to a Twelve Step program and a safe–house at night until, she said, "he was no longer a menace to society"; how people were appearing and disappearing all the time, wearing gang get–up, and mooching off her and the old man; how Leon kept his gun loaded even with kids in the house; how one of her sisters had lost her leg from diabetes and most of her teeth from fights or ill health, and how Shana had to care for her, too.

In a private conversation outside the house, Isabel told Anton that Leon had received little or no pain medication until a social worker had discovered him. "Even then, the people in the house used or sold much of his pain medication. We have no idea how many people are in this situation," she said.

As he opened the back door to Shana's car, Innocenti exhaled loudly. He seemed to wipe soot and darkness from his arms and clothing with silent eloquence as if to say, "God, I am glad to be out of there! Now I can breathe!"

As he drove Isabel back to her clinic in Watsonville, Anton could see new office buildings and a community college. People came and went on the boulevards and highways, and the city hummed with commercial activity. "So, Caritas exists for people like Leon," Isabel said along the way. "Who else would take a toothless old man who smells pretty strong and is hard to look at? Look at all this activity…the busier it is in our cities, the easier it is to lose sight of 'the least of these.'[249] No one has any time or space for him. Give him a home in Caritas, Anton, and maybe he will have real peace in the few days remaining to him. The daughter and Innocenti will want to stay, too. They can help with the laundry and have some energy to re-connect emotionally with each other. They have been so good to him. Your hospice is a place where a whole family can lay to rest all their frustrated intentions and old hopes."

"You don't think that Leon will miss his home?" Anton asked.

"No doubt he will. But I think he has missed his home for many, many years. 'Failure to thrive' is what is taking him more than the cancer, and that can mean that he is simply dying from grief and loneliness. The least we can do is bring him safely home and care for him at the end of the journey."

Alone again in the car and with Isabel's words fresh in his ears, Anton's mind wandered back to the people of the Great Valley. The poor are those who cling to God, he thought. Strong people can get on their feet to greet the God who visits them, but the poor cling like they are drowning. They cling tightly because they need to be reminded that they are alive, that life is close to them even as they teeter on the brink of homelessness and ostracism in a world that worships productivity. The poor are those who must expose their need, often at great cost to their human dignity and pride. And this is exposure is both indecent and a public indictment at the same time. Who could blame them for their rawness and anger and even hysteria that shocks us comfortable ones? Anton also remembered the table in Cyntheia's bungalow home; its four candles for the three at the table reminding them to invite the unknown guest. The place was now being filled.

When they arrived at the Caritas House, Shana, Innocenti and Anton carried old Leon from the car to the *Totenbaum*. Penelope invited Shana and Innocenti to move into the second room, and asked Anton to spend the night in the third room in case he were needed. The old man settled into the new bed with a sigh and closed his eyes. His daughter lovingly arranged pillows under his head and feet and between his knees, and set medicines on a side table, along with a glass of water and lotion. Then, as Leon slipped into the wordless passivity of the dying, she sat down on an easy chair and to rest herself. Overhead the great tree caught the sea breeze and gently rocked the bed in its arms below.

"Your bed welcomes Leon," Penelope said. "Look how it receives him. And now he can lay down his burden at last. Shana and Innocenti, this is your home, too. You may come and go whenever you please. You will not disturb him." Outside, in the gathering evening she said softly, "Leon will not be with us long, but all he will hear are happy and peaceful voices, most of all his family's, and a child's young voice, too, and the choir and some musical instruments. After a wee bit we will bring communion over to him from the cookhouse. It isn't right that his last sip of wine be from the chalice of anger, but rather from the chalice of new life."[250]

Leon's rest grew deeper and deeper throughout the day. He slept most of the time. His only utterances now sounded like distant whispers, undecipherable words offered to the human world which they interpreted as requests for a change of position or a sip of cool water. He chose not to eat, and with Penelope's counsels, his family accepted this as his desire for a different kind of nurture. Shana and Penelope bathed him, and Innocenti gave him a fresh shave. Medicine was always available, and Leon was comfortable.

Innocenti spent time exploring the Garden. Sounds of music drew him to the Green of the Octaves, where a choral festival was beginning. He sat to watch Akamu, who was dancing with the celebration. When the presiding spirit of the Garden danced, his Hawaiian shirt flowed and billowed out around his ponderous bulk. He moved with surprising grace back and forth with rollicking steps, in sweeping, dipping circles, his hair waving. With his hands held high he snapped his fingers in the glee of the percussive rhythms. As Innocenti was watching, he was approached by the artist from the Propylaeon gate.

"My, your arms!, such color! They're like stained glass windows at a cathedral!" she exclaimed. "How the sun shines on them! I wonder if we could make such color on canvas."

In short order, Innocenti found himself back at the Caritas House with the artist, sitting on the porch with a brush in hand. She laid out the four primary colors on a palette and showed Innocenti how to blend them for different tints and effects. With her encouragement he raised his eyes to the landscape reaching out to the sea and began daubing at the canvas. Soon on the canvas one could make out the Natural Bridges, then the waves rising and falling as the sea battered the durable rock. Beyond, the infinite expanse of blue spread out to a cloudy horizon.

As his drawing emerged, Innocenti's only comment was, "If I can learn to paint, maybe I can learn to dance. Just don't ask me to talk."

Hearing this, Anton said privately to the artist, "When I was building the *Totenbaum* I had very little sense of what it meant. It was as though someone had suggested it to me, and I just built it. Then Penny told me how the arms of the tree received Leon. Innocenti came along and now sits outside the door of the room where his old friend lies dying, and picks up paintbrushes. So much happens here, things I would never expect."

"From what you told me, Anton, Innocenti loves the out–of–doors, and has been inside a darkened hut for many months, caring for Leon. Up here there's a great view, both ways: out to the horizon, and inside, into the depths. Do you think Innocenti understands what is happening in Leon's life, and in his own life? Do any of us? His old friend is near death; he neither eats nor drinks. The tree of life pulls its sap away from him so that he might drop freely to the ground. From there, the religions suggest pathways. Some say we prepare to return to the earth or we may find our way to our ancestors' bosom, or we may rise again with our bodies all hale and hearty. By and large, the stories of religion can help bring a good death. In any event, Innocenti needs light to find his way, and the colors catch the light, don't they?"

"The religions can also fill the living with terror, visions of unspeakable horrors," Anton commented, "as though death begins a free–fall into nothingness or a perpetual torment."

"Unfortunately true. Religion alone cannot make a good life, a fact often forgotten outside the Gate, where people often center all their hopes in religious circles. But I think that more is needed. The arts, the dance, painting, music…How else could it be? Everything here is for life, including the bed you made for Leon. Innocenti is discovering himself in the colors, like the people discover themselves in the chorus. We will see his moods emerging though the colors and shapes that fill his painting.[251] He doesn't like conversation, so he is as much at risk of suffering the old nightmares as anyone. His painting will tell him much about who he is. With his brushes he will commune with his most intimate companion, his own Self."

Now that Leon was resting comfortably Anton felt ready to work in the earth again, to feel the flow of water and marvel at the rich, brown–black soil that covered the bluff above the coast. As he dabbled and played with plants and earth, he paused frequently, lost in thought. He whispered Cyntheia's name. From where he knelt he could dimly make out the peninsula of Monterey. He knew that she was there, still on the horizon, yet pointing beyond herself to the horizon that exceeds our capacity to encompass. Gathering paper from the Caritas House, he sat on the steps in the sunshine. Pausing occasionally to touch the necklace of seashells around his neck, he wrote the following letter –

Dear Cyntheia,

From where I sit the bay of Monterey lies bounded by the soft tan of the coastal strand, its water glittering in the morning light, its blue astoundingly bright, soft where it is reclaimed in the morning fog. How the sight reminds me of your eyes! In the mid–day I can see your distant home, high on the hill above the Cathedral, nebulous now in the mists of memory. You call me from your remote place of the spirit, voiceless, persistent as nature. Your homeland rests before me as the softest swipe of color between sea and sky. I know you are there. How my eyes long to see your face!

    And now to tell you: Easter is now. Easter is here. Please join me.

Anton

Then he sealed and sent the letter.

    Still later in the week, in the deep hours of the night, Anton awoke to what sounded like guitar chords from the old man's room. While it was not in the least bit disturbing, he was curious about who might be visiting at such an unlikely hour, for he had not heard anyone come in. He arose, put on pants and a sweater, and walked down the hall barefooted.

    Inside Leon's room another old black man with a white beard sat by the bed, playing a guitar. His hands moved smoothly up and down the frets in quiet chord progressions.

    "That sounds nice," Anton said. "Very peaceful. How's Leon?"

    "He is doing very, very well," said the man.

    "Nice of you to visit. Where's home?"

    "Mississippi." The chords and arpeggios continued, freeform, but gathering toward a melody that was distantly familiar. The eyes of the player rested on Leon as he lay sleeping.

    Anton sat down on one of the chairs to listen. "Are you from Leon's family?"

    "Yup. Granddad," the old man said.

    Anton started in disbelief. He held his breath. The music played on.

    "Leon used to swing in the big tree in front of my house in Greenwood. We had an old tire on a rope and on those days when the fields rested white in the sun with the cotton a–bloomin', and when the gin was shut off and it was too hot even for the flies, he still liked to climb up in the tire hangin' from my old tree. He would swing to make the breeze blow across his face. He would lean back and swing almost upside down, so his feet was pointin' up to the sky. He'd say, 'Sing, Pop!' so I'd sing some lil' no–nothing song. Then he'd say, 'Push me higher, Pop! Higher!' So I'd say, 'I'm pushin' you as high as I can, lil' boy. Hol' tight.' Now, just a bit ago, he come to me and asked me to give him another little push. So I'm a–tellin' him he don't need to hold tight no more. Now, it's me that's holdin' him tight...Now let's see if he wants to sing. Singin's something he never did before these times."

At that moment, as the guitar chords formed into a melody, Anton looked over at old Leon. The dying man was sitting up, eyes wide open and gleaming, a rapt expression on his face as he beheld his ancestor. The old grandfather found a pitch with a strum of a chord, and began to form the words deep within his heart –

When this old world starts getting me down...
And people are just too much for me to bear...

Then he said to the man in the bed, "Now it's your turn, my boy." So Leon sang,

I climb way up to the top of the stairs,
And all my cares just drift, right into space.

The grandfather then said, "You've got it, Leon, come on now..." And together they sang –

On the roof, it's peaceful as can be,
And there the world below can't bother me.
Let me tell you now, when I come on home,
Feeling tired and weak,
I go up where the air is fresh and sweet.[252]

"Is Leon dying?" Anton asked. The old man in the bed lay motionless, eyes closed, the faintest rise and fall of his chest the only sign of life.

"Whenever he's ready," his grandfather replied. "What about you, young man? Are you living or dying?"

"I am very much alive, but I am not sure that I am awake," Anton replied.

"Sounds like most people I know," the old player said, and strummed a decisive chord with his thumb.

Anton returned to his room to continue his sleep. In his dreams the old poem from his night in the wilderness returned to him –

I saw Eternity the other night
Like a great ring of pure and endless light,

All calm as it was bright…[253]

In the morning, now Saturday, Anton descended to the lower side of the Lethe Creek to prune the newly–budding Japanese maples and birches. While he was working he pondered his dream, which had reminded him of the night in the Tehachapis and of the vigil with Elena and Gustavo. Below the woody outcropping he could see Gene walking with his old professor. Leaving off his work, he asked their consent to join them and to share his dream.

When Anton had finished, the old teacher said, "Leon is communing with the company of his soul's journey. You were invited to listen in, perhaps because you made the *Totenbaum*. That was a great privilege. You have learned that we are not alone in our departure from this life. We go when we are ready, and we know when we are ready through our dialogue with friendly spirits."

"So Plato was serious with what he has Socrates say about death?" Anton asked.

"Remind me."

Anton's words tumbled out of him. "He says that when a just person dies he either enjoys a dreamless sleep—at long last—or a stimulating conversation with his wisdom–figures. If I recall, Plato has Socrates after death enraptured with the idea of talking with Orpheus and Museus and Hesiod and Homer."[254]

"Our guides gather during dream–time.…I think you're on to something, Anton," the older man agreed. "Why else would Plato write all those dialogues if he were not working through the mysteries of his own life? Tell you what: Gene has been your boon companion. Let him be a commentator on your soul's pilgrimage. He can create a little stage play for us. He'll imagine who are the kin of your own soul. That way you will learn more about yourself, and Gene can apply his craft. What do you say?"

Anton's curiosity was piqued, and he agreed.

"Then we can watch it with you tonight. You might be surprised by what you find. What do you think, Gene?"

Gene was eager to try his hand at the task and repaired to the Writers Circle. Before the morning was out he had crafted a simple play, which he decided to stage in the Circle for the Perplexed. Players were easy to find. He even suggested a role for Innocenti, Shana's tattooed friend, who demurred until Gene assured him that he would not need to memorize any lines. Costumes were not necessary, and props were gathered from the barn or kitchen. The players enjoyed themselves more and more as they abandoned themselves to their roles.

That night, after dinner, when the sun was low to the horizon yet still standing strong and visible through the Propylaeon Gate, a large gong from the musical green invited the community to the Circle. When everyone was gathered Akamu lit the torches around the outside of the Circle, and the teacher introduced Anton and Gene. Anton settled by the teacher in a place where he could watch both the play and the sunset. The older man said, "So here we are. Ironic, isn't it? We're the ones who think we have written our own script. Our lives are so close to us, we cannot even see them unless someone magnifies it so that the truth, be it comical or tragic, is plain for all to see."

And so, the troupe offered the play –

[Several men enter the Circle. A short, stocky man with bulging eyes, portraying Socrates, begins:] So, who wants to be Anton's guide? I think that he has been laying claim to me for the longest time; I should be the one!
[Second speaker, played by the Japanese gardener and representing the Buddha, responds in a cheery voice:] But I know what is best for him, Socrates. With me, he can have peace of mind at last. He can also learn compassion, which even you need to learn.
[Socrates:] What's so good about peace of mind, Gautama? Even happy scoundrels want that. And compassion? This seems simple, not to say simple–minded. Shouldn't we be drawing people out of their suffering through reasonable speech?[255]
[Third speaker, representing Jesus of Nazareth, and played by a young homeless man with eyes that knew suffering and radiated joy:] Not for a second! You are swinging at gnats and about to swallow a camel. Behold the man! His own wounds have healed him. He has shown that he has capacity for passion, for love, for self-giving. Yet I am not so sure he has the courage to pay the high price for true grace.
[Two other men edged into the conversation. The older of the two, a scrawny and bedraggled character with a mournful countenance and missing teeth and with no apparent concern for protocol, says:] Jesus has it right! The whole comfortable world be damned! He knows that foxes have their lairs, and birds have their nests, but the Son of Man has no place to lay his head. I too know this from experience. I'm his man! [He bangs his gloved hand on his chest armor, a large pot cover

borrowed from the kitchen.] Without me, he would just loll about here, while his chosen lady is out there waiting for him and needing him to come knighting for her! He must move forward! ¡Siempre adelante!

[Fifth man, apparently much given to drinking and dissolution, interrupts in a scoffing tone:] Romantic drivel! If he follows Socrates here, all he will have is a perpetual conversation, endless babble. Saddle up with you, Quixote, and he will mistake a sow's ear for a fine silk purse. Follow me, and he will be lying in her arms by sunrise!

[The mournful Knight, in a sudden rage, half draws an old pair of pruning sheers from a burlap bag:] You insult the lady! On guard, Zorba!

[Zorba, stepping easily out of the way:] You exercise yourself needlessly, Knight! You protest too much! Here's what I think of your noble intentions! [He makes an indecent gesture by turning his back to the audience, raising one leg, and slapping his thigh.]

[Socrates, shouting over the impending brawl:] I am astonished at you, Zorba! Everything a burlesque, a bawdy show! How do you know what will make her happy? You think only of your wine and Cretan bordellos. You smell like the streets after a cattle run, a fitting image for all your vital animal spirits. You are unfit to touch the hem of a real woman's dress. You are a greater fool than I thought,—and a Greek at that!

[Zorba:] Just because I reject your famous restraint for a little freedom of the spirit, Socrates? At least I am not arrogant like you! Even a frumpy old woman who wraps fish in my village deserves a little happiness. [With an ingratiating, odd little bow, he turns to Gautama and pleads in a plaintive voice:] I am right about that, aren't I?

[Gautama smiles at Zorba and makes no attempt at a reply. The Jesus player enters the conversation at this point. He had been watching the repartee and chuckling with enjoyment:] Quixote, you are on the rocks,—as usual. Zorba, you are at sea. But you are both right. The man is looking for God. And neither of you really want him to follow you, for that reason alone. I believe that he seeks a soul after my own soul, and only the Woman can open his mind to learn the language of the heart. She is the Namer now, and her voice is in a remote place. Without her, even I cannot speak the language of that other world.

[A sixth man, played by Innocenti, pushes forward. Innocenti's portrayal of the archaic Wildman is enhanced by his size, his beard and painted skin. He wears tattered pants from homeless people at the Garden.

He has no shirt or shoes, and has lined his face with some of the artist's paints, primarily orange–yellow ocher.[256] One can see that his hands and arms are strongly muscled from physical work, or from bearing weapons and heavy loads. While the others had been speaking he had been pacing with barely contained energy. Now he begins to speak a strange language that captures the attention of the others. Indeed, they seem to understand its emotional meaning. However, when the Wildman expects a reply from them, even the wisest among them becomes silent. All appear embarrassed because the sounds have no organized grammar and not one of them can recall the atavistic, neolithic tongue of humanity. Using song–sounds and gestures and facial expressions, the Wildman invites spirits to rise from the earth like smoke from the fire. He makes it clear to his more erudite companions that Anton's innumerable and forgotten ancestors were watching the unfolding drama and were not idle spectators. One ignores or forgets them, who together compose the great and ancient spirit of humanity, only at great peril for one's self and the whole earth. The Wildman also invites the other characters to be ready to meet again at the Meadow of the Stars when Anton's soul signals its readiness to depart from the earth.]

At the conclusion of the play, the Wildman seized a torch and led the other players from the Circle up the hill in the direction of the Meadow of the Stars. The procession disappeared into the forest outcropping and the torchlight flickered through the trees until it disappeared. The audience applauded and burst into conversation, which continued well into the night. The teacher put one arm around Gene's shoulders, and said, "Thank you, my friend. You have listened well to your companion and heard his deeper voice. You have shown us how to listen to you."

For himself, Anton walked with a chastened spirit up the hill to the Caritas House to rest.

For he was more fond of traveling than of returning home to be buried in his own country; for he used often to say that the way to heaven was the same from all places; and he that had no grave had the heaven still over him.

Thomas More (1478–1535),
Utopia

Dem Dichter und Weisen sind
Alle Dinge befreundet und geweiht,
Alle Erlebnisse nütlich,
Alle Tage heilig
Alle Menchsen göttlich.

To the poet and wise one,
All things are befriended and hallowed,
All experience profitable,
All days holy,
All humankind divine.

Friedrich Nietzsche (1844–1900),
Epigraph in 1st edition of
Die Froliche Wissenshaft

"MORE LIGHT!"[257]

WHEN ANTON AWOKE the next day, Sunday, he was still weary from the emotional intensity of the previous days, the night dream with Leon, and the stage–play on his own life. After communion with others in the cookhouse he descended again to the vegetable gardens. This time he chose to work on a new plot that had been lying fallow for a year. Once planted it was to provide corn, carrots and beans for a garden co–op in Freedom, north of Watsonville.

Anton studied the proportions of the open space for a while, then fetched stakes and twine from the tool shed. Starting at the center of the plot he created a one–foot square. He then unwound the twine and created a rectangle with one side equal to the sum of the previous two sides, or two feet by one foot. He repeated the process again, expanding the rectangle to three by two; and again, enlarging it to five by three feet in length. After four more repetitions of this process his plot had grown to thirty–four by twenty–one feet. There he stopped. He returned to the tool shed and painted a sign with the single Greek letter

or *phi*. This he planted at the head of the new plot.[258] With a shovel and hoe he began to work the earth, digging deeply, turning steadily and breaking up clods to aerate the soil. He also ran a hose down to the freshly turned earth to soften it further.

Hour after hour flowed by, unnoticed in the rhythm of tilling. The brown circle of soft, receptive soil expanded and warmed in the sun to lighter hues. The chiming from the musical game could be heard in the distance, blending with laughter and occasional cheers. Anton refreshed himself from the running water and drenched his shirt to remain cool. He formed small furrows to guide the water into the harder soil where he dug. The ocean hummed in the distance, while the breeze spread its freshets over his labor. He worked and fashioned, lost in thought.

A shadow brushed him. He turned. It was Cyntheia. She stood before him, her hair and skirt fluttering in the breeze, her sweet smile bringing forth the radiance of her soul. In the moment Anton saw in her every instance of loveliness he had ever known. She seemed alive with wondering about what lay beyond the next day, the next hour, the next breath.

"I received your letter," she said. "I came immediately. I have been watching you from above, near the farmhouse. I watched you until I could wait no longer to hear your voice, to see your eyes."

He stood, filled with joy. The Garden in all its loveliness had become complete. He found the words, "You have come unto your own, Cyntheia. Come down, and be in this with me."

Cyntheia removed her sandals and rolled her dress above her knees and walked into the muddy soil to kneel beside Anton.[259] He took her hands in his to create a small bowl, and standing together they lifted up earth and water in a gesture of offering for all that had been, and all that was yet to come.

Late in the afternoon, Anton and Cyntheia sat on the bridge, dangling their feet over the Lethe creek that flowed below the Caritas House. They sat facing the hills above, with their backs to the meadows as they fell away to the coastline. The clouds lay across the sky like a sheepskin, frayed and odd–colored, red and textured with pink.[260]

"Do you remember the *mystagogia,* Anton?"

Turning to her, Anton was struck by the light shining behind Cyntheia's head and through her hair.[261] "Being led into a new Universe," he said, remembering her words spoken back at Monterey. "The word reminds me that the Universe is home to humanity. It has received us, and it will send us. Being received here into the Garden must be followed by an eventual sending. Each greeting hints at a future farewell."

"I guess that it is just this simple," she agreed. "But that does not make it easy to understand or to surrender to. Who can understand or surrender to the most simple proposition in all of Scripture, the great 'I Am that I Am'?"

"The word *mystagogia* does not say that we will pause or stand under anything. It tells us to keep walking, Cyntheia. The professor has invited me to meet his students up at the University. I am ready to walk up there."

"Go, Anton."

"Will you be here when I return?"

"Yes, I will. Your bliss has brought you here. I will see you when you return."

Anton found the professor and asked him if he could join him. The older man was agreeable and suggested that they go up the next day, the first day of the week. He was working with a class of new students in an introduction to the humanities. Anton also asked Gene if he were ready to walk back up the hill. Gene said that everything had pointed in that direction, and that he too was ready. He also said that he needed to walk part of the way alone, and that he would meet his companions halfway up the hill, at the old quarry.

The next morning Anton and the teacher set off up the trail that led between the Caritas House and the cookbarn, across the Meadow of the Stars, and up the slopes to the University. Anton was able to recount some of his experiences, such as the lonely night on the Tehachapis where he was serenaded by coyotes and visited by the low–flying owl and where the mighty snake pierced him with his remorseless gaze. He spoke briefly about his crashing fall and the pain of the burn accident in the badlands of Bakersfield.

It was less easy, and even embarrassing, for Anton to probe deeper memories, to recall his rise to positions of security and authority within the collegiate system. He felt that to do so would take him to the brink of banality. Rather than waste an iota of his guide's hospitality with maunderings about his plummet into despair, he was prepared to talk about great ideas and perennial questions, hopefully in an abstract, peripatetic fashion as they walked…Someday, perhaps, his real quandaries could be shared, such as why he felt no guilt at all at not returning to the comforts of his tenured existence; and why he felt no shame in shedding his old identity like a thread–bare suit. But such a conversation did not rise easily on this day of shimmering sunshine and waving meadow grasses, with his destination lying ahead.

Yet the teacher was aware that Anton preferred only the bright side of his pleasures and regrets.[262] "The ironies of your life continue," he probed. "You still need to learn how to live in Ordinary Time. Look how all your learning paved your way into your tidy, intellectual *cul de sac*. Everything in your life had a beginning and an end. Your instruction, your position, even your relationships with students who came and went:

all very nice, encapsulated, dust–free, neat with square corners! A nice, comfortable illusion! Real life cannot be so easily contained. That's like trying to put a torrent into a thimble. No one told you differently, I suppose…"

"I was finding it harder and harder to both listen and speak," Anton confessed.

"About that speaking, do you mean 'lecture,' or 'proclaim'? That speechlessness is actually a good sign. Otherwise, you were becoming a 'literary man, dumb with knowledge.'[263]

"All choked up. I was probably beginning to think that conversation was beneath me."

"So you lost your voice. Hopefully you have learned the healthy silence through your journeys."

"I became anathema to the institution; emotionally and spiritually bereft," Anton said. "I did not even have the spirit of the woman in the Garden who throws rocks at people; and they certainly have no spice gardens in the colleges these days."

"We have forgotten that we must cherish our eccentrics," the teacher laughed, "especially those people who throw rocks at us, just like we throw rules at them. Even a voiceless, crazy woman flinging her pebbles can make us dance with more agility. It was for her that Jesus said that his yoke of freedom would sit very lightly."

"At the college it was business as usual, a conspiracy of silence about the impossibility of adventure. What was happening to me scratched at their collective fears. I, and they, had no idea what to do with it. No one suggested a quest. That's the stuff in old books. Only the very naïve one who knows next to nothing can imagine taking a great risk. The only risks that are socially acceptable anymore are business risks which promise a lot of money."

"The naïve, you said…," the teacher mused. "Your journey has allowed you to begin to recover your own original naïveté. It had to be 'spirit, body, mind,' in that order, like the old Samurai culture used to stress. Not just 'mind' or 'critical thinking,' which our culture has enshrined in so–called higher education. All you get from that is a noxious condition, a kind of 'hypertrophy of the intellect' that feels like a form of mental illness."

"That's rich! Do you think that the condition will appear in the lexicon of psychiatry?"

"Only when the profession regains a sense of humor. Your humbling has been a good thing, Anton, but it should be taken only so far. Heaven help you if you believe that you are humble or if you have been flattered into believing it.

"Like everyone in this enlightened age, you were seduced into reading the Icarus myth as a pretty story. Rather than fly near the sun, you tried to bring the sun down to you. For all your enlightened talk, you had been taking the low road like Daedalus. You dragged your feet in tedium. Wouldn't dare to try your wings. But, it was killing your spirit until you flung yourself in the air, and you did not even know you had the wings to fly! Then you began to sing your *Te Deum!*

"Think what would happen if you began to listen to your teachers with the same desperate passion that you have lived with over the last few months! You would learn that wisdom is not a thing of the textbooks, but an avid affair with *Sophia,* the most elusive of lovers. The thought of being intoxicated by God would no longer make you squeamish. And you would not want to run for therapy or distractions whenever you felt loneliness or grief.[264] Instead, you would thank Heaven for such gifts of the spirit! Would you not then embark on your quest in consciousness rather than wait for consciousness to descend on you?"

Anton pondered this as they walked on the path as it left the road behind. The grass along the path was already nearly knee–high and deep green. Water from the morning dew still glistened on the blades. Beyond a fence a small group of Angus cows chewed pensively on the grass.

"What use is all that learning, then?" he asked. "To make us good and useful creatures like those cows over there? *Homo consumens?* Is it all a survival mechanism, or just delicious speculations that can be disposed of as easily as closing a book?"

"Spoken like a true discontent!" his companion responded with spirit. "There's nothing easier for a teacher to do than to stand up before learners and say, 'Here is what life is all about.' Yes, it is our task to help young people traverse their path, to lead them to alluring vistas of thought and action. Yet the teacher—and this is a difficult confession—must season the feast of his ideas with the bitters and gall of his own failures. Why else does the Buddha begin his journey with the awful and dismal sights?[265] Then there is Jesus: his first agony was in his own powerful drives where he imagined unlimited acquisition or unhindered power over others. Why call Jesus a 'redeemer' if we are asleep on our feet like those cows and have no lusts and cravings of the spirit to redeem? Why would people drop their nets and run after him, or climb trees to catch a glimpse of him, or go hungry for days to hear his words?

Even more than your Socrates, he believed that he had failed in the end. Socrates cheerfully walked to prison and its chains and the hemlock, and so diminished the total claims of the city of Athens. With tears streaming like blood, Jesus walked to the city of Jerusalem and died in heart-breaking misery, a failed prophet crowned with thorns. In both cases, the true teachers admit their dismal and complete failure to persuade others about what life should be.

"Part of our work, yours and mine, Anton, is to dampen the expectations of students through the examples of our own failures. Tastefully, of course. Students hate sentimental, self–absorbed pedagogues! Somehow we need to convey the idea that the goal of education lies beyond our grasp, but not beyond our aspiration. We are not utopian, nor are we satisfied with ends within our own capacity. So, we ask again, what is the best way of life? Is it the purpose of education to prepare people to be productive in a high–paying job? How solid and attainable, and how low! Can you swallow it, Anton? It wants to stick in your gorge! Is it to produce credentialed junior professionals that have met every requirement for graduation? That soulless marketing mentality has turned education in a Procrustean bed of courses and credits.[266] What about 'molding good citizens'? A far sight better, of course; but perhaps what we need are good human beings who can hold their defective regimes to account. They invariably bear the stigmata of being 'bad citizens.' So we are left with the question, what is a good human being? We're back where we started from. It's no wonder that the brightest often drop out and are condemned as failures. At least it is better to fail nobly than to succeed basely.[267] Gad! I am surprised that it took you so long!"

The trail through the meadows now approached an old sandstone quarry. Gene was there ahead of them, sitting on a large, flat stone that had been deposited long ago on the edge of the pit. With a wave and greeting, Anton stepped off the path to approach his friend.

"Whoa!" Gene called. "Easy there! The ground is very crumbly. I lived here longer than you, and have better footing. You may already be over the abyss, and not know it!"

Anton backed up, then started again through the long grasses, watching his footing. Near the edge he looked out over the wide rim into the many–colored strata. From where he was standing he could not see the bottom. Yet what he could see of the quarry exuded warm brown, tan, and glittering russet layers of ancient rock.

"'Look to the rock from which you were hewn, and the quarry from which you were dug'..." the teacher mused, standing beside him. "It is best to see the quarry from deep within. Down there it is very safe. One can even climb down the side with a guide beside you. When you are safely on the ground, if you have the patience and can sit there all day, you may watch the angle of the sun move across the sky. The light filters through the dust in the air, the shadows move, the air warms and cools. You listen to your heart. The Spirit speaks to you. It was this way at Delphi, and so it is here."[268]

The three men sat and looked out over the quarry for a few minutes. It held the antediluvian story of the Earth, and this but a footnote in the still greater story of the cosmos. The meadow was blanketed in silence, punctuated in the distance by the lowing of cattle and more closely by the bright chatter of a robin's sibilant sentences.

They continued their walk up the hill. Approaching the forest they stopped to watch a stellar jay swoop through the air. The bird flew into a redwood tree where it clung with mocking ease on a flimsy branch high off the ground. In a moment it abandoned the treetop, jetted downward with its wings folded back, its high pitched call singing its contempt of caution; it then scooped the sky with its wings and raced off, laughing with an irrepressible twitter.

Further up, with the garden community now well behind them and with the buildings of the University in sight among the madrone, birches and redwoods, Gene said, "Anton, we are getting close. I need to catch my breath. All I can hear is my own heartbeat. Let's stop for a moment."

They sat under the trees, each occupied with his own thoughts. Then Gene said, "Why don't you go on alone? I have an errand to run, into the wilderness of my past.[269] We can meet again later in the afternoon."

Anton and the teacher resumed their walk. Before entering the dense forest and losing sight of the hillside below, they paused to look back down past the grassy meadows and quarry to the Garden which spread out below with its orchards and cultivated contours.

"A lovely sight," Anton said.

"Yes. It's the best of me, what's worth sharing. I only planted myself there for a while. I don't think of it as my creation. An untold number of people have come and worked there. My life is the ordinary stuff of family, work, eating and drinking, all blessed normalcy. Our lives are but straw to be swept away, said the Psalmist.[270] The Garden is a project far more worthy than I, and it will outlive me for a while, that I know. Then it will be claimed by time like everything else. In the meantime, may it be worthy of your memory. What about you, Anton? Have you figured out what you need to learn?"

Anton thought about the question for a moment. Then he said, "What would my *te deum laudamus* sound like?[271] I have been wondering for months. What I want to learn is so vague, so different than anything I knew before! Probably, if I could be learning what I need to know right now, I would be a sorcerer's apprentice, Merlin's understudy, a bottleboy for an alchemist. My materials? the visible colors of the rainbow!"

Anton stopped and looked down the hill, falling away resplendent in colorful grandeur. His energy and his voice grew in force. "Yes! On a blustery day when the rainbow breaks on the waves beyond the Natural Bridges and the lighthouse, I would gather the shimmering, radiant colors before they vanish, and hold them in a chalice. Then, in the cup I would mix the tears of longing and sadness from mothers grieving their lost children. I would add the salt of the sweat of men and women held in bondage. I would take the cup to a secret place around the inlets and tide pools, where lovers would add their cool wine, then warm it in their embrace.

"Thus ripened, it would be ready to share. I would invite old men to arise from their laments over fallen comrades, to step forward and to take the cup of blessing. It would become theirs to offer in renewed service, not in the clash of arms, but in the still more dangerous service of care and justice for the poor, the single mother, and the homeless child,—and even those wounded by love and service itself! Together, with all those who long for their final home, we would gather before the sunset outside the Propylaeon, and fling the chalice of colors into the air, where it would shimmer again in a cascade of sounds as lingering, inviting, acclaiming as Mozart's *Laudate Domino!* That is what I would learn how to do!"

As his acclamation ended they could hear the booming and clanging from the musical game in the Garden, well down the path. Someone had struck the high steel C and the whole rambunctious ensemble was striking up a jubilant, percussive *tan–ta–ra!*

Soon Anton and the teacher were walking along the needle and cone strewn paths underneath towering trees that swayed at their tips with the lightest of breezes. Robins pealed out their primal code, bright, wordless whistles penetrating the spaces. Sunlight shown through at every angle. Time disappeared, its mortality overwhelmed by the cascade of brilliant light from the sky and the golden meadow of flowers.

"Here," the teacher said. "I want you to meet my class." He opened the door to the auditorium. Anton felt the old pounding in his chest and walked in behind his guide. The large room dazzled with light and space. Students were gathering, placing paper on their desks, rummaging in backpacks and chatting.

Like a seasoned actor stepping onto the stage, the teacher approached the blackboard and began to write,

Nel mezzo del cammin di nostra vita
mi ritrovai per una selva oscura
ché la diritta via era smarrita.

Ahi quanto a dir qual era è cosa dura
esta selva selvaggia e aspra e forte
che nel pensier rinova la paura!

As he wrote, the room quieted as students transcribed the words to their own notebooks. Then he turned and said, "Good morning, everyone. This reads,

> Midway upon the journey of our life
> I found myself within a forest dark,
> For the straightforward pathway had been lost.
> Ah me! how hard a thing it is to say
> What was this forest savage, rough, and stern,
> Which in the very thought renews the fear.[272]

"The translation is familiar to you. Dante's meaning is less clear. Of course it does not refer to the redwoods which lie outside our door…What you already know in your young years is that the dark contains many hauntings. Hopefully in a class such as this you will come to trust in your fearful gropings. Then, in the ceremonies of your mind, in the electric zeal of discovery, your questions will become the fireworks that cast sparkling light into the obscurity of life. Our work is with those who have stepped with fear and trembling into the dark night and have emerged to tell us about it."

Turning to Anton, the professor continued, "I would like to introduce you to someone who had no intention to make this larger journey, to find himself under the duress of life. He has trod the way that leads through Purgatory. Whether he has arrived at his Paradise is not for us to know.

But he will tell you that the way is often ungentle, and leaves us only with our own truth. He wishes to greet you." He then sat in the front row.

Anton stood in front of the class, his hands in his pockets. The sea of faces before him sparkled with eyes shining in anticipation. He drew a breath and spoke slowly,

"You are students. Here you live in the safety of your friends and teachers. Life is good...but do you know what the Good for you is?"

Anton paused and smiled at the teacher and touched his shoulder lightly and affectionately. He then continued speaking to the students.

"A necessary step will be to free yourself from the spell of authority, even from those you love the most. I hardly need to tell you that. In coming here you have stepped outside your parents' circle. Next you will step out of the seductions of your own teachers' wisdom. Even Dante needed to bid farewell to Virgil, who taught him heavenly and abysmal things. Think of it!: the Aristotle who could write poetry, who composed a hymn to Justice,—he, too, had to free himself from Plato, his teacher for seventeen years and the man he revered like none other. Only then could he find his own voice. Only then could he launch the project that became Science—this proclamation of the truth as he experienced it.[273]

"When you have taken this step, you have begun the search for the great goodness you do not yet know. However you might name your Good, as *Paradiso,* or Oneness with Nature, or Heaven, or Easter, or 'Aguilares'—a name suggested to me by a Salvadoran—it must entice you,...woo you. You will find that what you thought you were seeking, is actually in hot pursuit of you! And at those moments when you feel most empty, most alone, know that the emptiness you feel is preparing you to receive the light from the supreme good you seek.

"Then, as you search, you will be watched by an invisible assembly of villains and heroes, many your own ancestors. With bated breath they will watch and they will wonder: How will you mount the stage of life? With courage and self–offering? With verve and great feeling and a cause? Will you risk excellence, and throw yourself into the agony of its service?"

Anton's voice rose as the urgency of his vision claimed him. Opening his hands and striding closer to the students in the front row, so close that he could see into the bright, speckled irises of their young eyes, he continued,

"Will you ride the curve of life in an unrequited desire to discover truth and beauty and share it abundantly? Or will you throw your arms around the knees of ambitious and hubristic men and women, people with an appetite for war, who will tempt you to become the Caesars of your culture, your country, or even the whole future itself?"

Looking around to other students who had leaned forward, mesmerized by his energy, he asked, "Will you dally and hang–out, comfortable, indolent, waiting for someone to drag you up to 'strut and fret your brief hour upon the stage'? Will you know life only in the safety of books, and be assured of a dismal and dreary fate that earns the contempt of the prophets?"[274]

He paused for a moment. His heart swelled with love for the students in their hopefulness, their seriousness and their passion.

"No! I hope for something different for you!" he said. "I hope and believe that you will embrace life like a lover and wrestle with it until daybreak: Life will invite you to suffer. It may break your bones or break your heart, but it will not break your spirit.

"If at this day's end you believe in the artist, the poet and the prophet within yourself, and give form and voice to Life's message with more poems and hymns than even heaven can contain…

"If you join your quest with others and discover total self–giving and experience the sweet astonishment of total receiving, and have brought forth new life that carries the future beyond you…

"If you have made the world safer for children and the lonely and the aged…

"If you have discovered the Good that is within you and that is yours alone to give…

"If you have heard a hint of God's name for you, hidden away until you are ready to claim it…

"Then you will author your own story, and your life will be one more parable in the Great Romance that enchants us all!"

Late in the afternoon, when it was time to descend off the hill, Anton and the teacher were puzzled at the whereabouts of Gene.

"I think I know where we might find him: at the college with the patio and the trellis. There is also a library nearby."

"I know the place," the teacher said.

When they arrived at the small college courtyard they found Gene sitting on a bench by himself. Students walked by in pairs and small groups or alone. The small fountain poured forth a continuous flow of quiet sound. Evening sunlight, captured and released by the cotton cumulus clouds, brightened the tops of the redwoods. Gene appeared serene, youthful, utterly calm.

"I am home," he said. "The campus gardener has said he needs help in the planters. And I have talked to one of the writing faculty, and have offered to be a writing tutor."

"That's wonderful, Gene! How did that poem go,…something about 'out of the loam'?"

"Then Whole I dug it,/ Out of the loam,/ And to my garden,/ Carried it home," Gene replied.

As the three prepared to return to the Garden, Anton said to the teacher, "It is tempting to want to stay up here."

"Who does not want to stay on the mountain top, on the peak? But you yourself counseled against that. Who would the poems be for? The hymns? Whose quest can you join if you insist on staying at your destination? The questions take you back to the ground, to what holds the peaks, to the realm of the father and the mother and the ancestors. Jesus goes down from Mt. Tabor. Socrates goes down from Athens to the Piraeus.[275] So must we go down, and even out through the Gate. Then perhaps one day you may make the ascent anew; or have it forced on you. We are not allowed to know."

Leaving the buildings of the campus, they walked back into the forest, traversed the bridges across the large, fern–filled ravines, and wended their way down the hillside toward the Garden. As they walked down and around the quarry, Anton wondered whether he would travel still further, alone, and plant his oar in some solitary place like Odysseus, far from the sounds of the sea. How could I do that?, he thought. I may travel further, yet not alone, and always within a day's journey of the sea.

Soon they had crossed over the Meadow of the Stars and approached the cookhouse. There Cyntheia greeted them at the door, where she said,

"Just in time. You must be hungry. Everybody's here and waiting for you. The bread is coming out of the oven. Last year's wine is poured. Come, let's have supper."

Author's Note

THE CONVENTIONAL WISDOM OF A THERAPEUTIC CULTURE predicts periodic crises in the life of an individual person.[276] Developmental psychology, which has occupied the provinces of human spirituality once served by religious culture, has charted these crises and described them in a popular literature that is in general humane and hopeful. Similarly, the ministries of sacramentary and confessional have been claimed by the vast secular professions of social work, mental health therapy and clinical psychology; and no one can gainsay their benefits and blessings for persons in difficult times. Not content to leave these fields to altruistic professions alone, commerce capitalizes on vulnerable souls at life's pivotal moments by creating healing spas, resorts and remote, "other worldly" adventures for hardy tourists.

What is less appreciated in the modern age is the value of the "trial of the spirit." An older wisdom found in most of the world's religions suggests that this trial, also known as the "dark night of the soul," is not something from which one must flee or, heaven forbid, simply talk away (dismissively called "venting") or numb with pharmacology. The trial of the spirit is more than an emotional crisis or untoward mood. It is a necessary concomitant to the experience of enlightenment or *satori*.

The "dark night" is the day's long shadow. The classical Greek mind knew that the encounter with the Good which is both True and Beautiful, occurs after the arduous ascent through the Cave. The classic rendering of this ascent in the Seventh Book of Plato's *Republic* shows that it is a lonely, painful journey of uncertain outcome. Similarly, the Hebrew mind beholds the Promised Land lying beyond the Wilderness. In the contemporary language of Thomas Merton, "The only way out of suffering is through suffering." Paradoxically, this older wisdom even suggests that an ineffable radiance may penetrate and accompany suffering and illuminate the path. The light of the Good shines within the Cave; angels succor Jesus after his wilderness temptations. Unpredictable, unfathomable, uncontainable, the experience of joy born of suffering may come as sheer gift.

The Sojourns of Anton Reisen is a tale about a scholar whose discipline has explored this truth while protecting him from the agony of its demands. Comfortably situated in his academic setting and role, little did he know, in the old vernacular, that his soul was being required of him. Ineluctably, the service to the luminaries of his tradition, his own life memories, and the engagement with his own students were slowly dissolving the protective shield that kept fantastic dreams and demons hidden away from his conscious mind. At the crucial moment, when he might have rested peacefully in the knowledge of his personal and professional attainments, he begins to hear a relentless question echoing in the empty chambers of his loneliness. So begins his trial, his descent into the dark night that anticipates the day.

The genre of this story is a *bildungsroman,* an "educational journey tale." It looks to Thomas Mann's *Magic Mountain,* Goethe's *Wilhelm Meister* and Homer's *Odyssey* as fitting examples of sublimation in the novel of adventure. As an educational endeavor it explores the unfolding consciousness of the protagonist while serving at the same time as a vehicle for discovery by the author; perhaps it will serve the reader in a similar way. In briefest expression, the story traces the character's spiritual plummet and his awakening to compassion, creativity and service. The plot of the story unfolds through a physical geography that under-girds the transformation of the psyche of the protagonist. Our character travels from South to North and from East to West; from the bustle of the city down into abandonment in the desert; from the parched badlands of Bakersfield to the fertility of the Central California Valley; west through the enchanted valley of Carmel, and from thence to the coast and into the ocean around Monterey. The final foray takes our character to the city of holy cross, Santa Cruz, where lies the University, a symbol of the whole in its unity and multiplicity. These movements on the horizontal and vertical planes are meant to suggest the inner spiritual landscape, not only of an individual, but of the human community. The axes of travel suggest that life itself has a *telos,* a meaningful unfolding whose pattern is often obscured by life's sorrows and crises. Yet the intelligibility of life experience is suggested by the presence of the owl in twilight—a classical symbol of wisdom—on more than one occasion.

But as beginnings are decisive, as is the freedom to choose and to choose again. We see our protagonist being given a choice: faced with his great question and the terror of the unknown, he might "march with downcast eyes back to the land of the Philistines" in all its comforts and routines.[277] Or he might step forward into the mystery of life and nature. There he will be assured of suffering. He may also catch a glimpse of a joy that becomes less remote with every step. He makes the latter choice, not once but continuously, and in this he is redeemed. In allowing his complacency to be demolished, he is able to respond to the imperatives of justice and hear the clarion call of beauty and love.

BIBLIOGRAPHY

Adam, David. *The Edge of Glory: Prayers in the Celtic Tradition.* Kirkpatrickburg: Morehouse, 1985.
Arendt, Hannah. *Eichmann in Jerusalem: A Study in the Banality of Evil.* Penguin, 1994.
Aristotle. Oswald, tr. *Nicomachean Ethics.* New York: Macmillan, 1962.
Bach, Johann Sebastian. *Cantata 140.*
Becker, Ernst. *The Denial of Death.* N.Y.: Free Press, 1973.
Boff, Leonardo. *When Theology Listens to the Poor.* Harper, 1970.
Bowie, Fiona. *Beguine Spirituality: Mystical Writings of Mechthild of Magdeburg.* Crossroad, 1990.
Brickhouse, T.C., ed., *The Trial and Execution of Socrates,* N.Y.: Oxford UP, 2002.
Bommelyn, Loren, and Berneice Humphrey. *Xus We-Yó': Tolowa (Tututni). Language Dictionary.* 2nd ed. Crescent City: Tolowa Language Committee, 1989.
Brown, Norman O. *Love's Body.* Berkeley: UC Press, 1990.
Burkert, Walter. *Greek Religion,* tr. J. Raffan. Cambridge, Mass.: Harvard UP, 1985.
Burkert, Walter. *Homo Necans: The Anthropology of Ancient Greek Sacrificial Ritual and Myth.* Berkeley: UC Press, 1983.
Campbell, Joseph. "From Darkness to Light: The Mystery Religions of Ancient Greece," in *Transformations of Myth Through Time.* HarperCollins, 1990.
Carse, James P. *Finite and Infinite Games: A Vision of Life as Play and Possibility.* N.Y.: Ballantine Books.
Chambers, Frank Pentland. *The History of Taste: An Account of the Revolutions of Art Criticism and Theory in Europe.* N.Y.: Columbia, 1932.
Chernyshevskii, Nikolai. *What is to be Done?* 1863.

Coffin, William Sloan. *A Passion for the Possible: A Message to U.S. Churches.* Westminster: John Knox Press, 1997.

Davies, Olive, tr. *Beatrice of Nazareth, and Hadewijch of Brabant.* N.Y.: Crossroad, 1990.

de Coulanges, Fustel. *The Ancient City.*

Dodds, E. R. *The Greeks and the Irrational.* Berkeley: U. of California Press, 1971.

Dorr, Donal. *Option for the Poor: A Hundred Years of Vatican Social Teaching.* Maryknoll: Orbis Books, 1983.

Dostoevsky, Fyodor. *Notes from the Underground.* Vintage Books, 1994.

———. *The Brothers Karamozov.* New York: Modern Lib-rary, 1996.

Drucker, B. "The Tolowa and their Southwest Oregon Kin," *Proceedings of American Archeology and Ethnography.* Berkeley: UC Press, 36.4, 1943.

Eckhart, Meister. *German Sermons.* Walsh, M. O., tr. London: Watkins, 1981.

Eissler, Kurt R. *Goethe: A Psycho–Analytic Study.* Detroit: Wayne State UP, 1963.

Eliade, Micea. *A History of Religious Ideas: From the Stone Age to the Eleusinian Mysteries.* Chicago: U. of Chicago Press, 1978.

———. *The Sacred and the Profane: The Nature of Religion.* Willard Trask, tr. Orlando: Harcourt Brace, 1957.

Eliot, T.S. *Burnt Norton.*

Elytis, Odysseas. *Selected and Last Poems.* Port Townsend: Copper Canyon Press, 1998.

Emerson, Ralph Waldo. "The American Scholar Essay," in *The Essential Writings of Ralph Waldo Emerson.* Princeton Review, 2000.

Episcopal Book of Common Prayer. N.Y.: Oxford UP, 1990.

Faulkner, William. *Three Famous Short Novels: Spotted Horses, Old Man, The Bear.* Bt Bound, 1999.

Finn, Thomas M. *From Death to Rebirth: Ritual and Conversion in Antiquity.* N.Y.: Paulist Press, 1997.

Foley, Helene P. *The Homeric Hymn to Demeter.* Princeton: Princeton UP, 1993.

Frankl, Victor. *Man's Search for Meaning,* Washington Square Press, 1998.

Frazer, Sir James George. *The Golden Bough.* (First published in 1890) New York: Granmercy, 1981.

Gascoigne, George. *A Hundred Sundrie Flowers.* C.T. Prouty, ed. Columbia: U. of Missouri, 1942.

Gow, A.S. tr. *Theocritus.* Cambridge UP, 1965.
Gutiérrez, Gustavo. *A Theology of Liberation: History, Politics and Salvation.* Maryknoll, N.Y.: Orbis, 1988.
Gutiérrez, Gustavo. *The Truth Shall Make You Free: Confrontations.* Maryknoll, N.Y.: Orbis, 1990.
Harrison, Jane Ellen. *Ancient Art and Ritual.* N.Y.: Holt, 1913.
Hart, Columba. *Hadewijch: The Complete Works.* N.Y.: Paulist, 1980.
Hegel, George. *Phenomenologie der Geist (The Phenomenology of Mind).*
———. *Rechtsphilosophie (The Philosophy of Right).*
Heidegger, Martin. *Was heist denken? What is Called Thinking?* Wieck, tr., HarperCollins, 1976.
Herbert, George. "The Call," in *Selections of English Poems.* W. H. Auden, ed. Harmondsworth: Penguin, 1973.
Heschel, Abraham. *Man is Not Alone: A Philosophy of Religion.* N.Y., Farrar, 1951.
Homer. *Iliad and Odyssey.* Fagles, tr. *Penguin, 1999.*
Horace. *Satires, Epistles and Ars Poetica.* Leon Golden, tr. Miami: UP of Florida, 1995.
Iamblichus. *Life of Pythagoras.* T. Taylor, tr. London: J. M. Watkins, 1965.
Jaeger, Werner. *Early Christianity and Greek Peideia.* Harvard UP, 1961.
Johnson, Elizabeth. *She Who Is: The Mystery of God in Feminist Discourse.* N.Y.: Crossroad, 1994.
Johnson, Robert. *He: Understanding Masculine Psychology.* HarperCollins, 1989.
Jung, C.G. *Alchemical Studies.* R.F.C. Hull, tr., New Jersey: Princeton UP, 1967.
———. *Memories, Dreams, Reflections.* Vintage Books, 1989.
———. *Nietzsche's Zarathustra: Notes of the Seminar Given in 1934–1939.* Princeton UP, 1988.
———. *Psychological Reflections.* Jolande Jacobi, ed. Princeton: Princeton U. Press, 1970.
———. *Psychology and Alchemy.* N.Y.: Princeton UP, 1953.
Kazantzakis, Nikos. *Zorba the Greek.* Carl Wildman, tr. N.Y.: Simon & Schuster, 1952.
Keats, John. *Ode to a Grecian Urn.*
Kierkegaard, Sorën. *Stages in Life's Way.* 1845.
Kingsley, Peter. *Ancient Philosophy, Mystery, and Magic: Empedocles and Pythagorean Tradition.* Oxford: Clarendon, 1995.

Kirkpatrickon, Edward. *Darkness at Night: A Riddle of the Universe.* Harvard UP, 1987.
Lehte, John. *Fifty Contemporary Thinkers: From Structuralism to Postmodernity.* London: Routledge, 1994.
Lessing, Gottfried. "Laocoon," in *Prose Works.* London: George Bell, 1879.
Levine, Daniel H. *Religion and Political Conflict in Latin America.* Chapel Hill: U. of North Carolina Press, 1986.
Lewis, C. S. *Allegory.* Oxford, 1936.
Lewis, Sinclair. *Babbit.*
Lindsay, Jack. *Dionysios.*
Machiavelli, Niccolò. *The Prince* (1515). Harvey Mansfield, tr. Chicago: U. of Chicago Press, 1985.
MacIntyre, Alaisdair. *After Virtue.*
MacNaughtan, Don. *American Indian Languages of Western Oregon.* Lane Community College, Oregon, 1996.
Mainwaring, Scott and Alexander Wilde, eds., *The Progressive Church in Latin America.* Notre Dame: Notre Dame UP, 1989.
Marlowe, Christopher. *The Tragical History of Doctor Faustus.* 1589.
McFague, Sallie. *The Body of God: An Ecological Theology.* Fortress Press, 1993.
Menzies, Lucy. *The Revelations of Mechthild of Magdeburg.* London: Longmans, 1953.
Merkel, Ingrid and Debus, Allen, eds., *Hermeticism and the Renaissance,* London: Folger Books, 1988.
Merton, Thomas. *Learning To Love.* San Francisco: Harper, 1998.
———. *Praying the Psalms.* Collegeville: Liturgical Press, 1956.
Moritz, Karl Phillip. *Anton Reiser*, tr. Ritchie Robertson. Penguin, 1997.
———. *Die Götterlehre.* Unveränderte Ausgaba, 1804.
Neruda, Pablo. *Passions and Impressions.* Margaret Peden, tr., N.Y.: Farrar, 1978.
Nietzsche, Friedrich. *The Birth of Tragedy from the Spirit of Music.* 1872.
———. *Thus Spoke Zarathustra,* 1883.
———. *The Twilight of the Gods,* 1888.
Nobile, Nancy. *The School of Days: Heinrich von Kleist and the Traumas of Education.* Detroit: Wayne State UP, 1999.
Nouwen, Henri. *The Way of the Heart,* Ballantine, 1991.
O'Donohue, John. *Anam Cara: A Book of Celtic Wisdom,* San Francisco: HarperCollins, 1997.

Olson, Alan M. ed., *Transcendence and the Sacred,* London: University of Notre Dame Press, 1994.
Pascal, Blaise. *Pensées.* 1660.
Pelican, Jaroslav, ed. *The World Treasury of Religious Thought,* 1990.
Plato. *Complete Works,* J.M. Cooper, ed. Indianapolis: Hackett, 1997.
Plutarch. *Lives of Famous Greeks and Romans.*
Polybius. *Histories.* W.R. Paton tr, Mass.: Harvard UP, 1960.
Rilke, Rainier. *The Book of Hours: Love Poems to God.* Anita Barrows and Joanna Macey, tr., ed. N.Y.: Riverhead Books, 1996.
Rousseau, Jean–Jacques. *The Solitary Promenades.*
Safranski, Rudiger. *Nietzsche: A Philosophical Biography.* Shelley Frisch, tr. N.Y.: Norton, 2002.
Shakespeare, William. *The Tempest.*
Shields, Peter R. *Logic and Sin in the Writings of Ludwig Wittgenstein.* Chicago: U. of Chicago Press, 1993.
Sidney, Philip. *Old Arcadia; Astrophel and Stella.*
Smith, Carl. *Set My Heart Aright: A Michelangelo Portrait,* 1996.
Smith, Huston. *The World's Religions.* San Francisco: Harper, 1991.
Snell, Bruno. *The Discovery of the Mind: The Greek Origins of European Thought.* N.Y.: Harper & Row, 1960.
Sri, P.S. *T.S. Eliot, Vedanta and Buddhism.* U. of Columbia Press, 1986.
Sterne, Laurence. *A Sentimental Journey through France and Italy.* Berkeley: UC Press, 1967.
Stevenson, Robert L. *From Scotland to Silverado.*
———. *Old Pacific Capital.*
———. *The Bewilderment of the World.*
Strabo. *Histories.*
Swift, Jonathan. *Gulliver's Travels.*
Tennyson, Alfred Lord. *The Charge of the Light Brigade.*
The Bible, *Christian and Hebrew.*
Turner, Victor. *The Ritual Process: Structure and Anti–Structure.* Chicago: Aldine Press, 1969.
Ulanov, Ann and Barry Ulanov. *Primary Speech: A Psychology of Prayer.* Atlanta: John Knox Press, 1982.
Virgil. *The Aeneid.*
Von Goethe, Johann Wolfgang. *Faust.* Walter Arndt, tr., Norton: 1976.
———. *Poetry and Art.* 1813.
Walsh, M. O., tr. *Eckhart: German Sermons.* London: Watkins, 1981.
West, Morris, *The Clowns of God.* William Morrow, 1981.
Weston, Jessie L. *From Ritual to Romance.* Cambridge UP, 1920.

Whitman, Walt, *A noiseless patient spider.*
Wordsworth, William, *Lines Composed a Few Miles Above Tintern Abbey.*
———. *Perfect Woman.*
Xenophon. *Anabasis: The March of the Ten Thousand.* Brownson, tr. Cambridge, Mass.: Harvard UP, 1998.
Yarnall, Judith. *Transformations of Circe: The History of an Enchantress.* Chicago: U. of Illinois Press, 1994.

NOTES

These notes are left in rough manuscript form as resources for readers interested in the lineage of many of the ideas offered in this work. The Notes are not intended for critical review or substantiation of the theories and perspectives presented here.

[1] Used from the 16th through 18th centuries, the hornbook was a thin piece of wood shaped like a paddle. On one side of the hornbook was a sheet of text including the alphabet, a syllabary, an Invocation to the Trinity, and the Lord's Prayer. It was covered with a thin layer of horn material to protect it.

[2] John Keats. "A Letter to George and Georgiana Keats" in *The Vale Of Soul-Making* (1819). Cited in http://www.mrbauld.com/keatsva.html.

[3] Cited in Safranski 119.

[4] The name of the character is derived from *Anton Reiser*, the title of a story by Karl Philippe Moritz (1756–1793), a critic, educator, friend of Goethe, and author of numerous works, including a series on classical aesthetics and accounts of his travels. (See Moritz, *Anton Reiser*.)

The protagonist's name also recalls St. Anthony, the early Desert Father who left Rome to attend to the Spirit. He found excessive noise and distraction living on the edges of the city, and went deeper into the desert. Eventually like–minded seekers found him out even there, and he established a monastic community devoted to silence and prayer. See Henri J. M. Nouwen, *The Way of the Heart* (1999).

Finally, *reisen* is the German verb meaning *to travel*.

[5] Sophocles, *Antigone* 29-30.

[6] Selections of literature from Sophocles *Oedipus Tyrannus* and *Antigone*, Plato's *Republic*, Shakespeare's *Hamlet*, Machiavelli's *Prince* and *Discourses on The First Ten Books of Titus Livy*, and T. S. Eliot's *The Wasteland*.

[7] As John XXIII, Antipope of the Pisan party from 1400 to 1415, Cardinal Baldassare Cossa was one of the seven cardinals who deserted Gregory XII. He joined with those obedient to Benedict XIII in the convening of the Council of Pisa, where he became the leader. (See *The Catholic Encyclopedia.*)

[8] Giovanni Francesco Poggio Bracciolini (1380-1459), Italian humanist and historian, was responsible for the recovery of ancient manuscripts of Cicero, Lucian, Lucretius, Quintilian, and Tacitus as well as a translation Xenophon's *Cyropaedeia (The Education of Cyrus)*. In 1431 he wrote the four books of his

De Varietate Fortunæ, whose comparison of the visible ruins of Rome with descriptions of the city in ancient manuscripts may mark the inception of the science of archæology.

Roman statesman and philosopher, Anicius Manlius Severinus Boethius was often styled "the last of the Romans." He born at Rome in 480 ce and died at Pavia in 524 or 525. Descended from a consular family, he was left an orphan at an early age and was educated by the pious and noble–minded Symmachus, whose daughter, Rusticana, he married. As early as 507 he was known as a learned man, and as such was entrusted by the Ostrogothic King Theodoric with several important missions. He enjoyed the confidence of the king, and as a patrician of Rome was looked up to by the representatives of the Roman nobility. When, however, his enemies accused him of disloyalty to the king, alleging that he plotted to restore "Roman liberty," and added the accusation of "sacrilege" (literally, the "stealing of sacred things"; "sacred" fr. Hittite *saklais,* rite), neither his noble birth nor his great popularity availed him. He was cast into prison, condemned unheard, and executed by order of Theodoric. During his imprisonment, he reflected on the instability of the favour of princes and the inconstancy of the devotion of his friends. These reflections suggested to him the theme of his best–known philosophical work, the *De Consolatione Philosophiae.*

On the battles of Cannae and Trasimene Lake, see Polybius, *Histories,* Volume II.

[9] From Niccolò Machiavelli, *The Prince* (1515),

> I conclude therefore that, fortune being changeful and mankind steadfast in their ways, so long as the two are in agreement men are successful, but unsuccessful when they fall out. For my part I consider that it is better to be adventurous than cautious, because fortune is a woman, and if you wish to keep her under it is necessary to beat and ill-use her; and it is seen that she allows herself to be mastered by the adventurous rather than by those who go to work more coldly. She is, therefore, always, woman-like, a lover of young men, because they are less cautious, more violent, and with more audacity command her. (Chapter XXV, "What Fortune Can Effect In Human Affairs, And How To Withstand Her.")

[10] Sorën Kiekegaard, *The Journals, 1850–1854,* in *A Kierkegaard Anthology,* Bretall, ed. (1973), p. 432.

[11] Sorën Kiekegaard, *Purity of Heart is to Will One Thing* (1847), in *A Kierkegaard Anthology.* p. 272.

[12] This subject was suggested by the comments of Bruno Snell in "Homer's View of Man" in *The Discovery of the Mind,* p. 1-23.

[13] The Shandian mood is portrayed in Sterne, *A Sentimental Journey,*

Sweet pliability of man's spirit, that can at once surrender itself to illusions, which cheat expectation and sorrow of their weary moments I long, long since had ye number'd out my days, had I not trod so great a part of them upon this enchanted ground: when my way is too rough for my feet, or too steep for my strength, I get off it, to some smooth velvet path which fancy has scattered over with rose-buds of delights; and having taken a few turns in it, come back strengthen'd and refresh'd—When evils press sore upon me, and there is no retreat from them in this world, then I take a new course—I leave it—and as I have a clearer idea of the Elysian fields than I have of heaven, I force myself, like Aeneas, into them—I see him meet the pensive shade of his forsaken Dido—and wish to recognize it—I see the injured spirit wave her head, and turn off silent from the author of her miseries and dishonours—I lose the feelings for myself in hers—and in those affections which were wont to make me mourn for her when I was at school.

To compare Sterne's saccharine and detached views to the judgment of Virgil, see *Aeneid* VI:450-476.

[14] Goethe, *Faust,* I.360-372.

[15] *Phronesis* (prudence) is the form of practical wisdom much praised by Aristotle in the *Nicomachean Ethics* Book VI.

[16] Consider the critique in Emerson, *The American Scholar*, and in Plato, *Seventh Letter.* See also Ecclesiastes 12:11: "Beyond this, my son, be warned: the writing of many books is endless, and excessive devotion to books is wearying to the body."

[17] The *Carmina Burana* cantata as written by Carl Orff (1895-1982) was based on the renderings by Johann Andreas Schmeller (1847) of the poems contained in an early 13th-century German manuscript found in 1803. These poems or drinking songs came from the Benedictine abbey of Benediktbeuern, south of Munich in the Bavarian region. Orff's original melodies support the poems and their religious, political, moral, bacchic and satirical verses.

Babbitt was written by Sinclair Lewis in the 1920s at the advent of the acquisitive age. On the distinction of the Apollonian and Dionysian, see Friederich Nietzsche, *The Birth of Tragedy from the Spirit of Music* (1872).

[18] This portrait of Socrates borrows from Alcibiades' speech in Plato's *Symposium* 215ff. The reference to the Shadow suggests the protagonist's dawning consciousness of all that he had buried and relegated to the unconscionable and unacceptable.

The pitiful spirit of flight and retreat recalls Thomas Hobbes, a self–confessed coward who fled to the Continent from the dangers of the English Civil War.

[19] See especially Nietzsche, "The Problem of Socrates" in *The Twilight of the Gods* (1888).

[20] In Jungian terms, Anton has experienced a direct encounter with his "Shadow." In his *Collected Works,* Jung writes,

> The shadow is a moral problem that challenges the whole ego-personality, for no one can become conscious of the shadow without considerable moral effort. To become conscious of it involves recognizing the dark aspects of the personality as present and real. ["The Shadow," CW 9ii, par. 14.]...
>
> Confrontation with the shadow produces at first a dead balance, a standstill that hampers moral decisions and makes convictions ineffective or even impossible. Everything becomes doubtful. [Ibid., par. 708.]...
>
> If it has been believed hitherto that the human shadow was the source of all evil, it can now be ascertained on closer investigation that the unconscious man, that is, his shadow, does not consist only of morally reprehensible tendencies, but also displays a number of good qualities, such as normal instincts, appropriate reactions, realistic insights, creative impulses, etc. [Conclusion," CW 9ii, par. 423. See C. G. Jung, *Psychological Reflections,* Jolande Jacobi, ed.]

[21] Grigori Aleksandrovich Potemkin (1739–1791), Russian field marshal and one of Catherine's chief advisers. Potemkin played an important part in the annexation (1783) of the Crimea, for which he was created prince. As governor of the new province, he organized Catherine's fabulous Crimean tour of 1787. The expression "Potemkin villages" refers to sham yet pristine villages that he is reported to have built along the route of her travel.

[22] Matthew 26:10-12.

[23] Shakespeare, *Hamlet* 1:3:59-85.

[24] Blaise Pascal, *Pensées* (1670).

[25] See James Thurber, *The Secret Life of Walter Mitty* (1947).

[26] Plato, *Republic,* Book I, the conversation at the home of the aged and pious merchant, Cephalus, and Socrates, his younger and ever–curious guest.

[27] See Nicholas of Cusa (1401–1464), *On Learned Ignorance.*

[28] On the idea of "the City of Man," see Augustine, *City of God.* Also, on living a nightmare, see James Joyce, *The Portrait of the Artist as a Young Man* (1916).

[29] Thomas Hobbes, *Leviathan* (1651) offered the definitive statement of the bourgeois mind and view of human society, a vision which became a great lever in the social program of John Locke, from which point it influenced the authors of *The Federalist Papers* and the architects of modern liberal democracy.

To convey the spirit of insecurity—cultural, mental and spiritual—in the bourgeois world, Hobbes writes in Chapter XIII, *Of the Natural Condition of Mankind as Concerning Their Felicity and Misery,*

> Again, men have no pleasure (but on the contrary a great deal of grief) in keeping company where there is no power able to overawe

them all. For every man looketh that his companion should value him at the same rate he sets upon himself, and upon all signs of contempt or undervaluing naturally endeavors, as far as he dares (which amongst them that have no common power to keep them in quiet is far enough to make them destroy each other), to extort a greater value from his contemners, by damage; and from others, by the example.

So that in the nature of man, we find three principal causes of quarrel. First, competition; secondly, diffidence; thirdly, glory.

The first maketh men invade for gain; the second, for safety; and the third, for reputation. The first use violence, to make themselves masters of other men's persons, wives, children, and cattle; the second, to defend them; the third, for trifles, as a word, a smile, a different opinion, and any other sign of undervalue, either direct in their persons or by reflection in their kindred, their friends, their nation, their profession, or their name.

Hereby it is manifest that during the time men live without a common power to keep them all in awe, they are in that condition which is called war; and such a war as is of every man against every man. For war consisteth not in battle only, or the act of fighting, but in a tract of time, wherein the will to contend by battle is sufficiently known: and therefore the notion of time is to be considered in the nature of war, as it is in the nature of weather. For as the nature of foul weather lieth not in a shower or two of rain, but in an inclination thereto of many days together: so the nature of war consisteth not in actual fighting, but in the known disposition thereto during all the time there is no assurance to the contrary. All other time is peace.

Whatsoever therefore is consequent to a time of war, where every man is enemy to every man, the same consequent to the time wherein men live without other security than what their own strength and their own invention shall furnish them withal. In such condition there is no place for industry, because the fruit thereof is uncertain: and consequently no culture of the earth; no navigation, nor use of the commodities that may be imported by sea; no commodious building; no instruments of moving and removing such things as require much force; no knowledge of the face of the earth; no account of time; no arts; no letters; no society; and *which is worst of all, continual fear, and danger of violent death; and the life of man, solitary, poor, nasty, brutish, and short.* (Italics added for emphasis.)

[30] See Dante. *Inferno.* Canto II.108.

[31] Numbers 21:7-9: The people came to Moses and said,

We sinned when we spoke against the Lord and against you. Pray that the Lord will take the snakes away from us." So Moses prayed for the people. The Lord said to Moses, "Make a snake and put it up on a pole; anyone who is bitten can look at it and live." So Moses made a bronze snake and put it up on a pole. Then when anyone was bitten by a snake and looked at the bronze snake, he lived.

[32] See George Hegel, *Philosophy of Right,* Preface, at end.

[33] Henry Vaughan (1622–1695), *The World.*

[34] Cited in John O'Donohue 197.

[35] The motif of northern journey, associated with the word "Aguilares," the name of a village community in El Salvador. Aguilares was the home of Father Rutilio Grande, whose pastoral ministry guided the awakening of the people of El Salvador to the Gospel as a vision of human dignity, destiny and freedom. Fr. Grande's death also awakened Archbishop Oscar Romero from his complacency and equivocation, and led him in turn to become a national and international advocate for the poor.

The use of the name *"Aguilares"* suggests the life of the *águila,* or eagle, a symbol of divine care and providence in the Hebrew Scriptures. In Exodus we read, *"You yourselves have seen what I did to Egypt, and how I carried you on eagles' wings and brought you to myself."* (19:3-5) And in Isaiah we hear, *"Even youths grow tired and weary, and young men stumble and fall; but those who hope in the Lord will renew their strength. They will soar on wings like eagles; they will run and not grow weary, they will walk and not be faint."* (40:30-32)

The destruction of the *communidades de base* and political aspirations of the people of Aguilares and El Salvador did not quench their desire for freedom, and their courage and tenacity speak to all human desire for growth and fulfillment. Thus the echo of the city's name evokes the spirit of these people and their leaders, and calls our attention to their prophetic presence in our collective culture. (See Levine 58ff.)

[36] Aguilares is on the intersection of Highway 359 and the Texas–Mexican Railway, twenty-four miles east of Laredo in southeastern Webb County. It is named after the Aguilar family, who settled in the area in the 1870s.

[37] From Adam Smith, *An Inquiry into the Wealth of Nations* (1776),

> Every individual necessarily labours to render the annual revenue of the society as great as he can. He generally neither intends to promote the public interest, nor knows how much he is promoting it...He intends only his own gain, and he is in this, as in many other cases, led by an invisible hand to promote an end which was no part of his intention. Nor is it always the worse for society that it was no part of his intention. By pursuing his own interest he frequently promotes that of the society more effectually than when he really intends to promote it. I have never known much good done by those who affected to trade for the public good.

[38] As a classical physicist, Einstein resisted the statistical interpretation of the cosmos offered through quantum mechanics.

[39] From Hannah Arendt, *Eichmann in Jerusalem: A Study in the Banality of Evil.*

[40] On the definition and traits of tragedy, see Aristotle, *Poetics.*

[41] The idea of "reciprocal individuation" in the thought of Carl G. Jung.

[42] See Plato, *Republic* Book X, "The Myth of Er."

[43] *Timaeus.* Donald Zeyl, tr. in *Plato's Complete Works.*

[44] See Plato, *Phaedo,* end, and Peter Kingsley, *Ancient Philosophy, Mystery, and Magic: Empedocles and Pythagorean Tradition* (1995).

[45] Isaiah 53:4-6.

[46] The character of Father Gustavo (named after Peruvian theologian Gustavo Gutiérrez) has emerged from the author's associations with Jesuit priests in East Los Angeles. Gustavo's perspective and conduct reflects a reading of Luke's Gospel in particular. His orientation to contemporary life reflects the situation of the Latin American church and the Catholic bishops in their meetings at Puebla. See bibliographic references to Gustavo Gutiérrez. See also Donal Dorr, *Option for the Poor: A Hundred Years of Vatican Social Teaching.*

[47] Homemade tortillas.

[48] *Pescador de Hombres,* ©1979, Cesáreo Gabaráin. Published by OCP Publications. All rights reserved. Used with permission.

[49] See Matthew 9:36.

[50] See Matthew 6:25-27,

> Therefore I tell you, do not worry about your life, what you will eat or drink; or about your body, what you will wear. Is not life more important than food, and the body more important than clothes? Look at the birds of the air; they do not sow or reap or store away in barns, and yet your heavenly Father feeds them. Are you not much more valuable than they? Who of you by worrying can add a single hour to his life?
>
> Foxes have holes and birds of the air have nests, but the Son of Man has no place to lay his head. (Matthew 8:20)

[51] Kirk : "of the Church." Patrick: "nobleman."

[52] See Matthew 20.

[53] Immigration and Naturalization Service, sometimes known to Spanish–speaking immigrants as *La Migra.*

[54] See Deuteronomy 15:12-15,

> If a fellow Hebrew, a man or a woman, sells himself to you and serves you six years, in the seventh year you must let him go free. And when you release him, do not send him away empty-handed. Supply him liberally from your flock, your threshing floor and your winepress. Give to him as

the Lord your God has blessed you. Remember that you were slaves in Egypt and the Lord your God redeemed you. That is why I give you this command today.

[55] Alternatively "It is my angel (the one who is my brother)"; or "You are my angel, my brother (Gustavo)."

[56] Signifies the disappearance of the *machismo* attitude that consigns women to the kitchen.

[57] From a prayer in *Las Pequeñas Rosas* Home for Girls, Episcopal Diocese of San Pedro Sula, Honduras.

[58] See the Parable of the Loaves and the Fishes in Mark 8.

[59] Mark 5:1-20.

[60] "South Central" is a section of Los Angeles in the general vicinity of Adams, Jefferson and Figueroa avenues.

[61] "The Final Solution" was the name for the systematic extermination of the Jews and their culture by the Nazis in the 1930s and 40s.

[62] Isaiah 40: 30-31.

[63] The distinction between *los pobres* (the poor) and *los apobrecidos* (the impoverished ones, those who are *made poor*) was made by Archbishop Oscar Romero. See William Sloan Coffin, 37.

[64] Matthew 27:14.

[65] For the significance of Goshen in the Hebrew mind, see Genesis 45.

[66] See Nietzsche, *Ecce Homo* (1889), written in the philosopher's last productive year.

[67] A diagnosis of this perplexing condition is found in Dostoevsky, *The Brothers Karamozov,* in the chapter entitled "The Woman of Little Faith." There she admits that "The more I love humanity in general, the less I love man in particular…The more I detest men in individually, the more ardent becomes my love of humanity." (Dostoevsky, 55-62.)

[68] The "book of the world" is a medieval concept for life and the world that holds lessons for those who are paying attention.

[69] "Pure life!"

[70] See Hesiod, *Works and Days;* also the cosmogonic tales known as *Theogony* (8th century bce).

[71] Shakespeare, *Hamlet,* I.II.137-138.

[72] From Exodus 23:10-12,

> During the seventh year let the land lie unplowed and unused. Then the poor among your people may get food from it, and the wild animals may eat what they leave. Do the same with your vineyard and your olive grove.

[73] See earlier reference to the fictitious work entitled *Psyche and Thumos in Homer's* Iliad *and* Odyssey: *An Evolving Conception of the Human Soul.*

[74] A slight paraphrase of Kant's comment in 1784 that humanity must come of age, throw off its "self–imposed tutelage," and take responsibility for its own freedom.

[75] "Would you mind not standing in my sun?" This imprecation was offered by Diogenes the Cynic when approached by Alexander the Great, as reported by Diogenes Laertius in *Lives of Eminent Philosophers*.

[76] The decisive battle of 490 bce in which a small group of Athenians and local allies defeated a massive invading Persian force under Xerxes. Had the battle gone otherwise the phenomenon known at "the Golden Age of Greece" would never have occurred, nor would Western civilization as we know it have unfolded. For an account of the conflict, its roots and progress, see Herodotus, *The History of the Persian Wars*.

[77] Aristophanes, *Ecclesiasuzae* (392 bce.)

[78] Pascal, *Pensées* (1660),

> The heart has its reasons, which reason does not know. We feel it in a thousand things. I say that the heart naturally loves the Universal Being, and also itself naturally, according as it gives itself to them; and it hardens itself against one or the other at its will. You have rejected the one and kept the other. Is it by reason that you love yourself? (277)
>
> It is the heart which experiences God, and not the reason. This, then, is faith: God felt by the heart, not by the reason. (278)

[79] Delphi: One of the major religious centers of ancient Greece that had a thriving international worship from approximately 700 bce to 400 ce. Delos: the small island near Mykonos that served as the pan-Hellenic shrine to Apollo.

[80] "Faience" is a moderate to strong greenish blue hue, characteristic of earthenware from Faience at Florence, Italy.

[81] Robert Louis Stevenson, *Pueribus Virginibus*.

[82] In 1502 Christopher Columbus was to first European to explore the territory of today's Nicaragua and seized it for Spain. After several changes of government Nicaragua proclaimed independence in 1821. In the following years the country gradually declined in fights between conservatives (especially landholders) and liberals (followers of civil liberty). With help of the United States the conservatives got power in the country that lasted in various forms till 1979. Then guerrillas led by Sandinista National Liberation Front (FSLN) overthrew the government of dictator Anastazio Somoza and established the government of national unity. So-called "contras," the core of which was formed by the former Somoza soldiers that were helped both with arms and money especially by the President's Ronald Reagan's administration, gradually started to rise and consequently fight against the Sandinista government. This civil war lasted till 1990 when—mainly under strong international pressure—the Sandinistas were forced to negotiate with the opposition. This war took a toll of 50,000 dead. (Source: www.projektnews.cz/index_en.htm.)

[83] From Shakespeare, *Hamlet*, the elder Polonius speaking to the younger Hamlet.

[84] See Plato, *The Apology of Socrates*, during the sentencing phase at the end of the dialogue.

[85] "Destroy, expunge the infamy!" Françoise-Marie Arouet de Voltaire (1694–1778) wrote: "What is tolerance? It is the consequence of humanity. We are all formed of frailty and error; let us pardon reciprocally each other's folly—that is the first law of nature."

[86] From Anita Barrows and Joanna Macey, *Rilke's Book of Hours: Love Poems to God*, 84.

[87] From Odysseas Elytis, *Selected and Last Poems* (1998) p. 153.

[88] For an elaboration on these themes, see Gustavo Gutiérrez, *The Truth Shall Make You Free*, 10.

[89] Writing of the Psalms, Thomas Merton said ,

> If we have no real interest in praising Him it shows that we have never realized who He is. For when one becomes conscious of who God really is, and when one realizes that He who is Almighty and infinitely Holy, has done great things to us, the only possible reaction is the cry of half-articulated exultation that bursts from the depths of our being in amazement at the tremendous, inexplicable goodness of God to men and women. (*Praying the Psalms,* 7, 10-11.)

[90] See Robert Pirsig, *Zen and the Art of Motorcycle Maintenance*.

[91] The image of the open road implies new freedom; the potholes are difficult learnings.

[92] The name of Don Quixote's dilapidated horse. See Miguel de Cervantes Saavedra, *Don Quixote de la Mancha*.

[93] The figure in this encounter is the feminine whose fertility and fecundity has been thwarted by sorrow and grief. The appeasement, healing, and invocation of the feminine—without which we witness the sterility of the earth and depression among mothers—was a primary object of the Greek Eleusinian mysteries. These rituals, which flourished from 1200 bce or earlier until several centuries in the Common Era, recognized both the sacredness and mystery of new life and our complete dependence on the fertility of the earth.

Closely related to the Eleusinian Mysteries celebrating Demeter and Persephone were the so-called "Thesmophoria" (from *thesmoi,* meaning "laws," and *phoria,* "carrying," in reference to the goddess as "law-bearer"). These rites were celebrated by women only, and only women, throughout all Greece in the month of Pyanepsion (late October), their characteristic feature was a pig sacrifice, the usual sacrifice to chthonic deities. The Greeks attributed special powers to pigs on account of their fertility, the potency and abundance of their blood, and perhaps because of their uncanny ability to unearth underground tubers and shoots. It was believed that mingling their flesh with the seeds of grain would increase the abundance of next year's harvest.

For further information, see Burkert, Walter, *Greek Religion* (1985). Also Campbell, Joseph, "From Darkness to Light: The Mystery Religions of Ancient Greece," in *Transformations of Myth through Time*. Public Media Video, William Free Productions. Vol. 1, #5. See also Eliade, Micea, *A History of Religious Ideas: From the Stone Age to the Eleusinian Mysteries* (1978); and Sir James George Frazer (1854–1941), *The Golden Bough,* ch. XLIV on Demeter and Persephone.

[94] The tree standing in its noble and indistinct isolation is a symbol of the philosophic tree of the hermetic and alchemical traditions. For images of the tree, see Carl Jung, *Alchemy;* also Genesis in the Bible; and Antoine St. Exupéry, *The Little Prince*. The Meadow is the symbol for the mystery of the Earth with her covering of green vegetation (See Carl G. Jung, *Memories, Dreams, Reflections,* p. 13).

[95] Reworded from Pascal, *Pensées* (1623–1662).

[96] See John 17.

[97] On the *agon,* or competition for the beautiful and noble, see Aristotle, *Nicomachean Ethics,* Book II. On the moral value of beauty, consider Nietzsche's anecdote in *The Twilight of the Idols,* "On Socrates," where the philosopher sardonically says that "Socrates' ugliness was a refutation of this way of life." In contrast to Nietzsche, Plato's Alcibiades reminds us of the irresistible attractiveness of Socrates and the appeal of his way of life in the *Symposium*.

See also Gottfried Lessing, *Laocoon* on the sympathy deserved by a beautiful soul housed in a worn and unattractive body.

[98] A symptom of the rising to consciousness of the feminine archetype. "So the Lord God caused the man to fall into a deep sleep; and while he was sleeping, he took one of the man's ribs and closed up the place with flesh." (Genesis 21)

[99] From Walt Whitman, *A noiseless patient spider,*

I mark'd where on a little promontory it stood isolated,
Mark'd how to explore the vacant vast surrounding,
It launch'd forth filament, filament, filament, out of itself,
Ever unreeling them, ever tirelessly speeding them.
And you O my soul where you stand,
Ceaselessly musing, venturing, throwing, seeking the spheres to connect them,
Till the bridge you will need be form'd, till the ductile anchor hold,
Till the gossamer thread you fling catch somewhere, O my soul.
Surrounded, detached, in measureless oceans of space.

[100] As noted earlier, the allusion to lions and bees and honey may be traced back to the fantastic gifts given to Samson in Judges 14 in the Hebrew

Scriptures. For additional insight into the nature of lions as divinity, see C.S. Lewis, *The Chronicles of Narnia*. Jesus was also known through the tradition as "The Lion of Judah."

The woodpecker may be understood through the tale of Picus and Canens told by Ovid in *Metamorphoses*. There, an arrogant prince fails to respond to the amorous intentions of the goddess Circe, who avenges the dishonor by turning him into a woodpecker. Thus, the woodpecker portends Anton's opportunity and obligation toward the Circe–figure whom he will meet after a few more turns in his journey.

[101] "The Poet is supposed to leave his companions, who are proceeding on a hunting expedition in winter, in order himself to pay a visit to a hypochondriacal friend, and also to see the mining in the Hartz mountains. The ode alternately describes, in a very fragmentary and peculiar manner, the naturally happy disposition of the Poet himself and the unhappiness of his friend; it pictures the wildness of the road and the dreariness of the prospect, which is relieved at one spot by the distant sight of a town, a very vague allusion to which is made in the third strophe; it recalls the hunting party on which his companions have gone; and after an address to Love, concludes by a contrast between the unexplored recesses of the highest peak of the Hartz and the metalliferous veins of its smaller brethren." (From website http://turn.to/goethe.)

[102] Xenophon, *Anabasis: The March of the Ten Thousand* IV.7.

[103] The personality of Gene and his setting in the storied isolation of Carmel Valley was suggested by the later life of Jean-Jacques Rousseau. While the philosopher had a highly public and somewhat notorious life that eventually produced a measure of paranoia in him, he remained productive and attentive (if retiring) to the very end. See especially *The Solitary Promenades*.

This particular scene of dirt, grime and exhaustion, followed by refreshment and conversation, was suggested by Niccolo Machiavelli's *Letter to Vettorio* in which the Florentine described his unwonted life in the country following exile from the Medici court.

[104] See Aristotle, *Nicomachean Ethics* I.

[105] *The Odyssey,* Book V.

[106] The first question is uttered by the "Last Men," those possessed of a "False Consciousness" as described by Hegel in the *Phenomenology of Mind IV.B.251,* and Nietzsche in *Thus Spoke Zarathustra* I. The second is the dismissive question of Pilate when confronted by Jesus in his silence during the prosecution.

[107] The central insight of this tribute to Gene's teacher is derived from Norman O. Brown, *The American Scholar Address* at Columbia University in 1960.

[108] In all matters of ritual passage and transformation, there is a profound silence; in fact, sounds such as spoken words, applause, and so on are often simply the expression of anxiety and discomfort in those who have become

detached from the ceremony itself. Outsiders encounter the conspiracy of silence as a secret.

The Eleusinian mysteries appear to have emerged in the post–Myceneaen period (after 1200–1000 bce) and survived until their proscription by the Christian Emperor Theodosius in 393 ce. During this time there was only one known profanation of the mysteries:

> How could something be kept a secret when it was shown to thousands every year? At the time when the great Telesterion was being built, the secret of Eleusis was violated by Diagoras of Melos, who 'told everyone the mysteries, thus making them vulgar and mean, and dissuaded those who wished to be initiated.'
>
> Told on the street, the secret of the mysteries is no blessing, no gain; rather, it is a nothing, like faerie-gold that turns to charcoal by daylight. The Athenians condemned Diagoras to death and pursued him throughout their realm. The Eleusinian mysteries, however, continued to be celebrated until eight hundred years after Diagoras. (Walter Burkert, 252.)

An account of the gravity of the crime of divulging the mysteries was offered by Libanius in his *Apology of Socrates:* "You, people of Athens, were wise when you promised a reward to the one who killed Diagoras, for he made a mockery of the Eleusinian mysteries and the sacred rites." (Brickhouse, 127. See also Strabo IX.i.16, and Chambers, *The History of Taste*, 281.)

[109] One of the primary tasks of the Garden community described later in the story is the "re-enchantment of the world." To give the reader a sense of the breadth and depth of that task, the author offers the following,

> In Roman mythology, the Penates ("the inner ones") are the patron gods of the storeroom. Later they gradually changed into patron gods for the entire household. Their cult is closely related to that of Vesta and the Lares. They were worshipped at the hearth and were given their part of the daily meals. The whole Roman state looked to the *Penates Publici.* They were rescued by Aeneas from burning Troy and via Lavinium and Longa brought to Rome. Upon their arrival, the Penates were housed in the Temple of Vesta, on the Forum Romanum.
>
> The Lares are Roman guardian spirits of house and fields. The cult of the Lares is probably derived from the worshipping of the deceased master of the family. It was believed that he blessed the house and brought fertility to the fields. Just like the Penates, the Lares were worshipped in small sanctuaries or shrines, called Lararium, which could be found in every Roman house. They were placed in the atrium (the main room) or in the *peristylium* (a small open court) of the house. Here people sacrificed food to the Lares on holidays. In contrast to their malignant counterparts the Larvae (Lemures), the Lares are beneficent and friendly spirits.

There were many different types of guardians. The most important are the Lares Familiares (guardians of the family), Lares Domestici (guardians of the house), Lares Patrii and Lares Privati. Other guardians were the Lares Permarini (guardians of the sea), Lares Rurales (guardians of the land), Lares Compitales (guardians of crossroads), Lares Viales (guardians of travelers) and Lares Praestitis (guardians of the state). The Lares are usually depicted as dancing youths, with a horn cup in one hand and a bowl in the other. As progenitors of the family, they were accompanied by symbolic phallic serpents. (See *Encyclopedeia Mythica*; also Fustel de Coulanges, *The Ancient City*.)

[110] Maenads were female devotees of the God Dionysios. Their ecstatic possession culminated in his sacrifice.

[111] The Yahoo's were the brutish and obscene human–like creatures in *Gulliver's Travels*. Gulliver says of them, "For as to those filthy Yahoos, although there were few greater Lovers of Mankind, at that time, than myself; yet I confess I never saw any sensitive Being so detestable on all Accounts; and the more I came near them, the more hateful they grew, while I stayed in that Country. (Jonathan Swift, *Gulliver's Travels* IV.II.)

[112] Consider the Clemente Program offered by Bard College, New York. See http://www.humanities.org/clemente/.

[113] Calypso addressing Hermes, the messenger God, in Homer's *Odyssey*, V.130-135.

[114] William Shakespeare, *Sonnet 65*,

Since brass, nor stone, nor earth, nor boundless sea,
But sad mortality o'er-sways their power,
How with this rage shall beauty hold a plea
Whose action is no stronger than a flower?
O how shall summer's honey breath hold out
Against the wrackful siege of battering days,
When rocks impregnable are not so stout,
Nor gates of steel so strong, but Time decays?
O fearful meditation! where, alack,
Shall Time's best jewel from Time's chest lie hid?
Or what strong hand can hold his swift foot back?
Or who his spoil of beauty can forbid?
O none, unless this miracle have might,
That in black ink my love may still shine bright.

[115] The amazement of encounter described in Shakespeare's *Tempest* (I.ii.409ff.),

Miranda (spying Ferdinand):

What is't? a spirit?
Lord, how it looks about! Believe me, sir
It carries a brave form. But 'tis spirit...
I might call him
A thing divine, for nothing natural
I ever saw so noble...

Ferdinand (seeing Miranda):
Most sure, the goddess
On whom these airs attend! Vouchsafe my pray'r
May know if you remain upon this island;
And that you will some good instruction give
How I may bear me here: My prime request,
Which I do last pronounce, is, O you wonder!
If you be maid or no.

Miranda:
No wonder, sir;
But certainly a maid.

On Ferdinand's willingness to bear burdens for Miranda, see *The Tempest,* Act. III, sc. I.

[116] An allusion to the standing of Helen in Homeric literature (see one example among many at *Iliad* IX.35-145).

[117] The nature images, stirring wildlife, color purple and grapes are all Dionysian similes intended to awaken the reader to the interplay of passion, ecstasy, and the influences of Aphrodite.

[118] From Andrew Marvell (1621–1678), *The Garden,* I.49-52.

[119] Goethe, *Found* (1813). The flowering plant may be a symbol of human culture. Like a plant, a culture can be uprooted and destroyed. With the plant goes the bud and blossom, symbols of the beauty of the culture as a whole. Carl Jung wrote,

> I was attracted to plants for a reason that I could not understand, and with a strong feeling that they ought not be pulled up and dried. They were living beings which had meaning only as long as they were growing and flowering—a hidden, sacred meaning, one of God's Thoughts. They were to be regarded with awe and philosophical wonderment.
> *(Memories, Dreams, Reflections,* p. 283)

[120] A dithyramb refers to the odes and hymns, sometimes solemn, sometimes frenzied and impassioned, that were sung to Dionysus at his festivals. The epithet "Dithyrambos" was often applied to Dionysus, possibly meaning

"he of the double door," i.e. twice born, alluding to his premature birth and seasonal restoration.

[121] The basic action of rescue from near–drowning is borrowed from the Calypso story in Homer's *Odyssey* V.

[122] John Keats, *Ode to Melancholy*.

[123] Juvenilia: creations of one's youth and immaturity.

[124] Jonathan Swift, *Gulliver's Travels* X.

[125] Homer, *Odyssey*, Book V.149, 225ff.

[126] Faustus lamenting to Helen in Christopher Marlowe's *The Tragical History of Doctor Faustus* (1589), I.1379-1383.

[127] "The name 'Zarathustra' in Persian is written *'Zarathushtra'; ustra* is typically Persian and it means camel. There is a family story about him and all the names in his family have to do with mares and stallions, horses and cattle, camels, etc., showing that they are quite native and that he belonged to a sort of cattle people. Also his idea of a perfect reward in heaven was exceedingly archaic. He himself hoped that after a life full of merit he would be rewarded in the land of the hereafter by the good gift of one stallion and twelve mares, as well as the possession of a perfectly youthful and beautiful body..." (C. G. Jung, *Nietzsche's Zarathustra: Notes of the Seminar Given in 1934–1939* (1988), p. 7.)

[128] This dream borrows figures from Nietzsche's "Three Metamorphoses" in *Thus Spoke Zarathustra* (1883), but with a wholly different intention and direction. The allegory reads, in part,

> Three metamorphoses of the spirit do I designate to you: how the spirit becometh a camel, the camel a lion, and the lion at last a child. Many heavy things are there for the spirit, the strong load-bearing spirit in which reverence dwelleth: for the heavy and the heaviest longeth its strength. What is heavy? so asketh the load-bearing spirit; then kneeleth it down like the camel, and wanteth to be well laden. What is the heaviest thing, ye heroes? asketh the load-bearing spirit, that I may take it upon me and rejoice in my strength...
>
> All these heaviest things the load-bearing spirit taketh upon itself: and like the camel, which, when laden, hasteneth into the wilderness, so hasteneth the spirit into its wilderness. But in the loneliest wilderness happeneth the second metamorphosis: here the spirit becometh a lion; freedom will it capture, and lordship in its own wilderness...
>
> But tell me, my brethren, what the child can do, which even the lion could not do? Why hath the preying lion still to become a child? Innocence is the child, and forgetfulness, a new beginning, a game, a self-rolling wheel, a first movement, a holy Yea...
>
> Three metamorphoses of the spirit have I designated to you: how the spirit became a camel, the camel a lion, and the lion at last a child.

[129] Job 4:10-15,

> The lion roareth, and the fierce lion howleth--yet the teeth of the young lions are broken. The old lion perisheth for lack of prey, and the whelps of the lioness are scattered abroad. Now a word was secretly brought to me, and mine ear received a whisper thereof. In thoughts from the visions of the night, when deep sleep falleth on men, Fear came upon me, and trembling, and all my bones were made to shake. Then a spirit passed before my face, that made the hair of my flesh to stand up.

[130] Isaiah 11 (emphasis added),

> A shoot will come up from the stump of Jesse; from his roots a Branch will bear fruit. The Spirit of the Lord will rest on him, the Spirit of wisdom and of understanding, the Spirit of counsel and of power, the Spirit of knowledge and of the fear of the Lord, and he will delight in the fear of the Lord. He will not judge by what he sees with his eyes, or decide by what he hears with his ears; but with righteousness he will judge the needy, with justice he will give decisions for the poor of the earth. He will strike the earth with the rod of his mouth; with the breath of his lips he will slay the wicked. Righteousness will be his belt and faithfulness the sash around his waist.
>
> *The wolf will live with the lamb, the leopard will lie down with the goat, the calf and the lion and the yearling together; and a little child will lead them.*
>
> The cow will feed with the bear, their young will lie down together, and the lion will eat straw like the ox. The infant will play near the hole of the cobra, and the young child put his hand into the viper's nest. They will neither harm nor destroy on all my holy mountain, for the earth will be full of the knowledge of the Lord as the waters cover the sea.
>
> In that day the Root of Jesse will stand as a banner for the peoples; the nations will rally to him, and his place of rest will be glorious.

[131] See Goethe, *Faust, Part II.*

[132] The Asclepiads (those who are "Unceasingly Gentle") are linked to the Egyptian school of the Bronze Age priesthood of Thoth from the early second millennium bce. Thoth, the Egyptian god of wisdom, established a school in Phoenicia which carried on the Hermetic teachings. Around 1400 bce this group was expelled from Phoenicia and took refuge in the Greek islands of Cos, Thasos, and Delos of the coast of Asia Minor. The new immigrants established a lineage of Thoth which later became the Greek school of the Asclepaids.

In classical mythology Asclepius is often pictured with his two daughters, Hygieia and Panacea. Hygieia represents the prevention of disease and is the root of the word "hygiene," and her sister Panacea symbolizes all healing potential of the *materia medica*. (David Little, *Thoth, Asclepius and Hermes,* in web reference: www.simillimum.com.)

[133] See Kierkegaard's *Journals* of August 1849.

[134] See Geoffrey Chaucer, *The Legend of Good Women* (1386), where his disciple Lydgate says that "It must have encumbered his wits to think of so many good women."

[135] Nikos Kazantzakis, *Zorba the Greek* (1952), p. 24. Also the hymn by Charles Wesley (1707–1788), "Changed from glory into glory, till in heaven we take our place, till we cast our crowns before thee, lost in wonder, love, and praise."

[136] Different features of this picture are drawn from Robert Louis Stevenson's descriptions in *Old Pacific Capital.*

[137] The old man's name is suggested by *The Idea of Order at Key West* by Wallace Stevens. See footnote on R.L. Stevens below.

[138] Purification rite in a sweat lodge.

[139] From Bommelyn, Loren, and Berneice Humphrey. *Xus We-Yó': Tolowa (Tututni). Language Dictionary.* 2nd ed.

[140] The observations that follow are examples of Tolowa culture as described by B. Drucker, "The Tolowa and their Southwest Oregon Kin," *Proceedings of American Archeology and Ethnography* (1943), pp. 221ff.

[141] The Chetco-Tolowa people of Western Oregon share in the Athapaskan family of languages...a region of incredible linguistic diversity. In only a few other areas of the world—New Guinea, the Caucasus, and Northern California—were so many tongues spoken in such a small area. In this complex region of mountains, bays and valleys, seventeen languages were spoken, some as different as English is from Japanese. (See Don MacNaughtan, *American Indian Languages of Western Oregon,* Lane Community College, Oregon, www.lanecc.edu/library. See also Sir William Frazier, *The Golden Bough* 121.)

[142] For the life cycle and migratory patterns of the Chinook salmon, see www.state.ak.us/local/akpages/FISH.GAME/notebook/fish/chinook.htm.

[143] Sonnet for Tommase de Calalieri from *Set My Heart Aright: A Michelangelo Portrait.*

[144] From Foley, Helene P. *The Homeric Hymn to Demeter* (1993), p. 26-27.

[145] See Plato, the shadow images at the base of the cave in the Allegory in *The Republic,* Book VII.

[146] As in Keats, *Ode to a Grecian Urn.* The encounter that invites Anton to fathom Nature's intention in fashioning humankind. See Karl Phillip Moritz,

> Nature fashioned humanity in order to be conscious of herself. In exchange for this extraordinary and patient creation and embodiment, humankind is learning how to re-express Nature in his own form. For the

expression of the divine form, nothing nobler could be found than eye and nose, brow and eyebrow, cheek, mouth and chin; since only from a living thing which has this form, can we know that it has conceptions like ours, and that we can exchange thoughts and words with it.
(Karl Phillip Moritz, *Die Götterlehre,* unveränderte Ausgaba, 1804). Also Pico della Mirandola.)

[147] "Daughter of Eve! Such sadness, such beauty!..." A complex image: archetypal woman in the tradition of Adam and Eve, Plato's Diotima of Mantinea, sorrowful *theotokos* (Christ–bearer), Helen of Troy. All of these figures converged in the character of Cyntheia portrayed here. On the necessity of the indirect praise of extraordinary beauty, and the authority and privilege of the elder in this regard, see Homer in his commentary on Helen in the *Iliad,*

There they found Priam, Panthous, Thymoetes,
Lampus, Clytius, and lord Hicetaon,
With wise Ucalegon and Antenor,
Counselors seated at the Scaeon Gates.
Too old for battle they were, but in words superb,
Like crickets that sit on some tree
where they pour their lily-like voices forth–
thus those elders sat on the city wall.
When they saw lovely Helen coming near
They said in a flurry of murmured words:
"No wonder the Trojans and Achaeans
have suffered so long for that lady's sake–
she's marvelously like a goddess to see.
Yet let her go home, go home to the ships,
Or she'll ruin us and our children too."

(Homer, *Iliad* III.148-160. See also Gottfried Lessing, *Laocoon* (1879), ch. XXI. See Plato, *Symposium,* "The Speech of Diotima of Mantinea.") Note also the "classical" austerity of Aristotle on matters of pleasure, even the pleasures of seeing –

Now in everything the pleasant or pleasure is most to be guarded against; for we do not judge it impartially. We ought, then, to feel towards pleasure as the elders of the people felt towards Helen, and in all circumstances repeat their saying; for if we dismiss pleasure thus we are less likely to go astray. It is by doing this, then, (to sum the matter up) that we shall best be able to hit the mean. (Aristotle, *Nicomachean Ethics* II.)

[148] An insight into the universal significance of the human face,

> The face of the Other is an epiphany that solicits us; it is that face which comes to us from the exterior. In [this perspective], thought, the future, the infinite, the face, and language become extended epiphany. It the astonishment of the Other speaking in me which enables me to become a self in language. In other words, through language, the Other enables me to have an identity.

(From John Lehte, *Fifty Contemporary Thinkers: From structuralism to postmodernity* (1994), p. 117-118.)

[149] Cyntheia's name emphasizes the Hellenic spirituality which merged with the Hebrew experience and insight to form original Christianity. The Greek name, the dark interior of the cathedral, and the brilliance of the sun's radiance outside symbolize that convergence. The universality of our human aspiration is suggested any sacred center where sacramental words and liturgical action emanate from the encounter of the human community with the ineffable. Her name borrows from "Cynthia," an Artemisian goddess said to have been born on Mt. Cynthus (from Gr. *Moon*).

For literary usages of this name, see Milton *Penseroso* 59 (1632), "While Cynthia checks her dragon yoke"; Caius Marius iv.i., *The reflection of pale Cynthia's Brightness*; Lord Byron *Lara* ii.xxiv (1814), "When Cynthia's light almost gave way to morn."

The name conjures the mood, the mists of Carmel, the forest spirits, the animals, the moonlight, our psyche's need for truth and goodness to be tempered instead of experienced directly like the brilliant sun. This person was envision to have blue-grey eyes that reflect the colors of the sea and mist, and a graciousness, gracefulness and poise worthy of her name, her beauty, and her humanity.

A note on Cyntheia's ancestry: Ramón's Tolowa grandfather married a Mexican woman. Their daughter married a man from Ireland. The two children from this marriage (Ramón and his sister) were thus one-quarter Tolowa and one–quarter Mexican, and one–quarter Irish. Ramón's sister consorted with a Greek–Norwegian man, and Cyntheia was born. Thus, she is one-quarter Greek, one-quarter Norwegian, one-quarter Irish, one–eighth Mexican and one–eighth Tolowa.

[150] Compare *Song of Songs,* ch. 7.

[151] Virgil, *Aeneid,* I.401-405,

> Speaking, she turned, and there flashed from her shoulder a roseate splendor;
> Not of the earth was the fragrance exhaled by her tresses ambrosial;
> Shimmering down to the earth, her robe flowed over her sandals,
> And, as she glided away, she showed herself truly a goddess.

[152] Wallace Stevens (1879-1955), *Peter Quince in the Clavier,*

> Beauty is momentary in the mind—
> The fitful tracing of a portal;
> But in the flesh it is immortal.

[153] A reference to the oppression of the Hebrews by Pharaoh, who not only compelled them to build his temples, but deprived them of the materials to do so (see Exodus 5).

[154] An expression borrowed from Thomas Mann's early work, *Disorder and Early Sorrow* (1926).

[155] Plato, *Theaetetus* 174a,

> Socrates: Do you know the story about the Thracian slave girl enjoyed great mirth at the expense of Thales, when he was looking up to study the stars and tumbled down a well? She scoffed at him for being so eager to know what was happening in the sky that he could not see what lay at his feet. Anyone who gives his life to philosophy is open to such mockery. It is true that he is unaware what his next-door neighbor is doing, hardly knows, indeed, whether the creature is a man at all; he spends all his time on the question, what man is, and what powers and properties distinguish such a nature from any other. You see what I mean, Theodorus?

For an analysis of the differing perspectives of philosopher and poet, see Plato's *Apology of Socrates* and *Republic.*

[156] In 386 bce Plato's friends acquired the Grove of Academe, the memorial site for an Athenian hero, thus providing Plato with the space for one of the world's first universities. It was destined to become the intellectual center of Greece for over nine hundred years. The academy was technically a religious fraternity. The students paid no fees but most came from rich families and were expected to donate. Women were also admitted to the student body. The chief studies were mathematics and philosophy. Over the main entrance was the motto "Let no one without Geometry enter here," i.e., the main requirement for entrance was a passion for Geometry.

[157] See Pascal, *Pensées.* Also Sallie McFague, *The Body of God: An Ecological Theology* (1993).

[158] See Deuteronomy 32, 33.

[159] Alfred, Lord Tennyson, *Ulysses,* 20-21.

[160] On the conversation between Croesus and Solon that addressed this question, see Plutarch, *Life of Solon.* Also, Herodotus, *History of the Persian Wars* I.

[161] See Homer, *The Odyssey,* Book X (the Circe encounter).

[162] See Dietrich Bonhoeffer's distinction between "cheap grace and costly grace."

¹⁶³ From the Hindu Sanskrit word, "Sacciananda," as in *sat* (Being), *cit* (Knowledge), and *Ananda* (Bliss): the trinity of the Brahman in which the human soul enters into its rest and finds peace.

¹⁶⁴ In the Hindu vision, human development and life is divided into four periods like the four periods of the day: morning, noon, afternoon and evening. Each chapter in the life follows the requirements of human nature. The day has the waxing and waning of its light; so the human person has the waxing and waning of his bodily powers...First comes *brahmacharya,* the period of discipline in education. Then comes *garhasthya,* that of the world's work; then *vanaprasthya,* the retreat for the loosening of the bonds; and finally *pravrajya,* the expectant waiting of freedom across death. (See Rabindranath Tagore, "The Four Stages of Life," in Jaroslav Pelican, ed. *The World Treasury of Religious Thought,* 1990, p. 153.)

¹⁶⁵ From Meister Eckhart, *German Sermons* (1981), p. 166-168.

¹⁶⁶ Rabbi Yisrael Baal Shem Tov (1698–1760).

¹⁶⁷ *Stasis* and *kinesis* are Greek for "stability" and "motion," respectively. They are the two poles of human dynamism as conceived by the ancient Sophists. See especially Thucydides in his *History of the Pelopponesian War.* On the notion of the unmoved mover in Aristotle, see *De Caelo,* I.9.

¹⁶⁸ Eckhart's commentary on Luke 21:25-36,

> There will be signs in the sun, moon and stars. On the earth, nations will be in anguish and perplexity at the roaring and tossing of the sea. Men will faint from terror, apprehensive of what is coming on the world, for the heavenly bodies will be shaken. At that time they will see the Son of Man coming in a cloud with power and great glory.
>
> When these things begin to take place, stand up and lift up your heads, because your redemption is drawing near."
>
> He told them this parable: "Look at the fig tree and all the trees. When they sprout leaves, you can see for yourselves and know that summer is near. Even so, when you see these things happening, you know that the kingdom of God is near.
>
> "I tell you the truth, this generation will certainly not pass away until all these things have happened. Heaven and earth will pass away, but my words will never pass away. Be careful, or your hearts will be weighed down with dissipation, drunkenness and the anxieties of life, and that day will close on you unexpectedly like a trap. For it will come upon all those who live on the face of the whole earth. Be always on the watch, and pray that you may be able to escape all that is about to happen, and that you may be able to stand before the Son of Man."

¹⁶⁸ Probably Hosea 7:12: "When they go, I will throw my net over them; I will pull them down like birds of the air. When I hear them flocking together, I will catch them"; or Ezekiel 12:13: I will spread my net for him, and he will be

caught in my snare; I will bring him to Babylonia, the land of the Chaldeans, but he will not see it, and there he will die.

[169] On the darkness of the night sky,

> For most of human history, the darkness of the night sky was taken for granted, and the question was why it was so. In an infinite universe filled with stars, every line of sight should eventually meet the surface of a star. The dimming of starlight with distance should be exactly canceled by the increase in the number of stars you see as you look farther out, so the night sky should appear as bright as the surface of the sun. Day and night should blend into one.
>
> This puzzle, known as Olber's paradox, was solved in 1848 by Edgar Allan Poe. In his prose poem *Eureka,* he argued that the stars must not have had enough time to fill the universe with light. The darkness of the night sky, then, tells us that the universe has not existed forever. Not only has that hypothesis stood the test of time, it eventually proved crucial to formulating the big bang theory.
>
> Still, the night is not pitch-black; it is pervaded by the cosmic background. Although we have made much progress in explaining it, we have much left to do. Whereas 19th-century thinkers had to explain why the night sky isn't bright, modern cosmologists must figure out why it isn't completely dark.

(See Gunther Hasinger and Roberto Gilli, "The Cosmic Reality Check," in *Scientific American,* March 2002, p. 67. Also, on Olber's Paradox, see *Darkness at Night: A Riddle of the Universe,* Edward Kirkpatrickon, Harvard University Press, 1987. Also www.weburbia.com/physics/olber.html.

[170] Considered by Crusaders and others who had to face its formidable blade and the confidence of the warrior who bore it, the Damascus sword of Syria was considered to be the finest hand weapon of the 1500s. It was distinguished by the damascene pattern of wavy metal tones and incredible sharpness: it could slice through a silk handkerchief floating in mid-air. (See John D. Verhoeven, "The Mystery of the Damascus Sword," in *Scientific American,* Jan. 2001, p. 74ff.)

[171] See Matthew 3.

[172] Psychologist of human development Erik Erickson (1902–1994) described the mid-life task to be one of "generativity versus stagnation."

[173] "All wisdom begins with wondering at the ways of the Gods." Aristotle, *Metaphysics,* I.i.

[174] *The Hymn of St. Patrick,* also known as *The Deer's Cry,* anon. 8th Century, translated from the old Irish by Kuno Meyer.

[175] At Kierkegaard's funeral in Copenhagen in 1856, a riot broke out between his friends and supporters and those who saw him as a heretic and

cynic. His casket was nearly tipped over in the cathedral, until a phalanx of students gathered around it in protection.

[176] "Do not be quick with your mouth, do not be hasty in your heart to utter anything before God. God is in heaven and you are on earth, so let your words be few. As a dream comes when there are many cares, so the speech of a fool when there are many words." (Ecclesiastes 5:2)

[177] Drama: Gr. d*romen:* action, ritual. See Jane Ellen Harrison, *Art and Ritual.* The *Oberammergau* or "work of Ammergau" is first mentioned in 1633 in connection with a vow made by the village to obtain relief from the Black Death. The people of Ammergau vowed to produce the play every ten years, beginning in 1634. (See *The Catholic Encyclopedia.*)

[178] The story is drawn from Luke 7:36-50. Cf. John 11:1-3, Mark 14:3-9, Matthew 6:6-13. The dialogue is selected from several passages in the Song of Songs in the Hebrew scripture.

[179] "The five senses are the vehicles of Christ's love for man...In the spiritual sense the rose is an allegory of Mary, but in the worldly sense it is the beloved, the rose of the poets, the *'fedeli d'amore'* of that time...so also has the rose the significance of the mandala, as is clear from the heavenly rose in Dante's *Paradiso.* Like its equivalent, the Indian lotus, the rose is decidedly feminine. In Mechthild of Magdeburg it must be understood as a projection of her own feminine Eros upon Christ." (See C.G. Jung, *Alchemical Studies (*1967), p. 294-295.)

[180] Adopted from Isaiah 35:1-2,

> The desert and the parched land will be glad;
> the wilderness will rejoice and blossom.
> Like the crocus, it will burst into bloom;
> it will rejoice greatly and shout for joy.
> The glory of Lebanon will be given to it,
> the splendor of Carmel and Sharon;
> they will see the glory of the Lord,
> the splendor of our God.

[181] Shavuot, the Feast of the Weeks, is the Jewish holiday celebrating the harvest season in Israel. Shavuot, which means "weeks," refers to the timing of the festival which is held exactly seven weeks after Passover. Shavuot also commemorates the anniversary of the giving of the Ten Commandments to Moses and the Israelites at Mount Sinai.

Pesach (Passover) begins on the 15th day of the Jewish month of Nissan. It is the first of the three major festivals with both historical and agricultural significance (the other two are Shavuot and Sukkot). Traditionally, it represents the beginning of the harvest season in Israel, but little attention is paid to this aspect of the holiday. The primary observances of Pesach are related to the

Exodus from Egypt after generations of slavery. "Pesach" comes from the Hebrew root Peh-Samech-Chet meaning to pass through, to pass over, to exempt or to spare. It refers to the fact that the Spirit of Gd "passed over" the houses of the Jews when he was slaying the firstborn of Egypt. "Pesach" is also the name of the sacrificial offering (a lamb) that was made in the Temple on this holiday. (See Exodus 1-15.)

[182] The action of the play is taken from Luke 7:36ff and Mark 14. Cyntheia's script is adapted from *The Song of Solomon*. Exact or approximate quotes from Scripture are placed in quotation marks.

[183] Caravaggio (1573–1610) combined naturalism, luminism and chiaroscuro, and was copied by many seventeenth century artists, the so-called "Caravaggesques." His use of light brings out the state of mind of all the characters, many of whom are simple commoners are dressed according to the fashion of the time, and living in squalid settings.

[184] Song of Solomon 4:9-10.

[185] Song of Solomon 6:5. (The prior stanza is not scriptural.)

[186] See Mark: 14:6.

[187] For example, John 15:14-16,

> You are my friends if you do what I ask. I no longer call you servants, because a servant does not know his master's business. Instead, I have called you friends, for everything that I learned from my Father I have made known to you. You did not choose me, but I chose you and appointed you to go and bear fruit—fruit that will last. Then the Father will give you whatever you ask in my name.

[188] See Robert Louis Stevenson, *From Scotland to Silverado*. Also Homer, *Odyssey,* Book X, and Ezekial 38:12.

[189] Baleen are plates or blades of whalebone from two to twelve feet long and up to a foot wide. In genus *Balaenoidea* these structures are attached side by side along the upper jaw and form a fringelike sieve which holds food in the mouth. The image is appropriate in view of the great fecundity of the Monterey Bay caused by the rich plankton layers brought closer to the surface by oceanic upwellings.

[190] With Cyntheia before him, Anton has been able to perceive both beauty and goodness inseparably joined in the same person. Thus, though his mind is perplexed by this mysterious nexus, his feelings are unambiguous. The reeling and perplexity of one's mental faculties is what produces religious language. The human person who unites beauty, goodness and wisdom, and whose presence itself is *perikalia,* awakens our awareness of the numinous.

[191] The old literature showed that both men and women could acknowledge the intrinsic nobility of the other with no mis-understanding or unspoken claims. See Laurence Sterne, *Tristram Shandy* (1765).

[192] Luke 21:25-27,

> People will faint from fear and foreboding of what is coming upon the world, for the powers of the heavens will be shaken. Then they will see the Son of Man coming in a cloud with power and great glory. Now when these things begin to take place, stand up and raise your heads, because your redemption is drawing near.

[193] Published after the Robinson Jeffer's death in 1914.

[194] Percy Brysse Shelley (1792–1822), *Hymn to Intellectual Beauty*.

[195] There is speculation in the Jewish *Kabbala* about the language Adam spoke before the Fall. He was esteemed as "the great name–giver." Much more than a symbolic interpreter (since a symbol suggests an idea) Adam's name for a thing was the idea itself. After him, a cloud could never be a whale, although it could look like one. A raging fire is not a feeling, although flames and tongues of fire are sometimes the only words and images we can find to describe our inner life. (See Merkel 15ff.)

[196] See Wallace Stevens, *The Idea of Order at Key West* (1935).

[197] The lens of ethics views only one aspect of God. God's ethical presence is like the first glimmer of light to reach our eyes after a solar eclipse of the whole sun. The whole light, the whole truth is too bright for our eyes. As Yeats wrote, "People and animals, trees and stars are like hieroglyphics...Woe to anyone who thinks they can be deciphered." Yeats seems to have believed with Plato that even Nature itself is but a "froth that plays upon the ghostly paradigm of things." (See Yeats, *Among Schoolchildren.)*

[198] Adapted from T.S. Eliot.

[199] Words by Philip Nicolai (1556–1608). The melody of *Wachet auf* is by Hans Sachs (1494–1576). J.S. Bach was the arranger.

[200] The final section envisions the welcome to Heaven for the wandering soul. Cyntheia's account of her meeting with the survivor of the bride–burning in Calcutta has prefigured this moment. This characterization of Cyntheia is drawn from *She Was a Phantom of Delight* by William Wordsworth (1770–1850),

> She was a phantom of delight
> When first she gleam'd upon my sight;
> A lovely apparition, sent
> To be a moment's ornament;
> Her eyes as stars of twilight fair;
> Like twilight's, too, her dusky hair;
> But all things else about her drawn;
> From May-time and the cheerful dawn;
> A dancing shape, an image gay,
> To haunt, to startle, and waylay.

I saw her upon a nearer view,
A Spirit, yet a Woman too!
Her household motions light and free,
And steps of virgin liberty;
A countenance in which did meet
Sweet records, promises as sweet;
A creature not too bright or good
For human nature's daily food;
For transient sorrows, simple wiles,
Praise, blame, love, tears, and smiles.

And now I see with eye serene
The very pulse of the machine;
A being breathing thoughtful breath,
A traveller between life and death;
The reason firm, the temperate will,
Endurance, foresight, strength, and skill;
A perfect Woman, nobly plann'd.
To warn, to comfort, and command;
A yet a Spirit still, and bright
With something of angelic light.

Cyntheia's effect on Anton and his emotional storm are drawn from George Herbert' poem (1593–1632), *Love,*

Love bade me welcome, yet my soul drew back,
Guilty of dust and sin.
But quick-eyed Love, observing me grow slack
From my first entrance in,
Drew nearer to me, sweetly questioning
If I lacked anything.

"A guest," I answered, "worthy to be here."
Love answered, "You shall be he."
"I, the unkind, the ungrateful. Ah, my dear
I cannot look on Thee."
Love took my hand, and smiling, did reply,
"Who made the eyes, but I?"

"Truth, Lord, but I have marred them; let my shame
Go where it doth deserve."
"And know you not," says Love, who bore the blame?"
"My dear, then I will serve."
"You must sit down," says Love, "and taste my meat."

So I did sit and eat.

[201] Johann Sebastian Bach, *Cantata 140 (Wachet auf)*, music conveying the entrance to the heavenly banquet.

[202] The stanzas are from George Herbert, *The Call*.

[203] This scene borrows from the "Banquet Scene" in Kierkegaard's *Stages in Life's Way* (1845), a depiction of the aesthetic moment that has few rivals in world literature. The dinner in Cyntheia's home contrasts to Constantine's in Kierkegaard in the purpose and composition of participants (traveler, aged fisherman and the host herself), the simplicity of setting (the absence of fine cutlery and crystal), the priority of conversation over palate, and gradualness of completion compared to the crashing conclusion of Kierkegaard's more famous Banquet. Thus Cyntheia's dinner signifies a dethroning (but not the abolition) of our smaller worldly pleasures as an appropriate antecedent to the discovery of the Garden.

[204] Psalm 36,

Contend, O Lord, with those who contend with me;
fight against those who fight against me.
Take up shield and buckler; arise and come to my aid.
Brandish spear and javelin against those who pursue me.
Say to my soul, "I am your salvation."
May those who seek my life be disgraced and put to shame;
may those who plot my ruin be turned back in dismay.
May they be like chaff before the wind,
with the angel of the Lord driving them away;
may their path be dark and slippery,
with the angel of the Lord pursuing them.

On the conclusion of the Arthurian romance, see Walter Scott, *Lochinar*.

[205] On the idea that hidden, interior realities can be discovered through the act of looking at something very large, such as a city, see Plato, *Republic* Bk II.

[206] "Nor can a soul see Beauty without becoming beautiful." (Plotinus)

[207] A commentary on Friendship,

Genuine friends, whether of the same or different sex, age, race, or class, whether married to each other or not, whether family members, neighbors, professional colleagues, or any of the myriad combinations possible to human friendship, dwell within each other, in each other's hearts and minds and lives, with an affection that engenders broad scope for individuality to develop. The better the friendship the more potent its capacity to generate creativity and hope, as experiences of trust, care, delight, forgiveness, and passion for common interests and ideas flow back and forth. In addition to its person–creating power, the love of mature friendship has the potential to press beyond its own circle to offer blessing to others. Befriending the brokenhearted, the poor of the damaged earth with its threatened creatures are but some of the ways the strength of this relation can overflow.

(Elizabeth Johnson, *She Who Is: The Mystery of God in Feminist Discourse* (1994), p. 235)

[208] The term for the Australian Aboriginal vision quest.

[209] See Dostoevsky, *Notes from the Underground,* beginning.

[210] A palinode: a poem or recitation of retraction for something said earlier. *Solitudo placet musis, urbs inimical poetis:* Petrarch's statement about his bucolic life in the country where he lived in the memory of his Laura.

[211] Shakyamuni Buddha.

[212] "The poem is a cell or seed, a germ of living thought, growing from nothing into ripeness. Instead of the dead wood of systems, ramifications, branched thoughts now grown from pain." (Norman O. Brown, *Love's Body* (1990).

[213] Aristotle describes three general types of human behavior in his *Nicomachean Ethics* I.3 (ca. 310 bce). The first and most prevalent type, he believed, were oriented completely to sensual pleasure. They wish, he suggests in his dry humor, to be like Sardanapulus, the gourmand and petty tyrant who prayed for a neck longer than a goose in order to more enjoy the taste of his food.

The scene in the coffee shop illustrates the proximity of the Cave—the symbol of spiritual and intellectual imprisonment—as depicted in Plato's *Republic* Book VII. In the Cave all pathos of human suffering and exultation is trivialized into "news" to be displayed as flickering images on a blank wall or screen. The plethora of words contained in the "news" paper has a cheapening effect on human experience.

In a situation which stirs the most abject pathos, Lear willingly proceeds toward prison as the only realm of freedom in a world gone askew. There with his daughter Cordelia, he will dismiss "the poor rogues who talk of court news" as he prepares himself,

To take upon the mystery of things as if we were God's spies;
and we'll wear out,
In a walled prison, packs and sects of great ones
That ebb and flow by th' moon."
(Shakespeare, *King Lear* V.iii.13ff.)

[214] Plato, *Republic* III. 408d-e,

...The judge governs mind by mind; he ought not therefore to have been trained among vicious minds, and to have associated with them from youth upward, and to have gone through the whole calendar of crime, only in order that he may quickly infer the crimes of others as he might their bodily diseases from his own self-consciousness; the honorable mind which is to form a healthy judgment should have had no experience or contamination of evil habits when young. And this is the reason why in youth good men often appear to be simple, and are easily practised upon by the dishonest, because they have no examples of what evil is in their own souls.

See also Socrates' earlier comment,

> Will you be able to produce a greater sign of a bad and base education in a city that its needing eminent doctors an djudges not only for the common folk and the manual artisans but also for those who pretend tohave been reared in a free fashion? (405a)

[215] From the *Tao Te Ching,* ch. 24, quoted in Huston Smith, *The World's Religions* (1991), p. 211.

[216] *"U-topia":* literally no-place, or nowhere.

[217] The design and setting of the Garden is intended to combine aspects of both Hellenic and Hebrew traditions in a harmonious and healthful way. Unlike the simple innocence of the Garden of Genesis, this Garden is a setting for healing and expanded wholeness occurring through *paideia.*

Propylaeon was also the name given by Goethe to a scholarly circle and journal which he supported in his early period.

The hill of the Holy Cross as a symbol of the self–offering and sacrifice needed for ultimate emergence from our benighted condition; hence the emphasis on light in the Universe and illumination in the University.

[218] This reference alludes to the task of Plato's *Republic:* to approach the obscure question of justice in the soul by describing a just city as a whole. This method, Socrates suggests, allows one to "see the smaller in the larger," to know that the city is "the soul writ large."

[219] This notion of a Semicircle was derived from the example of Pythagoras (560–475 bce). According to Iamblichus writing in the third century AD,

> Pythagoras formed a school in the city of Samos, the 'semicircle,' which is known by that name even today, in which the Samians hold political meetings. They do this because they think one should discuss questions about goodness, justice and expediency in this place which was founded by the man who made all these subjects his business. Outside the city he made a cave the private site of his own philosophical teaching, spending most of the night and daytime there and doing research into the uses of mathematics. (Iamblichus, *Life of Pythagoras,* 1818, 1965.)

On the reference to Limbo, Dante (1265-1321 ce) placed the great classical philosophers, notably Plato and Aristotle in a higher ring of Hell. I disagree with this valuation, but acknowledge the limits on Dante's horizon in the Italy of his time.

Huston Smith has written,

> In a striking but as yet unpublished paper titled, 'Philosophia as One of the Religious Traditions of Mankind,' Wilfred Cantwell Smith argues that the Greek legacy in Western civilization deserves to be ranked as one of the world's great religions. We could not recognize this earlier, he says, because our notion of religion was too tightly tied to Judaism and Christianity. A century of work in comparative religion has now loosened this parochial mooring; it has enabled us to bring the entire human heritage into view, lining up its components in our mind's eye, arraying them side by side, and according reasonable justice to each…("Western Philosophy as A Great Religion" in *Transcendence and the Sacred* (1994), p. 19.)

Smith goes on to point out that the predominance of the Judeo–Christian worldview has been immeasurably helped by the epistemology of science, which seeks to control the physical world. (For the objectification of nature and the ethics of manipulation and control that modern science learned from Christian metaphysics, see Stanley Jaki, OSB, *The Savior of Science* and other essays.)

This attitude toward nature was not reserved to Christianity. Equally infected by Aristotelian logic, the Spanish Jewish commentator Maimonides (1135–1204 ce), the Italian Christian Aquinas (1225–1274 ce), and the Spanish Moslim, Averröes (1128–1198 ce) believed that the truths which God has revealed would harmonize with the findings of the human mind in science and philosophy. They would have rejected the modern dilemma and denied that the universe "is stranger than we understand, and stranger than we can ever understand" (Einstein).

Finally, this author believes that one cannot appreciate *Philosophia,* especially in Plato, without acknowledging the presence and power of Hellenic *mythos* and Homer above all.

[220] Hawaiian for *Adam.*

[221] An allusion to the legendary movements of Aslan in C.S. Lewis, *The Chronicles of Narnia.*

[222] A flower with legendary healing qualities. Apollo the Healer derived his name from *peonia*, the plant found in the near Mid-East in Bronze Age cultures. See Jane Ellen Harrison, *Prolegomena to Greek Religion.*

On the effects of beneficial and harmful music and its modes, see Plato, *Republic* 410A.

[223] This scene draws upon the pivotal teaching of Plato on the importance of musical tones and rhythms *(Republic* III). Also pertinent to the healing and humanizing role of music, see Polybius, *Histories,* 4.20ff, as follows,

> For the practice of music, I mean real music, is beneficial to all, but to Arcadians it is a necessity. For we must not suppose, as Ephorus, in the Preface to his *History,* making a hasty assertion quite unworthy of him, says, that music was introduced by men for the purpose of deception and delusion; we should not think that the ancient Cretans and Lacedaemonians acted at haphazard in substituting the flute and rhythmic movement for the bugle in war, or that the early Arcadians had no good reason for incorporating music in their whole public life to such an extent that not only boys, but young men up to the age of thirty were compelled to study it constantly, although in other matters their lives were most austere.
>
> For it is a well-known fact, familiar to all, that it is hardly known except in Arcadia, that in the first place the boys from their earliest childhood are trained to sing in measure the hymns and paeans in which by traditional usage they celebrate the heroes and gods of each particular place: later they learn the measures of Philoxenus and Timotheus, and every year in the theatre they compete keenly in choral singing to the accompaniment of professional flute-players, the boys in the contest proper to them and the young men in what is caned the men's contest. And not only this, but through their whole life they entertain themselves at banquets not by listening to hired musicians but by their own efforts, caning for a song from each in turn. Whereas they are not ashamed of denying acquaintance with other studies, in the case of singing it is neither possible for them to deny a knowledge of it because they all are compelled to learn it, nor, if they confess to such knowledge can they excuse themselves, so great a disgrace is this considered in that country. Besides this the young men practice military parades to the music of the flute and perfect themselves in dances and give annual performances in the theatres, all under state supervision and at the public expense.
>
> Now all these practices I believe to have been introduced by the men of old time, not as luxuries and superfluities but because they had before their eyes the universal practice of personal manual labour in Arcadia, and in general the toilsomeness and hardship of the men's lives, as well as the harshness of character resulting from the cold and gloomy atmospheric conditions usually prevailing in these parts conditions to which all men by their very nature must perforce assimilate themselves; there being no other cause than this why separate nations and peoples dwelling widely apart differ so much from each other in character, feature, and colour as well as in the most of their pursuits.
>
> The primitive Arcadians, therefore, with the view of softening and tempering the stubbornness and harshness of nature, introduced the

practices I mentioned, and in addition accustomed the people, both men and women, to frequent festivals and general sacrifices, and dances of young men and maidens, and in fact resorted to every contrivance to render more gentle and mild, by the influence of the customs they instituted, the extreme hardness of the national character. The Cynaetheans, by entirely neglecting these institutions, though in special need of such influences, as their country is the most rugged and their climate the most inclement in Arcadia, and by devoting themselves exclusively to their local affairs and political rivalries, finally became so savage that in no city of Greece were greater and more constant crimes committed. As an indication of the deplorable condition of the Cynaetheans in this respect and the detestation of the other Arcadians for such practices I may mention the following: at the time when, after the great massacre, the Cynaetheans sent an embassy to Sparta, the other Arcadian cities which they entered on their journey gave them instant notice to depart by cry of herald, but the Mantineans after their departure even made a solemn purification by offering peculiar sacrifices and carrying them round their city and all their territory.

I have said so much on this subject firstly in order that the character of the Arcadian nation should not suffer for the crimes of one city, and secondly to deter any other Arcadians from beginning to neglect music under the impression that its extensive practice in Arcadia serves no necessary purpose. I also spoke for the sake of the Cynaetheans themselves, in order that, if Heaven ever grant them better fortune, they may humanize themselves by turning their attention to education and especially to music; for by no other means can they hope to free themselves from that savagery which overtook them at this time.

[224] A calliope is a musical instrument equipped with steam whistles, played from a keyboard. The character recalls the Muse of epic poetry. A Maenad was one of the female followers of Dionysios.

[225] *Paideia,* Gr. for education, derived from *paides,* Gr. "child" and "play."

[226] Use of the *sol-fa* syllables to note the tones of the scale.

[227] Forgetfulness (Gr. *lethe*) must somehow be overcome to attain truth (*aletheia*). According to Plato's theory of knowledge as recollection, the moment of birth holds the greatest portent for both forgetfulness and mindfulness. At the moment of birth the soul may either forget or retain its learnings and memories from the sojourn in heaven. (Compare the Tibetan Buddhist concept of *Bardo.*)

[228] Akamu's paean to the simple but attentive life is inspired in part by the vision of the healthy city in Plato's *Republic* Book II. See also Theocritus, *Idyll* XXIX.22.

[229] See Plato's expulsion of poets from the philosophical city in *The Republic* Book III-IV, X. See also Matthew Arnold, *Essays in Criticism: The Study of Poetry* (1880).

[230] *Lethe* (Gr.) means *forgetfulness*. Etymologically the word for "truth" *(aletheia)* can be understood as the overcoming of forgetfulness. For Plato, all deep learning is recollection of what one already knew. In his Myth of Er, desperately thirsty souls tend to drink too much from the river of Forgetfulness, and thus forget what they have learned. One may be refreshed by a measure of forgetting, just as too much truth may gag someone. Therefore the caution from the elder cook to the disheartened woman in the story. See Plato, *Republic* 621a, and *Phaedrus* 248b. See also Martin Heidegger, *Was heist denken? What is Called Thinking* (1976). Compare Virgil, *Aeneid* vi.714f., and Milton, *Paradise Lost* ii –

> Lethe, the river of oblivion, rolls
> Her wat'ry labyrinth, whereof who drinks,
> Forthwith his former state and being forgets.

[231] As mentioned earlier, the Meadow is the symbol for the mystery of the Earth with her covering of green vegetation. The Meadow of the Stars symbolizes the intersection of the inner and outer universe. Standing there, the human person is rooted in the earth, with eyes and mind on the universe.

On July 11th, 1991, a total eclipse was visible from Hawaii, Mexico, Central America, and South America. More than 30,000 people traveled from the United States alone to witness this event.

[232] Marcus Tullius Cicero believed that God has made human beings tall and straight with eyes looking to heaven in order to acquire knowledge of the Divine Being. This was a privilege shared so distinctly with no other animated creature.

Compare Victor Frankl: "Our generation is realistic, for we have come to know man as he really is," Frankl writes. "After all, man is that being who invented the gas chambers of Auschwitz; however, he is also that being who entered those gas chambers upright, with the Lord's Prayer or the Shema Yisrael on his lips." *(Man's Search for Meaning)*.

The Shema Israel is, "Hear, O Israel, the Lord our God, the Lord is one." (Deuteronomy 6:4)

[233] Sister Penelope recalls another, earlier Penelope, Odysseus' wife, who exemplified the woman who keeps the home safe and secure for the family. The religious sister in the Garden scene accentuates the possibility of generativity in all people, regardless of celibate or spousal state. Thus, she is linked with the *Totenbaum*, the bed for the dying, as much as Odysseus and Penelope are bonded in the mighty tree bed in Ithaca, Odysseus's homeland.

[234] Mircea Eliade wrote,

> [In antiquity] generation and childbirth are microcosmic versions of a paradigmatic act performed by the earth; every human mother only imitates and repeats this primordial act of the appearance of life in the womb of the

earth. Hence every mother must put herself in contact with the Great Genetrix, that she may be guided by her in accomplishing the mystery that is the birth of a life, may receive her beneficent energies and secure her maternal protection…

Still more widely disseminated is the laying of the infant on the ground. In some parts of Europe it is still the custom today to lay the infant on the ground as soon as it has been bathed and swaddled. The father then takes the child up from the ground to show his gratitude. In ancient China "the dying man, like the newborn infant, is laid on the ground…To be born or to die, to enter the living family or the ancestral family (and to leave the one or the other), there is a common threshold, one's native Earth…When the newborn infant or the dying man is laid on the Earth, it is for her to say if the birth or the death are valid, and if they are to be taken as accomplished and normal facts…(*The Sacred and the Profane: The Nature of Religion* (1957), pp. 142-143.)

[235] Anonymous, England, 1210 ce

[236] On the tree as archetype, see C.G. Jung, *Psychological Reflections* (1970), p. 145.

On the medium of the laurel tree at Delphi, see references in E. R. Dodds, *The Greeks and the Irrational* (1971), p. 72-73.

The significance of the linking of Penny (Penelope) and the tree is found in the final chapter of Homer's *Odyssey*. The tree is also a Christ or Cross symbol.

[237] The image of the "True and Healthy City" in Plato's *Republic* Bk. II.

[238] A reference to the Battle for Hill 1243, known as "Heartbreak Ridge," September 3, 1951.

[239] The personality, presence and teaching of this Teacher is a composite from several of the author's finest teachers, notably Norman O. Brown, psychologist, anthropologist and mystic; Paul Lee, philosopher and social prophet; Ray Alf, paleontologist and artist; and Steve Hanley, writer and poet.

[240] See Aeschylus, *The Oresteia* (ca. 475 bce).

[241] See Deuteronomy 23:25-26,

If you enter your neighbor's vineyard, you may eat all the grapes you want, but do not put any in your basket. If you enter your neighbor's grainfield, you may pick kernels with your hands, but you must not put a sickle to his standing grain.

[242] The spirit of generosity and gratitude that permeates this community is reminiscent of Exodus 16:15-19 where the Israelites receive as much mana as they need and are able to consume.

To finance and equip a chorus for a play or dramatic tragic cycle in ancient Greek society was considered a gesture of great liberality.

[243] Terpander (ca. 710 bce) is said to have started the first music schools in Sparta. He is thought to have sung poems similar to the Homeric hymns. His name is associated with the form of a song sacred to Apollo known as the *nome*. He is also considered the founder of lyric poetry. He won various musical competitions, four times at the Pythian games, and at Carneia.

[244] See John 4:7ff.

[245] Abraham Heschel, *Man is Not Alone: A Philosophy of Religion* (1951), p. 14.

[246] John Dos Passos: American poet and novelist (1896–1970). The comment on excessive learning comes from Horace, *Ars Poetica*,

> Most of us poets, O fathers and sons who are worthy of that father, deceive ourselves by an illusion of correct procedure. I work at achieving brevity; instead I become obscure. Striving for smoothness, vigor and spirit escape me. One poet, promising the sublime, delivers pomposity. Another creeps along the ground, overly cautious and too much frightened of the gale. Whoever wishes to vary a single subject in some strange and wonderful way, paints a dolphin into a forest and a boar onto the high seas. The avoidance of blame leads to error if there is an absence of art. (24-31)
>
> It is not enough for poems to be "beautiful"; they must also yield delight and guide the listener's spirit wherever they wish. As human faces laugh with those who are laughing, so they weep with those who are weeping. If you wish me to cry, you must first feel grief yourself, then your misfortunes, O Telephus or Peleus, will injure me. (99,113)

[247] A reference to the land grants to former slaves after the Civil War. Many were forty acres and included a mule for pulling a plow.

[248] In *The Odyssey,* Homer has his hero encounter the shade of Achilles in Hades. There, Achilles says that he would rather be the slave of the poorest serf on earth than lord over all the spirits in Hades.

Socrates in Plato's *Republic* Book III takes strong exception to this statement as unhelpful for a community that wishes to develop courage and civic devotion in the young. Still, the dying man's comment raises the question of the purpose of human freedom: *freedom for what, and how?* It implies that social responsibility for the well-being and development of all does not end with the provision of freedom.

[249] From the core teaching of the Gospel as found in Matthew 25:42-46,

> For I was hungry and you gave me nothing to eat, I was thirsty and you gave me nothing to drink, I was a stranger and you did not invite me in, I needed clothes and you did not clothe me, I was sick and in prison and you did not look after me.' "They also will answer, `Lord, when did we see you hungry or thirsty or a stranger or needing clothes or sick or in prison, and

did not help you?' "He will reply, 'I tell you the truth, whatever you did not do for one of the least of these, you did not do for me.' "Then they will go away to eternal punishment, but the righteous to eternal life.

[250] Isaiah 50:17, 51:22.

[251] From Hippocrates to Galen and medieval medical science, and continuing in Jung, Kretschmer and Isabel Myers, a consensus has been maintained that human personalities can be described as sanguine, choleric (or enthusiastic), melancholy, or phlegmatic.

[252] From The Platters, *Up On the Roof*.

[253] Henry Vaughan.

[254] Plato, *Apology of Socrates* 41.

[255] For a more complete account of *logotherapy,* see Victor Frankl, *Man's Search for Meaning* (1998).

[256] See Plato's description of *eros* in Diotima's speech in the *Symposium*. This figure connects the spirit of *eros* with the primal humankind.

[257] According to Johann Eckermann, *"Mehr Licht!"* ("More light!") were Goethe's final words. See *Conversations with Goethe* (1828). Also, the legendary last words of the Buddha were, "Make yourselves a light."

[258] The proportions of the new plot are along the lines of the Fibonacci series. The ratio that came to be known as the Golden Mean is present in the growth patterns of many natural forms, such as the spiral formed by a shell or the curve of a fern, for example. Both the ancient Greeks and the ancient Egyptians used the Golden Mean when designing their buildings and monuments. Artists as diverse as Leonardo da Vinci and George Seurat used the ratio when constructing their paintings. Actual determination of the ratio governing the series is done by dividing the length of each new side by the previous width:

$1/1 = 1$
$2/1 = 2$
$3/2 = 1.5$
$5/3 = 1.6666...$
$8/5 = 1.6$
$13/8 = 1.625$
$21/13 = 1.61538...$
$34/21 = 1.61904...$

Ultimately the number 1.619... is an irrational number. Artists and architects discovered that by utilizing the ratio 1:1.619..., they could create a feeling of order in their works. Artists are still using this proportion in their works, and scientists are discovering new things about the Golden Mean and its place in science, mathematics, and nature.

[259] The image of raising the skirt (the *anamcerma*) is one of the classic gestures of Aphrodite. Cyntheia's return to the water at this moment, as in the earlier walk to the ocean with Anton, recalls the element of her origin.

[260] The "sheepskin" signifies the college diploma.

[261] See Dante, *Paradiso* XXX:70,

> Without reply I lifted up my gaze,
> And saw her making for herself a crown
> Of the reflection from the eternal rays.

[262] From the title of Marcel Proust's masterpiece, *Pleasures and Regrets*. "Peripatetic" refers to the teaching style of Aristotle in the Lyceum, where he was famed to discourse while walking with students. One could imagine that much of the Aristotelian corpus was collected by students as they walked in Aristotle's wake, later to be transcribed and edited for posterity.

[263] Thomas Mann, *Tonio Kroeger*.

[264] Plato, *Phaedrus*.

[265] Gautama's "sightings" that compelled him to forsake his comforts and affluence: a corpse, a sick man, and a poor man.

[266] Procrustes was the nickname for Damastus (or Polypemon), a legendary robber of ancient Attica. He lived in the area of Eleusis, and captured passing travelers to fit them in one of his two beds. Whether the captive was too long or too short, they were either stretched or trimmed to fit in the bed. The founder of Athens, Theseus, ended this atrocious practice. (See Plutarch, *Life of Theseus.*)

[267] An aphorism by Leo Strauss, professor of political philosophy at the University of Chicago and Claremont Graduate School (d. 1973).

[268] On our elemental origins, see Isaiah 51:1-2. On the illumined depths: when asked who the Christ is, Franz Kafka answered, "An abyss of Light."

[269] An expression adapted from the title to William Frazier's classic, *Errand into the Wilderness.*

[270] See Job 21:18. Also Psalm 90:4-6,

> For a thousand years in your sight
> are like a day that has just gone by,
> or like a watch in the night.
> You sweep men away in the sleep of death;
> they are like the new grass of the morning-
> though in the morning it springs up new,
> by evening it is dry and withered.

[271] The *Te deum laudamus* has been a vital part of the Catholic liturgy since the early sixth century. In addition to its use during Matins in the Divine Office, the *Te Deum* is occasionally sung in thanksgiving to God for some special blessing, such as the proclamation of holy vows and orders.

[272] Dante Alighieri, "The Inferno," in *The Divine Comedy,* Canto I.

[273] For Aristotle's decision to separate from Plato see *Nicomachean Ethics* I. For the binding ties of intimate familiars, see Luke 9:57-60,

> As they were walking along the road, a man said to him, "I will follow you wherever you go." Jesus replied, "Foxes have holes and birds of the air have nests, but the Son of Man has no place to lay his head." He said to another man, "Follow me." But the man replied, "Lord, first let me go and bury my father." Jesus said to him, "Let the dead bury their own dead, but you go and proclaim the kingdom of God." Still another said, "I will follow you, Lord; but first let me go back and say good-by to my family." Jesus replied, "No one who puts his hand to the plow and looks back is fit for service in the kingdom of God." (Luke 9:57-60)

[274] Shakespeare, *Hamlet.* Also Ecclesiastes 12:12-13,

> Be warned, my son, of anything in addition to them. Of making many books there is no end, and much study wearies the body. Now all has been heard; here is the conclusion of the matter: Fear God and keep his commandments, for this is the whole [duty] of man.

[275] On the experience of the disciples with Jesus, see Mark, chapter 9. On the descent to the Piraeus followed by the beginning of the ascent to Athens, see Plato, *Republic* Book I. (Instead of arriving at Athens, the Republic culminates in the vision of the city in speech.) Compare Socrates' suggestion about the necessity of the descent into the Cave in *Republic* Book VII. For Zarathustra's descent after ten years in solitude in a mountain cave, see Nietzsche, *Thus Spoke Zarathustra*, I.i.

[276] The term "therapeutic culture" was coined by Robert Bellah in *Habits of the Heart.*

[277] From an old student drinking song (source unknown).